THE THIRD
REVOLUTION

www.anthonylewisbooks.com

ISBN 1-59113-500-1

Ten Mile Press second paperback edition: March 2005

Printed in the United States of America.

To my parents, who always insisted that I finish my homework before allowing me to run wild in the streets.

THE THIRD REVOLUTION

ANTHONY F. LEWIS

Ten
Mile
PRESS

~ Acknowledgments ~

I must first recognize and thank my editor, Liz Schevtchuk Armstrong, for her many insightful suggestions, and for her overall tempering influence on the manuscript. *The Third Revolution* is unquestionably a better book for her efforts. Many thanks to my sister, Lesley, for the cover design. They say you shouldn't judge a book by its cover, but just try telling that to the marketing people. And to all my many friends who took the time to read scattered pieces of the manuscript over the past year—your comments and suggestions were greatly appreciated and indeed influenced the final development of the story and of its characters.

"If ye love wealth greater than liberty, the tranquility of servitude greater than the animating contest for freedom, go from us in peace. We seek not your counsel, nor your arms. Crouch down and lick the hand that feeds you; may your chains set lightly upon you, and may posterity forget that ye were our countrymen."

~ John Adams
First Continental Congress, 1774

PROLOGUE
April 2013

There wasn't a fence anywhere in sight.

Thomas Running Wolf gingerly prodded his truck up the modest ridge, stopping near the top and shutting down the engine. Grabbing his 45-70 Marlin—this *w*as Grizzly country, after all—he eased his 61-year-old knees up the peak and took a seat on his favorite ledge. The view before him could've been enjoyed on any given day in the past 5,000 years—the Montana high-grass country, green and lush in its springtime effervescence, breathtaking mountain peaks framing the scene off to the west, the rolling hills dotted with buffalo as far as the eye could see. The bison seemed a bit ragged after having survived another brutal Montana winter, and were now in the process of shedding their thick winter coats and replenishing the fat stores that insured their survival during those tough, lean months. The herd clustered in what appeared to be loosely organized bands, with cows nursing and chasing their newborn, golden-fleeced calves towards the center of the group, and the young bulls grazing nearer the periphery. They spent their day eating, playing, enjoying a nice wallow, but mostly just lounging around, ruminating, resting their heavy, but surprisingly nimble, frames. The mature bulls were plainly obvious to even the most naïve observer—they were noticeably larger than their neighbors, weighing upwards of a ton or more, and carried themselves with a huffy, muscled strut to broadcast their power and authority (and the status of their kind as the largest land animals in North America). The big boys were strategically spread apart across the prairie, lest the need arise to challenge someone their own size. There would be plenty of time for those challenges during the fall rut.

Running Wolf took enormous pride in the herd. His people, the Blackfeet, had roamed the North American plains for over 5,000 years, as best anyone could tell, and had been calling this particular part of the country home for over 300 years. They'd lived in harmony with the bison and its Great Plains grassland ecosystem for all but about the last 100 of those years. They had been left no say in the matter; the buffalo were effectively exterminated around the turn of the 20th Century, predominately for their tongues, hides and horns, but also to "encourage" the native peoples to give up their traditional way of life and adapt an imposed version of a civilized lifestyle. The strategy was unquestionably successful in extinguishing the native people's way of life—the world as they knew it was forever laid to waste. So successful was the Great Slaughter, that in 1907, the Bronx Zoo sent 15 of its New York City bison to Oklahoma's Wichita Mountain Preserve as part of an effort to re-establish a public breeding herd in the wild.

The Armageddon plan was far less successful in effecting the natives' psychological adoption to the white civilization. The U.S. federal government managed only to anchor the traditionally nomadic Blackfeet to reservations, and establish within the native tribes the nation's first and longest-running welfare state. *They moved us physically but never spiritually*, Running Wolf often thought.

But the buffalo under his gaze belonged to the tribe: 412 head carefully raised and managed by the Blackfoot Confederacy for a decade. More than just a financial venture (though the market for buffalo meat was indeed profitable and growing), the herd represented a 100-year step backwards for the tribe, and a clearly welcome one. Many of these native people hadn't truly integrated into the post-19th Century American state. In their view they remained, as best they could, creatures of the organic Earth, one small piece of the miraculous puzzle of nature. The buffalo were a central piece of the puzzle (there the 19th Century western expansionists got it right), and were now being returned to the mix. Native grasses were allowed to grow back and the great bison permitted to graze unaffected, for the most part, by fences and small pastures. The renewed presence of the huge ungulates, their grazing behaviors, their instincts for finding water and digging shallow wallowing holes, the impact of their hooves upon the turf, even their droppings, induced a positive effect on the prairie, further encouraging the growth of native flora and the insects living upon them. A resurgence of indigenous birds soon followed, thriving on the seed and insects. Then came increased populations of small mammals and reptiles, feeding on those birds and their eggs. In turn came the larger birds of prey, elk, mountain lion, the recently re-established gray wolf, and the great grizzly bear. Balance and health were slowly returning to the remote grasslands of Montana.

In the old days the tribe would have been divided into several hunting bands, each headed by a chief qualified predominately by success in war. Today, this "success in war" requirement was understandably dropped in favor of at least some degree of political success—in this regard Thomas Running Wolf had earned his title. A five-term member of the nine-seat Blackfoot Tribal Business Council (the ruling body of the Blackfoot Confederacy), Chief Running Wolf proved himself effective in both internal leadership and in representing his nation to the U.S. federal government and the State of Montana. Active in the InterTribal Bison Cooperative (an organization of nearly 50 tribes across 17 states), the chief was known by tribal leaders throughout the west for his passionate work in bringing the buffalo herds back to Indian lands. Though respected by all who knew him, he was in ways far more conservative than many in the Bureau of Indian Affairs (BIA) would have preferred. Meaning Running Wolf's concerns lay more with returning his nation to a more holistic spiritual existence than in speeding their assimilation into modern economic and secular society. This attitude was problematic for the career bureaucrats at the BIA, whose mission it was to pour hundreds of millions of dollars annually into native populations in an effort to assist them in achieving economic self-sufficiency. The BIA had been following this plan for about 130 years or so and had yet to reach any discernable level of success.

Running Wolf slowly hefted his thick, still-muscled frame to his feet, drank in one more broad view of the future, turned and walked to his vehicle. Checking to make sure there was no cartridge in the chamber, he placed his weather-beaten rifle behind the driver's seat, climbed in and headed back to the small town of Browning.

CHAPTER 1
May 2013

"Hey chief!"

"Don't call me 'chief.' How's business?"

The two old friends smiled as they shook hands and walked to a booth in the back of the brewpub, out of the way of the boisterous lunch crowd milling about the bar. The taller of the two, a breath under six feet, with broad shoulders, a ruddy complexion and tawny brown hair flecked with grey, removed a cowboy hat and waved to the friendly faces in the dining room.

"Who's on today?"

"Diane. She'll be a few minutes. She's got a bunch of out-of-town exec's up there who are clearly through with their meetings for the day."

Ben Kane nodded, placed his hat on the seat next to him, and started fiddling with a paper bar napkin left on the table. A moment later he sat back and looked up, taking in the sights and sounds of his fabulously successful American Outback Brewing Company.

"I miss this place. I really do."

"You want to switch jobs, boss? There are people who'll pay real money to see me in a suit!" Joe Adams chuckled. His unruly mop of jet-black hair—now flecked with gray—framed an otherwise youthful face sporting a perpetual five o'clock shadow. A former party animal now in his early 40's, Joe worked for Ben as the general manager for the popular boutique brewery and restaurant.

"Not today. Ask me again in a couple of months."

"Gentleman, what can I get you?" Diane, a brassy blond of indeterminate middle-age, nimbly swept up the old napkin from in front of her boss and placed fresh place settings on the pine tabletop.

"Hey! Diane! Good to see you! How's life treating you?" Ben hadn't seen her in several weeks.

"Oh, same old stuff. Things could be a little quieter, I suppose." She motioned to the rowdy crowd at the bar.

"Should we send the wild man here up front to smack them around a bit?" Ben winked and nodded in Joe's direction. The three laughed.

"No, they're fine. Just enjoying the home brew a bit more than we're used to at this time of day." She pulled out her order pad. "What'll it be?"

"Why don't you get me a buffalo burger with a short beer. I've got a 1:30 I have to get back to."

"You got it! Joe?"

"Nothing, Dee, thanks. I'm just keepin' the boss company. You know how people talk when he drinks alone."

"They talk no matter whom I'm drinking with."

"OK, funny boys, I'll be back in a few minutes." Diane swiveled her chunky hips around and went to fetch Ben's glass of his own American Outback beer.

"Where do you think this One Nation thing is going?" Joe asked.

Ben sat back, shook his head and stared out the window at the Sanders Street mid-afternoon traffic. "I really don't know. I've been so wrong for so long about how far people would let this kind of thing progress. I mean, I wouldn't think you could find 10 people in a thousand-mile radius who would even suggest such a thing, much less vote for it. But here we are. That son-of-a-bitch Henderson has got an even-money chance of taking over the entire social inner workings of the whole country. And he makes people feel cheated if we stand in his way. It would be wonderful theater if we weren't talking about our lives here."

"I was in Billings last week," Joe said, "visiting the Crow buffalo operation. Nobody's happy about this, and everybody's getting less shy about letting their feelings known. Even the Crow are laughing at us! They think it's funny—they say all the white men are going to end up working for the federal government, just like them. But the folks in Billings, Ben, not pretty."

"Who'd you see?"

"I stopped into Hawk's place for lunch, then to Rino's parts yard to pick up some hardware for the Norton. Rino sees a lot of the motorcycle element—you know, not really your typical political policy-wonk discussion group." Joe lowered his voice. "He says everybody's pissin' blood over this thing. True, these are people who'd be prone to an 'us-against-them' attitude under the best of conditions. But they're pissed. Everybody's pissed."

"What about the non-outlaw types in town?"

"Not a whole lot better. The local business owners understand we have more federal money flowing into the state than we have going out in taxes. These aren't stupid people. But if Washington takes over education and law enforcement it means local officials lose control over their own tax policy, along with everything else. Nobody likes their life being yanked out of their hands and being treated like a child."

Ben was staring out the window again, considering Joe's comments. The approaching aroma of a sizzling buffalo burger and a pile of home fries commandeered his attention.

"Thanks, Diane. Tell your boss you deserve a raise."

"Very funny. Enjoy!" She hurried off to attend to her paying customers.

Ben glanced at his watch and made quick work of his lunch. Joe flipped through paperwork, organizing it for later in the day when he would have to take a more serious look at it. Chewing the last of his meal, Ben looked up at the crowd at the bar as they started moving toward the door, cheerfully saying their goodbyes to anyone who would listen. He drained his beer and started collecting the papers he'd scattered across the table.

"I've got to get back. Keep your ear to the ground for me. Things are going to get worse before they get better. And I'm not sure how they're ever going to get better."

"I'll walk you out. I have to run to the bank and pick up some change."

The two slid out of the booth and headed for the door. Joe waved to Diane to signal their departure; Ben stopped and said a few words to some friends at the bar. As they exited and entered the bright sunlight, both slipped on sunglasses. Ben snugged his cowboy hat to his head; Joe walked to the sleek, black motorcycle with gold lettering parked at the curb.

"I'll talk to you later, chief." Joe opened the fuel petcock, switched on the ignition, and with two swift kicks, started his vintage, meticulously restored 1972 Norton Commando and coaxed it to a throaty, rhythmic idle.

"Stop calling me 'chief.' Take care."

Ben watched Joe roar off, gently shook his head and smiled. He turned and headed south on Sanders Street. The Capitol building was only five minutes away, just one block over on Sixth Avenue. Benjamin Kane, the 25th Governor of the State of Montana, needed to get back to the office.

A half hour later, Joe was back at the bar, spread out in a booth doing the food order for the weekend, including a sizable supply of buffalo meat from local Crow meatpackers. The Crow Reservation was less than four hours southeast of Helena. The tribe owned a nifty portable meatpacking plant—a large, specialized trailer they could truck out into the field to process freshly killed bison. The resulting product was as fresh as it gets, and was a huge hit with both the local patrons and the tourist trade. The Governor's brewpub moved some steaks and sausage, but it was the buffalo burgers everybody was crazy about: Big 12-ounce patties with almost no fat, grilled to perfection on the well-seasoned, open flame grill. Served with a frosty pint of fresh draft American Outback beer, it was the simplest expression of gastronomical perfection one could casually enjoy in downtown Helena.

The television caught Joe's attention. The CNN talking head was pontificating on the promised benefits of the President's "One Nation" program presently working its way through Congress. The bill had just easily been passed in the House; the only question remaining was whether there were the necessary 60 votes in the Senate to break the threatened filibuster (promised by Montana's Senator Nancy Taylor, and a few others).

Joe dropped his pencil and sat back against the cushioned bench. "Damn," he said out loud, to nobody in particular. Behind him, the entire bar was watching the broadcast in silence.

CHAPTER 2
May 2013

President Robert Henderson stood at the French Doors in the Oval Office, looking into the Rose Garden, hands folded behind his back. It was good to have a few minutes alone to contemplate the direction his administration, in office now for 5 months, was taking the Nation.

The intercom interrupted his solitude. "Mr. President, I have the Majority Leader returning your call, and Senator Taylor has just arrived."

"Put the Leader through, and show Senator Taylor to the study, Liz. Thanks."

Liz smiled at senator Nancy Taylor, the junior Senator from Montana. A conservative Republican, the 48-year-old was two years into her second term. This was her first private White House visit with the liberal President, called on short notice by his invitation. No shrinking violet, the tough-talking Nancy Taylor was seldom at a loss for words. She was afraid one of those rare moments was upon her, though.

"The President will see you now, Senator." Taylor followed the businesslike aide into the President's study adjacent to the Oval Office.

"He just picked up the phone, he'll come and get you in a few moments."

"Thanks."

Nancy Taylor looked around the masculine, private study. While not terribly well lit, the small room seemed comfortable, deceivingly casual, and was impressively appointed with historical artifacts and artwork. The nice-sized fireplace looked too clean to have been used recently. *It doesn't look functional. Didn't Harry Truman have it moved in here during a major renovation?* An old, large walnut tree shaded the private terrace just outside the office. She could hear the muffled voice of the President through the door. In eight years, this was her first trip alone to the White House, her first glance at the inner sanctum of power. Leaning back against the doorjamb through which she'd entered, the door to the Oval Office to her left and in her sight, she reflected on the events leading her to this place.

Three weeks earlier the President had presented his "One Nation" package to the House of Representatives. With the smallest minority representation in 40 years, the Republicans stood powerless against the Democratic juggernaut. The proposal sought the federalization of all teachers, day-care workers, police, social workers—including all child protective services—and prosecutors as so-called "national agents of social enforcement." When it was first announced, Republicans, conservatives and the like-minded had been drop-jawed stunned that such an idea could even be suggested, much less seriously considered. But the President made his case to the people, the elected representatives parroted their daily talking points, and the mainstream media provided the uncritical, supportive stage on which they were able to perform. The bill authorized the transfer of just over one trillion dollars directly from the state treasuries to the federal government to support the endeavor. While the bill's opponents screamed about blatant violations of the 14th Amendment, nobody seriously thought the Supreme Court would find fault with it. Sixteen years of Democratic administrations saw the high court stocked with progressive, left-leaning justices who rarely saw a problem with a generous, expansive interpretation of the Constitution. The only thing preventing the bill from becoming law was the U.S. Senate.

Now the bill sat in the upper house, where the Democrats held a 58-42 majority, just two votes shy of the 60 votes needed for cloture—the ability to stop a filibuster and bring the bill to a vote. It was the threat of a filibuster that had brought Senator Taylor to 1600 Pennsylvania Avenue.

The door to the Oval Office opened suddenly; Senator Taylor snapped to attention and turned to the tall, striking man with a Hollywood smile walking toward her with his hand extended.

"Mr. President," she said crisply, extending her hand to shake his. "A pleasure to see you again, sir."

He guided her into his office, motioned toward a chair, took his own, and filled a minute with the obligatory social chit-chat before regarding her directly. "Senator, I understand you have a few reservations about my One Nation package. Let's hear it."

So she explained her concerns, speaking openly, confidently and without a lot of political beating-around-the-bush—or intervening questions from him. Her efficiency was providential, as it turned out. As she was just beginning to summarize her key points, he was already rising, flashing that celebrity smile again, and thanking her for "taking the time to share those most interesting perspectives."

Before she hardly even knew it, she was out the door once more.

"Liz, see if you can find Raul Fuentes. Put him through as soon as you get him. Thanks." Fuentes was the President's Special Assistant for Policy and Political Affairs.

"Yes, Mr. President."

Bob Henderson spun around in his chair, grabbed a folder from his desk and headed off to meet an aide rushing into the Oval Office at full speed. The aide hit the brakes as he saw the President of the United States on a collision course.

"Mr. President, the Physician's Union people are assembled in the Roosevelt Room. We're ready for you." The aide was now walking backward as the President shot past him.

He got two steps past Liz's desk when she looked up. "Mr. President, I have Mr. Fuentes on the line—he was at his desk."

Henderson spun around without missing a stride and shot back towards the Oval Office. "Paul," he shouted to the aide now behind him, still rushing down the corridor, "Entertain them for a minute, will you? I want to take this."

"Yes, Mr. President."

Henderson closed the door behind him, settled into the high-backed, black leather chair behind his desk and hit the speaker button.

"Raul! I'm glad I caught you."

"I was surprised to hear from you, Mr. President. There's a senior staff meeting scheduled for this afternoon—do we have a problem?"

"No, no, not at all. Just a little business I thought you might take care of for me."

"Yes sir, what do you need?" Fuentes hated special requests—just something else (he sometimes cynically mused) that he would have to lie about in front of a Congressional committee someday.

"I don't know if you've heard the One Nation package just passed the House?"

"Yes, sir, I did. Congratulations."

"Thanks, Raul. Listen, I need a clear head on this. Nancy Taylor from Montana is hell-bent on stopping this thing—she's threatening filibuster, and at this point I don't think we have the votes to bust it. I mean, if we have to, we can scare up the votes; most of those whores are just holding out for a bridge or a water purification plant or something. But it's going to cost us. She's a straight shooter; I don't think this is just a party-politics position with her. Find out what's going on, will you?"

"Sir, didn't we lose Montana by something in the neighborhood of 80 percentage points?"

"Yes, and Idaho, the Dakotas, Wyoming, and Indiana along with it. I know they love me out there, Raul, but nothing has stopped them from getting on the chow line before. I threw a lot of sweetener into this bill for those ungrateful cowboys; I need to know why all of a sudden they're not biting!"

"I'll check with our state-local team here; they should have a handle on what the local hot-button issues are out there. And I'll see what else we have. I should be able to piece together what might be percolating out there under the radar and let you know as soon as we have something."

"Thanks, Raul. See you this afternoon. Gotta go." The President hit the speaker button and once again headed out to his meeting.

"Mr. President, I put together a short briefing document." Fuentes handed the brief across the desk.

"Thanks, Raul. I appreciate you pulling this together on such short notice." The President opened the padded, black leather portfolio and studied the three sheets of paper within.

"Looks like pretty standard demographic migration stuff…shifting voter patterns, income distribution…the usual. How does this help me?"

"Well, you're correct about the demographic migration, but the patterns out there are not what we would traditionally call standard, sir. Normally, when we see these big moves from rural to more urban populations, you start developing a more collective voting preference."

"Right," agreed the President. "They change from rugged individualist, cowboy gunslingers to neighborhood-minded soccer moms and dads."

"Correct, sir. At least it's what we're used to seeing. But the patterns in Montana, and several of the other western states just aren't following suit. We're getting the traditional rural-to-urban migration all right, but voting preferences haven't changed accordingly. In addition, there's been a significant influx of new populations."

"You're talking about the Hollywood and media crowd, buying up the hobby ranches?" Henderson knew several close friends and contributors who had done just that.

"They're out there, sir, but aren't really a factor. I mean one person can buy up 10,000 acres, but it's still only one vote. The family who sold the property is now living in a three-bedroom ranch house outside of Missoula, and is still voting conservative. *Very* conservative. And the people who are moving into the state are coming in from the eastern and western coastal areas."

"Sounds like good news for us, no? It's an influx of more progressive thinkers who should eventually dilute the conservative voting bloc. Just like when New Hampshire became a bedroom community for Boston."

"Not so, sir. The people moving in are very conservative, libertarian, really. We're seeing lots of people moving away from the once conservative, now progressive suburbs to what they consider safer territory. And the local and state politics are reflecting that. They've got the highest percentage of libertarian politicians—including the Governor—of any state in the Union."

"That's why we can't get a Democrat elected dogcatcher out there."

"Yes sir. And from their perspective, this legislative package is right in their face."

"Almost 28 percent of the acreage out there is federal land," the President pointed out, taking a greater interest in the brief and eyeballing some of the statistics.

"Yep. And until very recently the federal government was the largest single employer in the state. Toss the Bureau of Indian Affairs into the mix, and you've got the most government-hating concentration of people in the country living in the middle of what is essentially a federal protectorate."

"We've pumped a lot of money into that state over the years," the President agreed.

The Special Assistant nodded. "Dependence can sometimes breed as much resentment as respect, I suppose. We haven't even touched on the gun issue..."

"I understand the state government has been a little lax in enforcement."

"Understatement sir. ATF thinks practically every unregistered assault rifle hidden since the Brady Bill has made its way into the state."

"The Governor isn't going to give us any help with that, is he?" Henderson mumbled sarcastically.

"He's a real piece of work. I understand he's calmed down a bit since being elected governor—he was a true bomb throwing, revolutionary nut job when he was in the legislature—but the truly frightening thing, sir, is he was elected by huge margins. And he's incredibly respected in the neighboring states."

"So the bottom line is Nancy Taylor isn't holding out for a deal. She reflects the state. They believe all that stuff and so does she, so she's operating on principle," the President concluded.

The Special Assistant nodded affirmatively.

"Anything else?" Henderson placed the briefing folder on his desk.

"Well, I did find someone who has spent some time in Governor Kane's eating establishment—you know he still owns the place. It's just two or three blocks from the Capitol."

"I remember reading as much."

"He used to hold court there before he got involved in elective politics. Now he just pops in for a drink once in a while. Anyway, the cocktail talk from off-duty legislators indicates all the noise over the One Nation bill is not just a lack of political support; there is serious talk of some sort of civil disobedience across the state. And of course the militia nuts are going berserk. Bill Barrett, the Flathead County state senator, is really worried about possible bombing or assassination attempts. You remember the book, *Unintended Consequences*? The one where the gun nuts go ballistic and start shooting all of the pro-gun-control politicians? It's the new Bible out there. And believe me, this guy Barrett is no friend of the federal government. If he's worried, we should be worried."

The President's cheeks reddened and his voice hardened a notch. "How the hell did I just go from trying to get a piece of legislation passed to possible assassination attempts?"

"Sir, when you went to president's school, do you remember the lesson about not shooting the messenger?"

"What's the governor doing about it?"

"We think he's planning a quiet trip up to Kalispell with Barrett to try to keep a lid on things."

"Keep me posted." The President shifted in his chair, now noticeably uncomfortable. "We've got a meeting to get to."

Henderson and Fuentes stood together. After picking up another briefing folder from his desk, President Henderson and his Special Assistant quickly headed out to their meeting in silence.

CHAPTER 3
Mid-May, 2013

"Governor. Senator. We've been cleared for take-off. Why don't you get yourselves buckled in and try to secure any loose papers or whatever." The pilot of the sleek, state-owned Gulfstream V-SP paused for a moment to be sure his two passengers heard him. "I'll hit the gas on your signal, Governor."

"Thanks Bruce. Give us a second here."

Governor Kane buckled the lap belt on his plush, white leather seat, then scooped up the paperwork scattered across the compact, rustic-style pine table bolted to the floor. Across from him, state Senator William Barrett followed suit.

"You ready Bill?"

"Let's go." The Senator took a second to loosen the belt a bit to fit around his 44-inch waist and snapped the buckle.

"OK Captain! Ready when you are!" Ben shouted to the front of the cabin.

The two Rolls-Royce engines rapidly and loudly spun up to power, drowning out the pilot's response. The jet shot down the runway, then unexpectedly leapt into the air at a frighteningly steep angle.

"Whoa!" The Senator, who didn't spend much time in what was essentially the Governor's jet, grabbed the edge of his seat for support.

"Yeah, this bird really moves out. We'll be at altitude in a minute; it'll smooth out real nice," Ben explained. Barrett still hung on, working on reclaiming his breath.

Bill Barrett was the conservative Republican state senator for Flathead County. When he wasn't busy representing his constituents in Helena, he lived just outside of Kalispell, the county seat, which was their present destination. Normally a two-and-a-half-hour drive from Helena, the 200-mile trip would only take them about 30 minutes, runway to runway. The plane quickly reached its cruising altitude of 41,000 feet, well under its 51,000-foot ceiling, and would stay there for a mere 10 minutes or so before gradually heading back down.

The town of Kalispell, frequently regaled as the most right-wing city in the country, hadn't done much in recent times to shake its reputation. Once the home of small-town merchants, outdoor enthusiasts and militia nuts, the population had grown to just over 20,000 with the recent influx of new economy, electronic urban cowboys. Advances in technology, as well as the general expansion of the service economy, allowed these upper-middle class knowledge-workers to relocate and live in an area that 10 years earlier would have been considered the middle of nowhere. They were there for a reason, though, beyond the still-pristine environment, endless vistas, and reasonable housing. Montana's reputation as a libertarian hub was well known. The new residents were folks who, for the most part, shared that libertarian streak. And Kalispell was the epicenter of this particular brand of political unrest.

The election of Benjamin Kane had a lot to do with spurring the immigration of the libertarian refugees and businesses from the coastal regions of the country. It was a physically stunning space in which to live, and for those few remaining folks who still refused to believe government, courts and lawsuits were the only way to advance in life, it was a friendly place as well.

But a friendly state was proving no protection from the federal government. The thought of the One Nation legislation becoming law, of living under an overarching federal civil-service regime heralded by the coastal majorities as the answer to issues of social inequities and better integration into the world economy, was too much to bear. Rumors were flying; threats were heating up. People were getting nervous. They wanted to know where their Governor stood.

"So what are we looking at here, Bill? How bad is this?" Ben was gazing out the small window.

"Bad. We've got two different, related problems joined at the hip." Senator Barrett unbuckled his seatbelt with a grunt and sat back a bit. "The militia members are an inch away from taking up arms and blowing up government buildings. And they're serious, Ben, it's no joke this time. They're ready for jail, they're ready for a lethal injection, they're ready for the freakin' guillotine. They don't care anymore. They think it's over. Their only concern is doing as much damage as they can before they're caught, and trying to figure out a way to protect their families."

"Should we even be talking to these people?" Ben shuffled through his papers looking for the militia-briefing sheet.

"They're citizens, they're taxpayers, and they voted for you. They haven't done anything illegal yet. I don't think we can hurt anything here, and we ignore them at great peril, in my judgment."

"How many are we talking about?" Ben asked, not finding the answer on the brief.

"At this meeting? I don't know. If you're asking how many of these birds we have to worry about…"

Ben nodded.

"Well, I'd say it's an excellent question, and one we really don't have an answer to. If I had to guess, I'd say we're looking at about six-dozen true believers. You have to figure each one of those has family or friends willing to help out with logistical issues—buying supplies, storing and hiding stuff, blowing smoke at investigators, and the rest of it."

"What you're saying is we've got 60 to 70 Tim McVeighs up there?" Ben had his head in his hand, staring at Senator Barrett.

"Well, sure, we could have that many in the Flathead County area. Likely some more scattered about the state, and God knows how many cells across the country." Barrett leaned back in his seat, giving the Governor a chance to digest the information.

"We're looking at a lot of blown-up buildings. A lot of bodies. A lot..." Ben snapped his head up and looked right at his old friend. "You said there were two problems?"

"Yep. The bulk of the people up there don't want to blow up buildings, and they don't want the militia to start blowing up buildings. But they don't want to accept this new way of doing things, either. And they're just as adamant as our gun-nut friends."

"I'm guessing that's the good news."

"Yep, that's the good news." The Senator slid forward in his seat, his knees almost touching the table. "I'm sorry for pulling this on you on such short notice, Ben, I really am. I didn't know what else to do. I mean, I could've gotten law enforcement involved, but I'm feeling things are too far gone; at this point everyone would just go underground and start lighting fuses. Besides, if we have to, we can certainly get them involved later. I'm sure there are some FBI or ATF undercover agents snooping around, but you know how tight everyone is up there—there's no way they're inside."

Ben nodded in agreement.

"The bottom line is they trust you, Ben. They'll listen to you. You need to tell them, well, I really don't know what you need to tell them." Barrett finished the thought softly, and glanced up at the

Governor.

Ben was again staring out the window, deeply lost in thought. *What do you tell people who are essentially right, but can't act on their conviction? Agree with them, tell them we're all screwed and we should all just get used to it? Tell them they're wrong, it'll all be OK?* He didn't believe it, they didn't believe it, and he knew they knew he didn't believe it.

The captain opened the cabin door and stuck his head in the passenger compartment. "Gentleman, time to buckle up and get organized; we're going to start descending. We should be on the ground shortly."

"Thanks, Bruce." Senator Barrett collected the Governor's papers, placed them in their file folder and stuck them in his briefcase. Ben continued to stare at the passing clouds.

The Governor's large, powerful, black SUV (like new firearms, the muscular vehicles were now essentially only available to government officials) pulled up in front of the community college building where the meeting would take place. Ben rarely traveled with bodyguards; tonight, his driver, a state highway patrol officer, was armed, and would accompany him in and out of the auditorium. And Senator Barrett usually packed an old snub-nosed .38; he would be seated next to Ben at the front of the room.

"Showtime!" Ben opened the rear door of the vehicle and stepped out. He really should have waited for his driver to get the door, but this was not a crowd likely to be impressed with formality or even some understandable security protocol. There was a small crowd of people scattered about just outside the doors—almost everybody grabbing a last smoke before the start of the meeting. Ben immediately recognized a familiar face.

"Coz!" Hand outstretched, Ben headed over to a giant, fiercely bearded biker. Vince Cozzentino, now balding but with ponytail still intact, stamped out his smoke and turned to greet the Governor.

"Hey! Governor Ben! How ya been?" The two shook hands heartily, then gave up pumping and embraced. Ben's driver watched nervously as the big man's heavily tattooed arms engulfed the Governor. Coz stood 6'4", weighed in at 350 pounds, and had spent a lifetime making law enforcement personnel nervous.

"I'm good, thanks. Busy. They don't let me out much. So tell me, what am I in for in there? How bad is this?" Kane got right down to business.

"This is ugly, Governor. *Major* ugly. I don't know what to do. Nobody up here knows what to do. We're looking to you for direction, chief, but nobody's in the mood for any political weasel words. You know what I mean, chief? We need to hear what YOU think, not what you think you're supposed to say, you know what I'm saying, chief?" Coz playfully poked his big finger into the Governor's chest for emphasis. The security officer felt his pulse jump.

Ben gave the aging, black-leather-vested biker his full attention, listening intently. Coz continued. "You know 20 years ago I would have been the first in line to strap 100 pounds of C-4 around my waist and volunteer to get shot out of a circus cannon right into the capitol rotunda. But times have changed, Gov. I'm married, I've got three kids, and there's no fuckin' way I'm fitting into a circus cannon any more!" He patted his expansive gut with both hands as the small, friendly crowd gathering around the two laughed loudly. "So what DO you think about the Big Brother takeover?"

"It sucks." Ben responded quietly. "But they don't ask me."

"Well, they should, my friend, maybe you could talk some sense into them." Coz smacked Ben on the shoulder. "You better get inside before the natives get restless." The big man stuck out his hand. "See ya inside."

Ben shook his huge paw. "Thanks for the heads up. Tell your wife to start cutting back on your portions." He patted Coz's protruding stomach and laughed. He started walking to the door.

"Shit, she's been trying since she's known me. If it weren't for my secret stash of little chocolate donuts I would have shrunk down to nothin' years ago!" He laughed again and lit another smoke.

Ben shook a few more hands before entering the building and slowly working his way to the now-packed auditorium.

The head of the local town council had the microphone, and was busy singing Ben's praises to a restless audience. *This is going to be a tough crowd*, thought Ben. Typically, a politician faces two different types of crowds. There are the "friendlies," like those at a political convention or party-fundraiser, where the speaker's job is to toss red meat to the crowd (as the pundits like to say), and simply preach to the choir. The other group, the "hostiles", may appear during unscripted moments during election year town meetings, or while elected officials are getting slapped around on a Sunday morning talk show: "So governor, is it true you just recently stopped smoking marijuana during office hours?" Ben, like most sane politicians, made a point of avoiding hostile encounters. With his victory margins and popularity ratings, there was no political upside in getting the crap kicked out of him in public. But the type of crowd sitting before him today was different—these people were friendlies, hence unavoidable, and hostile, though not specifically at him. They were going to be asking the very simple questions understandably asked by those who had grabbed the short end of the stick in a political contest: "What do we do now?" Ben scanned the audience, looking for familiar faces (he did notice a lot of newcomers to the area were in attendance), looking at expressions, body language and style of dress. Dress code tonight, like every other night in Kalispell, was definitely casual, outdoor-work casual.

Worn blue jeans, NASCAR t-shirts, cowboy boots. He noticed almost all were freshly cleaned, some even pressed. *Funny. People want to respect their government, even when they feel they don't have any reason to.*

If Ben Kane could credit any one thing for his ascension to political and popular power it was his ability to read people. Countless hours spent leaning over a bar in the smoky, post-midnight hours, sore feet sliding on soggy, beer-soaked mats, fingers puckered, listening to drunks babble on about the inane minutia of human existence, had honed his skills at patiently reading between the lines of personal expression. He knew overheated talk and emotion, while frequently running parallel, couldn't ferment an explosion until they intersected. He could spot a bar fight before it started, ever keen to the difference between foggy, alcohol-fueled, angry bellyaching and the sharp, clear look in the eye of a bona fide belligerent about to physically attack. Ben saw those clear eyes on many in the room with him tonight.

The increased fidgeting and nervous coughing focused his attention on the speaker, who was at the end of his remarks and was preparing to slide the mike over to Senator Barrett for a few words. There were eight people seated at two folding tables facing the audience. Six of them were members of the town council whose essential purpose tonight was to be seen with the Governor; the Governor was seated to the far right, with Senator Barrett next to him. The single microphone, with its weighted table stand, was being slid from speaker to speaker, working its way over to Ben. Senator Barrett didn't buy him much time.

"I've heard from quite a number of you over the past month," Barrett started. "You all know how I feel about this thing and don't need to hear any more about it from me. I've discussed the issue with the Governor and he agreed, as is his style, to join us tonight and let you know where he stands. So here we are. Governor?" He slid the mike over to Ben.

The Governor accepted the mike with his right hand, centered it in front of himself, placing both hands on the weighted base, and stared into the mesh tip of the instrument as if it were a crystal ball. He gradually lifted his warm, brown eyes to the crowd, as if surprised to see everyone there.

He opened with the usual litany of thank you's and perfunctory greetings. Not quite knowing where to go next, Ben resorted to the tried-and-true—the story of how he got to his present position. It was a well-worn tale among the true believers, repeated as frequently as Ronald Reagan shared his stories of being a teenage lifeguard in Dixon, IL.

The Governor's public story started at the place he continued to gravitate to whenever the opportunity presented itself—the American Outback Brewing Company in downtown Helena. It had already been a popular watering hole when he had first bought it some 10 years earlier, but he had invested a ton of money and reincarnated the place as a microbrewery and restaurant. Located on Sanders Street, between 6th and 8th Avenues, it was less than a 10-minute walk to either the executive residence (two blocks southeast) or the capitol building (two blocks southwest).

Given the location so close to the state Capital and Ben's political temperament, the place became popular with the more conservative members of the legislature. After years of complaining about industry regulation, minimum wages, taxes, etc, he finally decided to take everyone's advice to stop complaining and run for office himself. A popular representative from his district was retiring, and Ben was encouraged to make a run at the seat. Having decided that the only way he was going to do this was his way, he switched affiliation from Republican to the Libertarian Party and essentially ran his campaign out of his brewpub. It was an easy campaign—he was very well liked in town, and people loved his radical rants about personal liberty and the role of a constitutionally limited, non-coercive central government. His only competition was a woman running on the Democratic slate on a platform of increasing property taxes to improve school conditions. Hell, Ben wanted to privatize all of the public schools and slash property taxes by 60 percent. He won with 70 percent of the vote; he made the news all over the state. Nobody was really sure if he was elected seriously, or just to cause trouble and piss off the more "reasonable" members of the legislature, or even just for laughs, but elected he was.

Ben spent a mostly frustrating first term learning the ropes, measuring new personalities, and developing a feel for how the game was played. What set him apart right away was the fact that he was serious, he wanted to change things, and was willing to take his opinions to the public, especially to the voters outside of his district. He really had little choice in this regard—state level politics is about horse-trading projects and budget money; since all Ben was there for was to cut the budget, taxes, and government intrusiveness, he essentially had nothing to trade. But by targeting sympathetic politicians and speaking directly to voters in their districts, Ben was able to make the case for cutting some programs and provided fellow politicians with the necessary political cover for voting his way. Ben easily won reelection to a second, two-year term.

About a year and a half into his second term, the popular, conservative Republican state senator from his district unexpectedly dropped dead from a heart attack. Ben was the obvious choice to serve out the remainder of the term; he was appointed to do so by the governor. By this time, Ben also was very well known in Lewis and Clark County and in the subsequent general election easily won as one of 50 state senators. Borrowing a page from Ben's playbook, the candidate who won his old House seat ran as a Libertarian.

A good number of sitting legislators, both in the House and

Senate, switched their party affiliation to the Libertarian banner. It actually wasn't a terribly difficult thing to do in a state like Montana. Most voters there were fiscally conservative, "leave-me-the-hell-alone" types anyway—great fodder for the Libertarian platform. People were jumping ship from both the Democratic and Republican parties, if for no other reason than to demonstrate their independence from the national, Washington-leaning parties—another easy sell in Montana. By Ben's fourth year as a state senator, the Libertarian Party, though still in the minority, frequently controlled a ruling coalition in the state. What they didn't have was a governor who would stop vetoing their legislation.

Ben, of course, was the logical choice to carry the party's banner into the governor's office. In a Jesse Ventura-style campaign, Ben took to the Internet, to horseback, to tractors, speaking at rodeos, speaking from behind his bar, speaking anywhere the voters were. In a three-way race, Ben was the "bad boy," the "wasted vote," the one who was going to make the state a laughingstock. The Democratic candidate ran on the status quo; he was going to bring big Washington bucks to the state. The Republican said he admired Ben, but his radical platform was just too unrealistic in this day and age. Ben ignored them both. He talked about their beautiful state and how it was, in actuality, nothing more than a ward of the federal government. He talked about the state's weak, federally dependent economy, and how they could become a low-regulation, low-tax haven for business. He talked about the Native Americans, and how they could benefit from his policies. He became the embodiment of Montana's independent spirit.

In the three-way race, Ben took 55 percent of the vote. Even in a presidential election year, his victory made big, "above the fold," news across the country. Clips of his inspiring, common sense, but very radical, acceptance speech were played everywhere. Especially in Washington, where jaded political observers could only be darkly amused by the turn of events.

Ben could see his presentation was being politely received, but clearly wasn't going over well. The applause was frequent and in the right spots, but short and obligatory. The legs were crossing frequently, the arms folding this way and that; silent glances were being shot across the room. Ben Kane's rise to power in the state was legendary, and everyone enjoyed hearing the story from the horse's mouth. But it was clear he wasn't going to charm his way out of this one tonight.

Ben spoke for a few minutes about his opposition to the One Nation legislation, but could see he wasn't getting any traction. He sat back in his chair and pulled a piece of paper out of his jacket pocket. "I wrote this down for you earlier today; I'd like to read it for you."

He unfolded the sheet of paper slowly and laid it out on the table in front of him. He cleared his throat, then picked up the sheet with his left hand, moving it closer, then further away from his eyes, obviously struggling to find a comfortable focal length from which to read. Sighing audibly, he placed the paper back down on the table and sheepishly reached again into the inner, breast pocket of his jacket and pulled out a pair of reading glasses. As he rubbed the lenses clean on the lining of the jacket, Ben turned to the audience.

"Excuse me a moment, folks. I started out as a tavern keeper with a big mouth and ended up a tired Governor who can't read his own writing." Ben continued cleaning his glasses, then set them in place and once again prepared to read.

Ben's subtle, self-effacing gesture had the intended effect— many in the audience smiled and nodded sympathetically. The tension softened a little.

"May it be to the world," Ben started reading, "what I believe it will be…the signal of arousing men to burst the chains under which ignorance and superstition had persuaded them to bind themselves, and to assume the blessings and security of self-government. All eyes are opened or opening to the rights of man. The general spread of the light of science has already laid open to every view the palpable truth that the mass of mankind has not been born with saddles on their backs; nor a favored few, booted and spurred, ready to ride them legitimately, by the grace of God. These are grounds of hope for others; for ourselves, let the annual return of this day forever refresh our recollection of these rights, and an undiminished devotion to them."

Ben looked up from the sheet and peered at the crowd over his glasses. "So wrote Thomas Jefferson on June 24th, 1826, in reference to the upcoming 50th anniversary celebration of the July 4th, 1776, Declaration of Independence. At 83 years of age, gravely ill with only 10 days left to live, old man Jefferson still had his fastball."

He continued, his voice now clear and firm. "This government now giving you the so-called 'One Nation' legislation may not think much about restricting your liberty, but previous governments on this continent thought differently." Heads nodded in agreement throughout the room. "I know there's a lot of anger in this room. But we cannot afford to sacrifice, no matter how high the level of anger and frustration, the flame of liberty burning in this great state of ours. That flame has been all but extinguished in vast portions of this country; there can be no lasting value in allowing them to snuff it out in Montana, this land where it burns the brightest. Don't let Jefferson's dream end here.

"I know there's a temptation to want to strike out and do harm to those who seek to harm you and your families. It's an emotional response, and I believe, a normal one. But, trust me folks, guns and bombs aren't going to get the job done this time around. Everyone's talking about East versus West, the heartland versus the coast, as if we were talking about a North versus South thing here—like the Civil War. Well, the Civil War is the wrong model for what we're facing. We can't force liberty and responsibility on a population who view those things as being selfish, as somehow unfair and dangerous. And we can't afford to be wiped off the earth in the process of trying—the ideas we're fighting for are too big, are too important. We cannot fight; we must lead."

"Look," Ben pushed his chair back from the table a bit, "is it fair to say, generally speaking, people are safer with increased restrictions on personal liberty? Perhaps. Has anyone here ever been on a New York City subway train?" A couple in the back raised their hand. "I know I wouldn't feel safer if everyone on those trains were armed!" The crowd whooped and laughed at the thought. "What about the government-controlled security cameras keeping a 24-hour eye on our cities and roadways? Are you safer? Almost certainly. Unquestionably! And we'd be safer still in a martial-law society with imposed curfews and scheduled commutes. But the deal the Founding Fathers made with the government was not for safety and government involvement in every aspect of our lives; it was to secure and safeguard personal liberty. What did Ben Franklin say? Those who would give up essential liberty, to purchase a little temporary safety, deserve neither liberty nor safety. This country's been going there for the past 40 years, folks, under both Republican and Democratic Party rule. Safety over personal freedom at every opportunity. Exactly the way the ruling majority wants it—a least common denominator, collectivist society.

"Collectivism," he continued, "is where societies go to die." Though he wasn't real clear as to exactly what the phrase meant, Ben liked the sound of it, and knew it would elicit the right response from his audience. And it did, as the screaming, stomping and clapping grew louder.

Ben knew he was on a roll, one of the best in years. He spoke for a few minutes more, and was hoping to leave on a high note so he could hit the bricks without hanging around for any potentially sticky questions.

Voice surging to a crescendo, he wrapped it up. "The revolution in this country, this *third* revolution, is not going to be at the end of a gun barrel; it will be, once again, with the stroke of a pen. Thank you all for coming out tonight."

Ben stood and acknowledged the loud cheering and standing ovation. Senator Barrett, like many in the audience, wondering exactly what he had just heard, joined him in shaking the hands of everyone on the dais. They waved enthusiastically to the cheering crowd as they hurried out of the auditorium to their waiting car.

CHAPTER 4
Mid-May, 2013

"He said WHAT?" Mitch Steere couldn't believe his ears.

"You should'a seen this, Mitch. You should'a been there." Senator Barrett took a deep, satisfying pull on an icy, longneck American Outback Beer. Their host was kind enough to leave an emergency supply in a small refrigerator right there on the screened porch.

"It was a remarkable performance on two levels." Barrett continued. "Firstly, he instantly defused a very hot, touchy situation; a lot of those folks were ready to blow."

Mitch slowly nodded his head in agreement. Mitch Steere was a Republican representative in the Montana State Legislature from the 67th House district in Helena. A rising star in the state's political arena, Mitchell Steere had been recently elected Speaker of the House, and was considered a near genius when it came to mastering the details of practical government operating policy. The reason he didn't join the rush of legislators to the Libertarian Party was not so much for ideological reasons—he did see eye-to-eye with most of the free-market, non-coercive government policies of the Libertarians—but for more practical reasons. Libertarians had almost no hands-on experience running a government. As a national party, they tended to voice a fairly dogmatic and philosophically rigid platform. Extreme would be the word most frequently used to describe them, and most often, it was the correct word. Mitch recognized this as typical of a political movement busy spending the bulk of its time and money talking (mostly to itself), not winning elections and governing. This was the first time in American history that a libertarian political movement had won legislative, executive, and increasingly significant judicial influence over a state government. As might be expected, they were having a tough time translating long-held party dogma into practical, governing policies acceptable to the voting public. Mitch Steere was an invaluable ally in this regard.

As soon as he had dropped the Governor off at his residence the previous evening, Senator Barrett had called and left Mitch a cryptic message. He wanted to meet, first thing in the morning, at Kim Lange's small, hobby ranch. The message was brief; something about Mitch's need to "hear about what happened," before the media started running with it. The cozy ranch was just under a half hour south of Helena, about five miles north of Boulder, little more than a mile west off of I-15. When he pulled up in front of the ranch house, Kim was nowhere in sight, but Barrett's car was already in the small parking area across from the residence.

"Secondly, and more importantly," Barrett continued, "was his framing of the situation."

"How's that?" Mitch prodded, knowing this is what he was called down here to hear.

"I wrote this down; I didn't want to take a chance on misquoting him." Barrett pulled a sheet of lined yellow paper from his pocket. As he unfolded it, he leaned back in the Amish rocker, crossed his legs, and let gravity settle him into his new position.

He cleared his throat "...the revolution in this country, this third revolution, is not going to be at the end of a gun barrel, it will be, once again, with the stroke of a pen." The Senator allowed the paper to drop in his lap and flopped his arms to the side. He looked over at Mitch. "So what do you make of it?"

Seated in an identical rocker (Kim had fallen in love with the hand-hewn, rustic pine chairs during a Lancaster, PA, business trip), Mitch kicked back and shifted his gaze to the pasture just beyond the gravel roadway. "Revolution," he mused. "A nice way for a governor to talk. Did he plan it? Was he working from prepared notes?"

"Nope. He didn't have any idea what he was going to say on the trip there. He was stumbling around for the first few minutes, then he found his footing and it just came out. Mesmerizing, actually. Very much the way he used to be before he got talked into running for governor, the way he was in the legislature. Shhhh...hear that?" Barrett held up his hand and cocked his head towards the growing, deep pounding, staccato thump of a heavy equine in full gallop. "It must be her."

"Over there." Mitch pointed across the road, to the horse and rider racing toward them on the other side of the high-tensile woven fence separating the pasture from the house and roadway. "The fence looks new, doesn't it?"

"Yeah. Heavy-duty stuff. Fixed knot. And tight. What's she got in there?"

"The ranch used to run cattle before she took over, but she bought the property bare, if I remember correctly." Mitch stepped off the porch into the morning sun and ran over to the gate to greet his host.

Kim Lange reined the big stallion to a walk about 50 yards before the gate, letting the winded animal blow as she approached her guests. Cato was a large, magnificently groomed tobiano American Paint Horse, with bright white legs and feet. The white from his front legs crossed over his shoulders and neck, presenting a striking contrast to the solid, dark brown coloration of his rear haunches, head, and breast. Another shock of white ran from his nose to just above his eyes. In a part of the country where people knew their horses, Kim's stallion drew approving comments wherever she went.

"Well hello there, Mr. Speaker! It's been a little while. And I see you brought a friend!" Kim gave a nod to Senator Barrett, who remained on the shady porch. Mitch swung open the wide gate, and walked with horse and rider as they headed to the paddock adjacent to the barn.

"It has been a while, I know," said Steere. "Looks like the private sector's been good to you!" Kim, armed with an Ivy League MBA from the Tuck School of Business at Dartmouth, made a good living as an independent organizational design consultant, and had worked for Ben Kane on his political campaigns.

"I've picked up a couple of nice corporate clients in the last few years, steady systems-project type work. Financial planning and insurance companies, mostly. Beats the hell out of political consulting!" Kim grinned as Mitch jogged ahead of her and unlatched the gate to Cato's pasture. Horse and rider plodded on through.

"What's your situation like now? Are you working?" Mitch closed the gate behind them.

"I just finished a major project a couple of weeks ago. I was going to start working on another proposal for the same client— watch your step, Mr. Speaker!" Mitch deftly sidestepped the sizeable mound of fresh manure.

"Thanks. I've been riding a desk too long. My ranch-radar must be rusty."

Kim dismounted, led Cato inside the barn, and unsaddled him. Reaching under the huge animal's midsection, she unbuckled the back strap, then the front cinch. Mitchell watched as she hoisted the 40-pound western trail saddle from Cato's back. She was wearing a sleeveless blouse, providing a clear view of her well-developed upper body. Her triceps, tanned and glistening with sweat, were as hard and defined as a woman's arm could naturally get. A former amateur fitness competitor and all-around gym rat, she remained in enviable physical condition for a woman in her mid-30s. She pulled the saddle pad, then the red and white Crow-patterned saddle blanket from his back and started brushing down the deeply contrasted white and brown coat. "I'll just be a few minutes. So tell me what you boys are doing here?"

"I'm going to let Bill tell you—he called this meeting." Mitch turned to the fencing across the road. "What's with the new fencing? Decided to start running livestock? Those clients of yours MUST be paying you too much money!"

"No, not a business venture. Just a couple of new pets!" She tossed aside the brush and firmly scratched Cato's shoulder. "You go find something to eat, cutie." The horse wandered over to a bale of hay.

"Pets?" Mitch looked again at the tight, high-tensile fencing. He shook his head. "I'm afraid to ask."

"Let's pick up the Senator and I'll take you to see them; come on." Kim headed away from the barn across Cato's front yard. "Watch your step!" Mitch followed her carefully back through the gate.

Senator Barrett was already heading over to meet them. "This way!" Kim pointed to her pickup in the driveway. "We're going for a little ride!"

The sudden, jarring rattle of a large diesel engine ruptured the silence of the late prairie morning. "There should be enough room for you back there, Mitch." Kim looked over her shoulder as the Speaker of the Montana House of Representatives squeezed into the jump seat behind the driver. "Our Senator looks like he needs to stretch out."

"Oh, yeah." Senator Barrett settled into the spacious "captain's chair" after closing the gate behind the truck. Kim eased the big 4x4 into the gently undulating green meadow, turning onto the narrow trail she had just traveled on horseback. Mitch glanced up at the rifle mounted above the windshield. "Bill, look at the grain on that stock! What do you have there, Kim? Looks like a big Winchester. And exactly what kind of guests are you expecting?" The three laughed.

"Winchester Model 70 Custom. Fancy-grade walnut stock, match-grade barrel, in .338 Winchester Mag. Three an' a half by ten Leupold scope…" Kim rattled off the weapon's specs as she bounced the truck along the trail.

Senator Barrett laughed, "You don't want to be too close to anything needing that much punch to put it down!"

Mitch Steere looked out the small window at the thigh-high grass. "Hey Kim, didn't the previous owner run livestock on this land? This looks like virgin, mixed-grass prairie."

"He did and it is—sort of." Kim raised her voice to be heard over the chatter of the diesel laboring in low gear.

"This field was planted in western wheatgrass—my understanding was there were no cattle grazing here for over a year before I bought it. They planned to lease it out for a hayfield but decided to sell instead."

"It's in wonderful condition. It doesn't look like it's ever seen cattle," Steere commented.

Kim continued. "I know a professor down in Bozeman who teaches rangeland management at Montana State. He was able to give me a rough idea of what grasses this land would have supported before it was ruined by decades of grazing cattle. We spent two days driving the property in the truck, taking turns sitting in the back and scattering seed—sideoats grama, little bluestem, bluebunch wheatgrass, and a little buffalo grass—along the perimeter fencing and over there," she pointed, "along the streambed. Who knows if we got the proportions right, but I think it looks pretty good. And it feels much happier." She smiled. "That was two years ago, so this property hasn't seen a cow in at least three years."

"It's a recovered natural Montana prairie, Kim" Mitch observed. "Well done. All you need now is the buffalo."

Kim smiled broadly. She eased the jumpy pickup across a shallow, narrow stream. "Just over the hill!"

Senator Barrett glanced over from across the transmission console. "I knew it. I knew we were looking at too much fence for horses or cows." He glanced up at the rifle. "And way too much gun for coyotes."

As they crested the top of the hill, what could only be described as a classic "big sky" vista opened before them. Distant mountains to the north and south, with the broad, green valley in front of them, speckled with small pockets of timber, running west to eternity. Two dark shapes were visible a ways to their left. The truck slowed to a crawl as it crept within 150 yards of the animals. The smaller of the two, the cow, looked up at the visitors. About 30 feet behind her right side, the bull, standing six feet at his shoulder, gave a disinterested snort. He turned sideways to afford the trespassers a better view of his size, but kept his huge head in the grass.

Kim shut the engine. "Aren't they beautiful? They're probably the first members of their family to graze this land in 125 years."

"Look at them!" Mitch exclaimed. "They're magnificent—they look like they belong on a postcard. When did you get them?"

"I bought them both last November at the Custer State Park public auction. You know, the Fall Classic?" Kim explained. "She's a two-year-old, big for her age, almost 1,000 pounds. The big boy is 4 years old, probably 1,800 pounds. They auction their excess cows every year, but it's very unusual to get a 4-year-old breeding bull. They must have been way overstocked."

Senator Barrett's eyes were actually misting a bit. "Damn, Kim," he whispered. "They're just beautiful." The three sat in silence for a minute, soaking up the sight.

Mitch asked, "So you're getting into the bison business? You've got a ways to go to build up your herd."

"No, this is it for now. I'm not going into business. I've got just under 200 acres here—enough to support four bison all year without additional food supplementation. These two will probably calf next year; maybe I'll pick up another cow along the way. Who knows? I just wanted them here because they belong on the land."

"Ain't that the truth" muttered Barrett, still engrossed at the sight. The great beasts continued their methodical munching through the shimmering ocean of bright green grass.

Mitch finally got around to the subject at hand. "So Kim, when's the last time you spoke with the Governor?"

"We exchanged Christmas cards. But I don't think we've spoken since a few months after the election—almost a year now, I guess. Ben is an operations guy at heart—once he got settled in the job he just got lost in the day-to-day. You didn't see it so much while he was in the legislature because it's not as much of a management job. Lots more face time with constituents; more opportunity to talk with people and get his blood flowing. He was that way in the restaurant. He would pontificate for an audience when he was behind the bar, but once he took the bar-rag off he would bury himself in the books. I'm sure the bureaucrats in Helena and D.C. have him so buried in paper he needs a snorkel just to find his pen."

"Well," Barrett shot a glance back at Mitch. "I can't be sure, but our Governor may have just surfaced. Did you hear anything about this town meeting up in Kalispell?"

"Nope," Kim replied. "What happened?"

Barrett proceeded to lay out the events of the previous evening.

Kim listened carefully to the story, sitting back in the driver's seat and occasionally glancing out the window at her two pet bison. *You guys have the life.*

"So what's your take on all this, Kim?" Barrett asked. "The Speaker here is afraid Ben is going to talk himself into a mess of trouble, and I'm *hoping* he talks himself into a mess of trouble!" He chuckled.

Kim Lange turned serious. "You know, when we ran for the governor's seat, we really didn't have a road map. He was a conduit, a medium for the feelings and frustrations of people who related to his story and his politics. His attraction wasn't so much the platform as was his fire, his commitment. He was pissed off about the growth of government and the almost total dissolution of individual liberties and responsibilities. That's what sold. Once he found himself in office, his goals tended towards, you know, the regular Republican shtick—reducing regulation, strengthening property rights, reducing taxes, and privatizing as many government services as could be practically done. But once he's wearing his management hat, he's thinking evolution, not revolution. He's become part of the machine, and he hates it. It sounds to me like he found himself in front of a crowd who knew what buttons to push, and he responded. I don't know if I'd read much more into it."

"Shtick?" Mitch grinned.

"Oh, hush up! Turn on your TV once in a while."

"So you think there's nothing more to it? Just a reactionary moment?" the Senator asked.

"Yeah. Don't get me wrong—the TV people and the editorial pages will have their fun. And I wouldn't expect Ben to retract the statement or apologize. It'll just go away once his fever goes down and they lock him back up in his office," she smiled wistfully. She turned the ignition key down to light up the glow plugs, and then fired up the truck's engine. The loud chatter was enough to prod

both bison into raising their huge heads and to watch as Kim threw
the vehicle in reverse, and turned it back toward the ranch house.
"What do you say we go scare up some lunch, boys?"

"Sounds good to me!" Senator Barrett adjusted his seatbelt and
gave a parting look to the bison, now slowly wandering away from
the offending guests.

"Governor? Senator Taylor on line two."

"Thanks, Sherry. I'll take it."

Ben Kane picked up the secure satellite phone that he had
carried over to the executive residence, punched in his access code
to line two, and walked over to the window looking out upon the
modest lawn facing Carson Street.

"Nancy! How are you? How are things on your end?"

"Hi Ben. Well, weather-wise, it's cooler here, but the views
aren't as nice, unless, of course, your taste in landscapes runs to
white marble. Tactically, I have to tell you things are getting a bit
dicey for us."

"Humm, you don't sound very encouraging. No luck with the
filibuster?"

"I'm afraid not. I was hoping to get the western bloc with us,
but the President has been ladling pork into the bill to shore up
support. They only needed to pick up two votes on the Republican
side to guarantee cloture, and they got it. If I were to go ahead and
filibuster on my own, not only would it be a futile gesture in terms
of stopping the bill, but we'd be passed over by the gravy train."

"What's he offering?"

"He called me in the other day. He'll include 300 million above
and beyond the federal takeover allowances if we shut-up and go
away."

"How tight?"

"Every dollar is earmarked. Mostly for education and human

services, from what I've seen. The tribes are going to get a few extra bucks through BIA. I don't think they have any discretionary money in there for you, Ben."

"Well, there's a shock," Ben said sarcastically. "So our choice is to lose more autonomy and control and take the money, or lose more autonomy and control and don't take the money."

"That's about it Ben. Sorry."

"Not your fault, Senator. There's nothing any of us could have done." He paused for a second. "OK, it's executive decision time…let's see…I say take the money."

"Ah, that's why they pay you the big bucks, Governor! I've got to run to a committee meeting—anything else?"

"No. Just let me know when Washington decides it needs to elect our senators for us, I'll put in a good word for you. Thanks, Nancy!"

"Thank you Ben. We'll talk again soon. Bye." Senator Taylor terminated the connection. The Governor walked slowly to his desk and slipped the phone into the pocket of his sports jacket, draped over the back of the leather executive chair. He stood for a moment leaning on the chair.

"Shit," he muttered. He grabbed his jacket and headed for the door.

Kim Lange held court at the same corner of the bar she had regularly haunted during Kane's first political campaign for the Montana House of Representatives nine years earlier. Staff veterans who remembered her crowded around to catch up, while those who knew of her, but had never met, stood around the periphery to see what the excitement was all about. Behind the bar, Joe Adams kept splashing more Merlot in her glass against her protests. Kim was positively effervescing.

"Jooooooooe! Stop!" she squealed as she pushed the glass

away. "I'm meeting the Governor for lunch and I don't think he'd appreciate it if I passed out in the middle of our conversation."

Joe placed a fresh bar napkin under her glass and repositioned it back in front of her. "I'm sure any conversation the Governor has with you will so fascinate him he'll never notice your head down, face first, in the salad." They all laughed as Kim once again slid the glass towards Joe.

"Enough," she said, her tone now more serious.

A slam of the door and the click of cowboy boots against the worn hardwood floor announced the arrival of the state's chief executive. "Hey folks," Ben waved. "Kim, you hittin' the sauce already? Let's get our booth before the lunch crowd hits." He strode toward the back of the dining room at a businesslike pace. Kim hopped off her barstool and followed her soon-to-be boss. "See ya later folks! Duty calls."

The two slid into their accustomed places, nestled comfortably in a high-backed, green leatherette booth. "I appreciate your coming by on such short notice." Ben paused to take a sip of his icy diet cola, already in front of him. "I was surprised to hear from you last night. Glad you called, though."

"I've got some downtime now, Ben. This was a good time to touch bases with you. An important time, I think." Kim widened her eyes a bit, indicating to Ben she that was up-to-speed on current events.

"Yeah. It's an important time, all right. What's the old Chinese curse? May you live in interesting times? We've got it here in spades. Did you order?"

"I grabbed Diane at the bar. She's bringing me a chef's salad and a burger for you."

"Thanks. Do you think Pat Driscoll would make a good governor? I think he would." Patrick Driscoll was Montana's popular lieutenant governor. He was one-quarter Crow and appeared in many of the state's tourism commercials (a task Ben gratefully delegated to the handsome, athletic second-in-command).

Kim recognized the wistful undercurrent in Ben's statement. "Someday? He'll make a great governor when his turn comes. Not right now though."

"Why can't I quit?" He was whining now. "Why shouldn't I quit? Everybody else can. It's just a job." He sat back and looked around the room. "I came across this great recipe for a nice, crisp brown beer I'd like to try here. I think it would do well. And I think we could do a little radio advertising…"

Kim formed a megaphone with her hands. "Earth to Governor! Earth to Governor! Come back to us!" She put her hands down. "It's not just a job, Ben! You're the chief executive of the fourth largest state in the country, and you can't just bail out when parts of the job start pissing you off!"

"I know, I know. But I can dream, can't I?" he said with a wink.

Diane shuffled over with their plates and set them down. "Enjoy!"

"Thanks, Diane!" Ben and Kim said in unison. The waitress made a beeline to a table waving to her across the room.

Kim got down to business. "I know about the legislation; who doesn't at this point? And I know what your problem is with it philosophically, but what's the operational issue? I mean, I know it's going to be an administrative nightmare. But so is everything else they do. Where's the new problem here, Ben?"

The Governor nodded his head, seemingly in agreement with what he had just heard. "You're right. There's nothing really new here. But that *is* the problem, isn't it? We're looking right down the barrel at the practical elimination of even semiautonomous state governments. That's a problem. Almost every state in the Union is cheering the legislation—that's another problem." Ben put his head in his hands and massaged his temples. "And there's a gnawing feeling in my gut telling me I'm not going to be able to sit still for this. And that's *definitely* going to be a problem."

Kim chose to ignore his statement for the moment. "I understand they offered budget offsets?"

"Yeah," Ben muttered, almost to himself. "Nancy Taylor tells me about 300 million, mostly earmarked for education." He looked up at her. "Which just means they're paying themselves. They're taking over the whole freakin' education system. Where do you think the 300 million is going?"

Kim let him rant on for a bit. *How frustrating for him.* She knew this wasn't his ego talking, not just another politician pissed because his side lost and the other side won.

"What do you call a government like this?" Ben asked rhetorically. "Benevolent fascism? You've got the party of government, the Democratic Party, in charge of civil servants and government workers at the federal, state and local levels. They control the bulk of the easily accessible mass media, and the education system, from the childcare centers up to college campuses. Then you've got the loyal opposition, the Republican Party—Democratic 'lite.' They're mathematically locked out of the presidency and any hope of a Congressional majority, so all they can do is nip at the Democrats' ankles. The Democrats propose a new billion-dollar bureaucracy to regulate the redistribution of sunshine to previously deprived and clearly disenfranchised shady spots, and all the Republicans can do is counter with the same program with half the budget. They get painted as cheap and callous and lose the debate. Damn it, we've been watching this happen for the last 40 years. And if the Republicans are supposed to be such smart business people, how come they can't find a public relations firm to counter the lame, uncaring rap the Democrats have been throwing at them for the last 40 years?"

Thankfully, Kim was taking a gulp of her drink and was unable to offer a response in the brief time allotted.

"Equality of outcome," he continued, "involves massive government intervention and control of the economy, education and private enterprise. It requires a totalitarian state to accomplish. And it's immoral—in order to guarantee the equality of outcomes, the government must coerce or outright steal from some to give to others. It's just not right!" He finally paused to take a bite of his burger.

Kim knew better than to try to either encourage or discourage his current line of thought. She picked at her salad. A safe topic finally popped into her mind. "Joe says the new light beer is really catching on!"

He nodded, finished chewing and dabbed his mouth with his napkin. "It's doing very well. Not a light beer really, just a pilsner style. We need a new mash cooker to keep up with the volume. Damn it! I should just quit this governor crap and brew beer!" Kim watched as her safe topic flew quickly out the window. "I'm good at it, I can make a living at it, and Pat Driscoll would make a great governor, you said so yourself!" He took another bite of his lunch. Kim returned to her salad, determined now to keep her mouth shut.

The Governor finally returned to the subject of his immediate ire, the soon-to-be federal school system. "The public school system is where children are taught what to believe, what to think, what to value. It's where they're taught how to live, and what it means to be a citizen. From the day their mothers drag them kicking and screaming to their first day of kindergarten to their last walk down the auditorium aisle in their 12th-grade cap and gowns, those school teachers and administrators shape their hearts and minds, and directly determine the future of the nation." Ben paused and stared out the window separating their booth from the lunch crowds wandering sunny Sanders Street. He looked as if he had he just convinced himself of something.

He looked across the table at Kim, all business. "I need you to start looking at our options here."

"What do you mean?" Kim furrowed her brow. "I'm not a lawyer."

"I'm not interested in legal options," the Governor cut her off. "You think I need more legal opinions? This is government, Kim; I'm swimming in lawyers! I know what they're going to say, every last one of them: Don't say anything, don't do anything, don't write anything down; crawl under your bed, turn out the lights and don't come out. Ever! That doesn't help me."

"I need organizational options," he continued. "Plot me a way out of here. How can we operate without a government school system?" The Governor of Montana asked the question as if he were asking directions to the rest room.

Here we go! she thought.

CHAPTER 5
Mid-May, 2013

The hot asphalt of Interstate-15 rolled beneath the humming motorcycle's narrow front wheel, as if the vehicle were stationary and it was the earth itself rushing toward the rider, subject to the whims of the throttle controlled by Joe Adam's vibrating right hand. He'd left Helena just after 7:00 A.M., and was now approaching Great Falls, a little less than 90 minutes later. The city proper lay east of the highway, the Great Falls International Airport to the west, and the 200 Minuteman III missiles scattered about in approximately 23,000 square miles west, east, and northeast of the city. Joe would be surrounded on both sides by the nuclear-tipped weapons for the remaining 75 miles of his ride up I-15, right up until the turn west to jump on to US-2 heading into Browning. The missiles represented the long reach of American military power to the world at large, and a significant employment opportunity to the Great Falls locals. Officially under the aegis of the 341st Strategic Missile Wing operating out of the Malmstrom Air Force Base, the day-to-day operating management and missile personnel were attached to the 10th, 12th, 490th, and 564th Missile Squadrons of the 341st. This missile field was part of an arsenal of 530 intercontinental ballistic missiles scattered across Montana, North Dakota and Wyoming. In order to meet warhead levels set by the Strategic Arms Reduction Treaty (START II), a multi-billion dollar project was underway to reduce the number of warheads carried by the Mark 12 reentry system in each missile from three to one reentry vehicles (military jargon for the bombs) and to increase the accuracy of the system.

The city of Great Falls, population 57,000, was the second-largest population center in Montana. Billings, 225 miles to the southeast, was the state's largest city with a whopping 120,000 citizens. Since it was early Saturday, Joe was able to maintain a comfortable 70 mph through the I-15/US-87/US-89 interchange, a nexus of considerable traffic congestion on a weekday morning. It was a good speed for the vintage British motorcycle. Though capable, with the 20-tooth counter-sprocket Joe settled on, of a top-end speed of about 115 mph, it was far too light a vehicle—just 365 pounds dry—for a stable ride at top speed. At 70, it still produced enough midrange torque to aggressively pull itself out of trouble if need be, but wasn't moving so fast as to induce the infamous Norton rear-swingarm wobbles. Technically an attack of sympathetic vibration caused by excessive play in the rubber, isolastic mounts separating the considerable engine vibration from the bike's frame, the unwanted seesaw swingarm motion could start the rear wheel dangerously wobbling at high speeds. Nothing fucked up a good beer buzz like having your rear wheel suddenly and violently dancing side-to-side at 80 mph. Luckily, Joe didn't have to deal with either of those things this morning.

Another plus was that at 70 he was able to hold the engine at a hair under 4,500 rpms. It was a nice, comfortable spot for a motor redlining at 7,000 rpms and famous for its midrange power charge, and a safe one for a power plant with a well-deserved reputation for exploding ungracefully at the high end of its rpm range.

Motoring along with Great Falls receding behind him, Joe glanced at the odometer. The bike's small gas tank, holding just a few drops over 2 gallons of fuel, could only carry him about 90 miles at this speed. Shelby was 80 miles away, and he had already clocked about 15 miles on this fresh tank. *Probably stop for gas and grub in Conrad.*

Joe straightened his arms, lifted himself slightly on the footpegs and arched his back a bit to help maintain a sharp "ready" position on the bike. With head held high and chest arched into the wind, the position allowed the driver to use his upper body as a sail, lifting weight from his seat and legs. He took a deep breath of sweet, cool country air. *Poor Ben. What the hell is he going to do?* Joe went way back with the Governor and knew how troubled he was over this latest federal legislation.

Politically and culturally, California and Texas, along with their neighboring states, were, for all practical purposes, re-absorbed by Mexico. New York and its immediate neighbors were becoming part of the whole global, United Nations, European Union "New World Order" thing in their political and cultural nexus. Well, Ben didn't care much about Mexico's problems, and he certainly didn't give a rat's ass about the East Coast's problems in trying to tax their way to a global socialist utopia. He just wanted to do the best he could for Montanans. Like most people living in the American heartland, he identified more with the land, the wind, the wildlife, the history, and the people around him than with the growing priorities of the coastal states, places where, in his mind, there was no land, no wind, no wildlife, no sense of history, and more of a competition for capital resources than a shared appreciation of the natural ones. "They certainly have a right to live their kind of life," he would say, "but how come we don't have a right to live ours?"

Joe contemplated the Blackfeet reservation he was heading for this morning, and the growing parallels between their existence and his own. *Montana, Idaho, the Dakotas, Wyoming, Nebraska—we're all just becoming one big-ass reservation for 'classic Americans,'* he smiled at coining the phrase. *Just breathing museum pieces.*

And the demographics were showing fewer and fewer of those museum pieces remaining. A vast swath of mostly rural America just west of the Mississippi and east of Las Vegas had been rapidly depopulating for 20 years. As the migration spread to the east and western states, Congressional representation for those coastal states increased, at the cost of the mid-continental states that proportionately lost representation in the People's House. Economically, the mid-continentals were almost all experiencing federal tax net inflows—simply stated, they got more money back from the federal government than they sent in. Montana alone got back about $1.75 for every tax dollar sent to Washington. They were all left in the position of having increasingly significant portions of their state budgets dependent on federal largess, with less and less ability to have an effect on the policies controlling the distribution of those very funds in Congress. The governing policies of the mid-continental states became a largely take-it or leave-it proposition controlled by the coastal states through the federal government. This trend went largely unnoticed by the populous states, who were understandably focused on their own problems, but was increasingly noted by state legislators and newspaper editorialists in the affected states, who were consistently unable to deliver the more culturally and economically conservative policies preferred by their local voters. Frustration was building, to be sure, a frustration manifesting itself in the quiet but palpable depressed demeanor of a defeated population. A population who long ago had laid down their arms and stopped fighting. Except, perhaps, for Ben Kane.

The President pro tempore gaveled the Senate chamber to order. "The chamber will come to order! The chamber will please come to order! The Senators will take their seats please. Order!" Within a minute or so the Senate chamber settled down and the aging, blue-haired senator entrusted with the podium in lieu of the Vice-President of the United States proceeded to announce the results of the just completed roll call vote. The vote, taken at the request of an opposing senator, served to put on the record what had just been, to most observers, a fairly definitive voice vote. "The vote is complete. The ayes 78, the nays 22—the ayes have it; the bill passes." The gavel crisply struck the sound block, and cheers, though not overly enthusiastic, were heard scattered about the chamber. S.114-275, the "One Nation" bill, was ready for the President's signature.

CHAPTER 6
Mid-May, 2013

Joe Adams swung his very hot, annoyed Norton through the last lazy left turn on US-89 heading into the dusty, flat, depressed-looking town of Browning, Mont. The small settlement was in the south-central heart of the 1.5 million-acre Blackfeet Indian Reservation, home to approximately 7,000 folks of native decent— less than 20 percent of who could claim to be full-blooded Blackfeet. His initial, pressing priority was to pull into the first gas station in town to take the leak he'd been holding for the last 30 miles.

His face, he could see as he passed the dirty, ill-lit mirror, was red, sweaty, and painted with road grime and bugs. Thankfully, there were a few brown paper towels in the dispenser, allowing him a crude attempt at cleaning up. *Better than nuthin',* he convinced himself as he scrubbed something with wings off his cheek.

He exited the dank restroom still cleaning his sunglasses with a damp towel. Slipping on the shades, he sauntered over to the pumps to top off his tank. The attendant, a Blackfoot, too old to be pumping gas in most towns, walked out from the office, glad for the chance to get away from the afternoon talk shows on TV.

"Nice wheel! Haven't seen one of those around here in quite a while. Used to be a guy over in Kiowa rode one, a couple of Triumphs, too. Don't know what happened to him. Fast as hell, those Nortons."

"Thanks. It's a '72, Combat engine—runs hot as hell." Joe carefully pulled the nozzle out of the now full, jet-black gas tank and replaced the cap. He reached for his wallet and pulled out a $10 bill.

"Nice day for riding." The attendant made change from the wad of damp, greasy bills he pulled out of his pocket. "If you're stopping for lunch they've got fresh turkey at the diner." He pointed to the establishment farther on up the road.

"Not today. I'm meeting Tommy Running Wolf for lunch. I understand he's made some progress on the herd."

"Oh yeah. People are driving him crazy, driving up to the hills and watching those buffalo. Must have close to 400 head now, I think. It's very emotional for a lot of folks. Especially the old ones—they heard all the buffalo stories from their grandparents. Now the younger ones see as well. It's very emotional."

Joe smiled and nodded his head. "That's great. I'm glad things are working out. Listen, I gotta get rollin'. Maybe I'll catch you on the way back." Joe straddled the motorcycle, switched on the ignition, and gave the kick-start lever a swift, determined kick. The Norton responded with an aggressive idle. He squeezed the clutch lever with his left hand and punched the gearshift up into first gear with his right foot. Unlike practically every other motorcycle made in history, the Norton Commando shifted from the right side, and patterned one up, three down instead of the typical one down, four up from the left side.

"OK my friend—ride safe." The attendant took a step back, and Joe nodded and pulled away.

Ben Kane struggled under the weight of the 60-pound dumbbells. The phone rang, sparing him the trauma of realizing he wasn't as strong as he used to be. He dropped he weights on the heavily padded floor beneath the bench he was lying on. Sitting up with a grunt, he pushed his hair out of his face and reached for the cellphone resting on the small table near the entrance to his personal gym, set up conveniently in the Executive Mansion's basement.

"Ben Kane."

"Hey Governor. It's Kim! I've got a short update for you on the school issue."

The Governor reached for his water bottle and slumped into a chair. "Shoot."

"OK. Long story short, the government school system in this country is suffering from the largest, most ingrained case of mission creep I've ever seen."

"Explain."

"Mission creep is when additional goals are tacked on to a project or business operation on top of the original, clearly defined mission. Example—company XYZ produces the world's best, most popular, largest selling widget. Their entire operation—information technology, administration, marketing, sales, finance, human resources recruiting, training and development—everything and everybody is geared to producing, marketing and selling this premier widget."

"OK." Ben loved hearing Kim explain things.

"Then the board of directors gets ambitious. They replace the management team with a more 'creative' one. They start producing flavored widgets, extra-large widgets, color widgets, action-figure widgets, low-fat widgets, extra-fast widgets, good-gas-mileage widgets, extra absorbent…"

"I get it."

"OK. The company expands, hires the additional people, installs the additional internal systems. Then the stock price starts falling, for whatever reason. Nobody knows where to look first. Which product line is failing? What's our core business? What's our corporate identity? How did we end up here?"

"OK."

"The point is, nobody knows what kind of company it is anymore; nobody knows what the mission is. That's the story of government schools in this country for the past 100 years or so, Ben. In rural times, you got your schooling at home, with occasional visits to the local one-room schoolhouse. When urban industrialization expanded in the late 1800s and early 1900s, and most of society moved to a situation where everybody did the same work, in the same place, at the same time, for the same pay—that industrial model was transferred to the school system. All kids of the same age went to the same place, in the same class, and learned the same thing at the same time from the same person."

"OK. Makes sense."

"Whatever the weaknesses of that system, the mission was still pretty crisp—teach every student a fixed, age-based curriculum, to be built upon by the following year's curriculum. Students were held in the class, 'left back,' until they mastered the curriculum, before they were sent on to the next grade. By 8th grade, virtually everybody knew how to read, write and manipulate numbers at grade level. Again, whatever the weaknesses, everybody knew what the mission was."

"Got it."

"Things started getting really jumbled in the last 25 years of the 20th Century. Special groups got special classes—African-American studies, Latino studies, women's studies. Kids stopped getting left back because it was bad for their self-image, so they were either promoted without having mastered the grade, or the classes were dumbed down to the least common denominator so nobody with an IQ higher than a dandelion could fail. Nutrition was shown to effect academic performance, so proper nutrition became a priority."

"Is that why they put McDonald's in the school cafeterias?"

Ben thought he remembered having read something to that effect many years earlier.

"Ha! Yes, probably! Well, you get the picture here, don't you? Testing, class size, childcare services, healthcare services, after-school programs, food services, psychological counseling services, drug counseling, birth control services—the government school system has no idea what its mission is. In contrast, look at most private schools, or those for-profit learning centers. They know what their mission is. You pay your money, you pack the lunch, they teach your kid how to read and write. If they don't teach your kid how to read and write, nobody would pay them any money. It's not really too complicated. Except for the government schools. They're a monopoly, and they're accountable to no one. They've become job programs for teachers' unions, they have access to unlimited funding and budget increases every year regardless of performance, and nobody knows what the mission is. That's why nobody's figured out how to fix it; nobody knows what part of it is broken."

"Tell me about home schooling." Ben reached for his water bottle and took another long swig. This was getting interesting.

"OK, I'm sure you realize we have a relatively high percentage of home schoolers here in Montana."

"In the rural areas."

"Right. Nationally, there are about 9.6 million home schoolers, mostly middle-class families. Home-schooled children consistently outperform traditionally schooled kids on standardized achievement tests. Blow them away on the national tests, not even close. Home schoolers tend to be better socialized—they spend more time with adults, in an adult world, and more time with children of different ages."

"Downside?"

"The obvious. Time and motivation of the parents. Not every

parent wants to do it, can do it, or has the time to do it. And the law, in general, doesn't allow home schooling of someone else's kids."

"The law can be changed." The wheels started turning.

"Well, that's your department, Governor. You know as well as I do the entrenched interests out there—teachers' unions, civil rights organizations, and all of the political resources, civil servants, and politicians married to all of those interests. I mean, look at this latest piece of legislation, this latest fix. Nobody has even defined exactly which problem it is they're trying to fix—mission creep— remember? They're stacking the management structure even higher, increasing payrolls, broadening the mission further, and taking any and all responsibility away from the people on the ground in the name of holding them more responsible. It's really not even stupid, Ben, it's just laughable."

"Sounds pretty sad, Ms. Lange, but I expected as much. Look, I really appreciate the work you put in on this. Let's do this. Write it up for me, with some ideas on how home schooling could be extended to a broader population—forget the limitations of the law right now. How it would work, how it might effect the future of our economy, what government infrastructure would be needed, what the problems would be. You know the drill."

"Got it. Anything else?"

"That's enough for now. Thank you, Kim."

"Thank **you,** Governor. Talk to you soon." The line went dead, and Ben placed the phone down on the desk. He grabbed his water bottle and headed upstairs for a shower.

The Norton was ticking, clicking, knocking and making all sorts of strange noises as it cooled down after the 20-minute ride from the center of Browning to Chief Running Wolf's modest home. A small but steady drip of motor oil rhythmically plopped from the banjo connector linking the oil tank to the twin cylinder engine's sump.

The oil disappeared into the white gravel covering the chief's driveway. The chief didn't look concerned.

"Still riding that thing, Joe? Where do you find parts for it?"

"I've got a spare engine and frame at home I scavenge for parts. Otherwise I can order most stuff on-line. I actually ordered a front fender from England. Brand new—look at that chrome!"

"Yeah, beautiful. Some investment. Hope it gets you home."

"So far so good. I stay on top of the maintenance work. Ride an hour, work on it for an hour. But it sounds great, doesn't it?" They both shook their heads and stared at the bike with admiration. Sheltered from the early afternoon sun by a large umbrella covering the chief's picnic table, the two busied themselves with a generously iced cooler of bottled beer. The picnic table was situated on the chief's front lawn, between the gravel driveway and the flagstone walkway leading to the front door of the house. They waved to the occasional pickup careening down the dirt road running in front of the house. Life was good. Hot, but good.

"So tell me about the herd. The guy at the gas station said you're up to 400 head?" Joe pulled at the icy longneck until he was forced to gasp for breath.

"Just over. 412, I think. We'll go out and count again at the end of the summer. Wanna go take a look?" The chief stood up and grabbed the cooler. "Let's go. Let your bike cool down a bit. Just move it out of the way of the truck." He nodded at the Norton.

Eager to have somebody else drive, Joe put down his beer and rolled the bike farther up the driveway while the chief headed to the weathered 4x4 pickup. Joe retrieved his brew and hopped into the passenger's seat.

"Let's see if we can find them," said Running Wolf as he backed into the street and threw the vehicle into first gear. "I haven't seen them in a week or so, but I spoke to one of the crew yesterday, so I know where they should be. At least where they were yesterday."

"You don't know where 400 freakin' buffalo are! You got any smokes in here?" Joe flipped open the glove box and crumpled papers started falling out. "Oh man!"

"Forget it. Nobody knows what's in there." Running Wolf pointed to a ballistic nylon shoulder bag behind his seat. "In there." Joe lifted the bag and rummaged through its contents until he found an open carton of Marlboros. "Wow, four packs!" He gloated as if he had hit gold.

"Help yourself. I don't smoke much anymore." The chief turned north on to a recently repaved section of County Road 464.

"Excellent!" Joe ripped into the fresh pack of cigarettes and fished one out. "We have cold beer, cigarettes, and now—asphalt! Who said life sucks!"

"I guess it all depends on how high you set the bar."

"I like to keep success within reach; it reduces stress. How far we goin'?" The truck's cigarette lighter popped out; Joe fired up and took a deep drag. After the early morning start, a three-and-a-half-hour motorcycle trek, three beers and a suddenly smooth ride, the nicotine rush hit him hard. "Whoa!"

Tommy Running Wolf slowed his vehicle and steered around some sort of dead deer or antelope lying in the road. "What a shame. How far? We got about 18 miles here on 464, then about 4 or 5 miles east. Just south of Milk River. We've set aside about 25,000 acres for the herd. Beautiful, pristine, natural mixed-grass prairie. Plenty of water. We used to grow wheat there, years ago. A waste of time. Good year, bad year—you had no way of knowing what was going to happen. I don't think there's ever been cattle grazed on that land."

"What's the difference? Don't buffalo graze like cattle?"

"The bison are native to this land," the chief explained. "They've been here for tens of thousands of years. Cattle are from, I don't know, Southeast Asia somewhere. Lowland animals. You have to encourage the grasses they like to eat, shelter them in the winter, kill all of the predators on the prairie, shoot the prairie dogs so they don't step into their holes and break their legs. You have to fuss with the water access—cattle will hang out by their water source, they'll crap in the same water they drink. They're not very bright."

He continued. "The bison, this is their land. They eat the native grasses. They're fine on their own year round—even in the winter. They find their own food and water, and the rain and cold and snow don't bother them. Prairie dogs don't bother them; they don't step in the holes. We don't have to poison or shoot the wolves or the cougar or the coyote. They all live on their land together—the bison can handle the predators, and the predators know better than to attack a healthy bison herd. Especially when there are cattle around," the chief laughed.

"The return of the bison lets us restore the balance to the land. They were here long before my people were, and a long, long time before your people were," he smiled at Joe. "All we really have to do is make sure they're current on their brucellosis vaccinations, and only because the government makes us do it. Brucellosis doesn't bother the bison. It only bothers cattle and cattle ranchers. And government inspectors."

"And they're good eatin'!" commented Joe, thinking of the brisk market for buffalo burgers back down at the bar in Helena and the reason he took the ride today.

"Yes, they most certainly are," agreed the chief. "We haven't started a large-scale meat operation yet—we just take a few of the older bulls every year for our own use—but we're thinking about it."

Tommy Running Wolf steered the four-wheeler off of the paved roadway on to the narrow eastbound, hard-packed dirt road.

They bounced along for another 20 minutes or so, the chief talking about bison, Joe nursing another cold beer and smoking cigarettes, looking around and admiring the scenery. The uneven surface forced the chief to slow down considerably. Joe could now feel the mild, warm, spring crosswind blowing against his face. It was a live, rich prairie breeze—a full, sweet, grass-filled cross current in a dense ocean of air. He inhaled deeply and studied the bright, expansive grasslands to his right—technically, looking southwest towards Great Falls, though no hint of civilization was in sight. His eyelids grew heavy in the sun, as the mellow spring breeze, rising blood alcohol level and the long drive conspired to force the issue of an afternoon nap. He capitulated to their argument and drifted off into a light, but undeniable, sleep.

"Joe! Hey Joe!" Tom Running Wolf shouted, much louder than he needed to.

"Huh? Oh man, I drifted off. How long was I out?" Joe massaged the back of his neck with one hand while securing the beer bottle, still between his legs, with the other.

"About 10 minutes or so. Look up ahead." Running Wolf nodded to direct Joe's still-foggy gaze.

"Holy shit!" Joe sat up straight and lit a cigarette. "What do you have here? Jurassic Park?"

The truck now turned right on to less an unpaved road, more a worn rut running through the 3-foot high grass. Less than a half mile in front of them Joe could see an unusually tall, apparently endless livestock fence.

"Electric?"

"No," responded Running Wolf, now clinging hard to the less-than-cooperative steering wheel. "You're looking at about a quarter of a million dollars worth of fencing as it is; 8 feet high, runs across here," the chief motioned across the length of the dashboard, "about

5 miles, runs south almost 8 miles; 25,000 acres, totally enclosed with high-tensile fencing."

"How do we find the buffalo?" The truck stopped about 10 yards in front of a gate wide enough to let three trucks through. The chief opened the vehicle's door and stepped out.

"About a mile and a half down here, there's a rock outcrop with a little elevation to it. On top there's a nice wooded draw of ponderosa pine, a real nice spot. We might be able to spot them from there." He walked over to the gate and unlocked the large, heavy-duty padlock clasped through the latch. He swung the gate open and walked back to the truck. The padlock, with the key still in it, was tossed on top of the dashboard. Joe grabbed it and started playing with it. "Don't lose the key," warned the chief, "or you're going to contract for a lot more meat than you bargained for." He pulled the truck into the bison pasture and stopped again. He held his hand out for the lock.

"You're going to lock us in here?" Joe handed over the lock and looked around. He didn't see any immediate threats.

"Yes, I'm going to lock us in. We've got 40 square miles here—we can't watch the gate once it's out of sight. And the animals aren't going to ask permission to walk through an open gate. Don't lose the key." He jumped out of the truck, walked back, and closed and locked the gate. He returned to the truck and threw it into gear.

"How about you hang onto the key?" Joe suggested.

"Good thinkin'. Keep your eyes peeled." The truck bounced along the hint of roadway through the tall grass. After almost five minutes Joe could see the slightly elevated outcrop over to his right. The chief looped the truck behind the formation and drove it up the gently inclined hill running up to the edge of the cliff. He killed the engine and stepped out.

"I don't see anything. Grab those glasses out of my bag." Joe reached behind his seat and rummaged through the large duffle bag. He pulled out a pair of moderately expensive, variable power binoculars and jumped out of the truck. Running Wolf was standing near the edge of the outcropping, one hand shielding his eyes from the bright sun, scanning the horizon.

"Over there, maybe." He pointed to the southeast. Joe saw nothing but an endless sea of waving green grass speckled with tiny purple and yellow wildflowers. "Let me see those." Joe handed him the binoculars.

"Yeah. There's two, three, five. We lose some elevation as we head over that way. If they're down there we wouldn't be able to see them from here. There's a few animals down there, the rest are probably just below, out of sight." He handed Joe the glasses.

Joe raised the instrument and adjusted the focus. "I don't see shit." He moved his field of view a couple of degrees and fiddled with magnification adjustment. "Oh man, they're far away! How'd you spot them? How far are they?" He could only make out three of the five the chief claimed to have seen.

"Yeah, they're a ways off. Two miles maybe. Let's go." Running Wolf turned and walked back to the truck. Joe put down the glasses and followed. They hopped into the vehicle and backed down the gentle incline. He threw the vehicle into first and drove around the shady hill into the bright, infinite panorama of Montana's gently undulating green prairie.

The herd, as was its general inclination, clustered itself in various groupings—in some case family, in others, by previous herd relationships. In enlarging the herd faster than its natural reproductive rate allowed, the Blackfeet occasionally purchased 10 to 30 bison at a time, from other ranchers or government herds. Those brought in from the outside tended to stick together. But when it was time to move, for whatever reason, the herd moved as one.

Tommy Running Wolf inched the truck into a position he felt was about right; close enough to the herd so their presence could be felt, but not so close as to push or spook them.

"Awesome." Joe spoke quietly. "Just fucking awesome."

"They are beautiful," agreed the chief. The animals were spread out in a rough crescent in front of the truck, curving around well to their left. Coming from the northeast, the wind was skimming across the herd grazing to the left side of the vehicle, denying most of the beasts the scent of diesel, tobacco and humans, but providing the visitors with a continual noseful of sweet grass and buffalo. The air was thick and deep with scents and sounds—the herd was continually but softly grunting and barking—painting a reality very, very different from the one existing just minutes before for the two visitors as they bounced along the empty prairie—chatting, drinking beer and enjoying a smoke. The spirituality of the moment was plain to Running Wolf and perceived even by Joe, who spoke quietly, as if in church. In fairness, fear of causing a stampede contributed significantly to his newfound softness of expression, but in either case the mood was directly related to an evident power well beyond their immediate control. They sat silently for a while, windows open, drinking in the breeze, sights, sounds and smells of the Late-Pleistocene Epoch vision spread out before them.

"Wanna have some fun?" Running Wolf broke the silence.

"What do you have in mind?" Joe was starting to feel sleepy again.

"You see the white pail in the back? There's some buffalo cookies in there, and a scoop. Why don't you jump back there and shovel some out for the kiddies?"

"Buffalo cookies? What the hell are buffalo cookies? Is it safe to go out there?" Joe looked at the seemingly indifferent leviathans dubiously, really only caring about the answer to his last question.

"Sweet chops. Cubes of rolled oats and molasses. They love it. Just toss some out the back of the truck and I'll pull up a bit and give them some room. I do it all the time—what do you think it's doing back there? Go ahead, maybe you'll find one you like. Or maybe one of them likes you." The chief winked at Joe and pointed over his right shoulder with his thumb. "Scoop!"

"Oh man." Joe quietly eased the passenger door open, and stepped out of the vehicle, never taking his eyes off the herd, who were spread out some 70 yards in front of the vehicle on his side. He took a few soft steps back towards the truck's bed, put his hands on the rail and hoisted himself over the side. He remained in the squat position he landed in and surveyed his surrounding. *So far, so good.* The animals seemed not to notice him, or if they did, they seemed not to care. He could see Running Wolf watching him in the rearview mirror.

The rear, left corner of the truck bed contained a 10-gallon, white plastic pail, held in place with a couple of fat bungee cords. He eased over to the pail and tried to pry off the sticky top while kneeling next to it, still attempting to maintain a low profile. Poorly leveraged and not having any luck, he finally stood up and ripped the top off with a little too much force, sending it flying over the left side of the truck, about six feet away.

"Shit. Of course," he muttered. Now standing tall, he was feeling a little braver, and so hopped back over the right side of the vehicle, out of sight of the bulk of the herd, and walked around the back of the truck to retrieve the errant lid. After grabbing it from the ground and placing it in the truck bed, he stood for a moment and studied the animals in front of him. Most immediately noticeable was the large bull grazing just 50 yards off to his left. The size of the animal was a terrible thing to behold at so close a distance. Joe Adams stood 5'8" tall, so he was at eye level somewhere near the bull's shoulder blade. He could not see the top of the buffalo's hump, which was clearly over 6 feet tall. But the head! The huge, wide, black wooly head was pressed tightly against the grass, clipping it neatly but not pulling it out by the roots like regular cattle would. The striking thing about the animal's head was its disproportionate size when compared to those of the smaller cows or immature bulls. Theirs were regular "cattle sized" heads, proportionate to their bodies, scaled the way an artist might insist on drawing them.

But the large bull's head was positively prehistoric. Broad and heavy, from where Joe stood it looked to be the size of a clothes dryer—a dryer with 18" black horns sticking out on either side. The bull lifted his head from the ground and looked directly at Joe.

Joe landed safely in the truck bed before giving himself a chance to think about it. The bull snorted defiantly and tossed his freaky head from side to side, lifted his tail high, and turned to show the visitors his profile.

"OK, OK, I get it!" Joe reached into the pail, grasped the scoop lying atop the feed, and started tossing the moist, fragrant mixture over the side of the truck. *Humm…this stuff looks pretty good. I'm gettin' hungry myself, now that I think about it.*

Unbeknown to him, the animals knew exactly what he was doing. The moment the first scoop of the sweetened grain hit the ground, those closest to the truck started heading towards it—the big bull, of course, in the lead. By the time Joe looked up to see how his work was progressing, the bison were only 40 feet away and closing fast.

"TOMMY!!! HIT THE GAS!" Joe was banging frantically on the roof of the cab. "YO! MOVE! FAST! NOW! GO! TOMMY!!! MOVE THE TRUCK!!!"

Running Wolf, who had quietly watched the whole scene unfold, was now laughing uncontrollably. With tears streaming down his cheeks and Joe screaming hysterically, banging on the roof and jumping up and down, he calmly shifted into first gear and slowly eased the truck off to the right, away from the advancing animals. He stopped about 100 yards away from the growing cluster of bison and collapsed on the steering wheel, convulsing in laughter.

"Funny. Very, very funny." Joe was back in the truck, making a point of locking the door as soon as it slammed shut. His face was flushed and he quickly fished out a cigarette and lit it. The chief was still snickering, now watching the herd in the driver's side mirror.

"You didn't give them enough! Get back out there!"

"Yeah, that's going to happen. Shit." Joe cracked open a cold beer and took a well-deserved pull. "Are you going to sell us the big guy? He's a LOT of burger, man!" The whole point of the trip north was to arrange the purchase of an animal for the restaurant.

"No, not him. Too young; he's in his prime. We've got some 10-year-old bulls we are going to slaughter at the end of the season; we'll sell you one of those." The chief jumped out of the truck, quickly reached over the side of the rail, grabbed the pail and dumped the rest of the sweetened oats onto the grass. He tossed the empty pail back into the back and briskly returned to the cab. "Let's hit the road." He turned the truck around and headed back up the track, as the bison converged on their afternoon snack.

CHAPTER 7
Mid-May, 2013

Ben Kane was incredulous. "You're telling me you spent almost six hours on a motorcycle when you could have made a five-minute phone call? You could have gotten yourself killed!"

"Oh, you got that right! But not on the bike, chief. The Norton was the safest place I was all day." Joe was back behind the bar at the American Outback Brewing Company, counting out the bank for the opening register. His head was somewhere between a full-blown hangover and just plain feeling like crap.

"Not to mention getting your ass stranded up there for a week," Ben continued. "Did you hear about the snow? Major storm, must have blown in right after you left. I just got off the phone with the Red Cross. We're putting stranded travelers up in area hotels."

"Shit," observed Joe. "Me and Running Wolf were eating lunch on his picnic table yesterday afternoon! We had a nice cooler of beer; it was a beautiful day!"

Somehow Ben wasn't surprised to hear about the cooler of beer. "How's Tommy Running Wolf these days? I understand he's doing a great job with the InterTribal Bison Cooperative. They tell me the tribal herds are increasing dramatically. His herd is up over 400 now, isn't it?"

"Yeah, just over 400 head, minus the bull we're taking this fall. And the chief is doing well; he looks good. It looks like there's some new construction in Browning, too." Joe placed the cash box in the cabinet under the register.

"They're not doing too poorly up there, as tribal economies go. They've got a pretty good oil drilling operation, and a nice sized writing implement manufacturing facility—pencils and pens and such. And they run, I think, four big campgrounds, along with the outfitting and hunting guides. The business interests buy them a little financial wiggle room that allow them to grow their bison herd. If they could ever get out from under the federal bureaucracy they could actually make a run at building a real life for themselves up there. It's a shame." Ben shook his head and started stuffing papers into his briefcase. "I've got a meeting with the legislative leadership. Do you have everything under control?"

"Yes sir! Everyone should be in soon. The dining room was all set up last night, so we're ready to rock. See you later, commander!" Joe clicked his heels and saluted.

"Thanks Joe, you have a great day." Ben slipped his briefcase off the bar and rushed out the door. Joe came out from behind the bar to retrieve two cases of beer to pack out and ice down in the sinks.

State Sen. William Barrett lumbered up the appropriately named Grand Stair, which led from the state Capitol's rotunda to the third floor Senate chamber and related offices. The Grand Stair was bathed in an ethereal early morning light, pouring through windows positioned high in the copper-crowned Capitol dome and brightly illuminating both the staircase and the famous Golden Spike painting overlooking the steps.

His thoughts were interrupted by the patter of rapidly moving leather soles on marble quickly gaining on him. Before he could completely turn to see who it was, a hand firmly came down on his shoulder.

"Hey Senator!" Ben Kane pulled up alongside and slowed his

pace to match Barrett's. "What's going on? I see you guys more now with the legislature out of session then I do when you're all sitting!" The Montana Legislature met for a regular 90-day session every two years; they were scheduled to sit again at noon on the first Monday in January.

"It sure looks that way, doesn't it?" the Senator acknowledged. "I'm meeting with the Rules Committee later this morning, but the Speaker and I thought it wise to bring you into the loop on some of the buzz out there." The two continued up to the third floor, where they proceeded along the brilliantly polished stone floor to the Majority Leader's office. They settled in around the conference table in an alcove and an aide brought coffee.

"Thanks, Paula." Senator Barrett reached for the cream. "Have you seen Speaker Steere wandering the halls?"

"He was right behind me, Senator. Somebody stopped him for a word; he should be right in, I would think. Governor, can I get you anything else? Some pastries?"

"No thanks, Paula. I'm fine. Thanks." The aide excused herself and left them alone.

"Did your district get hit with the weather?" Ben asked Barrett. "I was on the phone with the Red Cross first thing this morning. It's a God-awful mess up there."

"Not badly." Barrett was working determinedly on a Danish. "We got heavy snow, but nothing like Shelby. Shelby, Cut Bank, all along Route 2—I understand they got 8-to-10 inches in about four hours overnight. They've got the big rigs backed up for 40 miles on Route 2." He took another healthy bite of sugar-glazed, almond-laden pastry.

"Springtime in Montana. You gotta love it!" Ben exclaimed. "You know Joe, the guy who manages the store for me?" Barrett nodded. "He was up there yesterday on his motorcycle, of all things. Said it was a beautiful day."

"Yeah—it blew in last night from Canada. One of the worst mid-May storms we've seen in a while. Took everyone by surprise. Have you seen the editorials, Ben?" Barrett, anxious to get to the business at hand, passed along a folder packed with photocopied newspaper editorials, the pertinent phrases already illuminated with a yellow highlight marker.

Governor Kane slipped on his reading glasses and opened the folder. "Is this about the Washington business?"

"Yep." Barrett got up to pour himself another cup of coffee and remained standing. "I know you're aware of the chatter out there, Ben, we just weren't sure—hey, here he is!" Speaker of the House Mitch Steere rushed into the room, closing the heavy mahogany door behind him.

"Hi! Sorry I'm late. I almost made it, but I got hijacked by a lobbyist. Gaming Industry Association." He shook his head and tossed some political literature on an empty chair. "You're never safe around here." Mitch settled in and poured himself some coffee.

"Mitch, I was just telling the Governor we wanted to be sure he's appreciative of the intensity of feeling out there."

Ben glanced up over his glasses and nodded to acknowledge Barrett's comments but was concentrating on reading the materials laid out in front of him.

"We've been buried, Governor," Steere chimed in. "Phone calls, faxes, e-mails—damn, more e-mail activity than I've ever seen!"

Barrett nodded in agreement. Ben turned a page and continued reading.

"You know what this reminds me of? And I know this is a bit before your time, Mitch, at least professionally." Barrett stared out the window as he spoke, as if the story he was about to tell was out there somewhere. "Do you remember in the early 90's, Ben, when Clinton started his attack on the Second Amendment? The Brady

Bill, assault weapons, limited-capacity clips...remember?" Ben looked up and nodded. "Remember how the whole militia thing crystallized so suddenly? Damn, every shoe salesman with a 20-gauge bird gun bought a pair of camouflage fatigues and joined a militia. The so-called militia experts were on *Nightline* every night for six months." Ben gave the Senator his full attention. Barrett, his hands stuffed casually in his pants pockets, turned from the window to face the Governor.

"It's like then, Ben, minus the hardware but at five times the intensity. We're hearing from a much broader demographic this time around." He bobbed his head towards the papers scattered in front of Ben. "What do you think of those editorials?"

"What's surprising to me," Ben commented, "is the degree to which they're starting to take aim not just at the government, which you would expect, but at the American citizenry in general. Kind of disturbing, actually. Listen to this." Ben picked up a sheet with some highlighted text and started reading:

> *"Our beloved federal government, expanding with gaseous alacrity, completely untethered from any bothersome constitutional ballast, didn't spring from some carefully orchestrated leftist conspiracy. It is merely the result of ordinary Americans attempting to get by on somebody else's nickel."*

"From the editorial page of the *Billings Gazette*." Ben let the paper fall to the table. "That's hard, man. Very tough." He sat back in his chair and looked at the two legislative leaders. "True, though. Unfortunately true, and very much on the money."

"Have you seen the bumper stickers?" Senator Barrett reached across the table and pulled a few stickers from the folder. "Look at these. One of my aides has a brother who's a trucker. He picked these up for me."

"Ha!" Ben laid out the bumper stickers in front of him and read the first one aloud. "I'M OLD ENOUGH TO REMEMBER WHEN AMERICA WAS A FREE COUNTRY." He laughed and thumbed through the rest. "Look at this one: LEGALIZE FREEDOM! Or this...THE BILL OF RIGHTS - VOID WHERE PROHIBITED BY LAW. Funny stuff," he chuckled. "Why is it truckers always seem to have their heads screwed on right? How come they don't run for office?"

Steere pulled a sheet of paper from a folder he was carrying. "Here Governor. This is a rough breakdown of the e-mails received by House members on this subject. Just the raw numbers by district."

"Wow! The bottom line is—am I reading this right—12,000 e-mails in April?"

"Actually, I think it's 12,000 from April through the second week of May." Mitch corrected. "But it's still a ton of reaction, Ben. I don't ever remember anything like this kind of volume, especially considering the legislature isn't in session, and it's so early yet in the election cycle. These are just reactionary opinions stemming from the federal action."

Senator Barrett pointed to a sheet in Ben's pile. "Our numbers are right there Ben; the Senate's being pounded as well. Never seen anything like it." The Senator reached across the table to the pastry-laden silver platter and grabbed a nice, glazed, blueberry fritter.

Ben glanced at the sheet. "And what's really amazing here is this is more or less just the conservative reaction to the One Nation legislation, right? We haven't heard from the liberal civil libertarians yet...just wait until the security legislation gets pushed through. What are they calling it? Safe Watch legislation, I think. Everybody will be in a frenzy then."

"Oh man, yeah, Safe Watch!" Steere exclaimed. "Bill, have

you been following that? This is rich…it's basically a compilation of the old Bush administration Homeland Security and National Security Agency measures updated with modern national-network and supercomputing technology. Video cameras with instant alarm, facial recognition capabilities everywhere—airports, casinos, stadiums, public buildings, highways, and all major urban streets."

"What about the microchip thing?" Ben asked.

"Yeah, last I heard, the House passed it, but I don't think it's going to make it through the Senate. They want to implant global positioning microchips under the skin of anyone who's been convicted of a Class A felony," explained Mitch. "They would transmit the person's location, heart rate, body temperature and other identifying information from anywhere in the country to the central monitoring facility—FBI, I think. They want to make it mandatory for the felons, and are suggesting it to parents as a good idea to prevent child kidnapping."

The Governor removed his reading glasses and gently massaged his temples. "What the hell are we doing? What happened to this country? When did it become this…this…whatever the hell it is now? Where are these guys leading us? And why is everybody following them? Damn!"

The two legislative leaders sat silently for a moment. Finally Senator Barrett pointed to the papers spread about the conference table and responded. "Ben, I think that's essentially what everyone else is asking."

"Yeah." Ben Kane stood up and gathered up his things. "People say I have a visionary grasp of the obvious. All right, are we all in agreement that nothing here is anything we haven't seen before—especially the bumper stickers—but that what's unusual is the timing and the intensity?" The two leaders nodded. "OK, thank you gentlemen. Thanks for your time…we'll talk later." Ben headed for the door.

The following day President Henderson signed the One Nation bill into law at a sunny Rose Garden ceremony, surrounded by proud, puffed-up senators and beaming Cabinet secretaries. The President handed out the special commemorative pens, embossed with the Presidential seal, used to sign the bill. Firm handshakes were exchanged all around.

CHAPTER 8
June 2013

Joe tossed his bag onto the king-sized bed and trotted over to the bathroom. It was a three-and-a-half-hour drive from Helena to Billings, and then it took another 15 minutes for Kim Lange and him to get checked into their separate rooms. Kim was fine in his book—a real cutie—but *way* too organized for his taste. Smart as hell, though, he loved listening to her talk. But after almost four hours in the car with her it was time for a break, and a cold beer or two.

Joe surveyed his home for the next two nights. He found the TV remote and clicked on the power. Cable stations were resplendent with talking heads jabbering on about the One Nation legislation. Conservatives were whining that it just added to the size of the federal bureaucracy; leftists crowed that it was just a "down payment on the legacy owed by the promise of freedom to the neediest among us."

What a load of crap, Joe complained to himself. *These guys can't POSSIBLY believe a word they're saying. The press certainly doesn't believe a word they're saying. Who's playing this game?* Joe shook his head, unpacked his shirts and got himself ready to meet Kim down in the lobby.

Joe stepped out of the elevator and started down the corridor toward the hotel's cocktail lounge. He could see Kim just ahead of him, now dressed in a snappy dark business ensemble and heels, and ran the few steps to catch up.

"Oh! You scared me! You all unpacked?"

"Yeah, I'm ready to rock." He glanced at his watch. "You have what, an hour?"

"Yes, I'm meeting the mayor and a few advisors for dinner at 7:30. They're going to swing by here and pick me up." The two entered the Yellowstone Valley Pub, the same cocktail lounge the Holiday Inn operated in every city in the country under a locally appropriate name. It was dark, not too loud, and populated by only about a dozen business travelers availing themselves of the happy-hour buffet, the same happy-hour buffet the Holiday Inn put out in every city in the country. Kim and Joe pulled up a couple of stools at the bar; the bartender efficiently slid two clean bar napkins in front of them and asked what they were having.

"White wine for the lady and I'll have an Outback beer."

"Sorry, we don't carry Outback. Bud, Heineken, and Olympia on tap. Bottles, we carry…"

"Olympia tap is fine. Thanks." The drinks were set up quickly and the server scurried to the other end of the bar to assist a businessman dejectedly swirling the melted ice cubes in what a minute ago had been a full glass of Dewars.

Joe took a sip of his draft and turned to Kim. "So are you expecting a late night out with the Billings brass?"

"No, not at all. The mayor is a busy man. Ben just wants me to take his temperature on the federal stuff."

"Wouldn't a phone call have been quicker?"

"The National Security Agency monitors all calls made in the country—in the world, for that matter. They have for years. But in the last three years or so they've actually installed the computing power they need to be able to process and screen the millions of calls they capture every day. Ben wants people to be able to speak freely to him without risking the chance the conversation is going to show up on some NSA junior analyst's radar screen."

Joe nodded his understanding, and then took a moment to relate to her the television commentary he'd caught earlier in his room. "So what's with these humps? I don't get it; do they just want to rule the world? Do they just feel they need to tell the rest of us how to live? Are we all just too stupid to be trusted with our own well being? How do they explain the previous 50,000 years of human history that somehow managed to squeeze by without all of their brilliant ideas?" He inhaled half his beer.

Kim cupped her wine glass in both hands and stared into the shimmering, golden liquid as if it were a crystal ball. She spoke thoughtfully and deliberately.

"To me it's all just organizations and organizational people gone amok. President Henderson may not be my cup of tea politically, but the man isn't Stalin; he's just a product of the system. I know the argument would drive most partisans crazy, but I think most of the issues we think of as government problems are not fundamentally philosophical issues. It's not a problem of a Democratic or Republican view of government. The government has grown out of control under both parties. They're organizational issues.

"If you have a hammer, every problem looks like a nail. Go to a doctor with a headache—the chiropractor thinks it's your posture, the internist wants to do a CAT scan, the psychiatrist wants to give you a tranquilizer, the dermatologist tells you to wear a hat and stay out of the sun. Go to any politician with a headache, and they'll see an opportunity for untapped votes and additional campaign contributions. They'll want to pass a law. Politicians pass laws; they don't do anything else. It's the answer to every problem you present to them; there can't *ever* be another answer, because it's all they can do. And of course they *insist* on being responsive, because it will net them votes and contributions. Once they get involved, they won't ever let go; they haven't let go of anything in 250 years. They may need it for an issue next election cycle, solved or not.

"There's no difference," she went on, "between them and an insurance salesman—you know I do most of my consulting work with financial services companies. They'll ask about your health, they'll ask about your spouse, your kids, your job. They'll look you in the eye, give you a big, sincere smile and shake your hand firmly. But if you don't buy the policy—you're dead to them. You've wasted their time and they hate you for it. Politicians are about power—about getting it, getting more of it, and keeping it. You're either there to help them, or you're just using up oxygen."

She took a sip of her wine and continued. "Look, if you have dozens of reporters groveling at your feet, begging for interviews; million-dollar, blow-dried network anchors chasing you around every week for TV appearances; the largest corporations in the world funneling millions of dollars to your campaign account, you'd start thinking you were pretty freakin' important, too. And powerful. Because you would be, the system makes sure of that. It's like being a comic book superhero where you're an ordinary guy until you put on the costume, or the magic ring, or whatever. It's not the man; it's the office. When they put on the office, they become superheroes. Out of office, they're just another Clark Kent—one who may have to actually earn a living like everyone else. There's nothing more important than staying in power. Creating or uncovering problems so government laws and regulation can fix them is simply the coin of the realm."

Joe needed to make it personal. "They all suck. Where do these people come from? I'm just trying to make a living, to live my life, and these pricks wake up every morning and try to pass laws to either force me to do this or prevent me from doing that."

"Well, you can't discount the possibility there are good, honest, hardworking people in the system. But they are *in the system*. The organizational structure and momentum will only allow so much deviation from one individual, honest or not. It's classic bureaucracy in the definitional sense—responsibilities and tasks are compartmentalized so work elements can be defined and responsibilities limited. Any one individual can only do a limited amount of harm. Unfortunately, the same individual can only do a limited amount of good. There's no difference between government systems and large corporations. The rewards of power and position go to those with longevity and finely honed social survival techniques, not to the most brilliant or creative minds, not to those who are best at their jobs. Don't get me wrong—I think the people who make it to the very top definitely have an element of brilliance, or creativity, or are, in fact, great at their jobs. I'm just saying those things aren't what got them there. *Politics* got them there."

"Wow!" Joe shook his head. "I have no idea what you just said, but if I did, I'd say it sounded like it made perfect sense." He smiled at her, drained his glass and signaled to the bartender. "What do you have in a seriously cold bottle? So cold it hurts. Cold enough to make me cry."

The bartender stepped over to an iced sink, rolled up his sleeve and bravely stuck his hand into the frozen slurry of green and brown bottles. In to his elbow, he grimaced as his stiffening fingers explored the bottom of the sink. He pulled out a naked green bottle, its label long ago dissolved to a soggy pulp. He toweled it off and looked at it with a studied eye.

"I think it's a Molson Golden Ale." He checked the bottle cap. "Yep."

"Sold!"

Kim enjoyed a sip of wine and continued, oblivious to the transaction stepping on her lecture. "There are many different ways of looking at the world. I just tend to look at things organizationally: How organizational structure forces or encourages people to act in certain ways, and discourages their acting in other ways. Some people learn how to work the system, some people learn how to game the system, some people think the system owes them something. The successful ones realize early on they're working in a maze, and need to give careful thought every time they come to a turn. Very few make it to the center."

Joe drank deeply from his icy green bottle. "And they wonder why I drink."

The rock, though large enough and relatively flat, wasn't quite as stable as he would have liked. He kept poking it with his walking stick hoping to find a spot to step where the stone wouldn't seesaw into the water, but it wasn't going to happen. A glance up and downstream eliminated consideration of any proximate alternative to crossing right here. Governor Kane steadied his stick in the cold, foot-deep, fast-running stream and stepped on the rock, testing gingerly for purchase. He cursed as his boot splashed four inches into the water, proceeded to the next stone and completed the crossing.

The trail continued up a fairly steep, but not terribly long, embankment. Thankfully some volunteer group, the Boy Scouts perhaps, had built a series of rough stairs out of some heavy, flat stones dragged from the stream. Except for a brief bubble of cool, sweet, breezy woodland humidity he had just passed through by the stream, the surrounding flora was dry, very dry. *There are fires burning in Idaho,* he thought. *I don't want to go through that again.* This area of the Helena National Forest had been burned pretty badly in wildfires past, but thankfully the lodgepole pine and spruce trees grew back quickly. Because of those fires, the resulting scarcity of easy fuel—overly crowded trees, along with dead trees and brush scattered on the forest floor—actually made this area relatively safe from a reoccurrence of those most spectacular of northwestern natural disasters.

He could hear the occasional twig snapping some distance behind him. He had asked the officer on his security detail not to get closer than about a hundred yards. He didn't like people within hearing distance when he was likely to be talking to himself. Personal safety was the least of his concerns. He carried his .40-caliber Glock in a fanny pack along with his PDA, a small flashlight, a Swiss Army knife and some lip balm. A cool bottle of water was secured to his belt. He sole concern in hiking alone would be if he were to sprain his ankle or something and might need help limping back to the car. It was a beautiful June day, sunny, low 70's, light breeze, a perfect day for a short hike. An hour out, an hour back—just enough to clear the cobwebs and perhaps kick-start some fresh thinking. And there was indeed some thinking needing to be done.

Twenty minutes after escorting Kim to the Mayor's waiting car on Midland Avenue, Joe stepped out of a late model, shiny black livery cab. The driver pulled away, his electric motor whirling up to speed, leaving Joe in front of the dingy-looking storefront. A booming, bass riff pulsed through the ill-fitted, wood-framed screen door.

Billings, like all American cities, had been affected by urban sprawl over the years, though not on nearly the scale of most. Hawk's Nest was a small, gritty saloon that at one point could only be considered to be in the middle of nowhere. When its doors had first opened some 25 years previous, the roadhouse had been well south of Billings proper, with just some scattered small homes and ranches as neighbors. It sat in the corner of a strip mall just a half-mile or so north of the Crow Indian Reservation, in the small town of Lockwood. The mall, which also housed a feed store, an auto-and farm-equipment parts store, a hairdresser and a beer distributor, serviced both the Crow and the local residents. The recent decade had seen considerable commercial and residential development in the area, but the strip mall still stood, and Sam Hawkins' gnarly little pub was still serving an eclectic local crowd.

Joe stepped into the dark, stuffy tavern. It reeked of stale beer and cigarette smoke. Federal regulations had long ago rendered it illegal to smoke in an establishment serving food, causing Hawk to have ripped up his menus years before. But there was free chili every Wednesday night and free spaghetti on Monday nights, both provided with a $3 service fee. And he was more than happy to grill up a burger for the regulars, and just tacked an additional five bucks on the price of their next beer.

Joe sidestepped a barrel full of roasted peanuts, one of several placed among the beat-up tables seemingly randomly scattered across the floor. Spent peanut shells crunched underfoot, an atmospheric effect blending nicely with the fresh sawdust already down there. The bar stood to his right, with no more than a dozen dowel-backed, swivel bar stools available; most were still tucked neatly against the brass bar rail. It was early yet; there were only three patrons in the place; a Crow couple, well into their cups, sloppily debating the next jukebox selection, and a lone biker playing a video game in the far corner next to the rest rooms. The bartender, Harry Spotted Horse, a Crow who had been working the bar for almost two years, greeted Joe as he slid into a stool at the bend where the bar curved into the wall, well away from the loud, oblivious couple.

"Dude! How are ya? We just saw you, what, a month ago?" Harry slid a bar coaster in front of Joe and shook his hand.

"Hey, Harry. I'm just here a couple of days. I drove down with Kim on some local business."

"Who's she?"

"Kim Lange. She's an advisor to the Governor. A real hottie. Smart as hell."

"You doin' her?" This was Harry's standard line of inquiry anytime a woman's name was mentioned.

"I wish. Great body, and a real nice lady, but half the time I don't have any fuckin' idea what she's talking about."

"Yeah. What else is new? What are you having?"

"Let me get a cold Outback."

Harry slid his sleeve up to his elbow, reached into the beer sink and fished out a bottle of beer. "I'll tell you this though," Joe continued, "the chick has her head screwed on right when it comes to knowin' the government is outta control. She's got those Washington humps nailed, and her job is to give the Governor an earful. By the way, how's our beer moving?"

Harry cracked open the cold, longneck bottle and slipped it over to Joe. "Good, actually. I think we took five cases from you four or five weeks ago? We've only got about a case left; a couple of regulars took a liking to it. Hawk was going to call you this weekend with an order."

"Cool." Joe took a long pull from his bottle. "I think Ben likes selling beer more than being Governor. He says it's not quite the ego trip, but at least it's honest work, and he doesn't have to wear a suit." They both chuckled knowingly.

"What about your Norton?" Spotted Horse rested on a well-worn stool behind the bar. He fussed with a strip of duct tape someone had used to repair a tear in the red plastic seat. "How's she running?"

"The bike is 40 years old, dude! If it's running at all, it's running good! You know what I mean? I took it up to Shelby a little while ago, up to see Running Wolf. It ran good; I owe it an oil change. How's your ride?" Joe walked over to the nearest barrel of peanuts and scooped up a huge pile with both hands. He eased the unstable mound back to the bar and dumped them by his beer.

"It's good. No trouble, knock wood." Harry reached over and rapped on the bar. "We went on a run to Sturgis last weekend just to get the kinks out. Partied at the Full Throttle Saloon a bit. Nobody broke down; nobody got arrested. Good weekend."

"Excellent!" Joe was already compulsively working the pile of nuts. "Who'd ya ride with?"

"Little Pete, Hammer, Pants—just the psychos. When we head down to the Sturgis Rally next month, man, the roads are going to be mobbed. Every dentist and marketing executive with a $40,000 Harley is going to be on the road. You goin'?"

"I don't know yet. I can probably get the time off, but it's a loooong hot ride for an old Norton. We'll see. I hate to miss it, though—the Norton always gets a good reception at Sturgis. People seem to like seeing it." Joe emptied his bottle and slid it out in front of him. "When you get a chance."

The bartender cracked open another cold one and placed it on the coaster, now barely visible in the growing jumble of peanut shells.

"Thanks, Harry. Hey, has there been any chatter about the political stuff in Washington?"

"Here and there. Everybody's fed up. We were talking about it in Sturgis last week. But you know those guys, Joe. They think the government should be building bombs, paving roads and nothing else. They like the bombs, and they think the roads could be smoother."

"I hear you."

"But the talk at the Full Throttle is they're bracing for a really big rally this year...you know, like a 'freedom' rally or something. They're saying close to a million people. The local law is freaking, big time. It looks to be a total fuckin' meltdown!"

Joe sipped his beer thoughtfully. "Man, sounds like something

I wouldn't want to miss. I'd probably end up getting arrested, though. The Governor won't like that at all."

"The Governor? I would think the Governor would be leading the parade! He should be the first one arrested, man—guaranteed reelection!" Harry laughed.

"Yeah," Joe agreed. "Right you are."

Joe continued to warm the barstool and catch up with Harry as the place slowly filled up. After about an hour or so the crowd reached critical mass and Harry was busy pulling beers, pouring shots of Jack Daniels and tequila, making change for the video game, answering the phone (always triggering a chorus of shouts: "If it's for me, I'm not here!"), and chatting up the ladies. Joe drained his last beer, left a generous tip on the bar, waved to Harry, who was busy washing glasses at the other end, and headed out.

Ben Kane slowed his pace a bit to catch his breath, indulging in as much of the cool, sweet evergreen air as possible before the end of his stroll. He was only about 15 minutes from the car, and deep in thought. He stopped for a moment and surveyed the peaceful woodlands surrounding him, one of many islands of federally controlled land in the midst of his state. *So whose land is it? The federal government purchased it from the French in 1803, granted the acreage to the Montana territories in 1864, then to the State of Montana in 1889. Before Washington's involvement, the white settlers took the land from the Indians, who took it from other Indians, who were borrowing it from God and the buffalo. And 100,000 years from now when humans are extinct, no one will 'own' this land anymore. But it will still be right here where we left it. For now, ownership is just a matter of paperwork...* The Governor paused to polish off his remaining water, and then picked up his pace to the car.

CHAPTER 9
July 2013

President Henderson was clearly agitated. "Look, we already know the punch line here, don't we? We've been telling this fucking joke for the last 50 years, but we somehow never get to the punch line. Socialism doesn't work. We *know* this. The Soviet Union collapsed. Red China, despite all the chatter about being the economy of the 21st Century, has only managed to stay afloat by manipulating its international monetary policy to keep the state flush with profits from the resultant low labor costs. And our good friends in Europe are a fucking economic basket case. Fifty years of cradle-to-grave, pay-as-you-go, social benefits and pensions, combined with a declining birth rate, have left the Europeans with massive immigration as their only means of paying the bills. They're what now? Up to almost 45 percent third world and Islamic populations? Their civilization is in the toilet, and they're reaching up with their last hand to help flush it. All because of collective economic policies."

He turned to his economic advisor. "You're the economist in this room. How much does the government take out of our economy, total? I'm talking federal, state, and local taxes, estate taxes, school taxes, bridge tolls, gas taxes, sales taxes, cigarette and liquor taxes, business taxes and fees, corporate income taxes passed through to consumers, everything. 40 percent?"

The advisor squirmed a bit. "Sure. Federal revenues are about 30 percent of GNP, state and local revenues account for another 10 percent. Personal income tax rates will run quite a bit higher for upper-income earners, of course. They pay most of the freight, with a little help from the upper-middle class."

The President stood and looked out over the Rose Garden. "So let me get this straight, Paul, and I say this understanding I'm not an economist. So keep me honest here, alright?"

"Yes, sir."

"Good. So then, we've got a $7 trillion economy, more or less, right?"

"Yes sir."

"And we pull out about 40 percent, close to $3 trillion, to run all government services at every level of government, from the most expensive stealth bomber to pencils for first graders, right? That leaves $4 trillion for the pure private sector—small business, Fortune 500 international conglomerates, cigarette money, money to buy a new or used car, vacation money, money for your grandmother's funeral, everything, right?"

"Some would argue with those numbers, Mr. President…"

"Round numbers, Paul. We both know nobody in the fucking universe knows what the real numbers are. Round numbers. Am I close?"

"Yes, sir."

"Very good. Now explain to me why you, the Treasury Department, Wall Street and all the shit-for-brains MBA, Ph.D. economists in this country are scratching their heads wondering why the economy has been in a slump for the past six years. Is it your position we can take 40¢ out of every dollar in the country and hope the 60¢ we leave behind will allow the economy to boom? Is this OUR position?"

"Sir, it's been a long-standing position of the Democratic Party that government spending does indeed stimulate the economy. We're not taking the money and keeping it, we're just taking it from one place and putting it right back into the economy somewhere else."

"Right. So we take some money out of Main Street 'A' and they suffer a little bit for it. A little less money to spend, fewer people hired there, fewer pets bought, fewer restaurant meals eaten, right? Good. Now we give the money, be it through tax breaks, raw government jobs, business, family, school or farming subsidies, to Main Street 'B'. So they have a few more bucks, they eat a few more meals out, buy a few more pets, and take a vacation or two more, right? I understand how we helped Main Street 'B', and I understand the argument saying maybe Main Street 'A' had too many successful people and we had a right to take their money and spread it around. But how does the money-shuffle boost the overall economic numbers for the country as a whole? It doesn't, does it?"

"Well, not in the scenario you've just described, sir. But look at all of the investment government has made in, say, the drug industry. We're spent billions over the years in research into the basic, raw science underlying the discovery of many of the most effective, and profitable, drugs of the last 20 years. Those drugs have generated billions of new dollars in the economy through drug company profits—all from government seed money."

"Very true. So...let me ask you this." The President returned to his seat behind the executive desk. "You're saying every dollar we've invested resulting in a successful, profitable drug has returned the taxpayer's investment, many times over, into the economy, into the private sector, right?"

"Yes, sir."

"Good." Henderson sat back against the stiff springs in the high-backed, black leather chair. "Can you tell me how much money we're sunk into research where it didn't pan out?"

The advisor returned to squirming. "Well, I'm not sure we track the numbers that way, Mr. President. At least I've not seen them broken out that way."

"Paul, if we were an investment bank, a venture capital firm, or some other sort of investment partnership, it wouldn't be enough to tell our investors how much we've earned with their money, would it? Wouldn't we be required to tell them how much of their money we've *spent* in order to secure those earnings? I mean, earning a million dollars sounds great. Earning a million dollars on a $100,000 investment is one thing. Big round of applause, right? But earning the million is something else if it costs you a hundred million to get there, right?"

"Of course, Mr. President."

"So if we don't know how much money we've sunk down the rat hole in order to get to the successful science adding so much money to the private sector, how do we know the economy wouldn't have been better off just leaving those trillions of research dollars in the pockets of the people on Main Street? Granted you'd have to account somehow for the economic gain of the actual health benefit of the successful drugs, but only against the economic harm caused by depriving people of the spending power of the investment."

"With all due respect, sir, you're as aware as I am that economic-policy analysis as often as not follows the politics. Both political parties spend millions convincing the voters it's the politics following the economic science. It gets tricky, sir. Our people feel…"

"I know it's tricky Paul. And I know how our people feel." Henderson drummed the desk with his fingertips and stared off through the French doors to the lush White House grounds just beyond the colonnade. "What I don't know is how long we can keep this up."

"Speaker Steere, please. Chuck Hardy returning his call."

"Hi Mr. Secretary! The Speaker is in his office. I'll put you right through."

Mitch Steere's administrative assistant transferred the call from Montana's Secretary of State to his phone.

"Chuck! Thanks for calling back. How's your day going?"

"Same old stuff. It's all in-basket, no out-basket. What can I do for you?"

"I appreciate your time, Mr. Secretary, I know how busy you are. I wanted to ask you about the fall elections. I've got something like 40 percent of the House term-limited out this year. Do you have a feeling for how the election filings are shaping up?"

"Oh, yeah. This is going to be a strange one, Mitch. We have some real pieces of work trolling for votes out there. If some of these guys end up in the Statehouse, I'm telling you it's going to be a whole different world around here."

Mitch grunted. "You're talking about the so-called freedom candidates?"

"Right," Secretary Hardy confirmed. "And they're coming at us three different ways. You've got..." Mitch could hear papers shuffling as Hardy searched for the numbers. "OK, got it...you've got 25 candidates who have filed for the Republican primary to challenge your sitting Republican representatives. It's unprecedented. I don't ever remember a challenge of this magnitude, Mitch. These guys usually sleepwalk their way to reelection."

"Wow," Steere stated flatly. "Not good. I knew there were going to be more challenges than usual, but we're getting close to half of the incumbent class."

"There's more. There are even more filings for the open seats...a few Democrats, but mostly it'll be Republicans running against Libertarians. And I've got a lot of write-in applications—very unusual considering we're five months out on Election Day. The law says they have to file at least 15 days before the general election. Usually we just get the 'Mickey Mouse' and 'none of the above' filings. But these guys are running for real."

"Well, this is really something. This political season is getting more interesting by the minute."

"Do you want the Senate figures, Mitch? I have 'em right here..."

"No thanks, Chuck, not now. I'm done. Barrett is going to want to see those, though. Do me a favor and have a copy sent to my office; I'll look at them when I have a moment."

"Sure thing, Mr. Speaker. Anything else?"

"Thank you, Chuck; I appreciate your time. We'll talk soon." Speaker Steere hung up the phone and sat back, clasping his hands to his head and massaging his temple and scalp. He needed a moment to digest the news. The major party primaries would be held in just a few days; this should have been checked out sooner. But either way there wasn't much, if anything, he could do about it now. Local Montana politics wasn't anything like the national scene. Nationally, the Republican and Democratic parties controlled everything—the primaries, the candidates, the debates, who moderated the debates, how the legislative districts were laid out, everything. They controlled every possible aspect of the elections just short of out-and-out appointing their candidates to office.

Not here. Not now. Not anymore, thought Mitch. The ability of the political parties to control the vote or even to direct the political agenda in Montana had been on the decline for years. The ascendancy of the Libertarian Party didn't as much shift the balance of power as it did simply stop fueling the political machine. They didn't appear overly interested in grabbing the levers of power. They seemed more concerned with making sure nobody else had their hands on those highly valued levers.

*Oh well…*Mitch stood and hitched up his pants. *If I lose the Speaker's chair I'll only have another year to serve before I'm term-limited out. It's almost time to start thinking about finding some honest work.* He glanced at his calendar and rushed off to his next meeting.

An understated but audible "ping" interrupted the small talk and general chatter buzzing the conference room, followed by a soft, disembodied female voice. "Governor, I have the Attorney General on the line. I can patch him through when you're ready."

"Thanks. Put him through, please."

The other participants quickly settled down, pastries and coffee in hand, and found their seats around the large, burled hardwood conference table. The high-tech Internet videoconference screen hung unused on the far wall; the AG was calling in from a Highway Patrol barracks in Bozeman where he was attending an awards ceremony. The small office there didn't have the requisite hardware to secure a video connection.

Governor Kane tapped the intercom icon on the communication control touch-screen. "John? Are you with us?"

"I'm here, Governor," responded John Gaffney. "I've got Col. Tommy Leech of the Highway Patrol with me. This legislation effects his people directly so I thought it would be helpful if he could sit in."

"Sure thing, John," Ben agreed. "Hello there, Colonel. Welcome to the inner sanctum."

"Thank you, Governor, the pleasure is mine," responded the head of the Highway Patrol.

Ben looked around the room. "OK, lets get started. For the benefit of our Bozeman guests, here in Helena I'm joined by our Lt. Gov. Pat Driscoll, by the Director of the Department of Revenue,

Rich Harrison, and by the Chairperson of the Montana Board of Public Education, Elizabeth Suarez." Greetings were exchanged all around.

Ben cleared his throat and started. "We're here to discuss the implementation of the next step in the federal government's plan to legislate utopia. Luckily for us, we get to facilitate this march to a more perfect world just by surrendering some more state sovereignty, a nice chunk of our state's treasure, and, of course, some individual liberties on behalf of our citizens. And as is typical and expected from our all-knowing federal protectors, we have been given no choice in the matter, and a tight deadline to boot—Oct. 1st of this year, if I read it right. Given the circumstances, I thought it might be fun if we got together and discussed exactly how we will go about surrendering our pride, our freedom, and our state to an administration which will likely be half run out of Brussels in a year or two. Any ideas?"

Ben's sarcasm wasn't lost on any of his associates. The group pressed forward, discussing how the complex transition of operational control of the state's law enforcement and educational infrastructure could be handed over in such a short time. The opinions were frank; the conversation occasionally heated. Nobody was having any fun.

At the close of the hour, Ben called an end to the discussion and reviewed the agreed-upon action points. Follow-up meetings were set, detailed reports were requested.

Ben stacked his papers, tossed his yellow pad on top of the pile and wrapped it up. "OK, so we'll proceed on the two tracks. The department heads will start defining the critical operational separation points and will delineate the budget impacts. We'll drill down from there the next time we meet." The Governor turned and directed his final comment to his director of the Department of Revenue, "and you'll do what we have to do to seek a waiver from the regulations. Temporary or permanent, partial or complete—we'll take what we can get. OK? Thank you everybody!" He turned to the Lieutenant Governor. "Pat, could you stay behind for a few minutes?" Pat Driscoll nodded and remained in his seat. The rest said their goodbyes, ended the conference call and exited the room.

Ben stretched back and grabbed the top of his high-backed chair. He leaned the seat back and stared at the ceiling. "What do you think our chances are with the waiver?"

"Not a chance," Driscoll stated honestly. "We're small potatoes—they've got much bigger fish to fry. They've got to worry about assimilating California, New York, Texas...not us. The federal government is already a large employer in the state; what's a few more people?"

"Agreed. We have to ask, though. Let them be the bad guys and turn us down. Fuck. A border and a flag—that's all they're going to leave us with. It'll take a few more years, but not many."

The Governor continued. "Politics isn't what it used to be. Two hundred forty years ago the issues were individual natural rights, liberty, freedom, self-determination. There were big fights, important fights, huge injustices to be fought, a raw society to be defined and structured. Today, all of the big battles have been won, except for the Indians, maybe, but they've just been written off. All the big dreamers are left with is the minutia...you're paying $50 too much on your prescription drugs? There's an injustice warranting a federal solution. Some asshole gets drunk and shoots his brother-in-law; clearly there's a societal crisis necessitating the continental banning of the particular brand and caliber of the projectile he used, including suing the manufacturer out of business and locking citizens in prison for five years if they get caught with that particular bullet in their bedroom end table. Government used to deal with broad, sweeping concepts, ideas clearly bigger than all of us. Now we're down to a one-on-one, bare-knuckle fistfight pitting one citizen against another." Ben shook his head in disappointment. "This can't be right; I can't believe any good comes of this." The subject needed changing.

"How's your family?" asked the Governor.

"Everybody's great, thanks. My little girl is starting 7th grade in September. It's unreal how quickly time goes by. How is it you escaped marriage?"

Ben freshened his cup of coffee. "I had my chances; maybe more than my fair share. Every time I try again I'm reminded why it hasn't really worked for me. It's the drama, man. I just can't take the drama." He shook his head thoughtfully. "You know, it's one thing to battle the dragons in your professional life. We get paid for handling the rough days, you know? The easy days run themselves. But in my personal life—I need smooth. I want smooth. I seek smooth. It's not to say bad things don't happen in your personal life. You know, shit happens, and you have to deal with it. No question about it. But when things aren't exceptionally ugly, why can't you have a smooth run for a while? Maybe it's my imagination, but the women I've been involved with seem to seek comfort, or stimulation, or shelter or something in continuous high drama. Love the women—can't deal with the drama. It's not that I think they're all unstable. I just think men and women must define stability differently."

The Lieutenant Governor smiled and shook his head. "Please tell me none of those observations are ever going to work themselves into a speech or a newspaper article or something. I was just starting to like my job!"

"Ha!" Ben laughed out loud. "No, I don't think so. And if you have any sage advice on the subject, I'm all ears." Ben collected his papers and stood up, ready to leave.

Driscoll shook his head as he rose from his seat and moved out from around the table. "Actually, Governor, there's not a single word of advice I could honestly give you. It's a path we each have to walk in our own way, at our own pace, and figure out for ourselves. You're just following the trail you see in front of you. Maybe someday you'll spot another trail."

The two exited the conference room still quietly chatting about personal paths and the curious twists they can take.

CHAPTER 10
August 2013

The temperature was approaching the mid-90's with the early August sun blazing. *Not good,* thought Joe. *This is not good.* He was heading east on I-90 to Billings, where he was to meet up with Harry Spotted Horse and his boys and push on to Sturgis. The Norton's sump was full of fresh, straight 50-weight motor oil, and Joe was trying to hold his speed to around 65 or so, trying to keep the engine temperature down while maintaining a decent airflow through the engine's cooling fins. He was thankful he'd taken the time to switch his everyday, street-friendly 20-tooth counter sprocket to a hard-to-find 23-tooth sprocket. The project had cost him all of the previous Saturday, but the change in the small gear pulling the bike's drive-chain dropped the engine's rpm from 4,000 to 3,000 at 65 mph, allowing it to run much cooler. Sadly, the bike now accelerated like a pig from a standing start, but the lower gear ratio was really a must for a long ride with a bunch of Harleys that had double his engine displacement. A small oil-cooler radiator was bolted to the front of the frame, just behind the front forks; it would help a bit too. But the Norton Commando was, after all, a British motorcycle, and loved to run in British weather and on British roads—cool and damp and all sorts of twisty-turnys. This run was hot and dry, straight and fast. And long. Five hours, including pit stops, from Helena to Billings, a short break if he was lucky, then another five, probably six, hours or so on to Sturgis. Five hundred hard, hot miles on a 40-year-old motorcycle not generally happy running in hot weather. He was pressing his luck and he knew it. His attention was focused carefully on the baritone drone of the exhaust overlaid by the frantic chatter of the intake valves, the tight hum of the gearbox and metallic whirling of chains. So much metal in motion, he just hoped it would all stay together. Hopefully Harry and his friends were putting on a buzz in the nice, cool, air-conditioned bar and wouldn't be in any rush to leave. An hour in the shade would do the bike good, and the later they left, the cooler at least the later part of the run would be. *Hang in there, kiddo,* implored Joe as he patted the side of the gas tank.

It was 11:45 A.M. when the Norton pulled into the south Billings strip mall, home to Hawk's Nest. Close to two-dozen motorcycles filled the parking lot; bikers congregated in small clusters in front of this bike or that, discussing the vagaries of life on two wheels and checking to see if their kickstands were sinking too deeply into the soft asphalt. Joe eased his bike over to where a large fir tree threw a nice bit of shade across a slice of the hot, gummy lot. The shade was already crowded with bikes, so he bumped the Norton over the curb and found a cool spot on the springy, pine-needle-covered earth. As he shut down the motor and switched off the gas petcocks, he quickly ran through a mental checklist—take a leak, wash his face, sit down on something solid and still, and guzzle down some cold water, hot coffee, and cold beer—in no particular order. The Norton's vertical twin engine ticked frantically as the blistering hot metal started contracting and shedding heat. Joe gave the bike one last look to make sure no fluids were squirting out from anywhere they shouldn't be, then wobbled out from the shade onto the bright, scorching parking lot and over to the bar's entrance.

Forty-five minutes later Joe had taken care of all of the items on his to-do list and had managed to grab a couple of burgers as well. The bar was pleasantly dark and cool, but uncharacteristically mobbed for this early in the day. Another half dozen bikers had shown up. No more than 25 or 30 percent of the crowd could be characterized as true outlaw, or former outlaw, biker types, and even most of them were in their late 40's or early 50's—their barroom fighting, hell-raising days well behind them. The remainder of the group was basically Middle America on motorcycles; jeans a little too clean, denim jackets a little too stiff, engineer boots not scuffed quite enough. Lots of husbands and their short, chubby, pink-cheeked wives riding passenger on 800-pound Honda Gold Wings with 100-watt stereos and short-wave intercoms. There were the expected groups of well-heeled, white-collar office buddies riding 3-year-old Harleys with fewer than 2,000 miles on them. A small group of grubby but clearly serious motor-heads—guys running stroked cylinders, high-compression pistons, hot cams and open pipes—were in the parking lot sucking down cold beers and talking horsepower. *Good luck on the highway*, thought Joe, shaking his head. One dude had what looked to be a dragster, with a stretched frame, café racer handlebars, a 15-inch thick back tire and a serious nitrous oxide injector system. But at least he'd had the good sense to lug it down in the back of his pickup. On arrival in Sturgis the bike would be cleaned, driven into town and used to cruise Main Street a couple of times, maybe thrill the crowd with a few screaming burnouts if the cops weren't watching. It'd then be parked in the middle of the street with several hundred thousand other bikes while the owner got plastered in one of the local watering holes. If all went well, after three or four days the bike, with perhaps 10 more miles on it than when it started the trip, would end up back in the pickup truck on its way home. Joe wished he could afford to have an obscenely expensive motorcycle that he didn't even have to ride. *Some day*.

Well, some day wasn't today. Today was hot as hell, and he was going to have to ride another half day on a close-to-antique bike likely to have balked at a trip like this when it was brand new. Joe walked over to the Norton and pulled a rag out of the knapsack he'd bungeed to the chrome bookrack mounted over the rear fender. He squatted down and slowly cleaned the many speckles of grease and road grime off the now-cooled chrome mufflers. The running joke for decades with Nortons—for any British motorcycle for that matter—had been that they leaked more oil than you actually put into them. This was an exaggeration, to be sure, but one not far from the truth. If it hadn't been for the invention of high-temp silicon sealant there wouldn't be many British bikes left on the road able to travel more than 50 miles and still manage to hang on to enough oil to avoid seizing their cylinders. But all of the external oil did have its advantages. Much of the chrome and polished aluminum of Joe's old warhorse looked pretty damn good. "All right...nice..." Joe softly whispered, just between him and the bike, as he wiped spots of chain oil from the heavily chromed rear wheel. "Good as new!" he said a little louder, as he finished and stiffly stood upright. A neighboring biker cleaning up an old rat Sportster smiled and nodded his approval.

"Yo! Fifteen-minute warning! Saddle up in 15 minutes!" A veteran biker of considerable girth used his thick hands as a megaphone and shouted to the crowd milling about the parking lot. "They've got copies of the motel directions inside the bar; let's get together for a quick meeting. Right now!" He trudged down to the far end of the parking lot to repeat the message.

Within a few minutes the small bar was jammed with the rowdy panoply of riders. A hard-core few were still sucking down their last beers; most stood around waiting for the coming announcements or reading the photocopied directions being passed around. The rest room lines grew by the minute. Harry dragged two full cases of beer to the wall beside the bar and climbed on top of them so everyone could see him. In addition to the social authority he normally carried as a local bartender, Harry was also essentially the only person everybody in the bar knew—hence became the de facto coordinator of the milling throng. He briefly glanced at a crinkled sheet of paper and prepared to address the crowd.

"Folks!" Harry cleared his throat and spoke up a little. "OK, folks—just give me two minutes here. I've got a couple of ground rules to review, then we can get on our way." The expected shouts of "bite me," "fuck you," "settle down," and "shush" died down after a moment and Harry was able to continue.

"A lot of you have heard this before, but I want to go through it all again so no one can say they didn't hear it. All indications point to this being the biggest rally ever. There is going to be a large, law enforcement presence at Sturgis. That's not unusual. We've been there before; they've been there before. We all know the drill. If you're going to ride with us—no reefer, pills, or blow in or out of Sturgis. If that's your thing, buy some in town, party there, bring nothing back. No funky serial numbers on the bikes—they *will* seize any bike with altered numbers. All your paperwork needs to be in order with photo ID, and no firearms."

The crowd settled down a bit and was now paying attention. Harry continued. "This is going to be a Boy Scout camping trip with Harleys and leather. Is anybody running open pipes?" Two brethren with beards and bandanas nodded. "You guys stay back from the rest of us about a half mile or so after we cross into South Dakota. No point in all of us getting strip-searched when they pull you over. We'll meet you at the Full Throttle later tonight." The two gave Harry the finger in unison and returned to their beers.

"There's a gas station a quarter mile up the road. Everybody be sure to tank up before we leave. For you guys with small gas tanks, we'll plan on fuel stops every hour if possible, otherwise no more than 80 miles between stops. We'll try to hold the stops to around 15 minutes each, or else we're never going to get there. If anyone wants to go faster than 75, or skip a pit stop, we'll meet you later on at the motel."

"Jodi and Stanley," Harry pressed forward, "will be following with the tool truck. They're gonna have 10 gallons of gas, two cases of motor oil, some spark plugs—what else—some tire tubes and a couple of taillight bulbs. They have a pile of tools, but don't plan on doing a valve job on the side of the road. The truck is the black F-250 super-cab at the end of the lot. Remember what it looks like, and stay in front of it when we're on the road. Questions?"

A couple of the finer points of allowable levels of intoxication and "exactly how much reefer is *no* reefer?" were reviewed, but the most of riders quickly dispersed and attended to their last-minute tasks. Within 15 minutes engines were started, passengers were seated, kickstands were lifted, gears were engaged, and the Montana riders of the Sturgis Rally hit the sticky asphalt and roared off into the bright, blistering, early August afternoon heat.

The ride to the small town of Sturgis, S.D., was exhausting, but uneventful. Most of the contingent stayed at a motor lodge about five miles outside of town. The last two hours approaching the rally was hell; traffic was thick and slow. Joe's Norton was hot and stalling at idle. He was grateful when at long last he pulled onto the white gravel driveway of the shady, pine-covered motel property and was finally able to shut down the balky, overheated motorcycle.

Despite the steep "rally prices," Joe had reserved a room for himself. Legs rubbery, hands buzzing, he tossed his bags on the bed, yanked off his steel-toed engineer boots and cranked the air conditioner to max-cool. He switched on the TV to keep him company, unpacked, got himself a glass of cold tap water and sat on the edge of the bed. It was only about 7:00 P.M. and still bright outside, but he had been on the road for the better part of 12 hours and was physically and mentally exhausted. He needed a shower, some sleep, and some cold beer but was incapable of deciding what to do first 'cause he needed all three so badly. A second glass of water restored enough essential brain function to force the executive decision. *Shower. Sleep. Beer tonight,* he concluded.

Attendance at the Sturgis Rally had been flat for many years. From a high of about 600,000 in 2000, attendance had fluctuated from between 200,000 to 400,000 in the years since. It could have been something in the air this year, maybe something in the water. Or maybe there was just something about riding a motorcycle, with its thundering power plant at your fingertips and the hard wind in your face, which evoked a tribal image of American freedom growing ever more distant in the collective memories of citizens who dwelled on such things. Whatever the reason, this year they came.

Officials estimated 800,000 to 1,000,000 people would converge on Sturgis—in a state where the year-round population hovered around 750,000, and in a town with a population of 6,500. This was not particularly worrisome for the locals. They had decades of experience gearing up for the rally and local businesses all knew the meaning of making hay when the sun was shining.

The first Sturgis Rally, held in 1938, was a weekend affair with nine racers scooting around a half-mile dirt oval track in front of a small local crowd. Attendance for the now 10-day event had grown into the tens of thousands in the early 1980's and ballooned into the hundreds of thousands through the late '80 and 90's.

So while the local residents of the Black Hills region remained sanguine facing the annual invasion of the rumbling mob, others were more uncertain at the prospect of a million like-minded, freedom loving, active citizens converging in one spot. So much potential human liberty could not remain unchallenged.

"Senator? It's Ben Kane. How are you doing?" The Governor shouted over his shoulder to the speakerphone as he fixed himself a fresh cup of coffee.

Senator Nancy Taylor, speaking from her Washington office, sounded crisp and businesslike, as usual. "I'm fine, Ben, thank you. I assume they're keeping you busy out there?"

"You have no idea," Ben declared, sounding like he was wound a bit tight. "I'm meeting with water resources people in a half hour. After them I've got some issues with livestock inspections, I've got to review some upcoming judicial appointments, then get with the Department of Revenue team this afternoon to run through the federal takeover. I wanted to touch bases with you before I meet with them. How are we doing on the waver issue?"

"Well, I don't have to tell you this is going to be an uphill battle. We've organized the entire delegations—both House and Senate—for Idaho, Wyoming, North and South Dakota and ourselves. They see eye-to-eye with us on this; there's no public support for the takeover in our part of the country and they just plain don't want to do it. We're obviously preparing to present a more nuanced argument. The President and his transition consultants have invited us to the Oval the day after tomorrow. Personally, I think we're just going through the motions. He lost all five states during his election, and the combined delegations consistently vote against him in Congress. We didn't want him and he doesn't need us. He doesn't owe us any favors and he probably wouldn't mind teaching us a lesson. Sorry I don't have a more positive assessment for you, Ben."

"Well," Ben had already been resigned to the bad news, but it sucked hearing it just the same. "You're giving it your best shot, Nancy, what else can you do? We all appreciate the work you're doing for us."

"My pleasure, Governor. I do what I can. Is there anything else, Ben?"

"That's it. Hang in there." Ben hung up and immediately hit Kim Lange's speed dial button. The phone rang six times before she picked up.

"Hello!" Kim was speaking just above a whisper

"Kim! Ben Kane. Where are you?" Ben stood, practically at attention, by his desk. Totally focused on the phone, he seemed prepared to compel good news out of the device.

"Hey, Governor! I'm on Cato; we're in the field watching my buffalo."

Ben smiled, relaxed a bit and sat back on his desk. "Oh yeah, your *pet* buffalo! How are the little beasts?"

"Ben, these things get BIG!" she giggled. "Hang on a minute, let me get some space between Cato and the wildlife. They don't always get along." She stuck the phone in her shirt pocket and trotted the horse through the tall, waving grass to about 100 yards clear of the grazing bison. Horse and rider slowed to a walk and continued back to the ranch house.

"OK, I'm back. What do you need, Governor?"

"Yeah, Kim, listen. It doesn't look good for the waiver. The last time we talked a little about home schooling—do you have any other options for me? Anything I can run with?"

"Ben, most of the educators I've spoken to are just horrified at the idea of a federal takeover. A LOT are talking about quitting. Principals and district administrators are just fit to be tied. Most of them would just as soon go drive a truck if they weren't so concerned for their kids. Teachers are saying the same thing; they don't want to be part of the system, but don't know if they can walk out on the students. I think there may be an opening for us there."

"Opening where?"

"Well, picture this. Lets say half of the teachers in the state resign. A disaster, right? The government schools won't be able to find enough qualified replacements; kids will spend half the day in study hall. A stupefied federal bureaucracy will go into collective brain-lock not knowing what to do first. Then to the rescue comes..."

"Private schools," Ben interrupted. "With plenty of trained, experienced, enthusiastic teachers itching to get back to work. And hundreds of thousands of parents ready to pull their kids out of a self-destructing system run by bureaucrats 2,000 miles away."

"My thoughts exactly. The law federalizes only civil servants; it doesn't affect private-sector workers. Now, any private-school network would likely look very different from our existing system: much smaller schools, combined ages and different grades in the same classroom, certainly much more sophisticated use of interactive computer technologies. Sort of a more formalized form of home schooling for neighborhood clusters of children."

"Sounds great, Kim. How do we pay for it?" He wanted to find a way to make this happen.

"Sorry, Governor. Balancing the checkbook is your department. Maybe some sort of voucher program? I don't know how much money the feds are going to let you keep."

Ben snickered darkly. "You and I both. And there's the issue of our state Constitution. It requires the legislature to provide a free, public school system. Well, hey, you've given me something to think about. I'm going to let the education people kick this around a while. Anything else?"

"Nothing more. It's hot as hell out here. I've got to give Cato a hose bath."

"Thanks Kim. We'll talk again soon." Ben hung up the phone and spent a few moments contemplating what he had just heard.

CHAPTER 11
August 2013

Joe tried turning over, but a spiking pain held his head pinned to the pillow. He was lying on his side, facing the window. Bright, streaming sunlight tormented his crushing hangover. Something was stuck to his lower lip.

He inched his hand along the side of the bed, up and across the pillow to an object which was at the same time crusty, soggy, smelly, and way too close to his face. Ponderously, but purposefully, he lifted his head up and away from the thing, too numb yet for proper revulsion. His eyes focused intently on a cold, half-eaten sausage calzone, leaking watery, curdling ricotta cheese on the pillow.

Staggering over to the door, Joe heaved the calzone across the parking lot. Then dragging himself into the bathroom, he swallowed three ibuprofens with several glasses of tap water, turned the TV on, and flopped back on the bed. He tossed the stained pillow on the floor and pulled the unused one into position under his throbbing skull. The medication overcame the opposing sunlight and he drifted back to sleep. So much for the early start for the ride home.

Joe had taken five vacation days and used four of them in Sturgis. Days were spent at BBQs, checking out bikes and attending various motorcycle contests and exhibitions, drinking beer, and doing a lot of walking. Intended plans to tour the scenic Black Hills countryside predictably didn't pan out. The annual destruction of a Japanese motorcycle (conducted, of course, by Harley riders) was fun, but as the owner of a British bike he felt it prudent to watch the festivities from a safe distance. Nights were spent in noisy bars listening to live music, drinking beer and doing shots of whatever his buddies slid in front of him. The plan was to spend today on the road and take 24 hours to recover before facing the working world again.

The law enforcement presence in the normally sleepy town of Sturgis was juiced up for the rally. Considering the thousands of revelers, crime and general misbehavior was statistically rare; arrests amounted to about 400 to 500 people over the course of the week-and-a-half. But you could reliably count on a certain percentage of hard-core, outlaw gang types floating around, so the town of Sturgis, Meade County, and the South Dakota state highway patrol added hundreds of law enforcement personnel to keep an eye on the streets and highways. The federal Drug Enforcement Agency, the FBI, and the Department of Alcohol, Tobacco and Firearms also had a number of people on the ground.

By the second day of the rally it became clear it would be a record-breaking crowd; television coverage was heavier than usual, weekly news magazines ran cover stories. The Department of Homeland Security (DHS) decided to get involved and requested assistance from the Department of Defense in keeping the event "contained." During the War on Terrorism, the Posse Comitatus Act of 1878, which prevented the military from exercising police powers within the borders of the U.S., had been amended to allow just that. The DHS had utilized the military in domestic law enforcement twice since the winding down of the War on Terrorism, once during a major power blackout in New York (which wasn't terribly controversial), and again during a border incident with Mexican police units on the U.S. side of the Texas border (which was). This would be the first time the U.S. military would be used for a non-emergency, domestic police action. The worldwide news media flocked to Sturgis right behind the four platoons of the 82nd Military Police Company out of Fort Bragg, N.C.

Nearly 200 MP's arrived at Ellsworth Air Force Base, about 30 miles south of Sturgis around 11:45 one night when the rally still had several days to run. Hours were spent unloading the complement of C-17 Globemaster III cargo planes they'd just arrived on. Equipment and supplies were laid out on the tarmac and assigned to squads after a quick inventory. Humvees, in troop carrier and lightly armored MP configurations, were rolled off the C-17's and likewise assigned. The MP vehicles were equipped with an M411A1 Suppressive Foam Dispenser on the weapons mount on the roof. Part of a new generation of non-lethal, crowd-control weapons, the device shot a heavy stream of various types of chemical foam over adjustable distances up to 50 feet. Today, the Army came equipped with canisters of slippery foam, which completely eliminates traction on any surface to which it is applied.

Most of the rank-and-file MP's carried only their 9 mm Beretta sidearms. Each squad was equipped with four Objective Individual Combat Weapons (OICW's), which had replaced the old Vietnam-era M-16's a few years earlier. The OICW fired both standard 5.56 mm cartridges at the same 850-rounds-per-minute rate as the M-16 it replaced and 20 mm High Explosive Air Bursting projectiles. The weapon utilized a sophisticated fire-control system incorporating a laser rangefinder to pinpoint the exact distance to the target, with the information instantly relayed to the 20 mm ammunition fusing system, enabling the fired munition to airburst precisely over the intended target.

By about 3:00 A.M. the company was geared up and ready to

roll. The roads, jammed to a crawl during the day, were clear, and the military's convoy to Sturgis proceeded quickly and uneventfully. The MP's set up roadblocks on 90 East, just east of the 79 tie-in; on 90 West, north of the 34/14A tie-in; on 34 just west of the 79 tie-in, and on 14A just west of 90. Individual squads were sent to several more highway on-ramps and important intersections. It wasn't really a lockdown in the strict sense; it certainly would have been possible to snake your way through the local streets and get past the roadblocks. It was left to local law enforcement to look after the holes in the net. The MP's mission was to perform random inspections for federal drug and firearm violations, to do on-the-spot inquiries using the DHS's remote access database to search for federal or state-level outstanding warrants, and to provide a generally intimidating presence to discourage misbehavior.

It took some time to set up the panoply of portable high-intensity lights, the orange warning blinkers, instructive signage, orange cones, and the other unmistakable trappings of a very serious highway checkpoint. Early morning riders were unpleasantly surprised.

The combination of water, painkillers and an additional two hours of sleep had the desired result of smudging the sharp edges of his hangover. Joe lay prone on the bed, running the impending day through his head—some more water, more ibuprofen, something easy to eat, maybe a Bloody Mary. Then he would need to check over the motorcycle to make sure it was mechanically sound and ready for another long day. He'd need to say a couple of goodbyes and see if anybody was heading home, maybe grub a cold beer or two out of somebody's cooler. Then bungee his bags to the bike, check out of the room and hit the road. He took a deep breath and eased himself up to the side of the bed. *Ugh…well, it's a start.* Another small push and he was off to the bathroom.

"Fuck!" Fat Bob suddenly realized the seriousness of the situation awaiting him just ahead on the crawling roadway.

"Look at this shit—do you believe this?" Bob's friend Panther was just catching on.

The traffic heading west on I-90 shouldn't have been this bad at just 11:00 A.M., but given the massive volume of people on the road, the military roadblock had traffic backed up for miles. The MP's tried to move things along as quickly as possible. Random riders and almost all groups were stopped and asked a few questions. Most people were waved through. A few were asked to pull over for further questions and, if deemed necessary, a vehicle inspection and luggage search.

Tempers were running as hot as the motors upon which they were sitting. Most motorcycle engines are air-cooled and simply weren't engineered to sit at idle for hours, especially on a hot August morning surrounded by thousands of other hot, running motors. Many riders were forced to switch off their engines and simply push their bikes forward as traffic inched ahead. Fat Bob and Panther, members of the Idaho-based Ghost Riders Motorcycle Club, weren't amused. Fat Bob already had one parole violation just by being out of state, and the two grams of crystal meth he had stuffed in the small leather tool pouch strapped between his handlebars wasn't going to help matters. Panther had a .45-caliber handgun of questionable pedigree wrapped in a pair of jeans jammed near the bottom of one of his silver-studded, black leather saddlebags. The Marlboro box sitting in the breast pocket of his denim vest had four fat joints keeping the cigarettes company. They sat just over 300 yards from the roadblock, with perhaps a half hour more to wait before they would face an almost certain search. Another half dozen Ghost Riders were scattered about in the general vicinity. Fat Bob shut down his chopped Panhead and walked from bike to bike and had a few words with his compadres.

Once their plan was hatched, one by one the group pushed their bikes to the shoulder of the roadway, half the group on one side, half on the other. The bikers in front, in the line of sight of the MP's, sat down and tinkered with their drive-chains, checked their oil, and otherwise fussed with their machines. The rest chatted and smoked cigarettes as if waiting for the others. One of the associates walked casually toward the checkpoint, stopping occasionally to admire a nice Harley, or to ask about an exceptional paint job. He returned to his group when he had seen what he needed to see.

"I don't see any police cruisers. They can't run us down with those Hummers. They're armed to the teeth, but they look like a bunch of 19-year-old kids playing soldier. No way they've got orders to shoot. Ten bucks sez those guns aren't even loaded." He straddled his black, hardtailed Shovelhead and lit another smoke.

Westbound I-90 was a three-lane highway, separated from the eastbound lanes by a 50-foot-wide grass divider. The MP's had the massive Humvee with the foam-gun mounted on top in the middle westbound lane. Soldiers stood on either side of the vehicle reviewing the motorcycles as they passed on the two outer lanes. The right lane had a nice, healthy sized paved shoulder; the left lane's shoulder wasn't quite as wide, but plenty wide enough for a motorcycle.

Fat Bob exchanged glances and nods with the guys standing with him and let rip a shrill two-fingered whistle to alert the riders on the other side of the congested road. The Ghost Riders mounted their iron and fired up the engines.

The sound of eight Harleys starting up simultaneously, all goosing the throttles to clear the engines, all with painfully loud open pipes, was enough to catch the attention of many of the hot, exhausted, frustrated riders in their vicinity. Transmissions thunked into gear, engines were gunned, and the fat rear tires spun furiously, spitting blue smoke and gravel. The riders launched themselves along the paved shoulders toward the roadblock.

As soon as the Ghost Riders initiated their charge, other riders started pulling from the blocked roadway onto the shoulders and blasted toward the checkpoint. Within seconds, scores of bikes filled the shoulders and roared forward as individual frustrations gave sway to communal ones.

Lieutenant Garvey had just handed a rider his driver's license back when he noticed the column of bikes racing down the left highway shoulder, now no more than 100 yards away, heading directly at him. A glance to his left showed the same thing on the opposite side of the roadway. "Get out of here—fast!" he shouted at the rider in front of him. The man stuck his Gold Wing in gear and gratefully gunned it down the highway.

"Sergeant, is the foam dispenser ready to go?" Lieutenant Garvey climbed aboard the Humvee as the Sergeant flicked a switch and checked the pressure on the swivel-mounted foam-gun.

"We're good-to-go, Lieutenant."

"Set the range to maximum, start laying down edge-to-edge coverage as far ahead of them as you can—on my orders, Sergeant!" Garvey could see the speeding riders were just about to pull even with his vehicle.

"FIRE! FIRE! FIRE!!!" the young Lieutenant shouted, pointing directly to the soldier manning the foam gun. A thick, 50-foot rope of rapidly expanding white foam shot out from the device, blanketing the roadway ahead. The operator zigzagged the stream from one side to the other, ensuring that the road would be impassable. The eight Ghost Riders, along with another dozen motorcyclists, were moving so quickly that they were able to get out in front of the stream of foam and escape unscathed up I-90 west. Behind them, though, other speeding bikes instantly flopped over on their side as soon as their tires made contact with the super-slippery stuff. Bikes were sliding across the roadway, still in gear with their engines racing and rear wheels spinning frantically, many riders pinned with their legs caught between the heavy bikes and the pavement. Screams resounded as red-hot exhaust pipes and engine-cooling fins burned trapped limbs. Gasoline poured out of split fuel tanks. Violently spinning rear tires smashed into heads and torsos. The bikes continued to slide until they either slithered off the asphalt and found traction in the grass, or found themselves so far down the road they just ran out of foam.

Two soldiers standing on the right side of the Humvee, opposite their lieutenant, heard his fire command above the din of racing motorcycle engines without realizing it had been directed only to the soldier at the non-lethal, riot-control foam-gun. Each leveled his OICW and used the weapon's laser rangefinder to place a red dot on the back of a Ghost Rider speeding away apparently scot-free, now some 200 yards past the checkpoint. Each released a 20 mm high-explosive grenade at the target locked in to the weapon's fire control mechanism. The projectiles exploded precisely over target, fragments from the bursting munition tearing into the unsuspecting bikers beneath them. Within 10 seconds, two additional bikers were targeted, two additional explosions were seen and heard about an eighth of a mile down the road. Motorcycles were falling away from beneath their riders. Pools of blood expanded.

Lieutenant Garvey was focused on working with the foam-gun operator when he saw the first two explosions. He was standing in the back of the tall Humvee just behind the gun mount; the two soldiers firing the 20 mm projectiles were below and behind him to his right. For a moment he thought the motorcycles had exploded due to some internal mechanical failure or something. It took him a second to realize what was happening…

"STOP! STOP! CEASEFIRE! CEASEFIRE!!!" He jumped

over the side of the Humvee and screamed just as the men were releasing their second fusillade. The Lieutenant got on his radio and started calling for medics, ambulances, fire-control equipment, medical evacuation helicopters, backup MPs, and anything and everyone who might assist in getting the situation under control. The one thing he didn't need to call for was a television news crew. There were three of them positioned around the checkpoint filming the entire event.

Joe Adams sat on the curb in front of the open door of his motel room. The TV was blasting so he could listen while he worked on the bike; the FOX News channel was doing a special in-depth segment on the Sturgis Rally. The Norton was getting its standard on-the-road inspection—oil level looked good, as did the transmission-gear oil and the tire pressure. The drive-chain had a little too much play, so Joe put the bike up on the center stand and took about 20 minutes to turn down the adjustment screws on the rear swing arm a bit. He applied a generous spritz of chain lube to complete the job.

A breathless announcer broke into the regular program with the initial report of an incident at a military checkpoint no more than four miles from where Joe was standing. He listened as the reporter at the scene described the carnage she had witnessed. Still numb with his hangover, he was powerless to muster much in the way of outrage. "Oh, this is nice," was the best he could manage. *Land of the free, home of the brave...* He finished tightening the locking bolts on the adjuster screws, stood up, stretched, took a moment to check out the gruesome images being shown on TV, and walked off to a small, gathering crowd to make sure everyone he rode in with was accounted for, and to see if anyone was going to attempt a ride home.

"Governor, Senator Taylor called from Washington while you were out. She asked me to give you a short message."

"Lets hear it." Ben leaned back heavily in his chair and let it rock him for a moment.

"She said to tell you the waiver has been denied."

CHAPTER 12
August 2013

Eleven Americans lay dead on the highway, sprawled broken and punctured in a perilous amalgam of motor oil, gasoline, slippery white foam and blood. Shattered motorcycles rested quietly and motionless among the carnage. Everyone, professional and volunteer alike, whose life calling caused him or her to mobilize at a time like this, had hours and hours of work ahead.

Seven of the helmetless bikers had been killed by the fragmenting munitions exploding above their heads. Sliding under their motorcycles in the foam, four more had lost their lives from snapped necks or severe head injuries. Many more were injured; everyone who'd hit the foam had significant damage done to their machines. Reporters were kept busy filming angry, tearful reactions from victims, loved ones, and witnesses. Coverage was beamed live nationally. Talking heads were being booked for television commentary by the second. The MP's had no comment. The Secretary of Defense ordered them to stay in the area and assist in any way they could—he didn't want images broadcast worldwide of departing soldiers juxtaposed with those of locals carrying away the dead and wounded.

A three-mile stretch of highway was closed to allow clear access for emergency vehicles, investigators and clean-up crews. Special solvents were flown in to remove the foam before the roadway could be safely opened. The severely injured were taken to hospitals in Rapid City. Due to the unusually massive number of people in the area, a lane on the eastbound side was sectioned off with orange cones to allow westbound traffic to cross over and bypass the site. All of the other military checkpoints set up in the Sturgis area were ordered to stand down; traffic was allowed to pass freely.

Most of the riders stuck on the highway behind the tragedy turned around and made their way back to town. Folks who had saddled up and left the rally hours earlier now found themselves crowded back into the bars, glued to television sets, watching news anchors 1,800 miles away explain to them what had just happened a few hundred yards in front of them. Nearly all sipped their drinks in silence.

By late afternoon the road was reopened. Military personnel still milled around the checkpoint locations, just collecting, organizing and cleaning equipment and awaiting their orders to withdraw completely. All checkpoints remained clear and open.

Back in town, though the rally hadn't yet officially ended, the unspoken word was that it was time to leave. The air had come out of the balloon; the party was over. Private conversations were held, drinks were finished, and generous tips were left for the bartenders. One by one, group by group, club by club…gear was collected, bikes were started, and the mass exodus from Sturgis began.

Traffic had been understandably light in the hour or so since the roadway had reopened. The soldiers were sitting around their equipment, enjoying a smoke, or digging into their MREs looking for a candy bar or something else to snack on. The approaching thunder caused several, the Lieutenant included, to stand up and stare down the highway. The deep, rumbling, endless blanket of sound approached more slowly than one might have expected; riders were holding down their speed out of respect as they approached the site of what would forevermore be known as the Sturgis massacre. The soldiers, now all gathered together on the grassy divider separating the east and westbound lanes, stopped what they were doing and observed in silence. The two remaining news crews loaded fresh digital memory cards and started filming the approaching host of riders.

They were riding two abreast in each of the three lanes, in close to parade formation. The sound, the thunderous, deeply physical bass rumble of Harley-Davidsons slowly rolling by in second gear, was impossible to capture in its ground-shaking, stomach-churning detail with the video-recording equipment. But what came next was very easy to record.

One of the first riders to pass the MP's took a long look at them through his dark sunglasses; he gave them the finger. It took just seconds for the surrounding bikers to pick up the salute. Right hands remained steady on the throttles; left hands were raised high, middle fingers rudely presented, suggesting the young men and women standing before them, working in service to their country, go fuck themselves.

The soldiers were young, 18, 19, maybe 21-years old. Lieutenant Garvey was only 24. Most of the attendees at the rally were over 30, probably two thirds were in their 40's and 50's. A great many were veterans themselves; many if not most displayed a picture of the American flag on their clothing, a helmet, a saddlebag, or on the gas tank. Wave after wave of riders rumbled by, arms raised, middle fingers extended, faces expressing disapproval and disgust. No words were spoken; no shouts or offensive comments were heard. The young warriors, understandably scared and nervous, stood stoically as the demonstration stretched out before them.

And stretch out they did. For miles and miles, hours and hours, the migration from Sturgis continued. An estimated 450,000 bikers traveled west on Interstate 90 that day, a crawling sea of rolling thunder, pausing only to offer an obscene gesture first to the military team, then to and through the television cameras remaining long after the MP's had left.

President Robert Henderson watched in silence from the White House residence, head in one hand, a 12-year-old, single-malt Scotch in the other, as the cavalcade slowly crossed his screen.

"OK, Governor, I think you're all set. They should be ready for you in a few minutes." The cosmetician dusted a little more makeup on Ben's forehead and removed the tissues she had stuffed along his collar to protect his shirt.

"Thank you." Ben hated doing television. Normally he never would have agreed to do a nationally syndicated Sunday morning talk show, but circumstances all but forced him. The White House was under a cloud of scandal due to the Massacre, his waiver for the One Nation program had already been rejected, and the Governor of South Dakota, originally scheduled for the program, was already up to his neck in the aftermath of the tragedy and had asked him to fill in. Ben had little to lose, and was happy to be handed the opportunity to kick the President when he was down.

The network sent a video crew and an assistant director from the local affiliate to get set up in Ben's statehouse office. Knowing how much pressure the formal, buttoned-down White House was under, he decided to dress down a tad in Western semi-casual: a deep blue, pressed denim shirt with a hand-worked sterling silver bolo tie crafted by a famous local Crow artisan. Anything to bother them. He would have worn his cowboy hat but the crew said it was impossible to light him properly. He walked over to his chair, now brightly lit and surrounded by two soft, gold-tinged reflectors used to enhance his skin tone. Backlights were directed on the bookcase behind him. A television monitor was set up so he could see the program's host who would be interviewing him from the Washington D.C. studio.

"What are we doing here?" Ben inquired. "Live feed, tape delay, or are we taping for later in the program?"

"We call it live, sir," the young director answered. "There'll be a standard 7-second delay between your conversation with Tom and air."

Ben chuckled. "Just in case I say a dirty word?"

"Pretty much, sir." It was awkward joking with a governor.

Ben took a sip of water and looked at the monitor. The Secretary of Homeland Security, the program's first guest, was dodging and weaving, trying his best to answer any and all questions put to him with only his previously prepared replies. A pound of plastic explosives would not have budged this man from his talking points. "It was a tragedy nobody could have anticipated...the administration will do everything in our power to assist the victims and their families in their time of need...now's not the time to point fingers, we need to pull together and show a united front at times like this...we need to withhold judgment until the investigation has been completed...the investigation is active and ongoing..." and on and on. Ben felt sorry for him. *The walls are falling in around them, and you get sent out to stand there and tell the country everything's fine, that no, those walls aren't really falling, we're in control, don't worry. What a load of crap!*

The show's host, Tom Russell, was almost finished chewing on the Secretary's leg. He shared a final humorous aside about his favorite baseball team and went to a commercial break. He was ready for Ben.

"And we're back and joined now by the Governor of Montana, Benjamin Kane. Governor Kane is a member of the Libertarian Party, the only sitting governor in the country not a member of one of the major political parties. Four of the people killed at Sturgis were citizens of Montana. Governor Kane, thanks for joining us."

Ben could hear Russell through a compact earpiece. "My pleasure, Tom, thanks for asking me."

"Governor, 11 people were killed this week at the hands of American military personnel. Those soldiers were on active duty on American soil. How do you feel about the policy of using American troops for law enforcement duties within our borders?"

"Tom," Ben started, "unlike yourself and most of our friends in Washington, I'm not a lawyer. I'm just a simple tavern keeper. So I'm not sure what I think is truly important here. Let me read a short couple of lines to you from a group whose opinion I believe carries a little more weight." Ben lifted a sheet a paper and read:

"He has kept among us, in Times of Peace, Standing Armies, without the consent of our Legislatures."

"Now Tom, over 235 years ago, the aforementioned grievance, along with numerous other complaints, was considered grounds for revolution and secession. Today, it barely rises to the level of discussion on a talk show. I guess that seems a little odd to me."

Tom Russell jumped in. "The quote was, of course from the Declaration of Independence. Governor, are you suggesting the federal government has the potential for becoming an occupying force in the states?"

Ben resisted the temptation to peak early. "I was just pointing out how our popular political perceptions have changed over time. What was once grounds for revolution is now something we seemingly just have to live with. What galls me is the perception that federal intervention of this kind is somehow necessary.

"For almost 75 years, the people of Sturgis, South Dakota, have been inviting guests into their town for a party. They're used to it; they cope with it. They know the drill. Have you ever been to a major state fair, Tom? You know, with 4-H livestock competitions,

agricultural exhibits, the latest farm equipment, rides for the kids?"
Ben knew damn well the closest his host had ever been to livestock
was the Black Angus resting on his dinner plate.

"Actually, I haven't, Governor."

"Well, there aren't too many people in this part of the country
who could answer that way. It's a part of life out here, Tom. There's
nowhere you can go in this state, or this part of the country for that
matter, where you can be too far away from the smell of hay and
manure," he smiled. "A small town of 3,000 to 7,000 people will
have an annual fair drawing anywhere from 100,000 to 300,000
people over a couple of days. We draw over 250,000 people to our
annual fair in the city of Great Falls, and we only have about a
million people living in the entire state. The local police direct
traffic to the fairgrounds, people enjoy their day, and the police
direct traffic away from the fairgrounds. It's pretty simple stuff,
actually. I think the point, Tom, is when you're the person doing the
inviting, you tend not to view your guests as threats or invaders. An
outside security force might, though."

Russell moved on to a related topic. "It's been no secret,
Governor, that the One Nation Act has not been well received in the
western states. In fact your own state, Montana, has had a waiver of
the regulations recently rejected by the administration. Is the federal
government infringing on the state's ability to manage its own
affairs?"

Ben smiled. "The short answer is 'yes, they are.' What the
administration has done is to render mute what little remains of the
principle of federalism—the concept of power being split between
the states and the central government. Hell, they've left the states
with little more than their name, their flag and their borders. We're
just little colored squares on a map." Ben paused for a second then
added, "I think the central government's little demonstration in
Sturgis makes clear the degree to which they hold state sovereignty

and individual liberty in contempt. These were people who were trying to get home, Tom, and were not allowed to do so until they were stopped and interviewed by an armed agent of the central government, asked to prove that their papers were in order, and shot and killed when they refused to do so!" Ben sat back in his chair. He knew the value of a good sound bite; he wanted it to hang out there for a second.

Tom Russell smelled blood. "Governor, you seem to be painting a rather conspiratorial picture of what most people in this country would consider a major obligation of the federal government—to assist state and local governments to meet their responsibilities to their citizens. Are you suggesting this tragedy was not an accident, suggesting it was some sort of a deliberate show of power by the federal government?"

Governor Kane maintained his calm demeanor. "You're half right, Tom. It does appear to have been an accident; I don't believe anyone out there was killed on purpose. Although in fairness I think you'd have a difficult time convincing surviving family members that having the military fire 20 mm grenades at their husbands, sons and fathers was somehow just an accident.

"But was it a naked show of power by the central government? Of a sort—they did it because they could. Who was going to stop them? Except for the fact it ended in an unspeakable tragedy, everybody, at least most people in your part of the country, seem to think it *is* the central government's job to use the military to patrol our highways. Some of us out here disagree with that view."

Tom Russell was clearly dissatisfied that Ben hadn't yet vomited all over himself on national TV. He pressed further. "Do you think your position as the only Libertarian governor of a state gives you a unique perspective on this tragedy? We haven't heard this strong an indictment of federal authority from either the Democrats or the Republicans."

"Tom, Libertarians stand for individual liberty and personal responsibility—on all issues, at all times. Look, it took the combination of Republican moralistic law-and-order principles and Democrat us-against-them, socialist politics to get us to the place where we're all so damn afraid someone is either doing something they shouldn't, or maybe has too much of something we want, that we think it's permissible for the central government to enter a state without being invited, and to attack and kill citizens who choose not to see things the government's way."

"I became a Libertarian because I didn't like politicians telling me what to do. I hadn't considered a strong third party necessary to keep from getting shot in the streets, but maybe now it is."

"Kent State, Ruby Ridge, Waco, Rainbow Farm, now Sturgis—how many times do we allow the central government to say *oops* before we stand up and say *enough*? Or do we all collectively stand up after the shooting, dust ourselves off and say, 'well, it wasn't me this time, let's have an investigation and get on with life?' I just think it's all very troubling, Tom, very troubling."

Tom Russell closed out the interview. "Governor Kane, I'm afraid we're out of time. Thank you for being our guest, and please pass on our condolences to the Montana families touched by this week's tragedy at Sturgis." He turned to the camera, "We'll be right back."

Russell chatted with Ben for a few moments during the commercial break. When they were through, Ben unclipped his microphone and allowed the sound technician to remove the earphone he had snaked up his back to his ear. Ben left his office to search out some coffee and some immediate feedback on his TV performance while the network crew packed up their equipment.

Joe Adams was normally not one for the Sunday morning talk shows, but Ben's appearance made it an imperative. He smiled when Ben commented about seldom being too far away from "the smell of hay and manure." He grinned every time the Governor referred to the "central government" whenever Tom Russell asked him about the federal government. One couldn't yet say the old Ben Kane was back, but it sure looked like he was peeking out from behind the curtain. "Walk toward the light, Ben!" Joe laughed and shouted at the TV, "Walk toward the light!"

Kim watched the Governor's performance from her living room couch, with a large mug of Guatemalan Antigua coffee and copies of the Sunday *Helena Independent Record*, the *Billings Gazette* and the *Washington Post* spread out all over the floor. *Oh-oh*, she thought. *We could have lived without the 'shooting people in the streets' comment. That'll have people twitching in D.C. But he was just expressing anger for the victim's families. They'll know he meant it. And they'll know the Secretary of Homeland Security was just covering his ass...* She muted the TV when Ben was finished and started reviewing the editorial pages.

Vivid white cotton ball clouds drifted leisurely across an otherwise translucent Montana morning sky. It was a magnificent late-summer day; temperature barely reaching 80 degrees, with just a hint of a cool breeze gently fluttering the leaves on the two old, gnarled oaks guarding the corners at the front of St. Francis Xavier Church. A modestly sized red brick structure, the church had stood on West Pine Street in Missoula since 1889, the year Montana became a state, and was widely renowned for its graceful steeple, the many interior paintings and murals, and its magnificent stained glass. A small, quiet, somber crowd milled about the stone steps at the church's entrance. Photographers and video crews were cordoned off across the street. It was a lousy day for a funeral.

He had been a professor at the Missoula campus of the

University of Montana, and was a native Montanan. His wife, a paralegal, was originally from New Hampshire. They had both been killed instantly when their 875-pound full-dress Harley slipped out from underneath them, trapping their legs and spinning then uncontrollably along the foam-covered roadway until their necks were snapped by the sudden impact of another wildly careening motorcycle. Governor Kane, wearing dark glasses, stood with his hands in his suit pockets looking uncomfortable. He spoke quietly with the deceased woman's sister, who had flown in from Nashua for the funeral service.

One of the governor's aides walked over to tell the press he wouldn't be doing any interviews. She took a moment to answer a few straightforward questions for them. "It was a Catholic service, a small group of family and close friends sat up front. No, the Governor sat back with all of the other non-family guests. Just the family will be going to the cemetery. Yes, he'll be attending some of the other services. No, I don't believe he's spoken with the President."

A soft breeze pressed gently against Ben's face. It carried on it the slightest early hint of autumn. He took a deep breath and exhaled slowly. *Change. Everything changes eventually. What's the saying? All things must pass...*

He stepped back and placed his arm around the sister's shoulder as the two caskets were carried down the grey granite steps and gently slid into the two black hearses waiting at the curb. He watched the loved ones following the coffins, all dressed in black, some crying uncontrollably, some already too emotionally exhausted to cry further. Ben couldn't help but to get choked up as well, his face flushed with emotion.

Oh, it was an accident in the strict sense of the word. The foam was an ill-advised tactic recommended by some pointy-headed analyst somewhere up the chain of command, and the soldier firing the grenades just panicked. It was an operational fuck-up, for sure. But ultimately, it was about power. It was about flexing muscle and telling people who was boss. It was about enforcing compliance, about using coercive power to make behavior compulsory. It was about power. Sure, those lowlifes tried to run a roadblock, dragging everybody else along with them. But since when is that a capital offense? These people are dead because one group of people deemed it necessary to enforce their will on another, less powerful group of people…

Governor Ben Kane suddenly straightened his posture, and shook off the emotion. Something clicked—he wasn't sure what. He knew he would attend more funerals; he needed first to help attend to the powerless. Then he would deal with the powerful.

"Governor? Governor Kane?" A deep, booming voice was making a determined effort to keep the volume down. Vince Cozzentino, dressed in a pair of clean denim jeans; black, recently polished steel-toed engineer boots, and a blue tweed sport jacket appearing close to the right size, made his way toward Ben. He moved slowly, so as not to spook the governor's small security contingent. Ben reached out to shake his hand.

"Hey, Coz," he said softly. "I saw you and your people in the church. Did you know the couple?"

"No, we didn't know them. We came down to show the flag. We have the bikes over in the municipal lot—we're running over to get them now to follow the funeral procession. I did know one of those Ghost Riders who bought it. A dude from Idaho we had some dealings with once. He was a dirtbag, but he didn't deserve that." Coz shook his enormous ponytailed head and looked Ben dead in the eye. "It ain't right Governor—it just ain't right."

The big man continued. "You know I'm a veteran, Governor. I supervised a team of Abrams tank mechanics over in the Persian Gulf. I love my country. I served my country." Coz looked around.

He was talking in a harsh whisper, trying not to disrupt the solemn mood. The news crews watched with interest from across the street. "I love my country—but I hate this fucking government. This government has nothing to do with the country I love; it has nothing to do with the Constitution I fought for. And I know *you* feel the same way, Governor, even if you don't have the balls to stand up and say it!" Coz was starting to smolder. He took a step back and tried to collect himself.

Ben, who had been talking toe-to-toe with his old friend, shifted his position to standing side-by-side to him, facing the family of the deceased who were now getting into the limousine for the drive to the cemetery. "Vince," the governor offered softly, "you're right. And I'm not ready to give up. But we have to choose our fights. We've got to keep our heads screwed on, you know what I mean?"

"Yeah, I know what you mean." Coz pointed to the hearse off to their right. "We all best hope they let us keep our heads long enough to fight that fight. You take care, Governor. Good luck to you." Coz stuck out his hand and gave Ben a meaningful handshake. He stepped back to join his friends; the group wandered off to saddle up and add a dozen Harleys to the funeral procession.

Over the next week Governor Kane attended funerals for slain bikers in Idaho, Wyoming, even Ohio. While a few of the instigators were hard-core, outlaw biker types (five of the eight Ghost Riders were killed), six of the victims were white-collar professionals who were just getting a little too adventurous. Four of those killed were women. One couple had stopped by Sturgis for just two days and was heading down to Graceland for the Aug. 16 gathering marking the 36th anniversary of Elvis' death. Ben diplomatically managed to skip the services for the more unsavory characters. He gave no interviews, offered no advanced travel schedule and made no statements to the press. Despite trying to stay in the background, or perhaps because of it, he was mentioned and shown in almost every newscast of the tragedy and its aftermath. One network went so far as to go to the American Outback Brewing Company to get some stock footage of the interior to use on its broadcasts, complete with a shot of Joe Adams smiling from behind the bar. The story wasn't yet Ben Kane, but Ben Kane seemed to be in every story.

CHAPTER 13
October 2013

Chief Running Wolf stood against the high-tensile wire fence separating the Blackfoot bison acreage from the outside world. To his left, a big Ford F-350 dual-axel pickup was slowly backing a 30-foot stock trailer through the open gate into the pasture. Muffled grunts and agitated stomping could be heard through the narrow ventilation slats running the length of the trailer's heavy-gauge aluminum body. The trailer sporadically bucked and shook as it inched back, its occupants clearly feeling cranky and cramped after the long, 10-hour drive.

"All right, Darrell," Running Wolf directed the driver. "Another foot and we're good. There you go." The chief walked over and slid the gate closed. He walked around the front of the truck and was joined by the driver, stiff from the long haul and walking gingerly behind.

"Got here just in time," Darrell offered. "We only have about an hour of sun left."

"Yeah. How was the ride?" They walked along the length of the trailer to the rear tailgate.

"Long. And rough. Those are big bulls in there. Could only take nine…"

"Nine?" Running Wolf's question had an edge of concern in it. "I thought we were going to take 10 on this trip."

"Couldn't do it, chief; they were too damn big. Ten tons is the limit, which'd be 10 bulls at 2,000 pounds apiece. Some of them fuckers are 23...2,400 pounds. I couldn't chance stuffin' 10 of 'em in there. Good thing, too. I don't know if they didn't like the company or whatnot, but they were rockin' and a rollin' for a while there. I had to pull over twice to get them settled down. They were gettin' real close to discovering an aluminum trailer can't really hold 10 tons of buffalo if they don't want to be held."

"OK. Get on the other side and let's get this done."

The two got into position on either side of the tailgate. Darrell unlocked the padlock and swung the safety bar out of the way. He gripped the 3/4-inch-thick steel T-shaped safety pin and made sure Running Wolf was well clear of the gate. With his free hand, Darrell grasped the handle located on the horizontal pipe, and slid it open, allowing the chief to raise the drop pin on his side of the gate. Running Wolf looked at Darrell and nodded. "Let's open it."

Darrell swung open the tailgate; Running Wolf grabbed it and held it clear. The trailer jumped and rocked sideways as the nine huge bison pushed out almost simultaneously, racing off into the distant pasture together in their unique, quick, loping gait. *Damn*, thought the chief, *they ARE big!*

He swung the tailgate closed and latched it shut. "Good job, Darrell, thanks a lot." The driver got a slap on the back and a firm handshake. "Just get the truck back to the ranch house and get some rest tonight. I'll have someone clean out the trailer." Darrell was going to be heading back down to Salt Lake City in the morning to pick up another load of bison.

The Blackfoot Tribe had purchased, by sealed bid at auction, 60 bison—50, 3-year-old cows and 10 large bulls, from the Antelope Island State Park herd. Located in the middle of the Great Salt Lake in Utah, the park was home to one of the oldest and largest bison herds in the country, one which inevitably grew to more than 700 animals after spring calving, about 100 more than the island park could safely sustain over the long term. Excess animals are auctioned off in the fall. Two independent truckers, contracted to deliver 40 of the cows in two trucks, had arrived earlier in the afternoon. Darrell drove the tribe's equipment down to pick up the bulls; he would make the return trip to pick up the remaining 10 cows and the bull he had to leave behind.

After Darrell got himself back on the road, Chief Running Wolf went out to the bison pasture, to the outcrop overlook. He wanted to see how the newcomers were adjusting. This was a pleasant time of day for late summer, not quite dusk, just past late afternoon. The wind was still; with the air cooling slowly, and a shimmering sun hanging low and red in the west. It was eerily quiet for such a large piece of land, just the sporadic, soft coo of a prairie grouse trying to get settled.

Thomas Running Wolf took the last few steps to the top of the brown granite outcrop and surveyed the broad expanse before him. Early summer's sea of lush verdant grass had faded to ochre, browns and ambers with just a lick of faded, pale greens remaining. Lengthening shadows added stark blacks and a startling contrast to the brilliant golden shafts. Running Wolf lifted his hand to shield his eyes from the glaring sun, and scanned the open grasslands for the bison herd. It didn't take long to spot them. He smiled.

No more than a half mile in front of him, scores of bison were chasing each other around in a series of large, looping circles. Clusters of animals would join in the chase, as others broke off from the core group and initiated small games of "tag" on the side. Running Wolf raised his binoculars and was able to identify the new animals from their oversized, bright red Antelope Island ear tags. They were still bunching together, but were evidently enjoying a vigorous welcome from the existing herd. Everybody was getting along just fine.

When the last truckload of Antelope Island animals pulled into the compound, the Blackfoot herd would have grown to 472 animals, now including 350 cows of calving age, with another 40 or so coming of age in the following season. In a well-nourished herd like this, nearly 90 percent of the mature cows would bear calves in the spring. With a few more purchases of outside animals to insure genetic diversity, the herd would be positioned for rapid growth in the years to come. "Welcome back, old friends," intoned Running Wolf, his eyes misting. "Welcome home."

"Thanks, Kim." Governor Kane accepted the tall, icy drink. He took a trial sip and placed the frosty glass on the table between the two rocking chairs.

"Jack's and Coke, twist of lime," she confirmed. She settled in to the second rocker and took a sip of her chilled white wine, a crisp New York State Seyval Blanc with its grassy overtones reminiscent of a French Sauvignon Blanc, but with much more prominent fruit. "Would you like something to munch on? Some cheese or fruit? Crackers?"

Ben lifted his glass and took another sip. "No, I think I've got everything I need right here. Alcohol for entertainment, ice for hydration, sugar and caffeine for energy, and a lime for a little vitamin C. Sounds like a perfectly balanced meal to me!"

They sat in silence for a moment, from the protective shade of Kim's porch, as the bright sunlight ebbed and reappeared in response to the fair-weather clouds drifting across the sky. A gentle wind challenged the now tall, golden grass in the enclosed bison meadow across from her home, adding a fluid-like dynamic to the alternating patterns of bright light and shadow being thrown onto the waving, wispy stalks. The wind felt cool and grassy as it brushed their faces. The air was sweet and clean as it was breathed deeply and became one with them. Ben's long week caught up with him all at once. His eyelids got heavy, his face relaxed, body untensed, mind let go. Sleep claimed him for the moment.

When he opened his eyes he shifted a bit in the rocker and glanced over at Kim. She was sipping her wine and quietly watching a hawk riding the thermals above her fields, searching for a meal. "Sorry about that," he murmured. "I left you for a minute."

She offered a friendly, dismissive flutter of her hand. "Oh please, Ben, I would have let you sleep until tomorrow if you hadn't woken up. My God, you've had a terrible week; if you don't deserve a nap I don't know who does."

"Not as bad a week as some."

She reached for the manila file folder sitting on the table between them. "Would you like to discuss these poll numbers now?"

He straightened up in the chair and gave a little push to initiate some assertive rocking action. "Let's do it!" After another quick sip of his drink, he inched the chair about to better face Kim as she talked.

"OK," she started. "But you have to understand these numbers are *very* soft. We rarely poll at this local a level, because the numbers of respondents are very low, and the margin of error very high. These are not snapshots—these are chalkboard sketches."

"Got it. Go ahead."

"Okey-doke." Kim spread a couple of papers out on the table and briskly leafed through a yellow legal pad to where she had outlined the important points of her analysis. She walked Ben through the numbers for the State Senate and House districts in play. Ben listened quietly, occasionally interrupting to request clarification of a point, or to probe in a bit more depth some of Kim's conclusions.

He finished studying some color-coded spreadsheet charts, then sat back in his rocker and looked up. "OK. Bottom-line this for me.

What does it all mean?"

"What we can say with reasonable certainty is there's an unprecedented level of ferment out there. People just don't generally throw their local, state representatives out of office. Ben, I'm preaching to the choir here, you ran for the Legislature three times; nothing's changed, you know all of this. These incumbent candidates are people from the neighborhood—former school principals, librarians, people who served on the school board. They're talking to their constituents about school taxes, building the new firehouse and changing zoning restrictions while their opponents are railing against the federal government's takeover and are running on a *nullification* platform, if you can believe it! And, for the most part, they're running ahead of the incumbents."

"Nullification?" Ben repeated the word slowly. "I thought the subject was definitively settled by Andrew Jackson in the early 1830s. South Carolina, wasn't it? Some tariff issue?" He continued idly. "Nice work if you can get it, though. You don't like a federal mandate? Just declare it illegal in your state! Hell, it works for me! We should have thought of it sooner."

"Funny." She responded flatly. "This is serious; these guys are actually promoting this stuff. Listen to this:" Kim pulled a sheet of paper from the folder. "I wrote this down while I was watching a local debate for the State Senate on a local-access cable channel. Fourth district, I think. In his closing remarks, one candidate said: *"If you abide by the truth that a free people have a right to choose their own form of government, then you must accept it is true for every people, at every time, in every nation—EXCEPT for the present-day United States. Here, we are NOT free to choose a government of our liking; we must follow the dictates of Washington or be thrown in prison."* Ben, this guy is running for the State Senate! These guys usually run on zoning issues!"

"Why am I finding it hard to dislike his position?"

"Because it's the way YOU used to talk during your first House campaign! Joe said you could have written some of these campaign speeches yourself when you guys use to rant in the bar at 3 in the morning. Their position is the country was founded on the principle of a sovereign people; it really doesn't matter what the federal government thinks about it, or if the Supreme Court disagrees. The people are sovereign. They choose to live under a particular government system or not. It looks like a lot of people are agreeing with their argument."

"Correct me if I'm wrong, but wasn't the argument effectively settled during the Civil War?"

"Yes. With guns and blood. It was settled by killing many of the people who thought that way and burning their society to the ground. Lincoln thought force was the answer. I think any reasonable view of history would conclude most of the Founders wouldn't have agreed; they would have held a free people have a right to choose their own government. I think they were pretty clear. I think our own state Constitution is pretty clear on the point as well."

"Looks like we have a real grassroots movement on our hands," Ben commented, enjoying another sip of his drink.

"Oh no," answered Kim. "This more than grassroots. This is a politician's worst dream—it's the real thing, Ben. The peasants with brooms and pitchforks are storming the gate."

"Hummph…good thing I'm not a real politician." The comment was followed by one of his patented little-boy grins. "I guess we'll just have to wait and see what happens."

CHAPTER 14
October 2013

The Speaker of the Montana House of Representatives settled into the comfortable black leather chair in the Majority Leader's office. Something caught his eye. "What *is* that ugly thing?" Mitch Steere pointed at the object of his inquiry.

Senator Barrett looked over at a faded, chipped, rather bizarre looking doll wedged against some books on a shelf. "Oh, it's an old Imus-in-the-Morning bobble-head doll. My wife picked it up at a flea market years ago for 50 cents. She thinks it might be worth something some day." He shrugged.

"Senator Barrett?" They were interrupted by a voice on the intercom. "Senator Taylor is on the line from Washington."

"Thanks, Paula. Put her through, please. Oh, and thanks for staying late. Why don't you go home now, the Speaker and I will figure out how to shut off the lights and find our way out of here alone."

"OK, Senator, thank you. Have a good evening." Paula laughed and put the call through. Barrett watched the touch-screen communications control panel on his desk for the blinking light confirming the connection.

It had been dark outside for a while. Just past 8:00 P.M. in Helena would make it after 10:00 P.M. at the Capitol in Washington. Barrett's office was a bit chilly; he liked fresh air, and had kept he window open all day. But the temperature had dropped aggressively this early October evening and the window had been closed a half hour too late. Barrett pressed the blinking speakerphone button.

"Senator Taylor?"

"Hi Bill! I appreciate your hanging around for my call." Nancy Taylor sounded tired.

"No problem at all. You're the one who's working late. You know we all get nervous when the U.S. Congress works late!" he snickered and heard her laugh along with him. "I have Mitch here with me."

"Oh, hello Mr. Speaker! I understand you have quite an election on your hands."

"Never a dull moment out here, Senator." Mitch deadpanned.

Senator Taylor got down to business. "Bill, I haven't spoken to the Governor yet—I wanted to touch bases with you first. The One Nation transition funding was supposed to be forwarded from the state to Treasury by Oct. 1st. We both know it didn't happen. Where are we?"

"Well," Senator Barrett spoke slowly and deliberately. "We had lawyers all over the state look at this. Everyone's clear about the fact that the Governor simply does not have the authority to divert Montana taxpayers' funds in any manner other than that which directly supports the State of Montana. The federal legislation wasn't written to accommodate our state constitutional concerns. The money they take goes into the Treasury, then they just spend what they want on our services. So we need a bill out of the Legislature to authorize the transfer. We're not in session, and we have elections in three weeks. Now, the Governor could have called a special session, but chose not to. You can ask him for the particulars yourself; but frankly, I don't blame him. A lot of members are in very tight races and would not appreciate being forced to take this vote. I suppose he could call the new Legislature to a special session in the middle of November, but otherwise they're not scheduled to convene until January. I don't know what he's going to do."

"So we're looking at being up to three month late," Senator Taylor concluded. "This may not be the end of the world. At last count there were, I think, 12 states missing the deadline. Most were facing computer system incompatibilities. A few just didn't have the funds—they were in between tax collection periods. And I think there are three with essentially the same issue we have; they need special legislation. I think Congress is realizing this is turning out to be more difficult than anyone here figured. I wouldn't be surprised if we extended the deadline through the end of January. We should have a decision in a week, I would think. So you guys don't need to knock yourselves out."

"Nobody's losing any sleep on this end, Nancy," Barrett responded flatly. "But we are certainly grateful for the news. Ben will appreciate the elbow room."

"Anything making a tough decision easier is good news, I suppose. There's no point in his calling a special session of a brand, spanking new legislature if it can be avoided. Are we going to challenge the One Nation legislation in federal court? I know Wyoming is preparing a case."

"We are." Barrett acknowledged. "The Attorney General is trying to get his ducks in order. We'll be in front of a federal judge some time in January, I think. A fool's errand, in my opinion. No judge is going to turn this thing back."

"I'm afraid I have to agree with you there, but I suppose we should take whatever shot the system allows. OK, can you update Ben on this call? I'll call him directly before your elections."

"I'll let him know. We appreciate your help, Nancy, and I know Ben does, for sure."

"I do what I can, Bill, I wish I could do more. You take it easy.

And Mitch, good luck with your leadership elections!" Goodbyes were exchanged and Senator Taylor hung up. Barrett and Steere grabbed their overcoats and headed out into the crisp Helena evening and over to the American Outback Brewing Company for some dinner and a couple of fresh, frothy dark beers.

The snow had stopped some hours earlier, but a stiff wind was still blowing out of the northwest. About six inches had fallen in this first, late October storm, but the turbulent air had been busy sweeping clean the exposed, high rolls in the land and building modest drifts in the lows. The bison herd stood stoically facing the wind, peacefully grazing on the still easily accessible grass.

The ground was hard and crusty but not yet frozen. Running Wolf walked softly toward the herd, eyes fixed on a large bull the herd handlers agreed was appropriate. A state meat inspector remained in the chief's pickup, having already approved the animal as appearing healthy. Running Wolf carried his bolt-action Remington Model 700 flush against his body, and positioned himself so if, on the slight chance, the bullet somehow managed to over-penetrate 1,800 pounds of buffalo, it wouldn't strike an unintended target.

The rifle was lifted into position and Running Wolf peered through the modest, but functional, 4X scope he had purchased some years ago through a Cabela's catalog. He steadied himself and set the crosshairs just behind and slightly below the bull's ear. The trigger snapped crisply and sent a 250-grain .338 Winchester Magnum on its way. *Thwump!* The animal crumpled into a black, wooly heap on the ground.

As with the four harvested before him, the herd seemed neither upset nor concerned that a member had just collapsed among them. The crack of the big magnum could just as well have been thunder, and thousands of years of instinct told them danger came from without, and ran towards them, as would a pack of wolves. This instinct, one unfortunately serving them poorly for the last 150 years, told them there was nothing to fear from a loud noise and a fallen bull. The chief walked back to the truck, where Darrell and the state inspector were waiting.

"Ok, that's done." He passed the rifle to Darrell. "Glenn," he addressed the inspector, "you need to stay with me—we'll bleed the carcasses. Darrell, why don't you go back and fetch the tractor and the flatbed so we can get loaded up. And chase the herd away from here while you're at it."

Darrell started up the truck as the inspector jumped out. "You got it! I'll be back in 20 minutes or so. They should have the equipment right outside the gate by now." Darrell pulled away and drove briskly directly toward the herd, still standing around the dropped animals. He zigzagged the vehicle, while blinking the lights and beeping the horn. It had the desired effect of causing the animals to lope off in the opposite direction. Once they started moving he ceased the commotion and headed off to the waiting team of men at the gate.

Running Wolf looked over to the inspector. "I need to do something before we get started." Running Wolf walked back to the last fallen bull. The others dotted the dusty, white prairie within a 75-yard circle of where it lay. He stood before the bull and removed a sweetgrass braid from his pocket—it looked like a small hand wound whiskbroom—and used his beat-up Zippo to light the fat end of the smudge bundle. As soon as it fully ignited he snapped it in the air a couple of times to extinguish the flames, allowing the dry sweetgrass to yield up a generous curl of spicy, incense-like smoke.

The Blackfoot elder fanned the pungent smoke about the bull— to the four points of the compass, then up, then down and to the center—creating a sacred space around the animal in hopes any lingering negativity would attach to the smoke and be carried away.

The buffalo spirit was thanked for its sacrifice and the way cleared for its welcome return. The smudging complete, Running Wolf bent down and snuffed out the glowing tips of the bundle in the dirt.

"You done there, chief?" Glenn walked up alongside Running Wolf. "These guys have to be in the slaughterhouse within an hour and a half."

"No problem," he replied. "Let's get to work." He unsheathed his well worn, but razor-sharp, hunting knife, positioned it over the animal's jugular and released the bull's hot, steaming blood, returning it to the prairie that had given it life.

CHAPTER 15
November 2013

Senator Barrett slid his plate across the bar, away from his bulging midsection, in the universal, gastronomical sign of "enough." A few twisted, ketchup-soaked French fries remained scattered about the plate, proof certain that the oversized carnivore was sated. "Man, that was some damn good burger!" Barrett declared, sliding back in his bar stool and swiveling to face the Governor. "Damn good burger!" he asserted again, in case everyone didn't hear it the first time. He reached over and grabbed one last, structurally sound French fry.

"Your burger was grazing on the Blackfoot prairie only a couple of weeks ago," Joe interjected as he picked up the empty plate and quickly wiped down the thick polyurethane finish protecting the rough cut, knotty-pine bar. "Ready for some coffee, Senator?"

"Yeah, that would be great, Joe. Thanks." Joe Adams strode to the coffee station to fetch a fresh cup. Taking advantage of the downtime, Barrett eased himself to his feet and plodded off to the men's room. The polls would close in 15 minutes and he didn't want to have to get up just as the early returns were being reported.

Kim Lange, sitting to the Governor's left, was sipping a glass of white wine, red pen in hand, fussing with the charts and yellow

legal pads spread out on the bar in front of her. A tablet computer
sat on top of the pile. A spreadsheet glowed softly on the touch-
screen, listing all of the local elections being contested this day.
Kim had set it up so it would instantly reflect the changing political
profile of both houses of the Montana Legislature as the evening's
election results were entered.

Governor Kane sat in between Kim and Senator Barrett. He
was swiveled around in his seat, his back to the bar, talking with a
female constituent about suburban sprawl and water rights. As he
spoke his eyes casually wandered around the crowded room,
scrutinizing the throng for familiar faces. It was going to be a big
night, with many politicians, legislative and executive aides in
attendance. Joe was behind the bar helping Caroline, the regular
night-shift bartender. The Sturgis Massacre was three months past,
but Joe was still sharing battlefield stories with enraptured
customers around the bar. The ambient noise level was high and
rising steadily. Three plainclothes State Highway Patrol officers
were unobtrusively moving about, keeping an eye on things inside
the bar, while two uniformed officers sat in a cruiser parked right
outside the entrance. Ben would smile and give a little nod of
recognition or subtle salute with his beer bottle when he caught a
known eye while remaining thoroughly engaged in his conversation.
He occasionally glanced up at the muted TV mounted high on the
ceiling at the far end of the bar. It was tuned to a regional cable
news program focusing on statewide results. Election returns would
start rolling in shortly.

The scene was actually fairly typical for an off-cycle election
gathering. There had been big, invitation-only parties, of course,
when Ben had won his legislative seats and later, the governor's
office. These off-cycle affairs were more casual; nobody in the
room was on the ballot, so the atmosphere was more akin to a major
sporting event than the otherwise life-or-death political struggle

upon which everyone's immediate employment, long-term career track and philosophical affirmation depended. Nationally, there were Congressional elections, but no big power shifts were expected or likely.

Within several hours, however, it became very clear that the changes in the Montana State Legislature would be significant, to say the least. Kim sat silently, hunched over her tablet PC, listening intently to the projections being presented by the TV announcer, staring at the news ticker running continuously at the bottom of the screen, and using her pen-like stylus to update her spreadsheet as required. Ben sat next to her, his gaze alternating between the TV and the two colored piecharts displayed on Kim's screen showing the developing composition, by political party, of the legislature Ben would be faced with in January, if not sooner. Bill Barrett was on his feet, standing just behind Kim and Ben, his hands resting on the backs of their barstools, head jammed in over their shoulders, mouth hanging open, staring at the same thing. The crowd in the bar had toned down quite a bit, with scattered exclamations of "Oh shit," "This is unreal," and "I don't believe this," every time an unexpected victory was projected. Only Joe Adams seemed to be truly enjoying himself.

A few yellowed leaves still clung to the majestic old walnut tree dominating the view from the President's private study. Soft classical music provided an understated aural backdrop for the easy exchange being traded around the table. Bright sunlight, normally filtered by the thick summer foliage of the large walnut, streamed unopposed through the thick, green-tinged glass panels of the double French doors, and the air smelled richly of fresh-brewed coffee. The 7:00 A.M. breakfast meeting slot was normally reserved for the President's national security briefing, but this morning the meeting was pushed back for a brief review of yesterday's election results. This meeting was more casual than classified; a White House culinary staff food server, a veteran of two previous administrations, was permitted to flutter about serving coffee, English muffins, croissants and fruit cups, continuously freshening the place settings. The White House Chief of Staff, Marty Cigala, and Raul Fuentes, the President's Special Assistant for Policy and Political Affairs, walked the President through an overview of first the federal, then the state-by-state ballot outcomes. Robert Henderson was already aware, of course, of the results of the national Congressional contests—the Republicans picked up two House seats, the Democrats picked up a Senate seat. He was still short of the veto-proof majority he would have liked; all in all, it didn't seem to be a terribly consequential election.

"Did you see this?" the President asked. Henderson held a sheet summarizing the legislative outcomes in the western mountain region. Fuentes and Cigala flipped through their briefs until they found the page. "Montana," the President said.

"Oh yeah," Fuentes acknowledged. "The governor out there— the Libertarian—what's his name? Kane? Yeah, Benjamin Kane. Anyway, he's going to have his hands full. His so-called Libertarian Party took the majority in both houses. This looks to be a real mess."

"Some of the campaign rhetoric was getting pretty hot out there," the President observed, enjoying his fruit cup.

"True enough," Fuentes continued. "But the party is just loosely organized, at best. If the governor out there hadn't very publicly bailed out of the Republican Party and declared himself a Libertarian a few years ago they wouldn't have any greater foothold there than anywhere else. They have a website, a small handful of volunteers for statewide administration, their over-the-top, radical national platform, but no local organization, no fundraising network, no party machinery. They're just a bunch of individuals, lone wolves, who share bits and pieces of a common antifederal government philosophy. I'd be amazed if they can organize themselves enough to even figure out how to elect a speaker and a majority leader."

Cigala sat back in the comfortable chair, munching on a buttered English muffin. He washed it down with a sip of fresh-squeezed orange juice and directed his comment to the President. "What the hell were the voters thinking?"

"Interesting," Henderson observed. "We know they're all ticked off about the One Nation legislation. But *everybody* out there is—Wyoming, Idaho, everybody. So Montana went ahead and elected a bunch of nuts to their Legislature whose entire platform consists of 'this law sucks.' So now what?"

It was meant as a rhetorical question, but Fuentes, generally unappreciative of the subtleties of public silence, attempted an answer. "What can they do? You could finance Montana's discretionary budget out of your own pocket. I suppose they could give everybody a $10 tax cut, stop paving the roads, and declare victory over government oppression! I don't know, but I doubt they'll last beyond the next election cycle. All I see is two years of non-stop headaches for the governor, same party or not."

"You're probably right," the President agreed. He sat back as the food server cleared the fruit cup and freshened his coffee, and then reached for the page titled Southeast Region. "Let's talk about Florida."

Kim Lange sat slumped in her easy chair, the morning prep work complete, with the warm, soothing aroma of roasting turkey wafting throughout her home. She enjoyed cooking, but as of late just hadn't been able to find the time. Inviting Ben over for Thanksgiving dinner provided the excuse to stretch her culinary muscles and break open a few special bottles of wine she had been hanging on to.

It took some doing to convince the Governor to accept her invitation; as was typical for a holiday, he had a heavy schedule. He'd be starting with a breakfast appearance with the Montana Army National Guard at Fort Harrison, then helping out at a Helena faith-based food bank and later eating lunch at a nearby homeless shelter. Next would be a drop-in visit to a nursing home a few miles out from the Capital district. Typically he would then call it a day, and enjoy his Thanksgiving dinner at the American Outback Brewing Company, but this time he would just mingle for an hour or so, maybe buy a few rounds of drinks. Kim's ranch would be the last stop this holiday, for his turkey dinner and a little well-deserved peace and quiet.

Kim took a mental inventory of her kitchen activities. Sweet potatoes had just gone in; turkey had about an hour and a half to go. Biscuits would go in after the potatoes came out. Veggies could wait. Fruit cocktails were being chilled down; the cheese platter should come out now to warm up to room temperature. *Time for a glass of wine,* she determined.

She'd selected a 3-year-old Napa Valley Chardonnay for the first wine of the day, a big, round, oaky wine with hints of butterscotch and vanilla. Kim uncorked the bottle and splashed a bit into the bottom of an oversized, 22-ounce, wine goblet. The large balloon-shaped glass allowed her to vigorously swirl the golden liquid to encourage the release of its aromatic personality. She inhaled the generous, toasty bouquet, took a small sip and let it roll over her tongue. The comfortable easy chair beckoned her return.

*Umm...*Kim took another sip of the wine and settled deeply into the chair. She let her mind drift back over the events of the past few weeks—both the good and the uncertain. The election of the Libertarian majority was essentially a huge question mark; everyone knew what they said, nobody knew what they were going to do. They had already proven themselves capable of making shrewd organizational decisions; when it became apparent there was going to be a considerable learning-curve before the new majority got up to speed on the complex maze of legislative processes and procedures, they did the unexpected and reached out to the former Republican leaders—Senator Barrett and Speaker Steere—and, after some careful discussions with the two of them, reelected them as leaders. The move bought the party instant legislative expertise and maintained a good deal of valuable institutional memory. *Unexpected and smart. Scary.*

The next move wouldn't be so easy. The first bill the Legislature would need to consider was the authorization to allow the governor to transfer Montana tax revenue to the federal government. Every one of the new Senators and Representatives had run against the One Nation legislation. *How are they going to finesse that?*

The crunch of a heavy vehicle rolling up the gravel drive interrupted her train of thought. A murmur of voices, a car door slammed, and footsteps fell along the path leading to her door. *OK, time to get up.* Kim lifted herself from the depths of the chair and tried to head off the knock at the door.

She swung open the door just as the Governor's knuckles were brushing against the wood. "Hey, Kim!" he exclaimed as he stepped into the house.

Kim stuck her head out the door in time to see the large, black SUV cruising away from the house. "Where's your driver going?"

"I'm not going to keep him sitting around on Thanksgiving. He lives 20 minutes from here; I'll call him when I'm ready to go." Kim shut the door and led Ben into the kitchen.

"Let's get you something to drink."

"Sounds good. Man, it smells great in here! It looks like you've got a real Thanksgiving working here! Oh, by the way—sorry for showing up empty-handed. I picked up a nice bottle of wine yesterday and left it at the residence. We were halfway here before I thought of it and I really didn't want to turn the driver around. Sorry."

Kim was pouring a glass of Chardonnay. She handed it to Ben and grabbed the cheese platter. "Lets go sit down. And don't worry about the wine—I've got it covered. What was it?"

"What kind of wine? Hmmm, red, I guess."

"Well don't worry about it. I've got a fabulous vintage Burgundy I've been hanging on to. It's a bright, vigorous, unrestrained 16-year-old, Grand Cru Gevrey-Chambertin. A bit much for turkey, I know, but I've saved it long enough."

Ben feigned concern. "An unrestrained 16-year-old? Is that legal?"

"Very funny. And for dessert we have a half bottle of Muscat de Beaune de Venise. It's a round, fortified sweet white wine from a small village in France's southern Rhone Valley, redolent with overtones of plump ripe pears with just the slightest hint of orange on the nose." She got up to check the turkey.

"*Redolent!* Jesus, Kim, where do you learn this stuff? You keep talking like a walking dictionary and you'll never find a man!" She tossed back her head and laughed.

When she returned from the kitchen she remained standing and finished the remainder of her wine. "Let's go."

Ben looked up, surprised. "Let's go where?"

"It's Thanksgiving. We need to go give the buffalo their holiday dinner." She walked over to the mudroom and slipped on a fleece-lined suede jacket.

Ben stood up and knocked-back his wine. "And what do buffalo have for Thanksgiving dinner?"

"I have a bushel of apples and some range cake I want to bring them. I like to bring them treats once it a while. It keeps them friendly."

The Governor threw on his jacket and placed his cowboy hat on his head. "I know range cake is just alfalfa buffalo kibble, but are apples good for them? I thought apples did a number on their gastrointestinal system?"

"I don't know," Kim replied, opening the door. "They seem to like them, and I suppose they might get a little gassy. Just one of many reasons we don't let the buffalo in the house. Let's go, cowboy! You can tell me about your week." They headed out the door into the chill, dull light of their late holiday afternoon.

CHAPTER 16
January 2014

The debate raged in Montana's House of Representatives for a week running. At the opposite end of the elegant corridor, in the Senate chamber, tempers flared as the body deliberated the disposition of the bill they had yet to receive from the House. Ben watched most of the deliberations from his office, via closed-circuit TV.

This new freshman class of legislators was very, very different. They were all young, in their late 20's, early 30's, even the senators, and almost all college graduates. Instead of seeing the usual collection of fat old ranchers, farmers and lawyers, folks historically attracted to state government for the opportunity to steer a few government bucks and laws in their direction, this new bunch had a whole new philosophical bend. They weren't there, so they said, to use government power, as much as to change the way and degree to which government power was wielded. *They would have all been kids when I first ran for office,* Ben realized as he watched them in action.

The young men and women had heard Ben ranting about the evils of oppressive government and the importance of individual responsibility. They had seen the attention he garnered; they admired him, and they wanted to be like him. Ben really didn't know if he should be proud, or scared.

For now he focused on the House chamber. Mitch Steere,

newly reelected as Speaker of the House, was presiding over the debate—an unusual event in itself. Seated at the original 1912 oak rostrum beneath the Charles Russell masterpiece, "Lewis and Clark Meeting Indians at Ross' Hole," Mitch toyed with the gavel as he listened to the debate. The House chamber was packed, with practically all 100 representatives in attendance. The chamber itself was showing in magnificent form, the warm, clubroom scent of recently polished wood and richly conditioned leather permeating the Greek neoclassic space, air dense with a loud buzz rising from scores of private conversations echoing off the hundred-year-old marble columns and glass skylights.

Jaded political reporters from the major state newspapers and regional TV stations, sitting together in the roped-off press section in the fourth floor gallery overlooking the House floor, were shooting puzzled glances at each other, noting the packed galleries, unusually strident debate, and overall electricity surrounding what would ordinarily be a routine statutory amendment to the appropriations process.

A newly elected representative held the floor, speaking forcefully in opposition to the measure, to the cheers and enthusiastic affirmations of the packed room. "The state is now demanding, or should I say *forcefully* coercing from individuals through threat of fine or jail, *responsibility* from parents. Instead of people being responsible for themselves—they must now be responsible to their government. Proponents will say: 'No, you're not being responsible to government, you're being responsible to society.' But this is not a concerned society simply shunning you for being non-responsive or irresponsible, is it? It's government workers with *guns* coming to take your stuff, your children, or your freedom, in response to your lack of communal cooperation. And to add insult to injury, we are here today to comply with a dictate demanding we PAY for the imposition of those demands! Mr.

Speaker, I, for one, was elected with a mandate to oppose such a measure, and oppose it I will!"

One of the few members who rose in support of the measure put a less-than-positive spin on it. "It is NOT our country!" he argued. "This country belongs to those who want government to solve any and all problems, to those who want government to right all wrongs, to make sure no one has too much, ensure everyone has the same, assure no one is ever hurt, even if it's their own fault, and if someone IS hurt, force everyone to pay. It is their country. They've won; we've lost. Get used to it." Reporters were taking notes as fast as humanly possible. Tomorrow would not be a slow news day.

"No votes." Mitch Steere plopped himself into an empty chair facing the Governor's massive mahogany desk. Senator Barrett, seated beside him to his left, had arrived a few minutes earlier.

The statement hung in the air for a moment. Governor Kane and Barrett exchanged a fleeting look; Ben cleared his throat. "No votes? What does no votes mean?" Ben was actually quite sure he knew what it meant, but he would need to hear this spelled out for him.

"No votes means the House of Representatives has rejected your proposal for amending the law to allow the Governor to pay state tax revenues to the federal government. We rejected it 100 - 0." Mitch held his hands up in a motion of surrender. "The People's House has said, 'sorry Governor, we don't think so.' "

Ben turned to Senator Barrett. "And the Senate can't act because this is technically a revenue bill and it has to originate in the House; am I right?"

"Right. Not that your luck would have been any better in there. I don't know if it would have gone down 50 - 0, but it wasn't going to escape alive. No way."

"Well," Ben looked aside wistfully, "at least I can sleep soundly at night knowing one or two more phones calls wouldn't have made the difference." The three of them laughed out loud and relaxed a bit.

Ben stared out the window. "OK. I guess this means we go to Plan B."

"Which is?" Steere asked.

"Plan B is we do nothing and wait and see what the Feds do. They can't force us to pass legislation. I don't even think the Ninth Circuit would uphold such a demand, though I guess it wouldn't shock me if they did." Ben was referring to the famously liberal Ninth U.S. Circuit Court of Appeals, the federal appellate bench that conservative Montana shared with the unapologetically socialist State of California and the rest of the West Coast. "All they can do is offset the amount due by withholding some funding they would normally send us. Highway money, I would guess. They can't hold back education or law enforcement subsidies—they'd just be fining themselves."

Ben continued. "I'll call Rich Harrison at Revenue and have him break the news to the Treasury people in Washington. I should probably give Nancy Taylor a heads-up. And for what it's worth, Attorney General Gaffney will be in federal court this week challenging the legislation. After that," he shrugged, "...we'll just have to see what happens. Anything else?"

Senator Barrett spoke up. "I'm afraid there is one more thing, Ben. A select committee has been formed. A joint-select committee."

Ben could tell by the slow wind-up he wasn't going to like this. "OK, a committee's been formed. A joint committee. Do I want to know why?"

"Yeah," Barrett continued. "You need to know why. Six members from the House Education and Taxation Committees will

join six senators from the Senate's Taxation and Finance
Committees to form the Joint-Select Committee on Montanan Self-
Government. They'll hold hearings to investigate the impact of the
new federal legislation on various related Montana constitutional
issues, and to suggest, and possibly sponsor, remedial legislation."

"What exactly is *remedial legislation*?" Ben knew he really
didn't want to hear this.

"Well, I suppose if we were being optimistic, and we thought
the new kids were going to play nice, it *could* mean they might
propose new amendments to the state Constitution to allow for the
changes imposed by Washington."

"But we don't think that, do we?"

"No, we don't think that. Ben, the committee is going to
consider if there are grounds to attempt to nullify the federal
statutes. If a bill nullifying the One Nation Act is pushed out of the
committee, I don't have to tell you how it will fare on the Senate
floor."

Ben looked over at the Speaker.

Mitch nodded slowly in agreement with Barrett. "It would pass
the House overwhelmingly."

"Have they considered it would be illegal, unconstitutional, and
has proven to be a failing strategy since the Andrew Jackson
administration?" Ben knew better than anybody that they could give
a shit.

"I think most of them know, but it's not going to count for
much in their deliberations. They think the federal action is in itself
illegal and unconstitutional; that's what they're focusing on. To be
blunt, they couldn't give a rat's ass what Washington thinks,"
Senator Barrett explained.

"This is going to be like talking a suicide jumper off the ledge
of a building," the Governor concluded.

The Governor slipped out the rear entrance of the Capitol, and was met face-first with an icy blast of winter wind. Dressed like a typical Helena urban cowboy in his western hat, dark glasses, full-length buffalo-hide coat and insulated hiking boots, he walked unrecognized along the Capitol grounds to the Roberts Street gate.

Though a car was available to shuttle him over, he'd decided a brisk walk was needed to clear his head. The meeting with the legislative leaders had left him numb. It didn't take him long to admit that had he been in the Legislature right now instead of the Governor's Office, he'd be doing just what they were trying to do; hell, he'd be leading the charge. But his role as Governor demanded he focus on different issues. For one thing, when the news hit the national media machine, every microphone and video camera in the country would be pointed at *him*, not at the 150 legislators who'd started the ruckus.

A more substantive concern was what he should do if and when a bill reached his desk. He could sign it, and become party to the paper insurgency. He could veto it in a transparent and hypocritical attempt to play the adult; the inevitable overwhelming vote to override his veto would render him irrelevant to the process. His third option would be the ultimate weasel move—he could table the bill for 10 days and allow it to become law without his signature.

Ben was aware this nullification thing was as dead an issue as could be imagined. Everybody had already had his say. Jefferson and Madison supported it, but neither attempted it. The Supreme Court, in 1803, asserted for itself the power to judge the constitutionality of acts of Congress. South Carolina, following the proclamations of John C. Calhoun, tried to nullify a national tariff law in 1832, but was turned back by Andrew Jackson and Congress under a serious threat of force. And the Civil War didn't work out real well for state's rights advocates. So there was no question but that Montana, or any other state, did not have the legal standing to turn back a federal law passing constitutional muster with the Supreme Court. *So what's going on here?* Ben wondered, as he swung around the corner onto Sixth Avenue, sidestepping a group of schoolchildren lining up for their visit to the historical society and museum. *A high-stakes protest vote? Petulance?* He didn't think so. They were too smart, too educated for such an empty gesture. He hoped.

Ben turned the corner to Sanders and crossed to his bar's side of the street. *I'm getting ahead of myself. There's no bill; nullification is not an option. All we have is a new committee and probably a modest media dust-up for a week or so. I'll deal with it...*

Ben opened the door to the American Outback Brewing Company, and was met with the wonderful, homey aroma of freshly brewed coffee and mulled cider (they kept a pot simmering just behind the kitchen door during the holiday months). The Governor said a few hellos and made his way back to his booth, where he would catch up on some reading and grab a bite to eat.

CHAPTER 17
January 2014

Senator Barrett contemplated the choices laid before him, and quickly formulated his action plan. He passed on the glazed donuts and instead selected a soft, oversized, chocolate chip cookie. Reaching for his cup of coffee, he quickly recalibrated and placed an oatmeal-raisin cookie on top of the chocolate chip. It could be a long meeting.

Ben swept into the conference room, accompanied by a legislative aide. State Attorney General John Gaffney followed closely behind, also accompanied by an advisor. Speaker Steere sat with the six House members of the Joint-Select Committee on Montanan Self-Government, while Senator Barrett joined the six Senate members on the opposite side of the long table. Introductions were exchanged all around as the executive entourage members helped themselves to coffee and juice and got settled into their places. The Attorney General confirmed the news everybody already knew: Montana had lost its bid to declare the One Nation legislation unconstitutional in federal court, and the Ninth Circuit had already rejected an emergency appeal. Wyoming had also lost in federal court and was still trying to get it before the Tenth Circuit. Appeals to the Supreme Court were being prepared, though with little hopes of success—over the past 10 years the Court had aggressively rolled back the pro-state decisions of the Rehnquist Court. It was the Henderson administration's comfort and confidence level in the acquiescence of the high court concerning this issue that had encouraged it to promote the One Nation package in the first place.

Ben made small talk with the new lawmakers, sharing some stories of his clumsy early days in the Legislature and eliciting more than a few genuine belly laughs from the group. After a short while the Governor circled back and got right to the point. "So what the hell are we trying to do here?"

Opinions were voiced around the table. Much of the dialogue centered on various guarantees listed in Montana's 1972 Constitution, a document that in many ways tracked more closely to the 1776 Declaration of Independence than the 1787 U.S. Constitution. Article 2, Section 1, stated: "All political power is vested in and derived from the people." Article 2, Section 2, clearly declared "The people have the exclusive right of governing themselves as a free, sovereign, and independent state. They may alter or abolish the Constitution and form of government whenever they deem it necessary." And Article 8, Section 12, required the Legislature to insure strict accountability of all revenues received and money spent—an impossible task if Montana tax dollars were to be forwarded to the federal government. They wondered if they could lawfully accede to the federal demands even if they wanted to.

The participants were smart, educated, rational and passionate. Ben would have much preferred it had they been obstinate, irrational or even clinically insane; it would have made his analysis of the situation so much simpler.

A young, newly elected representative made it more difficult still as he voiced his feelings. "Isn't the core issue here whether a truly free people have the right, or ability, to select a government of their own? This is *our* time on this earth, this is *our* society—this is how we would like to live. We want to run our own schools as we see fit, provide social services and law enforcement according to our societal mores and traditions. Are we asking too much?"

Ben sat silently. He had no answer for the idealistic lawmaker.

The young man continued. "Look, if California or the Northeastern states want to centrally control their societies in hopes of realizing some sort of utopian dream—we're not going try to stop them; we have no interest in stopping them. But what I don't understand is why they are so concerned about stopping us if we don't share the same vision. According to their political philosophy the only way to utopia is to force people into it. I was taught you had to earn your way into heaven—not be marched there at gunpoint."

"Nobody's got any guns out yet," interrupted Attorney General Gaffney. "I'd like to keep it that way." Everyone around the table was sympathetic, the Attorney General explained; here the young lawmaker was preaching to the choir. He reviewed the legal facts on nullification and made clear he considered it a lost cause. "This just isn't going to happen."

"But shouldn't we try? Or are we just supposed to swallow this?" The naïve, but compelling plea again left the room silent. Ben rubbed his face. *Three more years of this crap, and I can go back to brewing beer.*

Barrett turned to one of the newly elected senators. "Toby, why don't you share some of your ideas with the Governor—the stuff you were telling me the other day about religion and socialism."

Senator Toby Myers, from the 17th Senate District in the southwest corner of the state, spoke up. "I think we can make the case that the One Nation law is unconstitutional, at least at the state level, because it violates the establishment of religion clause."

Dear God, please take me now... "How so?" the Governor asked politely.

"Capitalism," explained Myers, "is at worst amoral. At best, it is linked by a common history through the Enlightenment with the American experiment of individual liberty and self-government. Privately controlled financing, production, and distribution of goods, services, and profits. Capitalism doesn't pretend to do good—unrestrained, unregulated capitalism can be very unfair. Hell, it can be downright cruel.

"Socialism, on the other hand, is a much more holistic philosophy—one in no way linked to our nation's roots in individual liberty. It's a Marxist philosophy, a reaction to the very real inequities of 19th Century unregulated capitalism. It essentially holds that government is better able to decide on the distribution of goods, services and profits than are individuals or the open market."

Ben interrupted the history lesson. "Where's the unconstitutional part?"

"We're getting there, Governor. My view is as religion has fallen out of favor in society, governments have seen fit to pick up the slack through collectivist utopian economic models like communism and socialism, both of which purport to direct a society's economic power to a common good—providing worldly goods equitably across all levels of society. Their economic policies are determined by political decisions—electoral decisions, really—based on a view of fairness at best, of constituent pandering at worst, but not on economic viability. Leftists talk about wanting and expecting *something more* from government. It's a moral conviction, a religious belief. It's a religion disguised as economics, its priests and rabbis masquerading as politicians and academics. Establishing a religion was supposed to be unconstitutional—most people think it still is. But the American people have taken a belief system and made it law."

The new senator took a sip of juice and continued. "Statism has become the new religion. Instead of looking to God, we have become conditioned to look to the state to provide for us. The left is doing what they've continuously accused the right of doing—trying to legislate morality—but are doing it with public cash instead of with blue laws."

He leaned forward and locked eyes with Ben. "Governor, socialism, democratic socialism, communism, hippie communes: No statist, collective economic model has ever proved itself effective on a large scale for a significant length of time—any time, any place, anywhere—ever. As economic models, they're particularly well tested—and they've always failed. *Always.* So why the persistence? Because it's a matter of faith, or moral conviction, for their followers. It's a religion! Look, this is not about passing judgment on whether it's right to take from the rich and give to the poor—or better yet, encouraging the rich to voluntarily give to the poor. I think that's a good thing. So do most of the major religious faiths in the world—that kind of behavior is codified in their doctrines. But when you use a tax system to redistribute wealth, you're forcing me into your moral view of the world. If that's not establishing a religion, I don't know what is."

Ben squirmed a bit in his chair. "Look, this can't be a real argument. Don't get me wrong; I like it. I might even agree with it. But the religion thing just isn't going to fly. It would involve the sort of bold, innovative thinking and willingness to go out on a limb you're just not going to find on the federal bench—or in any other mid-career professionals who value their job security."

Senator Barrett wiped his mouth and leaned over to the Governor. "Ben, capitalism assumes the economic environment can be shaped to allow the average man to create wealth and prosper. Collectivist systems assume that a society's elite exploits the average man. They say wealth must be redistributed by the state, since, in their mind, the prosperity of some either caused the poverty of, or somehow came at the expense of, others. In their world, economic power must be centralized; only government can be trusted with society's wealth."

Barrett continued. "They just want to legally certify goodness and fairness the same way those shit-for-brains idealists in Europe keep trying to make war illegal—with talk, paper, promises and other people's cash. Individual state sovereignty is just a technicality standing in their way. The One Nation legislation just eliminated that technicality."

Ben swirled the red-amber liquid until it climbed the sides of the thin, handblown brandy snifter. The aromatic, burnt-orange bouquet of Grand Marnier filled the air and Ben indulged in another sip of the sweet, potent cognac. Joe Adams sat on a stool behind the bar, sipping a beer, watching his boss and Governor get plowed. It was 3:30 A.M., well past closing. Ben had come in from the Capitol very late, eaten dinner alone, then moved to the bar for the first of three stiff Irish Coffees. He'd then switched to Grand Marnier, which Joe recognized as the boss's "contemplative" drink. Joe declined Ben's offer to join him—the last time Joe had indulged in the expensive treat, he had ended up asleep in his car on the side of the road, with a flat tire, being woken up by a Highway Patrol officer banging on his driver's side window. He had been too drunk to find the tire jack he knew was buried somewhere in the trunk, and had succumbed to the somnolent finale of the evening's reverie. The officer had not been amused.

The Senate debate had gone long into the night. The bill unanimously voted out of committee was, in fact, loosely modeled after South Carolina's 1832 Ordinance of Nullification. The bill, which was passed overwhelmingly and was now awaiting Ben's signature, declared the One Nation Act of 2013 null and void, on the grounds that the law ran counter to Montana's specific constitutional guarantees of personal and state sovereignty. The bill forbade the Governor from enacting any part of the federal legislation, and, in an unexpected move, empowered the Governor to use the state National Guard to enforce the Nullification Act. And they had voted on all this live, on C-SPAN.

Ben had his eyes closed, and was gently but unsteadily rocking to the soft country music now enveloping the bar area. It was an old song, and took him back 10 years, to 2004, when he was a freshman member of the House. He was alone in his radical views then, both houses of the Legislature packed with traditional Republicans and Democrats, representing their long-established investors, tolerant of his crazed tirades against federal encroachment into private enterprise, but essentially paying him no mind.

At the time the offending issue was the nationalization of the country's health care system—the old, discredited Clinton health plan back with a vengeance. Ben took the floor in the House chamber, delivering a fiery speech in opposition to the national universal health plan about to be passed in Washington.

"Mr. Speaker, having third-party payers and the lack of market forces will *inevitably* lead to higher costs. If a CAT scan were to cost $1,000 and people had to pay out-of-pocket, nobody would get CAT scans until the price dropped so most could afford it. Drug protocols costing $3,000 a month would go unused until the price dropped. If drug companies wanted to stay in business, they would be forced to price their products so the bulk of the population could afford them, just like every other business. But in today's world, hospitals and pharmaceutical companies would be insane to drop their prices as long as third-party payers—insurance programs, Medicare and Medicaid—were forced by law to pay. A single-payer system—the government—*has* to lead to rationed care, just as it has everywhere else in the world. Budgets aren't unlimited, and when the budget runs out of money, services are going to get cut, plain and simple. A single-payer system means continued rising costs and

certain rationed care. Period. It's *simply not possible* that there can
be any other outcome! Only a return to a system where individuals
are allowed to make rational spending decisions, like they do for
everything else in their lives, can return sanity to the system. Prices
cannot rise above what the market will bear if the company
providing those products and services wants to stay in business.
Insurance was originally designed to provide coverage for
catastrophic medical bills, not first-dollar coverage. That system
worked fine for a hundred years, and didn't stop working until the
utopian leftists decided health care was a *right*, instead of a
business. When it was run as a business, market rules applied—
prices couldn't rise above the market's ability to pay. When it
became a right, and government started mandating who got covered
for what, *somebody* had to pay, and those costs got wrapped into
rising insurance premiums. Mandated payments created an artificial
seller's market, where providers were able to set prices as high as
they liked. So now the utopians claim the solution to rising
insurance premiums is for the *government* to pay all of the bills! It's
so irrational, Mr. Speaker, I'm getting a headache just saying it! The
press calls it *free* health care. *Free health care!* It's free! Whoopee!
Nobody has to pay! It solves everything! We should have thought of
this a hundred years ago!"

Ben opened his eyes and partially focused on Joe, still sitting
behind the bar. "The promised road to heaven on earth," muttered
Ben "is always paved with somebody else's money."

Joe eased himself off his stool and walked to the front door. A
Highway Patrol trooper was waiting to drive the Governor to the
residence. "Let's go chief," Joe suggested wearily, "big day
tomorrow."

CHAPTER 18
January 2014

The national news media descended upon Helena like the plague. Governor Kane had yet to sign the Nullification Act. The talking heads on cable TV were frenzied with speculation as to whether he would or wouldn't, and what would happen if he did or didn't. Cameras and recording devices were banned from the American Outback Brewing Company, though reporters weren't. Sales were up rather nicely, and for the duration the staff followed Joe's lead in answering every breathless question with a polite, smiling "Sorry, no comment."

The U.S. Attorney General called Ben warning him the state legislature's act was illegal and unconstitutional, and advising him not to sign the bill into law. The administration, she counseled, would prefer it if he would veto the bill, forcing the Legislature to override, at least giving them a chance to think about it again. No harm was yet done, she intimated; let's just make this go away and we'll address the concerns about the federal legislation in due course, though she offered no specifics.

TV news trucks lay siege to the Capitol campus. Catchy titles, splashy graphics and dramatic music had already been produced to lead the newscasts. Journalists scattered frantically throughout the city, seeking interviews, commentary and outright speculation from anyone who was willing to sit still in front of a camera. Most of the smart money was on the Governor vetoing the legislation, which enabled more endless commentary about what the Legislature might do in response. Fewer speculated he would sign it or, more likely, let it pass into law by letting it sit for 10 days without his signature. Retired federal prosecutors, judges and academics offered legal opinions. Presidential historians and bestselling biographical authors provided perspective. Prominent Democrats supported the administration; well-known Republicans counseled caution. One former member of the Joint Chiefs of Staff even submitted his thoughts on the military options open to the President in case things got out-of-hand. Washington talk show hosts were apoplectic. Shielded references were made to the Governor's drinking habits and his possible relationships with unsavory militia types. A network news magazine ran a one-hour special on working for alcoholic bosses.

Ben spent a few days working the phones, talking to county-level politicians, mayors and local town council leadership. He met endlessly with his administration's officers and advisors, and several more times with Mitch Steere and Bill Barrett. He ate dinner twice more with Kim Lange. Eight days after the Legislature had passed the nullification bill, the Governor requested some airtime from the local network affiliates. They granted it immediately, as did the local public TV channel and C-SPAN. In an attempt to emphasize the uniqueness of the event, Ben finally acted on a suggestion both Joe and Kim had been making for the past year—he would do the broadcast from the brewpub.

This decision, of course, led to a frenzied, last minute scramble for the mobile video production crew. The Governor wanted to sit at his usual booth in the back of the restaurant. Joe had to close the dining room to the public and move the people already eating away from the far corner where the lighting crews would be setting up shop. There was a large, picture window to the right of where the

Governor would be sitting, and a framed western painting behind his head; the reflections and glare were driving the crew to distraction. After considerable trial and error, they finally settled on a lantern-style softbox hanging from an overhead boom for the main light, with a couple of carefully mounted, flat-black metal flags to block the light being reflected in the picture. A soft, gold-colored reflector was placed at the picture window—they would shoot the Governor straight on, from an adjacent booth, so the window wouldn't be in the shot, and the reflector would throw a mellow, warm light on the scene, especially at the Governor's face, which complemented the whole fireside chat thing they were going for. A couple of graduated scrims were placed over the fill and background lights to soften some of the harsher shadow transitions, and they were ready to go.

The Governor took his seat. It was a bit disorienting for a moment. He had been eating meals and reviewing the business books in this seat for years, and now the familiar views were blotted out by hot lights, strange reflectors, and clusters of people standing around facing him, talking into headphones and fussing with equipment. He opened the folder in front of him and reviewed the outline he had constructed earlier. No teleprompter would be used for this address; he would speak briefly, and from the heart. When they counted down the seconds to broadcast, Ben instinctively sharpened his focus, and projected past the camera to imagine he was talking to a small group of close friends.

Ben spent the first 10 minutes of the broadcast carefully reviewing the events running up to this point, and then summarizing the reactions both he and the state legislators were receiving from Montana's general public. "They tell me signing this bill into law would be illegal and unconstitutional. Now I'm not a historian, nor am I a lawyer, just a humble tavern owner who has been honored to be elected Governor of this great state—so I believe what the experts tell me.

"But if that's really true it would mean a few things, a few things we should all be a little uncomfortable with. It would mean the people of this state would, in essence, have no right to representative government; it would mean we have no right to choose a government to embody and stand-up for our views. It would mean the federal government stands alone as the sole legitimate authority on the continent, and low population states, like our own, would simply have to suffer our relative lack of input, and are destined—indeed, mandated—to live with the consequences. As your Governor, it falls to me to decide whether a free people may retain the right to shape the world in which they live. I believe they do. I believe I have no right or authority to choose otherwise."

Governor Kane slipped on his reading glasses and signed the bill into law.

Pen still in hand, he looked up at the camera, peering over his spectacles. "I think it was Benjamin Franklin who said *we must indeed all hang together, or most assuredly we shall all hang separately.*" Still talking directly to the camera, Ben slipped the cap on the pen and removed his glasses. "I guess we're about to find out."

A light, windswept snow blanketed Browning, giving the Great Plains outpost a more isolated, forlorn feel than normal. Running Wolf sat in his worn, but still comfortable, reclining chair in front of the TV. Lynn, his wife, snuggled at the corner of the couch closest to him, her feet tucked under her small frame and a blanket tossed loosely around her lap. Governor Ben Kane was talking to them through the television, sitting at his booth in his restaurant in Helena.

Running Wolf had been to the American Outback Brewing Company twice, and described it a bit for his wife. He shared a couple of old biker war stories; he and Joe had ridden together almost 20 years before. When they first met, Joe was working behind the bar of one of the toughest, most violent biker bars on the outskirts of Helena. "He still rides an old Norton. Nice bike, but too small for a big state. He's a good mechanic; gotta be to keep that old thing running."

Their conversation ground to a halt as they listened to Ben deliver the finale of his speech, and watched, with the rest of the state, as the Governor signed the nullification bill into Montana law.

Lynn spoke first. "Damn, can he do that?"

"I don't think so," Running Wolf responded. "I know we can't." He was referring to the Blackfoot Confederacy's relationship with the federal government. "Nice trick if they can pull it off, though."

President Henderson was watching the broadcast from the second-floor residence in the White House. He quickly reached his Chief of Staff. "Are you watching this? What the hell is this guy doing?" He paused for a second, his mind racing. "Look," he continued, "We need to get our ducks in order on this thing. I want a coordinated response ready no later than tomorrow morning, right after the cabinet meeting." The President terminated the connection and watched the avalanche of expert commentary following Governor Kane's unexpected action.

CHAPTER 19
February 2014

Ben held his gaze at the camera for an extra second. "OK…we're out! Thank you, Governor."

"Thank *you*!" Ben responded. "Thank you all." He collected his outline and notes and placed them back into the folder. The activity level around him picked up rapidly as the crew started unplugging lights and retrieving cases to stash their equipment. "Let me get out of your way." Ben slipped out of his booth and walked over to Kim Lange who was watching from outside the penumbra of tightly clustered broadcast equipment and personnel.

She placed her hand gently on his arm. "Are you OK?"

"Huh?" Ben responded with a puzzled look. "I'm fine. How do I look?" He brushed his hand across his forehead. "Oh, the makeup." He turned to the young lady who was already rummaging through her box for some moisturized wipes. "Can you help me with this?"

"That's not what I meant, Ben."

Men are so weird, she reminded herself. "You just took a big step over there. God knows what's going to happen now; we could be in for a rough ride. And you're in the driver's seat. How *are* you?"

Ben pulled out a chair at a nearby four-top and invited Kim to do the same. The cosmetologist quickly got him cleaned up and left them alone. "I'm fine. It wasn't too difficult once I got there. Do I support the will of the people, or don't I? Was the bill unlawful under Montana's constitution? I don't think so. So on what basis do I refuse to sign it? Is it unconstitutional at the federal level? Shit yeah! So the law will be declared unconstitutional and we'll see what happens next. At least we got their attention." His eyes darted to the procession of broadcast personnel now humping equipment out of the dining room to their truck. Joe Adams was manning the front door in an attempt to keep as much cold air out as possible. He wanted to get the room open for dinner business as soon as they could get it put back together. Hungry customers were backed up in the bar area.

The Governor sat back and continued. "The federal government appears determined to establish a centrally controlled, collectivist social and economic system. The Left support and defend that end with what borders on religious fervor. Personally, I really don't think they're moving ahead with this by design—I wouldn't give them that much credit. More likely the whole past several decades of incremental socialism is a result of entrenched special interests, elective pandering, political momentum and American citizens trying to live off of one another. But however we got here—we're here, and I think a free people have a right to have their feelings known."

"Have you heard from the White House?"

"Not since the Attorney General called to say signing it would be a bad idea. I thanked her for her advice and signed it anyway. I'm guessing I'm due for another call." He grinned sarcastically.

The full roster of departmental secretaries sat assembled in the elegant Cabinet Room, each laden with reports, opinions and options provided to them by armies of subordinates. Marty Cigala, the President's wiry Chief of Staff, carefully reviewed advance copies of all of the reports, and directed his office to produce the three-page brief being reviewed by the President in the Oval Office. It was a regularly scheduled cabinet meeting, but the agenda had been usurped by the recent events in Montana. The buzz in the room radiated energy, confidence, perhaps even a little amusement at the circumstances currently confronting them. They awaited the President.

The loud chatter in the room stopped abruptly as the heavy French door was swung sharply open at the hand of a crisply uniformed marine. The occupants stood as President Henderson entered and immediately signaled all to take their seats.

Henderson snapped open his leather portfolio and immediately addressed the Montana issue. He went on for a few minutes reviewing the various positions, asking questions and requesting an occasional clarification. Cabinet secretaries traded opinions.

Finally the President weighed in. "I sympathize with those who have voiced concern about us looking impotent or somehow limp-wristed if we don't respond strongly. My feeling is since we already know this is going to end with the repeal of their so-called nullification act and accepting the One Nation protocols, I'm less concerned about our saving face and more concerned with just getting this behind us. I agree with those who suggest the last thing we need after the Sturgis fiasco is to appear somehow intolerant or heavy-handed." He looked across the table to Mary Sullivan, the U.S. Attorney General. "Mary, this is your matter. Keep Marty in the loop." The President glanced down at the agenda. "What's next?"

A merciless Arctic wind blew in hard from the northwest. Chief Running Wolf faced the frigid blast to better taste it, to see what news it might be carrying. He detected a bit of pine scent from the surrounding, heavily forested Black Hills, perhaps a hint of wood smoke, and some more snow, but little else. The air was too cold and dry to carry much more. He turned to Gordon Bird-in-Flight, a white haired, well-sunned tribal elder from the Crow Nation.

"Who's idea was it to meet in South Dakota in February?"

"Tradition," responded Bird-in-Flight. "We've met here since 1991."

"Our people have been on this land for 5,000 years. It's time our traditions took us to Florida in the winter." They laughed and headed into the warmth of the doublewide trailer serving as the headquarters for the InterTribal Bison Cooperative.

The snow surrounding the trailer was hard packed and muddy. A lusty fire snapped and popped in an industrial green 55-gallon steel drum; a dozen rifle shots into the lower third of the barrel had provided two-dozen nicely positioned vent holes, allowing the fire to breath. Four guys stood around it, trying to keep warm while grabbing a smoke. One poked at the fire studiously with a well-charred stick. Pickup trucks of all makes, ages and conditions were parked haphazardly in a crude crescent around the trailer. Three dogs were chasing each other across the lot, providing the only visible sign of unadulterated enthusiasm on the property. Running Wolf and Bird-in-Flight smiled and nodded to the four as they walked past on the way to their meeting, a breakout discussion with the Northern Plains tribes.

Once inside, the two worked their way to a nice-sized meeting room in the back corner of the trailer. The room's décor was bordering on depressing; only several rather well done, colorful framed photographs of bison grazing in the local environs saved the room from going over the edge. Several ancient, fold-up, school cafeteria tables were arranged to form a horseshoe around which the attendees seated themselves. Two overhead fluorescent fixtures threw a harsh, almost clinical light on the proceedings.

Handouts were neatly and sequentially laid out on a small table by the door. Running Wolf and Bird-in-Flight collected their documents as they walked in, then grabbed a couple of beat-up, brown metal folding chairs and found themselves a spot together at the table. The representatives from North and South Dakota, Wyoming, and Nebraska and the remaining Montana tribes joined them over the next few minutes.

Discussions proceeded at a leisurely pace. The participants concerned themselves primarily with land-use issues, native wildlife reintroduction to lands occupied by bison herds, and genetic diversity programs. Running Wolf was gratified to learn about the progress made by the Crow Nation; they'd grown their herd to just over 4,000 animals grazing freely on 200,000 acres of native Montana grass.

Running Wolf studied the numbers and tapped the keyboard of a small calculator. "It looks like we're all in the same boat; we're victims of our own success." The five Montana tribes were carrying in the neighborhood of 5,500 bison on 260,000 acres—they had all reached the upper limits of the environmentally sound capacity on their allotted grazing land.

The discussion quickly turned to contiguous prairie lands possibly available to expand the bison herds, and to the expensive, maintenance-intensive, high-tensile fencing needed to accompany any expansion.

"We've got plenty of land," said Running Wolf, speaking for the Blackfoot. "What's stopping us is the damn fencing—the initial expense, really. The labor and the maintenance we can deal with; the young people are lining up wanting to work with the herds. We're got about 50,000 additional acres we could give to the bison immediately if we could afford to fence it."

Gordon Bird-in-Flight nodded affirmatively. "I agree with Tommy. We talk of seeing the Crow herd grow to 10,000 strong. At the rate they're reproducing we could easily be there in four years.

But we would need up to 500,000 fenced acres. Like the Blackfoot, we have the land, but finding the money for the fence is difficult. And the buffalo can't be controlled without it. We can barely control them *with* it." An understanding chuckle fluttered around the table.

"What about the Bureau?" asked a representative from one of the 10 regional Sioux Tribes, referring to the Bureau of Indian Affairs.

"I thought they were sending a representative to this meeting," said Running Wolf, thumbing through his papers searching for the agenda. "Ah, here it is...tomorrow. He's supposed to be here tomorrow. We can run it by him, maybe get him to fill out some of those grant proposals they're so fond of." Another laugh. "I doubt it, though. The bison are an Indian priority, not a Washington priority. We'll get another $3 million, understaffed birth control clinic with a beautifully paved parking lot before we get a single mile of fencing out of them."

Bird-in-Flight shook his head. "Ain't that the truth..."

CHAPTER 20
March 2014

U.S. Attorney General Sullivan slept fitfully on her flight to Helena. In her late-40's, she was tall, blond, and a native of Queens, New York. She had quickly risen through the ranks of the New York City Parks Department, then the New York State Department of Environmental Protection, and then, despite the New York accent, the U.S. Justice Department. Sharp as a tack, she was a determined, dogged advocate of whatever legal argument she was chosen to represent. Her rise to political power wasn't due to her exceptional legal skills, which were real, as much for the fact that, regardless of the argument, she was reliably able to chart the winning line of reasoning to greater government oversight, control or authority over some previously unregulated segment of American life. "It's not *your* country," she would say, "it's *our* country. And we all have a say in what goes on here."

The airplane's rushing descent snapped her eyes open for good. The dreary, monotonous Great Plains winter landscape greeted her as she yawned at the window. *Another 20 minutes and I'll be in a car on the way to the state Capitol. Why do I get the plum assignments? The President could have let me send a Justice Department deputy secretary to slap these clowns around.*

She didn't realize until she stepped off of the plane what an unusually beautiful winter afternoon it had turned out to be—a weak but bright sun shining in a cloudless sky, a balmy breeze, and temperatures in the low 50's. Her aide-de-camp lugged both of their overnight bags while the Attorney General burdened herself only with her own briefcase. In spite of the fact they were in an airport just outside one of the largest cities in the state, the air smelled distinctly rural—of soil and hay and open space, air gusting for miles and miles without anything larger than a barn getting in the way. Her mood improved despite herself.

Sullivan assumed there would be some horse-trading, assumed this was just another example of over-the-top political brinkmanship gone haywire. The crazed Montanans were surely positioning themselves for more federal money, for quietly relaxing some environmental or livestock regulations, for something, in return for repealing their nullification bill. Her job was to hear them out, to be serious, firm, but understanding, and to promise them nothing but the President's ear.

The discussion, by common agreement, would be restricted to the highest levels; only Ben and the two legislative leaders would meet with her. They convened in a small conference alcove just off the Governor's office. Ben had a few minutes alone with Senator Barrett and Speaker Steere before the Attorney General arrived; they had no feeling for how bad the pushback might be so they decided just to sit back and play it by ear. When she showed up, they all gathered around and exchanged small talk, offered the usual coffee and refreshments, and gave the two sides a brief opportunity to non-confrontationally size each other up. They brought their coffee and their marginally relaxed attitudes to the conference table as they settled in.

"The weather sure is a whole lot nicer than I expected!" said Sullivan. "I'm afraid I overdressed."

"Oh, don't worry," responded Mitch Steere. "It'll drop into the 20's tonight and probably won't rise again until April. You'll be fine. Oh, we saw you on TV the other day—how was your trip to New York?"

"It was great, thanks. But exhausting. You know how it is—the media is fighting for a piece of you, you're constantly living under a microscope, and here I was trying to do some shopping and sneak around visiting friends I haven't seen in a while." She thought for a moment, than added, "It's very tough on the friends, too." The Attorney General took a sip of coffee and dabbed her mouth with a napkin. It was time to get down to business.

"So gentleman," she scanned all of the faces at the table, "what are we doing here? You've caused quite a bit of commotion! 24/7 TV coverage, front page of *The New York Times*—if you wanted our attention, you got it! So where do we go from here?"

"Well, we're kinda already at where we were going," said Ben. He wasn't quite sure he'd expressed himself clearly, but he couldn't stop now. "Just to recap—the people in this state didn't want to live under the terms of the One Nation regime. They elected representatives who passed a bill nullifying the program in this state and I signed it into law. So we're pretty well done on our end. What are your people thinking?"

Sullivan maintained her game-face, but felt a little color involuntarily creeping into her cheeks.

She began. "Well, Governor, I guess *our* thoughts are these actions taken by your government have been irresponsible, illegal, and, some say, treasonous. I came here to see you in hopes we could find a way to defuse the situation. I'm sympathetic to the wishes of your citizens, but your Legislature simply cannot overrule an act of Congress. You'd certainly be within your rights to challenge the law in the Supreme Court. But until the Court strikes it down, the law remains in effect, here in Montana as in the rest of the Nation." The marginally relaxed attitudes hadn't lasted long.

"Look," Senator Barrett chimed in, "not to put too fine a point on this, Madame Attorney General, but what you have here is a community running out of options and refusing to capitulate. And we believe our own state Constitution, as well as America's founding principles, provides us with both a basis and an obligation to resist a government forcing an unacceptable lifestyle down our throats."

Before the Attorney General could respond Mitch Steere jumped in. "I think what the Majority Leader is saying is that as a state, as a community, we're at the end of our wits with this thing. If you don't allow people a sane way out of a situation, all you leave them with are the insane ways. We'd like to find a rational way out of this mess as much as you would."

The Attorney General responded in measured tones. "Mr. Speaker, with all due respect—this isn't a *mess* or a *situation*. It's an act of Congress, a federal law. You have the same weight in the Senate as every other state. In fact, my understanding is that your Senator Taylor made a valiant effort to turn back the legislation; her efforts subsequently failed. Your state had its chance, now you need to back off for the greater good, for your country and for your President." She looked over at Ben for a response.

He paused for a long moment. "All of us here," he waved his finger at the two legislative leaders, "were elected to represent a constituency. The people of this state speak through their elected representatives. That's America 101. We were not elected to jump every time the federal government directs us to jump. Now the people have given us here our marching orders," he shook his head as if in disbelief, "and I'm not aware of any basis for a supposedly representative government to be overtly non-responsive to the will of its people."

"Oh come on, Governor! Spare me the libertarian philosophy

lesson. This is the real world; these are public policy decisions you and your administration are responsible for enacting and enforcing."

"I'm afraid as things stand I will be unable to help you out there," Ben replied tersely.

"What are you going to do about it?" challenged Barrett. He had lost patience with this game.

Sullivan closed the cover of her leather-padded folder a little too sharply. "Mr. Majority Leader, I don't honestly know what the repercussions will be at this point. We were all hoping it wouldn't go this far. But I think we all know something *will* be done. Something *must* be done! Otherwise every state in the union would be free to do whatever it pleases, whenever it pleases."

The Montana contingent exchanged glances around the table. The Governor locked eyes with the U.S. Attorney General. "And what a terrible thing that would be," said Ben, so softly it was almost under his breath. Except for the fact he held his face expressionless, it could have easily been taken as a threat.

The U.S. Attorney General hadn't been back in Washington for much more than a week when Ben and State Attorney General Gaffney were both served with copies of pleadings made on behalf of the federal government to the Supreme Court requesting an emergency petition for a writ of certiorari. Invoking the high court's original jurisdiction under Article III of the Constitution, they were seeking a ruling on Montana's nullification law—they were, of course, seeking to have the law declared unconstitutional.

Within days of the petition, the Court granted cert, and scheduled oral arguments to be heard in a week. Gaffney managed to cajole an old friend with some experience arguing before the Court, now lecturing and writing for the Cato Institute in Washington, to present Montana's oral argument. The state's Attorney General, with a few less experienced but no less eager legal minds in tow, then flew off to Washington to assist in preparing the brief and outlining the state's oral argument.

The hearing before the Court went about as everyone had expected, and as the multitude of expert television commentators had bravely predicted—Montana's advocate was essentially eaten alive by the justices of the high court. Within three days the country was once again treated to the spectacle of sleep-deprived, panting reporters simultaneously ripping through, reading, reporting, and commenting on the 30-page decision on live television. The Court had declared the nullification bill unconstitutional by a vote of 8-1 (Justice Clarence Thomas dissenting).

The day after the decision was issued, the Governor's press office released a joint statement from the Governor and the legislative leadership. In it they thanked the Supreme Court for its opinion on the matter, while expressing regret for what the decision would ultimately mean for a free people's right of self-determination. The statement concluded:

> ...despite the learned findings of the Court, we feel it our responsibility to state here, unambiguously, that the Nullification Act of 2014 will remain in force within our borders, and that the One Nation legislation will not be imposed, nor lawfully enforced, within the State of Montana.
>
> Respectfully,
> Benjamin Kane, Governor
> William Barrett, Senate Majority Leader
> Mitchell Steere, Speaker of the House

CHAPTER 21
March 2014

President Henderson was furious. Congress was in an uproar. The national media was simply frothing. Even the Chief Justice of the Supreme Court placed a rare telephone call to the President to get a feeling for how the executive branch, charged by the Constitution with the responsibility for enforcing the laws passed by Congress, was going to respond to this situation.

The President did what every executive does when confronted with an unexpected crisis—he attended meetings. Lots of meetings. Nobody could remember the last time a state had so brazenly disregarded a Supreme Court decision, especially one directed specifically at the state in question. A measured, but serious response was called for and would indeed be delivered. The legal issues were clear, but this remained a politically delicate situation, and the President wanted to be sure everyone involved was on the same page.

Another meeting was taking place, this one on a Gulfstream V-SP climbing rapidly toward 40,000 feet, ripping through the 90 miles of airspace between Helena and Malmstrom Air Force Base. Maj. Gen. Paul McDermott, commanding general of the Montana Army National Guard, waited quietly while Governor Kane worked his way through yet another phone interruption. General McDermott, like most who rise to the top of military organizations, very much looked the part of a general officer. At 62 years of age, he was a few inches over 6 feet tall, trimly built, ramrod straight, and had a tan, angular face topped by a stubble of white hair. The General was proud of the fact he was a fourth-generation Montanan. His great-grandfather had emigrated from Scotland, first to the farmland of south central Pennsylvania, later to the Montana Territories. There he'd worked in the silver mines of Butte, then on the newly constructed railroads expanding across the state. His grandfather had also worked the rails, eventually settling down to a modest cattle operation in Townsend, which was later expanded considerably, and very successfully, by his son, the General's father. The latter had fought in the Second World War, but saw military service as a duty, not a career. The old man, now 92, was still down at the ranch, long since officially retired, remaining in good health, and still getting around quite well. Some time ago the business had been transferred to the General, who was hoping to retire there in just a few more years.

In response to a call from the Governor the evening before, General McDermott had met Ben alone at the airport early in the morning. No mention was made of the subject of the meeting, but McDermott, like everyone else in the state, had been reading the papers and knew this wasn't going to be just an early Easter visit for the fly boys at Malmstrom. This wasn't the first time he was meeting the Governor, but it was his first one-on-one encounter. He liked the Governor—he thought Kane was smart and personable, and generally supported his politics and his current dealings with the federal government. But like any National Guard officer, who reported to his state's Governor until the President said otherwise, he was a little queasy about where this crisis might lead. General McDermott liked working in straight lines, and this situation had none.

Waiting on the tarmac at Malmstrom Air Force Base for the Governor's jet was Brig. Gen. Jerry Calderone, the Assistant

Adjutant General for Air. Per General McDermott's directive, he was alone, which was fine with him as he got to drive his four-seat, command/communications-configured Humvee, something, as the senior base commander, he rarely got a chance to do. His command at Malmstrom was one of the most unique in the military, encompassing the 120th Fighter Wing, the 219th Redhorse, and the 341st Space Wing of the Montana Air National Guard. The 120th was a standard fighting wing, flying the new F-22 Raptor Stealth Fighter along with a few old F-16s. The 219th was a highly mobile, rapidly deployable, heavy construction and repair unit whose mission was the support of American airpower worldwide, primarily in the more isolated, austere operating theaters. The 341st Space Wing was a relatively recent addition to the command, inherited from the Air Force when it pulled out of Malmstrom in 2008 in a Pentagon-ordered base consolidation.

The 341st Space Wing was home to the "missileers", the approximately 55 men and women who sat at the ready, their fingers on the triggers of the 200 Minuteman III ICBMs buried in hardened silos scattered about the Great Falls area. It was a tough job with a high burnout rate...a 24-hour shift in a cramped, underground working environment, a culture with a zero tolerance for the slightest of operational errors, and a workday thick with endless, repetitive boring tasks to be attended to with unceasing vigilance. A sweet gig it was not, but a necessary one—the last, human link in a long chain of military and political events unleashing Armageddon on some unlucky society with a suddenly limited shelf life. It was a link unlikely to be usurped by a computer; it took the judgment, agreement and simultaneous physical collaboration of two trained soldiers to launch a nuclear intercontinental ballistic missile, and only one to stop it.

General Calderone cranked up the heat in the Humvee. He should have just waited inside, but he didn't want to entertain any more questions than necessary about the VIP visitors arriving shortly. He'd met Governor Kane a few times, and liked him. Kane was honest and a regular guy; he was hard to dislike. But, *Jesus*, he had really gotten himself into a pickle this time. Getting yourself into a nationally televised pissing contest with the President, the Congress and the Supreme Court all at once can't be good for your career. He wondered what they were doing, coming out to Malmstrom. *Probably he just needs to get the hell away from the press for a while.* Calderone reached for the intercom and called the tower. "How far out is the jet, Sergeant?"

Ben snapped his secure satellite phone shut and looked up at General McDermott. "Sorry, General; there won't be any more interruptions." He glanced at his watch. "We'll be on the ground in 15 minutes. We need to talk."

As the president of any corporation, large or small, in the country could attest, a significant, albeit less than glamorous part of the job was signing things. Many things. Every day. The Presidency of the United States was no different. As the senior operations officer for the entire national government, the President put his pen to an endless parade of proclamations, executive orders, legislation, appointments, commissions, regulations, budget authorizations, and other documents required to keep the United States federal government in business on a daily basis.

The two documents working their way to the Oval Office had been sifted and combed through for legal and political content, detail, and clarity by the Justice Department, the National Security Council, the White House Legal Counsel, the President's Special Assistant for Policy and Political Affairs, and finally, the President's Chief of Staff. The papers had successfully percolated their way through the hierarchy of government filters and now sat on Marty

Cigala's desk. The Chief of Staff read them through a hundred times. He now sat quietly in his small West Wing corner office, playing a game of mental chess trying to anticipate the recipient's countermoves and the likely chain of events possibly set into motion once the President affixed his signature to the papers. The unknown was unwelcome in the West Wing, and the unknown with a potentially devastating outcome was even more unwelcome. He meticulously slipped the stack of documents into a handsome, black leather folder for presentation to the President.

Cigala picked up the phone and called the President's executive assistant. "Is he ready for me?"

"He's finishing up a call with the Prime Minister. He should be ready for you in two minutes," she responded. He gathered the portfolio and some additional notes and headed down the hall to the Oval. By the time he reached the reception area the President's assistant was waving him through. "Go ahead, Mr. Cigala. He just hung up."

The Chief of Staff opened the door to the Oval Office and stuck his head in. The President was jotting down some notes on a pad; he looked up and waved. "Come in. Let's see how it turned out."

Cigala walked carefully across the sunny, historical space and placed the open folder on the President's desk. "Two executive orders, Mr. President. The first is titled a Proclamation to the People of the State of Montana. It reasserts the supremacy of the federal government to the citizens of the state and to their elected officials in the matters of the ongoing controversy. It doesn't specify consequences, but leaves no doubt there will be consequences if they don't back off and settle the matter once and for all." Cigala pulled a cluster of finely milled linen papers from the folder and handed them to the Chief Executive. "Signed copies will be delivered, by federal marshal, to Governor Kane, to his attorney general, and to the state legislative leadership."

"Very good," said Henderson. "What else."

"The second is a proclamation and executive order federalizing the Army and Air National Guard of the State of Montana, and directs the Pentagon to immediately use the Guard to protect and reinforce the Great Falls missile fields. It's pretty straightforward— we've got plenty of precedent for this type of thing."

The President started signing the many multiple copies of each of the executive orders. "What happens next on the National Guard thing? I want every single civilian position on the airbase filled by a Guardsman. I want Guardsmen serving lunch and collecting garbage if they have to. I don't want any of those lunatic civilians stepping foot on those missile fields."

"Yes, sir. As soon as the orders are signed, a copy goes to Attorney General Sullivan. She'll call the Secretary of Defense, who will in turn call General Byrnes. General Byrnes is the Commanding General of the Third U.S. Army—out of Fort McPherson, Georgia, I believe. My understanding is General Byrnes then calls Maj. Gen. McDermott, who is the commanding general of the Montana National Guard. General McDermott will then be informed his command will be under the purview of General Byrnes, and we'll proceed from there. We'll have direct command of the Montana Guard within the hour, and will be able to provide them with any assets or assistance they might need to carry out their mission."

President Henderson finished signing the last copy of the orders and handed the leather portfolio back to his Chief of Staff. "Sounds good! Let's hope things go according to plan."

Cigala accepted the portfolio and nodded. "Yes, sir. Thank you, Mr. President."

He left the Oval Office to start the ball rolling.

"Umph!" *OK…that should do it.* Joe Adams hoisted a last beat-up, dangerously full, cardboard box of old plates on top of a small stack of similarly bulging containers. He took a step back and brushed the dust off the front of his worn denim shirt, then slapped the dirt off his bare forearms, having worked up enough of a sweat to roll up his sleeves. "Diane! Check this out!"

The waitress stuck her head into the room. "Joe! Look at this place! Nice job—do you do windows? I could use…"

"Nice try! Not a chance, my dear. My place isn't much bigger than this room and the thought of cleaning it hasn't crossed my mind." He looked around the quickly made-over storage room. The old glassware and china were stacked somewhat precariously in the far corner. Some old, dusty, framed pictures were leaning against the boxes. A rolling service bar, complete with a brass bar rail, sat in the opposite corner. They used the portable bar for large, private parties held in the dining room and stashed it in the storage room to keep it out of the way when it wasn't in service. Joe had wiped it down and stocked it with fresh glassware and liquor. He'd bring out a couple of cases of cold beer and a full ice bucket in a little while.

Joe collared one of the busboys. "Help me drag those two four-tops in here. And I'll need a couple of tablecloths and about half a dozen chairs."

In just a few minutes they had the two tables fitted together and covered with a large, clean tablecloth, giving them the appearance of a small, if somewhat uneven, conference table. Since Ben had signed the nullification bill on live TV from his booth in the back of the dining room, the place had been mobbed with people of all sorts. Tourists had made it a must-see stop on the Helena itinerary, and would wait over an hour for a seat in the back just to eat a couple of their famous buffalo burgers. Media types were constantly drifting in and out, even with the imposed no-cameras rule, many eating lunch and dinner, then returning for cocktails later on after their evening broadcast. The regulars were afraid to get off their barstools even to take a leak, for fear some blow-dried TV anchor would steal the seat in an attempt to do a hidden camera interview with the bartender, and, in a potentially dangerous breach of barroom etiquette, refuse to give it up. All this was putting a crimp in the Governor's preference for conducting unofficial business in his favorite booth.

The circumstances led to Ben's request to Joe to see if anything could be done to make the storeroom at the back of the dining room fit for human habitation, or at least close enough for government officials. It took Joe just a couple of hours, in between interruptions, to drag the bulkier crap down to the basement, get the space swept up and mopped, and to replace the single, bare bulb burning in the center of the ceiling with an old brass, three-bulb hanging fixture used to light the entrance foyer some years ago. He also scraped up a short, shaded table lamp Ben could use to throw some light on his paperwork.

As one of the busboys was collecting the old prints and posters to bring downstairs, Joe noticed a framed print of the famous John Trumbull depiction of the signing of the Declaration of Independence. "Whoa—that's a keeper!" He snatched the idealized portrayal of the seminal moment in American history and wiped it down with a damp rag. It was still pretty grimy; he walked up front to the bar to find some glass cleaner, a hammer and a couple of nails. Minutes later, the refreshed rendering was hanging on the far wall of the room, readily visible to anyone walking through the door.

Later in the evening, Kim Lange was the first to arrive. At Joe's insistence, she went back and stuck her head in the storeroom; she returned to the bar with the compliment he was so obviously fishing for. He was somewhat disappointed when she turned down his offer to enjoy her dinner in what six hours ago had been a dank storeroom full of slimy slop buckets and broken furniture. Instead she opted for a light meal at the bustling bar with a nice glass of red wine. Figuring the Governor would be arriving shortly, Joe went ahead and stacked two cases of cold bottled beer into the rolling bar's steel-lined, insulated cooler and filled the ice bucket. *Ready for show time*, he thought with considerable satisfaction.

A cold air mass rolling down from the Canadian Rockies had brought with it a fairly fierce early spring snowstorm. The Governor and Senator Barrett barreled through the front door of the bar, cheeks flushed from their bracing walk from the nearby Capitol building, both shedding snowflakes and radiating cold air. The two spent a few minutes greeting the raucous well-wishers in the crowded room; Ben worked his way to the bar, where he signaled Kim to join them in the back and placed a dinner order for himself and Barrett. Then Ben and the Majority Leader headed down the narrow aisle in the packed dining room to their new meeting room. Kim hurried to join them, but stopped at the entrance to the dining room when loud applause broke out for the two politicians. She waited until Ben, smiling broadly and waving enthusiastically, opened the door to the newly christened conference room, then demurely and quickly walked through the room as the clapping and cheering died down.

"It's nice to know someone still loves us," commented Ben as he draped his sport coat across the back of a chair. "It's nice to get some applause without having to give a speech first."

"I don't know about you, ladies and gentleman, but I've had enough coffee for one day," said Barrett as he familiarized himself with the service bar. "Look! It's got a brass bar rail! Great stuff, Governor. It's good to be king. What can I get you two?" The Senator took their drink orders and entertained himself playing bartender.

"The applause was real, Ben," said Kim, wanting to insure he didn't miss the significance of the enthusiastic welcome. "I think you'd get a similar reception anywhere in the state right now. They're rallying around their leader."

"Rallying around their leader," Ben repeated softly. "I hope their faith isn't being misplaced. Can you really be considered a leader if you have no idea where you're going?"

"Yes, you can," Kim affirmed without hesitation. "Being a leader means being willing to do the right thing. You could have capitulated to the federal law, Ben. Forty-nine other governors did, including a great many who disagreed with it. They capitulated despite the fact their constituents opposed the law. I know *that* sure isn't leadership."

"Amen," added Barrett, nibbling on the cocktail olives Joe put out in a rock glass. *What the hell, nobody here drinks martinis.*

"The fact we don't know where this ends up just enhances your position," Kim explained. "You're doing the right thing *despite* the potential consequences. It's very brave, Ben, and true leaders are brave."

There was a sudden rush of noise and dining room clatter as the door opened and Mitch Steere walked through. He immediately drew large smiles from Ben and Barrett—he was wearing a cowboy hat, which was unusual for him.

"I usually don't go for the hee-haw look. But I have to admit, these things really work in the snow," he said as he removed and shook the ice off his hat. "Sorry I'm late—I got hung up at a meeting with the committee chairmen. They love you, Governor. The whole House is ready to canonize you."

"Isn't canonization what they do to martyrs sacrificing themselves for the cause? Great. St. Benjamin the Jailbird," Ben cracked.

"Nobody is going to be arrested," replied Kim. "They would have to arrest the entire state government—they didn't even try that during the Civil War. All they've done so far is to nationalize our National Guard. Pretty lame if it's the best response they could come up with."

Speaker Steere accepted a cocktail from the Majority Leader and turned to Ben. "How's General McDermott handling his end? He can't be thrilled having the steering wheel yanked out of his hands."

"Paul McDermott is a good man," said Ben carefully. "He's a loyal American, a good soldier and a fourth-generation Montanan. He's in a difficult position right now. We anticipated the call from the Pentagon, and, you're right, he wasn't feeling real good about it." Barrett and Steere exchanged glances. "I'll be hearing from him soon; tonight, I would guess."

Dinner arrived shortly. Considering the circumstances, the conversation and mood around the table were relatively lighthearted. Gallows humor, perhaps, but certainly there was a comfort being with like-minded spirits in the midst of the turmoil they had created. Ben was mildly concerned he had not yet received the expected call from General McDermott.

The reason the call never came became apparent when the General showed up in person later in the evening. As he entered the room, he paused for a moment and surveyed the strange scene—a small, poorly lit, windowless room, Senator Barrett standing behind a cluttered bar pouring himself a drink, empty beer bottles scattered about the table, with the state's political leadership hunched around animatedly talking.

"This is what you civilians consider a meeting? I missed my calling!" He walked over to the bar and helped himself to a generous single-malt Scotch splashed over a couple of ice cubes. He took a healthy sip. "We're in the middle of a revolution against the United States of America and you guys wall yourself off from the rest of the world and get plastered? Nice work, if you can get it." The General found himself a seat and gulped another mouthful of Scotch.

"We're not in revolution, Paul," responded Mitch Steere, a bit defensively. "We're just trying to make a point; we're just trying to hold our ground."

McDermott drained his glass. "Well, gentleman, and ladies," he tipped his glass to Kim, "if you weren't in revolution this morning, you are now." He walked back to the bar, dropped in another cube, and filled it with more of the smoky, amber liquid.

"I refused the order to turn over command of the Guard to the Pentagon. Congratulations, Governor, you still have control of your troops!" The General slumped back into his chair and took another big swallow. The room went stone silent. His limpid, moist eyes looked around the table, lingering for a second at each of the shocked faces staring back at him. The sounds of dinner conversation and clinking silverware on plates could be heard coming from the crowded dining room just outside the door.

McDermott looked up at the Trumbull print: Jefferson, Adams, Franklin and Madison regally standing around George Washington, who was shown seated, presiding over the signing of the Declaration. "Do you think they had good Scotch back then?"

"Hard cider, rum and grain whiskey," responded Ben. "And

lots of it. Washington himself was a whiskey distiller. Jefferson, of course, had his own vineyards, but was partial to expensive French wines... "

"Thanks, Governor," General McDermott interrupted. The alcohol was starting to hit him hard. "I get it. No Scotch." He took another sip of his drink. "Do you think they ever sat around drinking, wondering what the hell they were doing, starting a revolution against the most powerful empire in world history?" He squinted his eyes and looked hard at the painting. "I don't see any glasses in their hands."

There were a few snickers but the weight of the General's statement still hung over the room. He drained his glass. "How'd they know it was time?" His words were starting to slur slightly.

"Time for what, General?" Steere inquired.

"Time to get out. Time to pull the trigger. Time for revolution." McDermott stepped heavily to the bar and poured himself another. Barrett looked across the table at Ben. It was pretty apparent McDermott wasn't much of a drinker, and it was starting to show. The General continued. "The colonies had been taking crap from the British forever. The complaints never changed—taxes were too high, the prices they got for their goods were too low, the few government services they had at the time sucked, and there was no protection from the Indians. Two-thirds of the colonists either supported the British or didn't give a rat's ass whose flag was flying in the town square. What was going through their heads," he tipped his glass at the picture, "causing them to think it was time to go to war with their government, instead of just taking the crap, like they had for the past 100 years? All they had to do was to swallow their pride, accept the passage of the Stamp Act, pay out a little more of their hard-earned money in taxes, and go on with their business like good little colonists. What the hell were they thinking?" He gulped down half the glass of Scotch. "What the hell are *we* thinking?"

CHAPTER 23
April 2014

The press took a couple of days to catch on to the fact that the plan to federalize the Montana National Guard had hit a snag. The White House tried to keep a lid on the news in the hope cooler heads would prevail, but the executive order authorizing the action was still nothing more than ink on paper. Administration hawks were already confidentially advising the President to arrest the whole political leadership of the state—the Governor, the compliant cabinet officers, and the entire state legislature. Others in the administration argued that no one could be sure a new legislature wouldn't go ahead and do the same thing the jailed one had done. Then what would the President do? There were a million people in Montana; he couldn't arrest them all.

"Governor! Governor! What's your reaction to the statement by a militia leader that the President is going to bomb Montana?"

The media people were crazed. Ben was on the steps of the state Capitol, surrounded by microphones, cameras, and a frantic hoard of reporters, several with their eyeglasses knocked asunder. For the first time in his life, he almost enjoyed this aspect of his public responsibilities.

Since news of the National Guard standoff had started leaking,

Ben had been unable to appear anywhere in public without loud, sustained applause following his every move. The media sensed there was an magnificent train wreck of historical proportion building here, and they were going to be there, in the middle of it, a witness to history—to record, report, analyze, discuss, and prognosticate on every blessed minute of it.

A reporter shoved a portable television monitor in the Governor's face. It showed an interview with a gnarly-looking militia leader from the northwest corner of the state, who was asking, "Is the President prepared to shoot and napalm American citizens on national TV for exercising their right to political expression?"

"Do you have a reaction, Governor?" the reporter inquired, at the top of her lungs, brandishing a microphone in one hand and using the monitor to bash a fellow journalist out of the way with the other.

"My reaction?" Ben responded innocently. "Who cares what my reaction is? Has the President answered the question yet? Any rational citizen of Montana, or of any state, should be interested in knowing what the President has to say on the subject. Will the federal government react with overwhelming, violent, military force against a helpless civilian population for voting their conscience? It's a good question—I'd like to hear the answer. Wouldn't you?"

Joe Adams sat, intensely focused, in his cramped and cluttered office behind the bar, reconciling the latest inventory figures with the past month's sales receipts. The Governor stuck his head in.

"Are we still in business?"

"So far. But I hope you're not depending on my math."

"Don't worry," Ben chuckled. "I just keep my eye on the checking account. Hey, speaking of the inventory, are you still in touch with that friend of yours who set up our computerized business-control system?"

"You mean Angel?" Joe dropped his pencil, happy to entertain any interruption coming between him and his paperwork. "The dude's a genius with all things digital. If it's got a silicon chip and electricity running through it, he's your man. You need some help with a network or something up at the Capitol?"

Ben stepped into the room and quietly closed the door behind him. "Sort of..."

Joe listened attentively as the Governor carefully outlined his proposition. "What do you think?" Ben asked when he was finished.

Joe studied his boss's face for a clue as to whether he was serious or not. No clue. "Well...I...I guess I could ask him. I suppose you would prefer if I phrased the question as a hypothetical?"

"Yeah. Good idea. And if the answer is 'yes,' ask him if he would like to provide a much appreciated service to his state." Ben placed his hand on the doorknob, thought for a second, and continued. "I've spoken to General McDermott about this. We're not sure if it's a capital crime or not, but we think it's good for at least 20 or 30 years in a federal pen if he gets caught. I'll need an answer by tomorrow night. Thanks." The Governor slipped out the door and closed it behind him.

Just a few hours later, in the privacy of his office, Ben bluntly laid out his concerns to Senator Barrett. "We'll be crawling with CIA operatives inside of a week. They'll have to secure the missile fields and launch control sites. Then they'll send the FBI after us; probably arrest the entire Legislature. We've got about 100,000 square miles of empty prairie out there. They could drop in 10,000 paratroopers and it would be a week before we'd hear about it. If we're going to stay out of handcuffs we'll need leverage, and we'll need it fast." The Governor was in full-bore executive mode, speaking quickly and with authority.

"I don't know about the paratroopers, but you're right about the missile fields," Barrett opined. "Once the press picks up on the issue, the White House will be under immediate pressure to step up and declare they have them under control. They'll need to, for both domestic *and* international consumption. What kind of leverage did you have in mind?"

"The missile fields," the Governor stated flatly.

"I understand." Barrett, a little confused, wasn't sure if the Governor had heard him. "But what are you going to use for leverage?"

Ben smiled weakly. "Sorry. The missile fields...I want to use the missile fields as leverage."

The Majority Leader cupped his eyes with the palms of his thick hands, then worked his way a bit higher and started massaging his balding head. "Oh man—I figured we weren't in enough trouble yet. Do I really want to hear this?"

Ben grinned. "Oh yeah, you do. You'd be pissed big time if I managed to pull this off behind your back." He shifted his weight in his chair a bit. "*If* I manage to pull this off." Ben got up and walked over to the elegant wet bar and dropped a handful of ice cubes in a pair of smooth lead crystal tumblers with thick, heavy, rounded bases. He fixed drinks for the Majority Leader and himself.

He settled back in his chair. "I spent some time with Jerry Calderone last week. He's the Commanding General for the Air National Guard out of Malmstrom. Works for General McDermott. This guy knows more than anyone needs to know about how ICBMs are targeted and how the fire-control fail-safe systems work. I absorbed about one tenth of what he told me." The ice cubes clanked against the thick glass as he sipped his drink.

"I'm going to investigate the possibility of utilizing those missiles as—let's call them persuasive assets. It won't be easy. As I understand it—and for the record, I barely understand it—missiles can be launched, flight-controlled and monitored by a missile combat crew in a launch control center, assuming they receive the proper launch control codes, but not targeted from there. Targeting authorization comes from a remote headquarters: from the Pentagon, Cheyenne Mountain, Air Force One, an E-6B airborne strategic command post—the so-called doomsday plane—from wherever the civilian and military brass are hiding. Coordinates—the target's coordinates—are entered by the combat crew at the launch control site, but the system will only accept the approved coordinates. The electronic lockout is controlled by password from headquarters.

"As complicated as it sounds, the technology involved is apparently not very sophisticated. General Calderone is fairly technically savvy; he's been involved with these computerized targeting systems since the 1980's. According to him, our laptop computers use technology about two decades past the electronics controlling those weapons. The Minutemen were using a 1960's-era, tape-based targeting system up until the mid-90's. You had to climb down into the freakin' silo to physically load new target tapes if you wanted to retarget a missile."

"Do you mean to tell me those weapons have been sitting down there untouched from the Cuban Missile Crisis to the end of the Clinton administration?" Barrett sounded a bit incredulous.

"Sort of but not quite," Ben responded. "They've been tweaked a number of times. The rocket engines have been upgraded. The payload has been reduced from three warheads to one on most of them. And targeting accuracy has been doubled over the years, from about 250 yards down to a 120-yard bull's eye. Not terribly bad shootin' from 8,000 miles."

"But," the Governor continued, "it would be a mistake to underestimate the degree to which nobody thinks we're ever going to need to use these things. All of the state-of-the-art technology is in submarine and bomber-launched cruise missiles. The ICBMs are there for deterrent purposes only. If we needed to hit North Korea or some tin-pot dictator in the Mideast with a nuke, we'd toss a few cruise missiles from 200 miles out at sea and send them through the bastard's bedroom window. Or if we really needed to ruin someone's afternoon, we could drop a 9-megaton gravity bomb from a B-2 Stealth Bomber. Why would you take a chance on an unproven 8,000-mile flight of a 40-year-old ICBM? Those babies are there for the doomsday scenario only." Ben took another sip of his drink and returned the heavy glass to the darkened leather coaster protecting his desk. "Essentially, they're there for when we think there won't be anyone around to give a shit where they land."

"Have you shared your thinking on these—assets—with Mitch?" asked Barrett.

"No. He's frazzled enough trying to keep some semblance of order in the House. I don't know what I'm going to do, or even what I *can* do yet. I'll let both of you know before I pull the trigger." Ben paused for a moment then changed the subject. "Where are we on the budget and appropriations?"

"It'll be finished on time; we have two weeks before we end the session. The conference committee is just hashing out a few last details. I imagine it'll be on your desk in a week, assuming everyone behaves themselves."

"And what are the chances of everyone behaving themselves?"

"Slim to none," Senator Barrett stated bluntly. "Oh, the budget will get done. But I think we're going to see some more nullification action before we adjourn." The intercom pinged on the Governor's desk.

"Excuse me, Governor," the receptionist said softly. "Senator Taylor is on the line from Washington."

"Thanks." Ben brushed the touch-screen on his

communications console. "Nancy? How are things going out there? Do they have you in leg-irons yet?" Barrett, sucking on a nearly spent ice cube, got up to freshen his drink.

"No, I'm still on the loose!" the Senator laughed. "Though I'm not sure for how much longer. I don't have anything new for you, Ben, but I thought I should touch bases with you and give you a feel for the mood out here."

Senator Nancy Taylor, along with Montana's senior Senator, Bud Kingston, a 91-year-old, conservative Democrat former farm equipment salesman, and their single House member, Deb Heilman (a former Missoula schoolteacher), had been pulled into all sorts of "crisis" meetings in Washington. She described to Ben how she had seen, firsthand, the dismissive attitude of the national political leadership toward the Montanan citizenry, and the degree to which political and electoral calculations were dictating their decisions, rather than any real concern for making a judgment on the merits of the arguments. Taylor voiced her frustration at the other half of Montana's Senate delegation.

"Bud, God bless him, is healthy and chipper as ever. But Ben, he doesn't have a clue as to what's going on around him. He'd be just as happy watching TV in a nursing home, with a Roy Rogers bib around his neck and some pretty, young nurse spooning warm oatmeal into his mouth. He spent five minutes talking to the President of the United States about John Deere tractor transmissions from the early 1970's while Deb and I sat there smiling politely, sipping coffee. We're trying to coordinate things with his staff, but they're so mired in the partisan politics of the whole thing they're useless to us. Deb is trying her best, but she's still just one voice in the House."

"Should I give Senator Kingston's people a call?"

"I don't know. They think you're out of your mind. You could try, I suppose."

Ben laughed. "OK, I'll give it a shot. Maybe they'll want to come back home someday!" He laughed again. They wrapped up the conversation and said their goodbyes. Ben turned his attention back to Senator Barrett and continued their discussion on the remaining legislative agenda.

CHAPTER 24
April 2014

The short legislative term was winding down, but the legislators were not. Incensed by the media-fueled expectations they would all soon be arrested by federal officers, and boosted by an ever rising tide of popular local support, the Montana lawmakers reached the conclusion there was more work to do before the final gavel fell.

On the House side, speaker after speaker urged members to "remember the Sturgis Massacre." Another passionately pointed to the federal attempt to "commandeer our brave, hometown volunteers in the Montana National Guard to bear arms against their parents and neighbors." Both houses of the legislature whipped themselves into a lawmaking frenzy, nullifying federal laws and federal departmental regulations on the environment, forest management, education and testing standards, highway speed limits, gun laws and drug laws, and diverting federally-imposed communications and energy surcharges, gasoline taxes, and internet sales taxes to the Montana Treasury. Governor Kane signed the bills as soon as they hit his desk.

Majority Leader Barrett and Speaker Steere, with their senior committee chairmen in tow, made the media rounds explaining there was no intention to create a "lawless" society. "The people of Montana," they repeated, "have their own Department of

Agriculture, their own Department of Natural Resources and Conservation, their own Department of Environmental Quality, and their own Board of Public Education." The legislators forcefully and publicly declared themselves quite capable of governing their state with their own institutions. All state laws would remain in force.

A thin, muffled voice, emanating from a radio or a small TV, was chattering on from an office somewhere far down the corridor. Otherwise the air was still, and Mitch Steere sat quietly in his office, eyes closed, trying to let go of some of the day's tension. His stomach had tightened into a hard knot; he hadn't eaten a bite since breakfast. He hadn't bothered switching on the lights, hadn't checked his voice mail, and had no intention of doing either. *Good God Almighty*, he thought. He exhaled forcefully. *I know this is going to end at some point. But how...*

Advancing footsteps, snapping rapidly against the cold marble floor, could be heard echoing in the otherwise empty hallway.

What now? Before he had a chance to get up, Kim Lange, her blond mane bouncing enthusiastically, stuck her head in the doorway. "Mr. Speaker? Oh, Mitch, are you in there?"

He snapped forward in his chair and ran a quick hand through his hair. "Come on in, Kim. I was just trying to relax for a moment."

"I'm so sorry," she said as she stepped gently across the dense carpet to where the Speaker was rolling back his chair and starting to stand. "No, stop, don't get up. I was just talking with Ben and he asked me to give this to you personally. He already left for the night." She handed him an envelope.

"Hmmm..." he took the unmarked envelope and tore it open. "It's not my birthday; too early for Christmas cards. Lets see what we have here." Kim lowered herself into the soft, plush guest chair.

"I don't have to eat this note when I'm finished reading, do I?" Mitch held the note up so the floodlights from the Capitol's campus, leaking through the open blinds behind his desk, illuminated Ben's barely legible handwriting.

> *Mitch,*
>
> *I think we need to consider drawing up an alternative budget. If we keep going down this road I'm sure they're eventually going to cut off all of our federal funding. We need to start thinking about how we're going to survive without Big Brother's wallet. Now go home and get some rest.*
>
> *Ben*

Mitch waved the note like it was a little flag. "What do you know about this?"

"The note was prompted by the discussion I just came from downstairs. We think it's going to happen—especially after our latest little binge of legislative self-expression. The President's not going to have any choice. He's going to have to flex some muscle, and cutting off our cash would be easy, relatively non-controversial, and bloodless. The public will say we deserved it, and there won't be any messy TV pictures."

"They'd be right," Steere said quietly. "We would deserve it. Hell, it's what we asked for, isn't it?"

"Well," Kim responded, "I'd argue that we've used the political process to express our dissatisfaction with the administration's policy. Are we *asking* for a punitive response? I suppose…"

She stood up abruptly. "I'm sorry, Mitch, I'm really tired. You must be exhausted. I'm going to head home." She started toward the door. "You should try to get some rest. See ya soon."

"Take care," Mitch said wearily. "Thanks for stopping by." He closed his eyes, sat back, and breathed slowly and deeply. Kim's footsteps receded down the corridor.

Three old CRT computer monitors glowed harshly in the otherwise dark room. Two oversized black plastic ashtrays sat overflowing with stale, crushed cigarette butts. The small space was actually quite loud—between the two outdated PCs, the server and its networked disk array, there were eight spinning hard drives whining away in the room. A bookshelf sound system was cranking out a vintage Fleetwood Mac tune. Empty beer cans were everywhere, making it difficult for anyone without a trained eye to differentiate between the empties, the several still holding a small amount of stale beer swimming with foul, spent cigarette butts, and the one fresh, cold, full can.

Angel was sucking hard on a cigarette, like a thirsty child frantically drawing chocolate milk through a straw. He sat otherwise motionless, staring at the forbidden lines of code peppering the screen in front of him. Locked deep in concentration, he reached out for his beer and grabbed the first can he came to; it didn't feel right—too warm, and a slight shake warned of something knocking around inside. He put it down and tried the next one; cold condensation signaled a winner.

"Angel! ANGEL!" his wife screamed from somewhere beyond the closed door. His gaze on the code remained unbroken; he slurped some beer and pulled on a cigarette.

"ANGEL!!! YOU'VE GOT A PHONE CALL! PICK UP THE PHONE, IT'S YOUR SISTER!"

He tapped the keyboard methodically, slowly advancing the lines of code on the screen. He wasn't seeing what he wanted to see, wasn't seeing what he needed to see. *Dead end*, he determined.

"YOU CAN'T STAY ON THE PHONE LONG! YOU NEED TO DRIVE ME TO THE DRY CLEANERS! ANGEL!!! PICK UP THE PHONE!"

He copied a few interesting lines and phrases he thought might

come in handy at some later point, then terminated his unauthorized
excursion into the Pentagon server. After another sip of beer, he
stood up, lit up a fresh smoke, and looked around for the phone.

"Holy shit, look at those assholes," Joe Adams observed. He and
Diane were peering through the picture window of the bar, watching
a reporter and her video crew who had just ambushed Ben and Kim,
as they were about to step into the American Outback for some
dinner.

"Why are they so mean?" asked Diane. "Why can't they back
off and let him breathe once in a while?"

"Because he's a public figure in the middle of a crisis," Joe
explained. "After a while, everybody's got the same story, so then
they have to go out and try to find a unique angle. They're probably
trying to get him to admit he had sex with his cousin on camera.
Then the reporter can put it on her resume and take a shot at a better
job in New York or Washington."

They watched Ben smile graciously as he patiently worked his
way through the reporter's insightful, penetrating observations and
questions, the same ones he'd answered five times already for five
different news organizations during this day's news cycle. Kim
stepped back out of camera and let the Governor do his thing. It
took just a few minutes, and Ben swung open the door and allowed
Kim to enter the establishment. Ben followed, leaving his two-man
security detail to watch the front door.

"Hey chief!" Joe greeted his boss as he swept into the bar. "Do
you want your booth or the inner sanctum? The booth is open but
the dining room's pretty busy."

"Don't call me 'chief.' What do you think, Kim? Are we going
to be able to talk back there?" Ben and Kim both stretched their
necks to evaluate the situation. "I'm getting tired of barricading
myself in the closet."

"It's crowded, Ben. It's going to take us 45 minutes to have a 5-minute conversation," Kim observed.

"Right," he admitted. They placed their dinner orders with Joe and worked their way back to the converted storage room.

A half hour later they were digging into their meals and hashing over a topic rapidly rising on the Governor's ever lengthening list of things to worry about.

"Running cattle is a big chunk of our economy," Ben stated. "It's also probably the sector most heavily subsidized by the feds. I need to get a clearer picture of where we'd be if they pulled the rug out from under the ranchers." He shoveled up a large forkful of mashed potatoes and gravy, then glanced around the room. "I hate eating in here. I feel like I'm eating in a closet."

"We *are* eating in a closet!" Kim rolled her eyes.

Ben shrugged his shoulders and grunted in agreement, his mouth now stuffed full of potatoes. A sip of cold beer cleared his palate. "Look," he continued, "we'll run about 3 million head this year—three head of cattle for every citizen in the state. We've got 25,000 jobs in meat processing alone." He paused for another quick mouthful of gravy-soaked spuds. "And, when you include the upstream and downstream industry linkages, the beef industry provides about a billion dollars in personal income within the state."

Kim chimed in. "Not bad for an industry probably incapable of standing on its own feet."

"I know it's bad. Is it really *that* bad?"

"I think the fair statement would be the industry is precarious under the best of circumstances," Kim stated judiciously. "Livestock production in today's world is really more of a lifestyle choice than it is a rational business enterprise. The return on investment—between one-half and one percent, the last time I checked—is so thin you need massive scale to make it even remotely worth your while."

"True," agreed Ben. "I think only 10 percent of the state's ranching operations own over 50 percent of the cattle."

Kim paused to enjoy a sip of her wine. "That's right. And with profits so thin I think it's safe to assume any cutoff of federal assistance would plunge even the most efficient cattle operation deeply into the red."

"Where are we most vulnerable?"

"Hmmm," Kim pondered the question for a moment. "Like everything else in agriculture, it sort of depends on the weather. There are drought-relief payments, emergency livestock feeding programs, emergency grazing access to Conservation Reserve Program lands, and livestock-assistance funds in response to natural disasters. Essentially, the U.S. taxpayers insure livestock production against the natural ups and downs of the open agricultural market, in order to stabilize supply and, to a large extent, prices."

"So if the feds cut off those subsidies, the ranchers could stay in business, but they would have to raise prices?"

"Well, in a perfect world, yes, but we're not in a perfect world," responded Kim. "The federal government would cut off *our* payments, but not those to the rest of the country..."

"Meaning," interrupted the Governor, "Montana beef would be far more expensive than everyone else's, and we wouldn't be able to compete, home or abroad."

"Yep," agreed Kim. "And it gets worse. The very structural foundation of the industry is built around decades-old federal support policies. The taxpayers support livestock scientific research. Grazing fees on federal land are set *well* below market rates. Low-interest agricultural loans are available. In fact, you can use the value of your federal grazing permit—already set well below market—as collateral to get your subsidized, low-interest loan. The taxpayers subsidize your subsidy! So if a rancher had to pay market rate for grazing permits, pay market interest on his loans, and support those loans with his own property...frankly, Ben, I can't see how anybody would be in the business."

"Unless we were willing to pay $30 for a pound of ground beef," added Ben. "And we haven't mentioned the fact the state provides a generous agricultural exemption to lower their property taxes."

"Yep," Kim nodded, and returned to her meal.

"It doesn't seem possible Montana taxpayers alone could prop up the industry for any length of time if the feds turn off the faucet," Ben considered. He turned his head and stared off into nowhere. "The ranchers would be on their own. If they have a good year, if the weather cooperates, maybe they could fatten the herd and successfully close out the year. If not, they could sell off their stock and shut down the operation."

"I wouldn't lose too much sleep worrying about the large cattle operations," Kim interrupted. "Most of those guys are wealthy entrepreneurs who will just move on to something else. The problems will be in the upstream and downstream operations—farm and feed supply, equipment providers, meat packers, seasonal labor, all the industry support stuff."

"Any ideas?"

"Nope." Kim lifted her glass and finished her wine.

CHAPTER 25
May 2014

"Shit. It figures." Joe Draper stepped back into his small, cluttered cubicle to pick up the phone. It had, of course, suddenly decided to ring just as he took the first two steps down to the second-floor cafeteria to grab some lunch. A mid-level programmer working deep in the bowels of the Pentagon, Draper was tempted to let his voice mail pick up the line. But everyone he worked with knew he religiously went to lunch at exactly 12:25—so the call was either important, or from someone outside of his normal sphere of professional contacts. The phone number displayed on his caller-ID was not familiar, and in fact the area code indicated it was an out-of-town call. The voice on the other end of the line was likewise unfamiliar.

"Hi. This is Pat Forrest; I'm calling from Boeing world headquarters, out of Chicago. Listen, I'm really sorry for disturbing you, but I got shuttled over to your line by the switchboard. I'm really trying to reach Mark Capson. Is he in your area?"

"Not a problem," Draper responded. "I work for Mark, and his office is two aisles over—I'm looking right at it, actually."

"Is he in there? If you could transfer me over I'd really appreciate it."

"I haven't seen him today. It's really not unusual, he's typically in meetings all day. I could switch you over to his voice mail."

"I'm kinda in a bind, actually, I'd rather not leave a message. Maybe you could switch me over to someone else who could help me. Mr. Capson was the project manager and our contact person, for REACT—the Rapid Execution and Combat Targeting project. Is there anyone around your area who might have worked on the project with him?"

"Yep." Draper glanced at his watch. He was getting hungry. "I did some work on REACT. What can I help you with?"

"Cool. OK, I'll take it from the top. I'm a systems analyst working for Boeing, and I've been assigned to the Minuteman III Guidance Replacement Program project for the last 18 months. If you've worked on REACT, you're probably familiar with the two major components of the project—the weapon system control element and the higher authority communications and rapid message-processing element. The WSCE mediates all functions related to the actual weapon targeting system. The HAC/RMPE integrates all the command authority communications, and passes instructions to the WSCE side for processing."

"I'm familiar with the breakdown," Draper commented flatly. "I worked on debugging the original weapon system code, then helped out with a chunk of the weapon system element rollout. What do you need?" Draper got cranky when he was hungry.

"Great!" exclaimed Forrest, perhaps a bit too enthusiastically. "You're probably aware this whole system has come under increased scrutiny since the Montana dustup; we've been going over things at our end with a fine-tooth comb."

"OK," Draper responded tersely. He wasn't looking to drag out the conversation any more than necessary.

Forrest continued. "I'm reviewing the Higher Authority Communications logic tree and trying to confirm the presently active code is in strict compliance with the logic structure everyone originally signed off on. Again. I need to get into…" Paper could be heard rustling through the phone. "Ah, here it is, the Mountain States fire-control server."

Forrest read off a 12-digit alphanumeric code identifying the particular server. "Obviously, access to that server's directory is password-controlled, and, as I'm sure you're aware, those passwords are changed on a regular basis. The administrator's password I have would have expired long age—I figured Mr. Capson could hook me up with the current one."

"I haven't heard anything about a systems review," commented the Pentagon programmer, his stomach growling.

"Neither had I, until my boss dropped it on my desk. You know how it goes."

"Well, like I said, I don't know where Mark disappeared to, or when he'll be back. But he probably wouldn't have the password information anyway—only the techs would need that level of server access."

"Any ideas of who might be able to help me out?"

"Just a moment." Draper reached up into his overhead cabinet and selected a white binder labeled 'REACT' in bright blue letters along the spine. "What did you say your name was?"

"Forrest. Pat Forrest. Patrick D. Forrest, if you're looking me up."

"Thanks, Patrick. Hang on a second." He opened the project binder and found the subcontractor section. "Boeing, you said?"

"Yep. The HAC team. Higher authority communications," Forrest clarified.

"Hang on." Draper found the page he was looking for. "What's your work-group ID number, Patrick?" Forrest provided the number.

"OK, I found you. Now how about your personal security-clearance code?" Again, Forrest provided the requested number. Draper wrote it down and reached for another, smaller binder. He flipped through the laminated pages until he reached the index he was looking for. The passwords were indeed changed on a regular basis; updated, freshly laminated pages were circulated as necessary. Forrest's code checked out.

"OK. It looks like everyone in your work-group is cleared for this password. You know I can't give this out over the phone, right? I'll have to send it to the work-group e-mail address we have on file here." Draper read the address to Forrest to confirm it was current. It was.

"Cool," responded Forrest. "I really appreciate your help on this. I'll get back to you if there's any problem. Hey, tell Mark Capson I said hello!"

"Will do," said Draper.

"Thanks again." Angel smiled as he hung up the phone, and cracked open a fresh can of beer. He would have no difficulty accessing Pat Forrest's e-mail folder.

President Henderson came around from behind his desk and rested himself casually on the front edge of the massive mahogany block, his arms folded across his chest. He liked to hold standing, bang-bang update meetings for subjects he wished would just go away. He had bigger fish to fry—a recent revival of a long dormant rebel insurrection in Chile, the dollar struggling against the euro, an Israeli cabinet official suddenly assassinated by Palestinian gunmen in Tel Aviv. This Montana thing was cutting his legs off politically; they'd had their fun and it was getting old.

The Vice President, National Security Advisor, Secretary of Homeland Security, FBI Director, Chairman of the Joint Chiefs, the President's Chief of Staff and the Special Assistant for Policy and Political Affairs gathered around him in a semicircle, keeping a respectable distance.

The President started off. "The Montana Legislature claims to have the support of the people. That may be true, but it doesn't make them right. It's time to put a little pressure on those people. I want to squeeze those legislators from both ends."

Raul Fuentes, the President's Political Advisor, advised he tread softly—the Legislature was legitimately elected; the Governor, though in violation of federal statutes and Constitutional precedents, was apparently acting within the scope of the Montana Constitution. He pointed out support was building for their cause in the neighboring states—Wyoming, Idaho, and the Dakotas. "It's not a huge problem politically yet—only a handful of electoral votes are involved, just 16 of the 270 needed to win the Presidency. But a heavy-handed response might cause us more trouble than it's worth."

The President grunted and shifted his gaze to the Chairman of the Joint Chiefs. "What do you have?"

"Montana Air National Guardsman are patrolling the missile fields. They're using their new, fully-armed, state-of-the-art F-22 Raptors and their best pilots—retired Air Force and Navy fighter jocks with significant combat experience in the Persian Gulf theater. Quite frankly sir, we don't think now's the time to pick a fight. We'd prevail, of course—we could outgun them 5-to-1 if need be, but both sides would take casualties: We're talking about a dogfight over Great Falls. We'd have American boys shooting at each other, crashing and burning into their parents' cornfields, all live on the nightly news." The Chairman paused for a moment and let the unhappy image sink in.

He continued. "We're really not worried about the missile fields, sir; they can't physically target or launch those missiles without your approval, Mr. President, so there's no real danger there. We don't need them strategically; there's nothing going on in the world we couldn't handle with a submarine or strategic long-range bomber launch, if it comes down to it. We'd certainly like to have boots on the ground over there for public relations reasons, but I see no reason for people to die over them, sir. Not at this point, anyway. Not if all we gain is the ability to circulate photographs of our Marines posted outside of a couple of underground Launch Control Centers in order to appease our allies."

Fuentes leaned in to the President. "We don't want to see American boys burning up in their parent's cornfields, sir."

"Agreed," responded the President. "As I figured. This is what I want to do…"

Henderson had clearly given this a lot of thought. He laid out a plan cutting off all discretionary and entitlement funding to Montana. Included would be education funding at all levels, student loans, college scholarships, stipends for the arts and public TV, agricultural funds, aid to cities, job training programs and research stipends; all money earmarked for public construction—funds for building hospitals, bridges, waterworks, and so on, as well as entitlement programs. Food programs, welfare payments, Medicare, Medicaid, and Social Security payments would stop. The number was difficult to get a handle on, but they figured upwards of $9 billion in federal taxpayer money would stop flowing into the state—a devastating hit for a state whose own annual budget ran only about $2 billion. "The price of their so-called freedom just got a hell of a lot higher. This is going to end. Let's see how long the citizens of the great state of Montana support their legislators and Governor when their checks stop!" the President concluded.

It would take some time to get coordinated, but he gave his Chief of Staff the green light to line up the Cabinet secretaries and get the ball rolling.

The bar was mobbed. Troopers assigned to the Governor's security detail were on edge. The Governor, despite the ruinous budget news erupting out of Washington, was trying to have a little fun working behind the bar.

He grabbed a highball glass and jammed it with ice. Vodka poured with one hand, orange juice with the other. A red and white plastic drink straw was inserted with a nifty little stir, while his other hand positioned a fresh bar napkin in front of the waiting patron. Grab the cash; make change. Point to next customer. Highball glass. Ice. Dewar's with one hand, soda gun with the other. Straw, napkin, cash, change. Next. Hand dipped into the icy beer sink. Use bottle opener, toss bottle cap in trash, grab fresh glass, napkin, cash, change. Next. Rock glass, ice, a healthy splash of Chivas, napkin, cash, change. Next. Highball glass, ice, Jack Daniel's with one hand, coke from the soda gun with the other, lime wedge, straw, napkin, cash, change.

Thankfully, it was a mature crowd, so there were no requests for Long Island Iced Teas or other such silly concoctions to upset his rhythm. Every once in a while he'd toss an ice cube high over his head with one hand and catch it in a glass held in the other, all while looking away, pretending to be distracted by something across the bar. It wasn't much of a trick, but it could be counted on to get a chuckle and didn't cost him anything when he missed.

He worked furiously for about 20 minutes before things cooled down to a simmer. Joe stayed at the far end of the bar, letting his boss entertain himself and his enthusiastic public. "Let the old man have his fun," he cracked to a couple of regulars. "I just hope he doesn't stay back there long. He's going to wreck my tip cup." Everyone within earshot laughed. Nobody felt obligated to tip the Governor.

Ben thoroughly immersed himself in working behind the busy bar—waving a quick greeting to a familiar face, surprising a regular he hadn't seen in a while by remembering his drink, acknowledging the subtle nods and winks signaling the need for a refill. It was a welcome opportunity to be awake and active, to be surrounded by loud music and cheerful people. And, blissfully, it was a chance to be momentarily distracted from the decisions soon to be forced upon him.

Ben found a spot in the far corner of the bar where he could lean back and take some of the pressure off his feet. He turned to one of the regulars and grubbed a smoke. Everyone had been served; most were on their second or third drink, so the pace had really settled down now. He took a drag of the cigarette; despite the music and noise and shouts, he was, for the moment, at peace. Maybe because of the vaguely familiar combination of odors he had just caught a whiff of—the cigarette smoke, the orange juice splashed on the sleeve of his wool flannel shirt, the unpasteurized draft beer settling in the slop sink drain—he was transported back to the roadhouse bar he had worked during his college years.

It was a fairly sleazy gin mill, dark ski-lodge decor complete with the muddy parking lot, sawdust on the floors, local bands and fights on Friday night. Located off Route 200 just past Twin Creeks—about 10 miles outside of Missoula—it was strategically positioned between a college town and a ski area, the geography reflected in the youthful faces of its customer base. Back then, you didn't think twice about pouring a thoroughly soused college kid into his car and pointing him back to Missoula, if only to get him out of the bar. Oh, kids would routinely get pulled out of snow banks in the morning, but they hadn't been out there long enough to freeze to death—most stayed till closing, and were usually greeted before 6:00 A.M. by a highway patrolman banging unsympathetically on their window. Once, he remembered, there had been a bad wreck. A popular, but blind-drunk 19-year-old plowed into the forest at a high enough speed to leave him with legs that would never be of any use to him again. When first told the news, Ben spent a few very uncomfortable moments trying to recall if he'd been the one pouring the drinks—he hadn't; it was his day off. It didn't make the news any better, but it made it easier. For him, at least.

Summers were a whole different deal. The snow-revelers and ski-bunnies went home for the season, while the greasy bikers moved in. In some ways, the bartending tasks were less demanding—just shots and beers, and the crowds were a bit lighter. But it was a rough and surly crowd, and you took your life in your hands if you smiled at the wrong girl.

Girls. He looked around his crowded tavern...women flirting, guys trying their best material...*what about me?* He took a deep drag of his smoke. *Not now*, he mused. *Way too much going on in my life right now...*

A dark-haired woman at the bar caught his eye. He'd noticed her in here before. Flanked by two friends, she was sneaking glances in his direction and offering a reserved smile when caught. *Shy.* Very attractive, she had dark eyes with long, straight black hair draped smoothly down the length of her back. Her nose was a fraction larger than a modeling agent would consider perfect, and the hint of oval in the shape of her eyes spoke to some degree of Indian heritage. But she had an overall Mediterranean look about her. *Italian, maybe.* A bit younger than he was, for sure, but probably within 12 of his own 51 years, or 14, maybe. *What the hell...* Ben pressed out his cigarette, and walked over to the dark-haired lady to see if he could freshen her drink.

The mood was somber in the Governor's office. A blistering spring rain was drumming the windows; thunder could be heard rumbling off in the distance. General McDermott stood by the small conference table talking quietly with Col. Tom Burns from the State Highway Patrol. The Majority Leader, the Speaker of the House, and Attorney General John Gaffney clumped together in a small circle, engrossed in an animated conversation. Ben sat alone, leaning back deeply in his chair, feet propped up on his desk.

One of the Governor's research assistants strode briskly into the open door of his office and handed him a thin folder. After exchanging a few words, he thanked her and she exited the office, closing the door behind her. Ben reviewed the contents of the folder.

After a minute Ben cleared his throat, and stiffly worked his way to his feet. "Gentlemen, I think we can get started." He stepped over to the conference table as the others did the same. A heavy downpour pounded the pavement outside.

Ben lay open the folder on the table and passed a sheet of paper to each of the attendees. The five read the short statements in silence. Mitch Steere looked uncomfortable.

Printed on the handouts was Section 13 of the Montana Constitution:

> Section 13. – Militia
> (1) The governor is commander-in-chief of the militia forces of the state, except when they are in the actual service of the United States. He may call out any part or all of the force to aid in the execution of the laws, suppress insurrection, repel invasion, or protect life and property in natural disasters.
> (2) The militia forces shall consist of all able-bodied citizens of the state except those exempted by law.

Ben looked first at the Attorney General, and then addressed the group. "John, you and I have had a chance to kick this around for a few minutes in an earlier conversation. Our position has always been the government that governs best governs least. Apparently the Henderson administration has recently decided to agree with us. They've chosen to highlight their agreement by cutting off almost all federal funding to the state. Dealing with the situation is going to take some maneuvering on our behalf. It's not going to be fun; it's not going to be easy. Harrison's people over at Revenue are looking at our options. Those options, as you might guess, will be extremely limited. I've asked him to prioritize Social Security payments, and any retirement, disability and veteran's benefits. Maybe some Medicaid payments as well. We think we can continue payroll withholding at the current rate, shuttle the money over to a state-run trust fund instead of sending it to Washington and continue most of the payments ourselves for the time being. That would fill close to one-third of the hole. He's still running the numbers. I'll let you know what we come up with."

He shifted gears and continued. "Having said that, under the circumstances I can't think of any reason for federal employees in this state to be reporting to work. They've got no laws to enforce, so what the hell are they doing at work? They've cut off our money, the least we can do is cut off their paperwork."

"Should we really be escalating this?" asked Mitch Steere. "I mean, we've kind of reached the end of the line with this thing, haven't we?"

Ben looked around the table for other reactions.

Senator Barrett weighed in. "I don't mind turning up the heat a bit, Ben. But what's it going to look like when the pot boils over?" He tapped the sheet of paper lying in front of him. "What did you have in mind?"

"Fair enough," the Governor responded. "I want most, if not all, of the federal employees working in this state locked out of their workplaces. I don't know, maybe we can let the Post Office people do their jobs. Everyone else gets locked out. We can utilize National Guard personnel to lock out armed federal officers, and mobilize armed citizens, the militia, for the rest."

"Geez! Come on, Governor!" interrupted Mitch Steere, appearing visibly upset. "With all due respect—what's the point?

Don't get me wrong, Ben. Politically, you're on solid ground. But at this point the House is little more than a crazed mob in good suits. We need a leader, and you're it." He sat back in his chair and forced himself to relax. "Where are you taking us, Governor? That's all I'm asking. Where are you taking us?"

Ben responded calmly, with a measured tone. "Good question, Mitch. And a fair question. Honestly—where are we going to end up?" He shook his head. "I have no idea. All I'm trying to do is to keep us on a path maintaining our sovereignty as a state. I'm trying to keep us on a path where individuals can at least *pretend* they still live in a free country. I'm trying to keep us on a path where it *matters* when you petition your local town council, or state government, because they still have enough authority to make a difference in your life. I'm just trying to keep us on a path where the people in our state still have a voice in the determination of their lives. Clearly Washington is at odds with those goals, and there's no question they're bigger and stronger than us." The Governor paused and took a sip of water.

"The lockout?" he continued. "The lockout is for us, for Montana. I want to show we can still throw a punch, even if it's just a little rabbit punch. I want to get people involved, hence my decision to call out the militia—assuming we can do it safely, which is something we need to discuss here. But Mitch, if it's any comfort to you, they've already cut off our legs by cutting off the federal funds. All they've got left is to physically invade and occupy the state. Frankly, I just don't think Henderson's going to do it."

"I hope not," said General McDermott.

Everyone nodded in approval.

CHAPTER 26
May 2014

The media reacted to the Governor's activation of the militia with the expected hysteria. Reporters spread like ants throughout the countryside, seeking interviews with slow-speaking, surly-looking men with guns; attractive, petite women with guns; and the jackpot, one family, talking around the breakfast table, with three generations of men with guns. Talking heads flooded the airways engaged in debates about the meaning of the Second Amendment. Statistics were wielded like swords—how many children were killed every day by gunfire? How many children killed every day by gunfire were 17-year-old crack dealers killed by other 17-year-old crack dealers, and should they really be counted as children? The president of the NRA made the rounds of the talk shows, emphasizing, especially under the present circumstances, how the Second Amendment was the "first freedom," how when the right to own a firearm was restricted, all other rights could be denied quickly and easily. The showboat senior senator from New York argued, in front of any operating camera he could manage to jam himself in front of, that the individual right to own a gun was a late 20th Century fantasy, promulgated by right-wing fanatics who cared more about stockpiling weapons arsenals and allowing easy access of machine guns to terrorists than protecting suckling infants from armor-piercing, cop-killer, "high-powered" bullets.

As is often the case, things were a bit calmer off the airways. Working with personnel from both his Attorney General's office and General McDermott's staff, the Governor's office whittled down the definition of militia member to any citizen over 21 years of age, with a long gun of .223 caliber or above, and 250 rounds of factory-made ammunition. Every volunteer had to pass a firearms safety and maintenance exam and demonstrate the ability to pass a basic marksmanship test. It was estimated a quarter of the population of the state—250,000 people—could answer the call if needed, a number quickly picked up by the national news networks and repeated alarmingly, as if an army of camouflage-garbed, armed Montanans would be fighting their way eastward within days. In fact, fewer than 5,000 volunteers were called up between the state's 56 counties.

National Guard officers were tasked with the organization and management of local civilian, watch procedures, and provided basic sniper training to those willing, able and in possession of accurate, scoped rifles. Attorney General Gaffney's people produced a directory of all the known federal officials working in the state, with a separate list of those licensed to carry concealed handguns. They agreed regular National Guard soldiers would be used to lock out any armed federal law enforcement personnel, a list including officers of the FBI; the Secret Service; the Bureau of Alcohol, Tobacco and Firearms; National Park Rangers; the U.S. Marshals Service, and the Drug Enforcement Agency; and enforcement agents of the Environmental Protection Agency, the U.S. Customs Service, the Immigration and Naturalization Service, the Internal Revenue Service, the U.S. Postal Inspections Service, the Bureau of Indian Affairs, the Bureau of Land Management, and the nearly 60 U.S. Fish and Wildlife and U.S. Forest Service agents assigned to Montana. Militia volunteers were to be used to lockout all unarmed federal officials from their workplaces, and to escort the various rangers and agents from the vast National Parks and other federal lands.

Militia volunteers were called county by county, the numbers determined by General McDermott, in consultation with Colonel Burns and local Highway Patrol leadership, depending on how much territory they needed to cover. McDermott was surprised at the number of federal guns in the state, and somewhat dismayed at their widely scattered distribution. Nobody was surprised at the number of privately held firearms in the state.

Indian tribal officials, including Tommy Running Wolf, contacted the Governor's office to find out exactly what was going on and where they stood. Running Wolf mentioned the fact he was in the middle of a grant application with the BIA, still trying to secure financing for additional high-tensile fencing on behalf of the InterTribal Bison Cooperative and their expanding bison herds. Ben apologized for the inconvenience and authorized his Coordinator for the Office of Indian Affairs to release regular updates to all of the Montana tribal nations, and assured the nations their sovereignty would be recognized and respected under any and all circumstances. The federal government had not cut off funding to the tribes, and Ben made it clear any federal officials working on Indian land would be left alone.

Ben contemplated these facts as he sat in his office, sipping a small bottle of water while waiting for a meeting. It was the first he had heard of the InterTribal Bison Cooperative's plans for significantly expanding their herds. He liked the idea. *Hope I don't screw that up for them. Probably screwing up a lot of things for a lot of people…*

His communications panel pinged softly. General McDermott was on the line. "General! How's it going?"

"Good morning, Governor," responded McDermott. "It's going pretty well, actually. No trouble so far, and none anticipated."

"Good. Great. Hey, I'm sorry to hear about your court-martial—I heard about it on the news. I guess, well, I suppose under the circumstances it was to be expected."

"Yeah. Can't say I was shocked when I got the papers. It's not a court-martial, by the way, not yet, at least. It's an Article 32 investigation, in essence the equivalent of a civilian grand jury. I'm allowed to attend the proceeding with my lawyer, call witnesses, present evidence, cross-examine prosecution witnesses, all to determine whether or not they have enough to charge me. To tell you the truth, they're being nice to me—I'm being charged with two Article 92 violations—failure to obey a lawful order, and counseling insubordination, disloyalty, and refusal of duty. They could have asked for treason charges. If I'm indicted, they'll convene a general court-martial."

"Where are they going to hold it?" asked Ben.

"The lawyers are fighting over jurisdiction. I don't want to leave the state. There's no way I can ask my potential witnesses— you, for example—to leave the state and subject themselves to possible arrest. They're worried about putting together an impartial panel, of course. We'll work it out."

"Anything you need, Paul. Anything. Anytime," the Governor said in a firm voice. "I'm standing behind you. The Legislature is behind you. The whole state is behind you. If you need something you just pick up a phone, show up at my door, or throw a rock through my fucking window. Don't hesitate."

"Thank you, Governor," the General responded softly. "I'm pretty sure I'm going to have to take you up on the offer."

They paused for a second. The Governor continued. "OK. So how are the lockouts going? I've been following them on TV—I see we had a little excitement in Missoula."

"Oh yeah. Things got a little prickly out there, for sure. A couple of ATF agents didn't take kindly to the idea of being denied access to their office. There was a little pushing and shoving and yelling before our boys convinced them to make a few phone calls and settle down. The fact that we rolled up a Humvee with a .50-caliber machine gun mounted on top didn't hurt. Did you see the student protesters?"

"Briefly. What was that about?"

"It was actually pretty funny. You know how they say politics makes strange bedfellows? There was a crowd of about 150 protesters from the university crying about being cut off from federal money for this and federal money for that, and they decided to make their stand in front of the FBI office. It's not often you see the left wing college crowd claiming solidarity with the beleaguered FBI. Anyway, the FBI lockout went smoothly. The local Chief of Police is a pretty close friend with the Special Agent in Charge, and gave him advance warning. When we showed up there were more TV crews than agents. We made a show of denying them access to their office, and they backed off cooperatively. I spoke to the Special Agent in Charge, and we arranged to meet at a local diner with his guys. We bought them breakfast, and waited until all of the media hounds had packed up and left. Then we all went back to the FBI office, let them go in and collect their personal stuff, secure any sensitive files or computers or other stuff they had laying around and let them lock up properly. When they finished they all left to go set up a temporary office in one of the agent's basements. Most of the media people were more upset than the folks being locked out."

"No surprise there. Hell, the people being locked out are still getting paid—what do they have to worry about?" They both laughed.

McDermott continued. "All of the high-profile refusal of entries were in front of TV cameras, and, as far as I know, were expected. Everybody reads the papers. The only other excitement I've been notified of was some posturing over at the DEA offices in

Billings, but last I heard that was being sorted out. But overall, things have gone as well as could be expected. Nobody was looking for a gunfight to protect the office furniture. You know, except for a few of the FBI agents who got transferred here for pissin' someone off, practically all of these folks are Montana natives. No longer your most loyal supporters, if you don't mind my saying."

Ben chuckled. "All right. So we got wall-to-wall media coverage, no weapons have been discharged, and I've lost a few votes. Not a bad day's work. Anything else, General?"

"That's not enough?"

"Plenty!" Ben laughed. "Thank you, General. I have to run—keep those militia boys under control, will ya?"

"Will do, Governor. Take care of yourself." Ben tapped the communications panel and terminated the connection. He had more calls to make.

Ben placed calls to a couple of old friends to the north. The Premiers of Alberta and Saskatchewan, his counterparts in the conservative Canadian provinces just across the border, had more in common, politically, with Governor Kane of Montana than with their Socialist national leaders to the east in Ottawa. Montana National Guard troops had replaced U.S. Border Patrol personnel on the border crossings into Canada. Ben was aware the Canadian government had been asked by Washington to step up security at the border. The official purpose of the calls was to fill them in on what had been going on, and to assure his neighbors to the north that all border security protocols would be observed, and if anything, the physical security presence would be increased, not weakened.

The unofficial purpose of the calls was to secure safe passage across those borders for his people in case things turned ugly.

"Dude! What's happening?" Joe was surprised to hear his friend's voice. Angel rarely called him at work. "When are you going to come by and have a drink? I haven't seen your ass on a barstool in years!"

"I know. I know," Angel responded. "I don't get out as much as I used to. When are *you* going to stop by for a visit?" A grating voice screamed in the background; "ANGEL! ARE YOU ON THE PHONE? DID YOU TAKE THE DOG OUT? THE DOG HAS TO GO OUT!"

Oh yeah, I'll get married someday... "Umm," Joe responded aloud, "yeah, I'll stop by for a drink the next time I'm in town. What do you need?"

"Well, I looked into the situation you asked me about, and I think I've come up with a solution. Do I tell you? Or who should I be talking to?"

"Oh." Joe had no idea Angel had been seriously pursuing an answer to Ben's latest brainstorm, and worse, he had no idea who else knew (or didn't know). He took a sip of his ginger ale and Angostura Bitters—his stomach needed settling. "OK—so the message is you think you have a solution?"

"Yep."

"Alright dude, sit tight and let me think on this for a minute. I'll make sure somebody calls you, OK?" He wrapped up the conversation with a minimum of additional small talk then considered the situation. He knew he couldn't call the Governor at his office, and had no idea when he might show up at the bar. *Kim!* She was his only real choice. Plus it was an excellent excuse to reach out to a hot babe, even if he had no idea what she was talking about half the time.

He called Kim and she cut the conversation short as soon as she caught the drift; then she stopped by the bar later in the afternoon for a more secure personal conversation. She agreed to call Angel and try to get a read on what he had come up with.

Hours later, she called Angel from her ranch. She had no idea who he was, except he was an old friend of Joe's; she also knew nothing about any secret plan and wouldn't admit it if she did. He was expecting the call and sounded eager to explain his idea to someone.

After the initial introductions, Angel got right into it. "...it took some doing, and a little creative detective work, but I finally managed to get through their password server and enter my CPU's address parameters and user-preferences onto their LDAPv5 directory. Once I was in there, I was able to join their remote workgroup as a network administrator. Then I was able to use the server's operating system remote management tools to..."

Kim gently placed the phone down on the table, walked over and got herself a small bottle of water from the refrigerator. She twisted off the plastic cap and took a refreshing swig. Taking a minute to rummage through the freezer, she pulled a prepared meal from the frosty clutter, removed the aluminum foil wrap, placed her rock-hard dinner on a plate, and placed it in the microwave. She set the timer, the power level, hit the start button, and then stepped back to the phone. Angel was still talking.

"...pretty sure I covered my footprints, but if I try to commandeer any of the secure application software—targeting-control type stuff—they'll spot the incursion almost immediately. But..."

Enough! "Angel, let me stop you here. This sounds like it's way above my pay grade. I'm going to kick this up the ladder a bit and see if we can come up with somebody who speaks your language." She apologized for not being able to be of further help to him and promised someone would be in touch with him very soon.

The next day Kim managed to grab a few minutes with the Governor and let him know what was afoot. Ben immediately got in touch with General McDermott and slid the task over to his plate. McDermott knew just the man—Major Gus Walski, a technical expert on the Minuteman III's targeting and security systems. Major Walski was given the assignment of meeting with Angel and making a determination as to credibility of whatever scheme he'd cooked up.

Walski contacted Angel and arranged to meet with him the following day. A driver was sent to pick him up and shuttle him over to the Major's office at Malmstrom Air Force Base. The planned 90-minute meeting ran to more than 4 hours. Walski was impressed, flabbergasted, and scared. Angel's idea was so unpredictable, so outside the box—it just might work.

Running Wolf reined his horse to an easy, rhythmic walk. Five teenagers, three boys and two girls, experienced riders all, clustered their horses closely around the soft-spoken tribal elder, so he wouldn't have to shout to be heard. It was Saturday, their school week over, but all had eagerly signed up to extend their studies here, on their tribe's bison range.

Their day started early, with the dusty 25-mile ride up from Browning to the bison enclosure. They rendezvoused with the chief and a couple of leathery ranch hands at the spartan but comfortable bunkhouse recently constructed next to the horse stables. Only a bit more than a quarter mile from the main gate, the unfinished wooden structure consisted of a generous common room, with propane heat and modest cooking facilities, a couple of generators for power, and a small bunk room with a shower and a head. The building smelled of sweet, freshly sawn pine lumber, bacon and coffee.

The students were at the site to assist in moving the herd a mile or so south of their present location. New grass grows rapidly in the spring, so the handlers liked to try to keep the herd moving to prevent overgrazing. The bison relished new growth, and would nibble it down to the roots if not encouraged to move on. And a record number of calves had been born this year; the elders thought it would be a good time to familiarize the young people with a close-up observation of the herd's complex social dynamics.

Bison calves are born from late April through early June. They greet their first spring dressed in a reddish-brown, cinnamon coat. Most predators—wolves, mountain lions and coyotes—have difficulty distinguishing between red and green, so the coloration was nature's way of protecting the calves. They would darken to their adult shade in two or three months.

The herd was about two-and-a-half miles away from the bunkhouse; Running Wolf wanted to leisurely walk the horses to the bison as not to tax their strength so early in the day. He took advantage of the time to explain what they would be doing. The students had heard much of this before, but paid particular attention now, as the nervous reality of the pending encounter drew closer.

"These are not cows. They are not domesticated animals," Running Wolf warned. "They're wild, they're big, and they're not afraid of you. You can panic a herd, but you cannot scare an individual buffalo."

He continued. "At best, if they're being cooperative, they'll ignore you. At worst, they'll attack. If your horse gets hooked by a horn, you're screwed." He had his Marlin in its worn, weather-stained, tasseled leather, saddle scabbard, but knew there was no way he was going to manage a shot clean enough to stop a charging bull chasing a panicked horse. "They're not afraid of you," he repeated, "and they're faster than your horse."

They were going to bait the leaders of the herd, he explained. Darrell had driven the pickup ahead of them, with another ranch hand in the back manning a bucket of sweetened grain. The animals were familiar with the routine. The idea was simply to get some movement going, to influence the group leaders to move in the direction you wanted them to move.

"You can't *make* them do anything." The job of the riders, he said, was not so much to steer the herd to where they wanted them to go, but to politely suggest where they shouldn't go. "The trick is to get them to want to do what you want them to do. Keep your distance. Remember they're wild animals. Less is more. Persuade them, don't push them."

By the end of the day, the students were tired, dirty and exhilarated. The herd had been slowly and methodically persuaded to move almost two miles to the south, and would settle in for another few days of undisturbed grazing.

"Maybe some day we won't have to do this anymore," Running Wolf said wistfully on the ride back to the stables. "If we can give them enough land, the buffalo will take care of themselves."

CHAPTER 27
June 2014

Governor Kane quietly read through the long-awaited report from his Director of the Department of Revenue. It provided him with a broad overview of the state's financial situation in the aftermath of being cut off from all federal funds, with a fair degree of drill-down illustrating the economic impact on the state's major industries and employers.

The timber industry would emerge largely unscathed; it might even secure a slight advantage, since the state had assumed control of the federal lands constituting almost 30 percent of the territory within its borders.

Mining and mineral production should also be OK. Montana had the largest coal reserves in the country, with impressive undeveloped oil and natural gas reserves as well.

The impact on the farming industry would be something of a mixed bag. Those farms heavily involved in growing federally subsidized crops—corn, for example—could take a beating. But it might not matter in a good year. Montanans were used to ups and downs in their largely resource-based economy. Hard winters, excessively hot summers, persistent draught, apocalyptic forest fires, and fickle commodities markets were economic hurdles they had lived with forever. The subsidies and tax-advantaged crops just helped even out what was a naturally tumultuous economic base.

Of the 1 million people living in Montana, almost 40 percent lived in the seven largest cities: Billings, Missoula, Great Falls, Butte, Bozeman, Helena and Kalispell. They were largely middle-class, employed predominantly in various service industries—the type of people who paid taxes without the benefit of any special-interest handouts. The type of people who *paid for* the special-interest handouts. *As long as we can keep the schools and hospitals open, maintain the police and fire department budgets, and keep the roads paved, they'll be fine,* Ben thought hopefully.

The existing revenue collecting structure would be kept in place until things got sorted out or settled with the feds. All collection of federal taxes would continue—federal income taxes, Social Security taxes, gas, cigarette, alcohol taxes and land use and telecommunications fees—and would all be diverted to the Montana treasury. The situation wasn't as bleak as they originally had thought; federal employees, over 22,000 of them, were still drawing paychecks, Indian reservations were unaffected, and it looked like the state government would be able to maintain a good, solid degree of basic services.

But there would be problems, for sure, especially in the cattle industry. *We'll never be able to sell meat domestically without a USDA Inspection stamp. We might have to let the inspectors back on the job. Maybe we can come up with a superior Montana inspection protocol and brand it nationally...* He liked the idea and jotted it down. He returned to the report.

The federal government spent billions of dollars in the state, but it largely spent those billions on enforcement of laws and regulations it had imposed, on solving problems it had defined, on enforcing standards of its own making, on fulfilling responsibilities it had taken up on its own. *All for votes*, thought Ben. *First tell me I have a problem, then tell me you have the solution, and then, under penalty of financial ruin, jail or death, pick my pocket to pay for it.*

He shook his head in disgust. *Nice work if you can get it…*

Ben put down the report and gently rubbed his eyes. They'd make it economically. It would be tough, sacrifices would have to be made, state dollars and manpower would have to be redeployed, and some farmers would have to find more profitable crops. All he really had to worry about now was invasion. Ben knew he had no intention of ordering his National Guard troops, or the civilian militia, to open fire on American troops. Nobody else knew. It was the only card he held right now, and it was a bluff.

The soft ping of the communications panel interrupted his thoughts. General McDermott was on the line.

It was a beautiful, clear, balmy day, and Ben wanted to get outside and stretch his legs. He needed to speak privately, very privately, with General McDermott, so he decided to kill two birds with one stone and had his driver take them to Black Sandy State Park, on the western shore of Hauser Lake just 15 miles north of Helena. It was a weekday, and still a little early in the season for the boaters and water skiers, so the park would be relatively empty. There was a short hiking trail there where they could talk. The Governor's security detail followed at a discrete distance.

They started down the bark-covered trail at a good pace, stealing a few lungfuls of fresh, piney air before they got down to business.

"Who knows about this?" Ben asked.

"Three people," the General answered. "Myself, a Major Gus Walski, the technical specialist who evaluated the source and briefed me, and this…Angel, the apparent source. Major Walski wisely decided to bypass the normal chain-of-command and reported directly back to me."

"Plus Joe, and Kim knows something's going on," added Ben. "OK, bring me in."

A pillow of sweet, cool air rolling over to them from the nearby lake mixed with the nourishing spring sun. For a moment, Ben felt himself drifting into one of those warm and fuzzy déjà vu moments he couldn't quite place.

McDermott quickly snapped him out of it. "The Minuteman III ICBMs are deployed in circular clusters of 10 missiles. Each flight of 10 missiles is controlled by a single launch control center—LCC in military talk—located right smack in the center of the ring of missiles. The LCC is manned by a missile combat crew."

"There are 20 LCC's surrounding the Great Falls area. Apparently, our friend Angel has determined each LCC has its own targeting control server—a big computer. I would guess this way, in case a server goes down, you only lose 10 missiles. A 16-digit, alphanumeric code, changing every minute, is sequenced with a portable key code generator carried in the nuclear football following the President everywhere he goes. If he needs to authorize a launch, the President has one minute to read the code showing on his key code generator to the Pentagon before the number changes. The correct code clears all 20 servers to allow a fire-command from the field, from the missileers in the LLC in Great Falls."

"So the combat crew is unable to launch a missile without the President of the United States providing the launch code." Ben clarified to himself.

"Correct. And the missiles are actually targeted by the Pentagon. They set the strike coordinates from a preset list in the computer, and then authorize the missile combat crew to launch on their command. Those missiles can't be targeted on a city or a site not previously authorized and entered into the targeting control server."

"So the President couldn't order a nuclear strike on Los Angeles if he wanted to?" Ben asked half seriously.

"Not unless someone entered the approved coordinates into the

computer first," McDermott responded, way too seriously. "Don't
get me wrong. New targets can be and are added when necessary.
But it's a process. The President and his national security team sign
off on the proposed targets; cartographic specialists need to define
the precise global coordinates of those targets. Those numbers are
then passed over to the programming people who enter the stuff into
the computer. Once they're in the system, they can be selected for
targeting—like a pull-down menu, I suppose."

"What happens if the Pentagon is destroyed in a nuclear
fireball?" Ben asked. "The targeting computers would be toast and
the President's password would be useless. There has to be some
kind of a doomsday option to get those missile out of their silos."

McDermott looked over at the Governor with a hint of a smile
on his face and the high sun reflecting off his dark glasses. "The
answer to that would be 'yes,' there is."

The General went on to explain the super-high-frequency
satellite fail-safe signal, or at least his understanding of it.
Redundant super-high-frequency signals were continuously beamed
from the National Security Agency to a satellite in geostationary
orbit above the Rocky Mountain states. Those signals were relayed
from the satellite to the ICBM launch control centers scattered
around Great Falls. A signal loss would assumingly indicate a
devastating knockout punch had been delivered to the nation's
capital region, and the signal's loss would digitally release the local
missile combat crews to target and launch their missiles on their
own, pending orders from the surviving chain of command.

"So Washington goes boom, the signal stops, the missile crews
are on their own?" Ben repeated.

"Uh-huh," McDermott confirmed. "The assumption is the
President and the military chain of command would have escaped to
Air Force One or Cheyenne Mountain or some other secure
location, and will call the shots from there."

A playful, 20-something couple was walking arm-in-arm toward Ben and General McDermott. They instantly recognized their governor and offered shy waves and smiles of recognition. Ben smiled back and offered his hand. They briefly exchanged pleasantries about the weather and, yes, Ben agreed, things *had* been rather exciting lately.

"OK," Ben said as his young fans moved on down the path, past his not-so-happy security detail, "so where does this all leave us? What does this Angel guy have in mind?"

"Apparently he's snaked himself far enough inside their system that he's confident he can delete the fail-safe signal management software."

"Huh?"

"He thinks he can delete the software managing the fail-safe signal," the General repeated. "The way I understand it, it would be the digital equivalent of a nuclear strike—the fail-safe signal transmission to the LCC would be cut off, allowing the missile combat crew to retarget and launch the weapons under their control, at least for the LCC controlled by the server he attacks."

"Shit. Sounds a little too simple, doesn't it? Can't they just reinstall the software and regain control?"

General McDermott looked straight ahead and answered. "Too simple? Yes, it's *way* too fucking simple considering what we're talking about. But no, they can't regain control. Once the local missile crew fires up their targeting computer, it's over. Actual missile flight-control could be another matter, though."

Ben waved the General's last concern away with his hand. "We're getting way ahead of ourselves here. Will they know if we retarget some missiles?"

The General nodded. "They'll know immediately they've lost control. It'll take them a short while to figure out what happened; then, yes, they could use an airborne launch control center aboard an

EC-135 to read the target coordinates on the individual missiles. They'll know."

Ben abruptly stopped in his tracks. "Let's get back to the office."

They turned and headed for the car. "Heard enough?" asked McDermott.

"Heard plenty. I'm not sure running a brewpub and a year in the Governor's chair qualifies me for a career in nuclear brinkmanship, but I guess you have to start somewhere, right? Have the Major write up a report detailing the proposal for me. Handwritten, on a yellow pad, no copies. I want to see a timeline, what has to happen when, who has to do what, where, and when. You know the drill."

CHAPTER 28
June 2014

Within days Ben had Major Walski's report in hand. It was presented much as General McDermott had laid it out, but with the additional operational detail he'd requested. More detail than he needed to see, really, but he thought it wise he have a chance to look at it. He could see this Angel guy was a real freak. Sabotaging the system once he was in there was easy—getting in was a virtual act of God. Ben tried to picture the guy in his head. He'd met him just once—Joe had brought him in to set up the new computerized sales system in the bar and had introduced him as Ben was running out the door. Now the guy was sitting in a messy shit-hole of a room, fueled on smokes, cheap beer and Twinkies, waiting for the green light on a 20-minute telephone connection likely to bring the U.S. federal government to its knees, at least until they figured out what had hit them. *Imagine what he could have done if he'd finished college*, thought Ben, glancing at Angel's biography.

Ben was left only with the decision, and even then only the process, not the actual decision. He was going to do it; of that he was sure. The question was who should be brought in on the decision. He knew how everyone would react—Barrett would agree and tell him he was doing the right thing, Mitch Steere would flip out and tell them they were all crazy, and Kim would methodically want to review the pro's and con's of the proposal in more detail than any normal human could stand. Then he would go ahead with it anyway. His only real concern now was deniability on their behalf. At this point they all knew something was going on, but hell, the whole state knew something was going on. If things went badly, they could all be pumped full of sodium pentothal, strapped into a polygraph machine and still be able to honestly deny they had any idea what their crazy, treasonous Governor was going to do. There was a measure of comfort in that. He would be screwed no matter what; there would be no joy in taking everyone down with him.

He let his thoughts momentarily drift over to the dark-haired lady in the bar. He had spoken with her three times so far. Patricia was her name, Patricia Bennetti; her friends called her Trish. Deep-brown eyes; an easy smile; a terrific sense of humor; thick, long, dark hair, and a better body than he had a right to wish for at his age. He was well past the point of being able to keep his eyes off her. He knew she'd go out with him if he asked, but with his leading this spur-of-the-moment revolution and all, and the press following him everywhere, he would just be begging for trouble. Maybe he could have the Highway Patrol guys sneak her over to his residence, like Clinton used to do when he was Governor of Arkansas, and probably as President. But then they'd *have* to write a book about it, right? They'd *have* to. It wouldn't be fair to her. Dating was so difficult nowadays. Would she really want to get involved with someone who was about to threaten the federal government with nuclear war? What kind of future would she see with someone who would likely be tried and executed for treason in the next year or so? She did seem the understanding type, though. *It's so complicated. No wonder I'm still single…*

Hours later, in the darkness of night, Governor Kane lay alone in his thoughts, sprawled across his rumpled bed in the Governor's Residence, sheets twisted into an impossible knot. For the first time since this episode had begun some 13 months earlier, an otherwise exhausted Ben Kane was having difficulty sleeping.

"Do it."

"Good luck, Governor."

"Good luck to all of us, General. Let me hear from you as soon as you know something." Governor Kane was tired, very tired, his sluggish neural synapses firing only with the help of copious amounts of caffeine. He glanced at his watch; it was going to be a long day. He would have to grab a nap somewhere along the way.

"Got it," replied the stone-cold serious commanding general.

Ben terminated the connection and let McDermott get down to business.

Cruising east on Route 12, Joe Adams buzzed along on the Norton, heading back into Helena after a nice romp in the mountains. His day trip took him to the Garnet Ghost Town. Hidden high in the Garnet Mountain Range between Missoula and Helena, it was a nicely preserved old gold-mining ghost town, and as good a destination as any. As usual, the destination was largely beside the point—the ride made the day. Working the throttle with his right hand and smoking with the other, he zigzagged the nimble motorcycle across the width of the road, occasionally throwing the bike so low he was scraping the breakaway foot pegs. *Ya gotta love British engineering. Who needs the extra weight and complexity of a spring when you can just have the foot pegs snap off?* Seemingly out of nowhere, the Norton's almost useless vibrating rear mirror revealed flashing red lights rapidly closing on him. He chucked the butt, grabbed the handlebars with both hands, straightened his line and nervously glanced down at the speedometer. But the Montana Highway Patrol officer blasted by him without even a cursory look, siren screaming. He dialed down the throttle a bit, shook his head, and considered the fact that he had just been passed by an officer of the only remaining state-run law enforcement organization in the country.

It had been nine months since the so-called "national agents of social enforcement," ushered in by the One Nation legislation, had started down the path of solving everyone's problem by issuing federal paychecks with accompanying centrally controlled training and performance standards. Previously poorly performing government schools still largely sucked, with the added advantage of now having it be *completely* impossible to fire a substandard teacher or administrator. Daycare workers were obliged to attend a three-week training seminar, but were rewarded by having their salaries more than doubled and now enjoyed a lush, taxpayer supported federal benefits package. State and local district attorneys lay smothered in administrative requirements; prosecutions languished nationwide as promised funding got sidetracked to other federal priorities. Law enforcement organizations suffered from the same combination of increased process, balky funding and flat performance. Projects were underway tying the information technology systems from all of the services together, allowing information searches and investigations across all of the newly integrated federal social services, in all states. Police in a small New Jersey town would be able to query a child protective services database in Ohio. Prosecutors in Indiana could tap welfare and child support records in Arizona. School officials in California could peruse criminal records in Florida. Federal agencies could access all of the information in all of the states. Except for Montana.

Benchmark standards for all the new federal services were tweaked and adopted so the promised improvements in performance could be documented, whether realized or not.

Just a reservation for 'classic Americans,' he thought. *Just breathing museum pieces...* He shifted his weight a little in the Norton's saddle, goosed the throttle and raced his lengthening shadow home.

President Henderson backed away from the podium, stood to its side and waved to the enthusiastic crowd. He had just finished an address at a Georgia defense-contractor plant, one of several planned stops on a fundraising trip through the southeast region of the country. Since he had finished a few minutes early, he'd agreed to entertain a few spontaneous questions from the handpicked AFL-CIO representatives strategically planted in the crowd. As the moderator took the podium, the President's press secretary inconspicuously slipped Henderson a note. He blanched, waved to the crowd and signaled his hasty exit to the moderator.

"What do you mean, you've *lost* the ICBM's!" the President shouted into the phone. He was in the limousine being rushed back to Air Force One for the flight back to Washington. On the other end of the phone, the CINC/STRAT—the Commander in Chief, the U.S. Strategic Command—calmly explained they had lost the signal for a flight of 10 ICBMs, up by Shelby, Mont. There had been no explosions, no launches detected. All of the missiles were attached to a single Launch Control Center. They'd have more information soon.

Air Force One was cruising seven miles above the earth, high above the pillow of East Coast cloud cover, high above any other aircraft in the neighborhood, and was riding as rock-solid smooth as only a 747 can. President Henderson stepped out of his private suite and worked his way over to the conference room. Waiting for him there were his press secretary and the Secretary of Defense, who had come along for the ride to visit the defense contractor. Elsewhere on the plane were the Secretaries of Labor and Commerce, as well as Congressional delegations from a number of the states on the political outing. On the phone were the CINC/STRAT, and the Secretaries of State and Homeland Security. Henderson lost no time.

"What do we have?"

CINC/STRAT spoke up. "Mr. President, we've narrowed the problem to the targeting-control server mediating the security apparatus for the launch and targeting systems for a single Launch Control Center roughly 20 miles west of Shelby, Montana. It's been breached, and it's been trashed. Whoever was in there screwed up the operating system so bad it doesn't even recognize the hard drives in the machine, much less the software that's supposed to be managing launch security."

"Do we know who was in there and who has control of the missiles?" asked the President.

"We don't know who was in there, but the network I.T. guys are trying to track him down. The FBI is sending some talent over to help out. The missiles would be under the control of the LCC—at this point they can retarget and launch those birds on their own."

Henderson was steaming. "Are you telling me Kane has 10 nuclear warheads at his disposal?"

CINC/STRAT hesitated for a moment. "Actually, Mr. President, the LCC they've commandeered has not yet been DEMIRVED."

"Huh?" muttered Henderson.

"Under the START II treaty," explained the CINC/STRAT, "we are reducing the number of reentry vehicles—the physics package, the bombs—on the Minuteman ICBMs from three to one. We...haven't gotten to that LCC yet."

"Don't tell me..."

"Mr. President, those Minuteman have three W78 warheads each, 350 kilotons a pop—close to 25 times the punch of the Hiroshima bomb. Thirty warheads on 10 missiles."

"What are my options?" Henderson looked at the SEC/DEF, the Secretary of Defense.

"I don't believe I've ever seen any plans for invading our own missile fields," the SEC/DEF calmly stated.

"Mr. President," added the CINC/STRAT, his voice firm and authoritative over the speakerphone, "we don't think we're going to be able to re-establish Pentagon control over those birds anytime soon. Any solution is going to involve knocking on the door of the LCC and physically taking them back, sir."

The President grunted and nodded to the SEC/DEF. "I want to see contingency plans in a couple of hours. Even if it means we have to send in a couple of dozen special ops guys on horseback. I want to be able to take back that LLC when I say 'go'." The SEC/DEF nodded and jotted down some notes.

"Who's in the loop on this?" asked SEC/STATE. "If this is going to get out we need to stay ahead of the curve and reassure the E.U., the Russians, the Chinese, everybody. They're going to love this."

"The Pentagon. The FBI," responded CINC/STRAT. "All communication on the matter has been classified 'top secret.' So figure the *Drudge Report* should have it in a few hours, unless *The Washington Post* gets it first." His tone, unfortunately, was more serious than sarcastic.

The President shook his head. "And we don't know what's going on inside Montana yet," he stated slowly. Elbows on the table, he buried his face in his hands and massaged his temples. He looked up, his face red and drawn, as if just woken up from a deep sleep. "What the hell is this about? What does he want? Has anybody talked with this guy since this news broke?" Blank stares and silence on the speakerphone laid bare the answer. "Give me the room," he ordered. "And somebody get me that cowboy sonofabitch on the phone!"

"Nope, I gotta pay for my own lunch. The ethics police will have my ass if they find out you're buying me lunch in my own place."

Ben laughed as he signed the check. "If that's not double-dipping, I don't know what is!"

A good laugh arose from what was otherwise a rather serious group. Ben sat across from the executive officer of the Montana Department of Livestock. He'd dragged him along for a lunch meeting with the 10-member board of directors from the Montana Stockgrowers Association, representing the statewide cattle industry. The group took some small comfort in the, however temporary, suspension of the ever tightening and politically charged federal environmental regulations. And they liked the idea that the now-routine federal intrusion on private property rights would be curtailed for the time being. (Under the guise of the common good, and enthusiastically rubber-stamped by the courts, the federal government had assumed the right to demand essentially anything it wanted regarding land-use and development, to the point where the concept of private property was another one of those legal fantasies people enjoyed telling themselves still existed, when in fact it had no practical meaning.) But most of the discussions centered on the increasingly troubled family-owned ranches, the inability of ranching operations to secure bridge loans based on the value of their now-questionable federal grazing permits, and the concerns of some with the rapid increase in the Indians' bison herds. More bison meant a possible increased risk of the spread of brucellosis to their cattle. Brucellosis, a disease carried by many wild bison and free-ranging elk, was known to cause spontaneous abortions in domestic cattle and undulant fever in humans. But the group's primary concern remained financial—most ranching operations survived year-to-year, margins were tight in the best of years, and this clearly wasn't going to be the best of years. Many producers were already selling off their spring calves and some were liquidating entire herds.

After lunch, the Governor saw his guests to the door. Out of the corner of his eye, he spotted the best of reasons to excuse himself and linger for a moment before heading back to the office. Trish was there, eating a salad at the bar. She was sitting sidesaddle in the tall, swivel chair, facing the Governor, her shapely legs crossed, with a pair of snappy black flats capping one end and a proper, pleated grey skirt covering the other.

It was slow at the bar, and Ben thought it not unwise to step behind the bar to say hello. They talked pleasantly for a short while, about her job, about his meeting with the cattle people, about her salad. He absentmindedly leaned over and used his finger to pick at some pulpy beer labels, gummy with black slime, clogging the drain in the slop sink. She laughed, asking if he didn't have something more important he should be doing.

He laughed with her, and was wiping his hand on a bar towel when his cell phone chirped three times in quick succession—his office. He pulled the phone off his belt and flipped it open. "Excuse me," he said to Trish, then switched to his business voice. "Kane."

It was his secretary. "Governor, it's the White House, the President."

"Holy shit! Hold them for a minute; then put him through, OK? Thanks."

"I have to take this," he said to Trish, as he ran out from behind the bar. "I'll catch up with you later." He further excused himself and ran to the former storeroom turned office in the back of the dining room. Henderson hadn't yet been patched through, so he snuck over to the service bar and poured himself a couple of fingers of Scotch. He was a good sip into it and staring at the Trumbull print when the President's familiar voice addressed him through the tiny phone.

"I know they're keeping you busy out there, Governor, I hope I didn't catch you at a bad time."

"Any time is a good time to talk to the President, sir."

That was lame… he chided himself silently.

"Look, Governor, I have to be straight with you here. I've got crazies on both sides of me—the law enforcement people want me to have you arrested and strapped down with a needle in your arm, and the military folks want to invade your state. And you know how messy they can be when we let them play with their toys. I want to be reasonable here, Governor, but I don't have a lot of time. What exactly are you up to?"

"We're working hard to give you a third option, sir." Ben delivered it without missing a beat.

Henderson cleared his throat. "What third option?"

"The ability to change the subject, Mr. President," Ben stated. "You can make a big deal about the missiles, negotiate their return to your control, make the world safe again, and let the One Nation controversy fade into the mist. You get your missiles, and the citizens out here get to keep control over their police and schools."

There was a pause on the other end of the line, as if the President was waiting for more. "You can't be serious! We all know the punch line here, Governor—we're going to take back control of the missiles, and the federal legislation will continue to be the law of the land, whether you like it or not. Period. End of argument, step down, next case. That's how all this ends. Now…I certainly could find some wiggle room for you. We could drop the prosecution of General McDermott, and accept your resignation in lieu of a treason prosecution. And I don't have to tell you how many people are racing to get their hands on whoever the hell it was who hacked into the Pentagon's server. I can tell you he's going to be looking at a bit more than a parking ticket, if you get my drift. But this isn't a game, Governor, this is going to end, and it's going to end fast. It's up to you if it's done nice and neat, or if it ends messy. It's your call, Governor." Ben could hear the Chief Executive sipping a drink.

"Mr. President, do you remember when President Clinton got

up at a State of the Union speech and declared 'the era of big government is over'? Now nobody really believed him, but it gave the press something to talk about for a few days and served his purpose politically. I think a lot of people out here would like to see you get up in front of the nation and state, clearly and unambiguously, that the American founding principle of a free people being able to choose their own government is dead. Tell 'em it's over. You can say it was an 18th Century artifact whose time has past, you can say it's unrealistic, unworkable, even anarchistic if you need to, but stand up like a man and tell us all the truth as you see it. Make it work for you!" Ben was getting more sarcastic then he wanted to be, but it was difficult to reverse course, midstream. "Tell the nation it is unlawful and treasonous, in this 21st Century, for a state to elect a representative government of their choosing, and live under a set of laws passed by those lawfully elected representatives. That's what you're telling me, Mr. President, and I'm getting the message, clear as a bell. Do you have the stones to stand up and tell the rest of the nation? To tell them the era of self-determination is over? To tell them individual liberty and personal responsibility is no longer the American creed, but simply American history?" Ben gulped the rest of his drink, and splashed another generous serving into the oversized tumbler. "Or would you prefer if I carried the message for you? It's not like I don't have enough press out here."

The President hesitated for a moment. The truth is, for all of the insanity and commotion engendered by Kane and his band of merry men, the Governor really hadn't taken to the cameras in a big way. They'd been doing their own thing, however illegal and disruptive, but he'd never really done anything on camera other than defend an action they had taken, or rebut an accusation thrown at him by the administration. He hadn't taken this show on the road yet, and Henderson knew there'd be plenty of agreeable audiences waiting for him in the neighboring western states. He was right, of course, there was no longer any right of self-determination, and state governments were only there because somebody had to be available locally to take bribes for fudging zoning regulations and make sure the streets were cleaned and such. Everybody knew that. But you just didn't say such a thing. You could not say such a thing.

"I'm afraid this call hasn't gone as well as I had hoped," Henderson finally said. "If you don't make this easy for me, Governor, I can't make it easy for you. You need to understand that. It's something you need to keep in mind as you consider your moves going forward." His tone was subdued, but cold. "I know your intentions are sincere, but trust me on this, history is *not* going to treat you kindly. When this episode is over, however we bring it to a close, you're going to be the Governor who led his citizens down a very dangerous dead-end street, and I'm going to be the President who preserved the supremacy of federal power against an upstart state. Me and Lincoln!" He laughed out loud at his own characterization. "We're going to be in the history books together, Governor, you and I. We're going to be forever joined at the hip with this thing. Whether history gives us a just a short paragraph or a long, tortured chapter is up to you. Let's make it a short chapter, right, Governor?"

It was clearly Ben's turn to say something. He actually sort of agreed with the President on the long chapter/short paragraph thing. But he wouldn't mind the long chapter, assuming things didn't turn out the President's way. A sudden, welcome flash of common sense pushing its way through the Scotch fuzz in his head told him this was as good a time as any to keep his mouth shut.

"Yes, Mr. President. A short chapter."

The President hung up and Ben knocked back the rest of his drink.

CHAPTER 29
June 2014

After the call, Ben was a little shaken up, more so from his own swirl of emotions than from the President's thinly veiled threats. It was actually something of a badge of honor for him to be personally threatened by the President of the United States for enforcing the laws of his state. *I must be doing something right.* He walked through the dining room to the bar; Trish had already left. *Damn!* He entered Joe's office behind the bar and walked through to the "cold room"—the 1,000-square-foot home to his microbrewing operation.

The beer maker, Mark Wagner, was off today, so he could be alone with his thoughts for a few minutes. Mark was a Helena native, trained as a master brewer at the Doemens-Academy in Gräfelfing, Germany, just west of Munich. Asked during the job interview why he didn't study at the related Siebel Institute's Chicago campus, he quipped: "Why fuck around? You don't study brewing in Chicago when you can study it in Munich." The logic was inescapable and Ben had hired him on the spot.

Originally, he had wanted to set up the brewing operation behind a big glass wall, so the diners could watch the miracle of commercial fermentation while they enjoyed their meals. But the layout of the building would have made it difficult, if not impossible to do without rebuilding the entire restaurant, and truthfully, there wasn't much to watch. Most of what really went on back there was just the transfer of immature beer from one sterile-looking stainless steel tank to another, and cleaning, cleaning, cleaning; lots of cleaning. Tanks needed to be cleaned, transfer hoses were cleaned, filtration machines were cleaned, kegs were cleaned, the cement floor was cleaned, everything was cleaned. Every once in a while Joe would take a small group on an unscheduled, casual tour, as long as Mark was amicable to the idea, and they let it go at that. The regulars had all seen the cold room, and were more than happy to drink what came out of it than to worry much about how it got to them.

The brewing operation itself was a compact, 15-barrel system, with a small four-barrel trial setup for test-running new recipes. They had one cooker for boiling the wort, and two large primary fermentation tanks. With five days for a cold fermentation and another week for filtering and clearing, it took about two weeks to produce a batch of 15 kegs of beer. With the two fermentation tanks, he could produce up to 60 kegs a month, but rarely did. The fresh beer left the room in both tallneck bottles and kegs, but the decision had already been made to stop filling the bottles. The bottling was done by hand and all of the necessary cleaning, spilling, capping and attendant broken glass was just too much of a pain in the ass to continue. Most of his outside, bottle customers were willing to switch over to kegs, allowing a quick and painless decision in regard to the bottling.

His flagship brew, American Outback, was a typical western, light-bodied, robustly hopped, clean, crisp, Pilsner-style beverage. Served ice cold, it went down easy and was the perfect, unobtrusive match to the type of meat-and-potatoes menu featured in the restaurant. In addition to the popular American Outback elixir, he was also sure to have some sort of brown beer on tap—something with a little more bite and body (alcoholic bread, Joe called it). And there was usually a featured potluck beer of the week—something Mark cooked up that was new and different. If it went over well, they'd save the recipe and put it into a regular rotation. If it turned out to be a flop, they'd have a bon voyage party during the Friday happy hour, where the unwelcome brew was sold off cheap (even given away, if need be) and the staff would ceremoniously burn the recipe when the last keg was spent.

The Governor found himself a cold, pinched seat on an empty aluminum keg and considered his situation. The fact the President would be willing to let McDermott slide stuck with him. Ben figured this thing was going to blow up in his face sooner or later. If that indeed were the case, he'd like to see as many people escape with their lives intact as was possible, especially those who would have an exceptionally high price to pay—Paul McDermott was at the top of the list.

But he didn't want to fold his hand too soon. If the feds felt they had the political cover to safely muscle their way into Montana and force their capitulation they would have done so already—Henderson didn't owe him any favors and had no reason to give him a warning like he did.

Ben buttoned his sports coat and folded his arms across his chest; it wasn't called the cold room for nothing. They kept the room temperature at about 60 degrees. Unpasteurized draft beer was as perishable as milk—if you left a spill sitting around too long in a warm room it could get mighty funky very quickly. Maintaining the cool temperature kept things under control until they could get around to hosing the place down.

Ben could hear someone knocking around in the small office behind the bar, and knew the door to the cold room was going to swing open in a moment. When it did, Joe poked his head through the door. He looked more amused than surprised to find his boss in there alone. "Hey, chief! There you are!" He eyed the keg on which the Governor was sitting. "Hey—if you're thirsty, we have glasses out front," he grinned.

Ben shook his head. "I was just going to lay on the floor and open the spout on the clearing tank. What do you need?"

"I've got General McDermott on the public phone up at the bar. He said he couldn't get through to your cell phone, so he had his assistant look us up in the Yellow Pages."

Ben checked his cell phone—he had shut it off after the call from the President. He switched it on. "Tell him to try again."

Raul Fuentes, the President's Political Advisor, was talking animatedly with his boss as they entered the cramped White House Situation Room together. "They'd make it easier for us if they'd shoot somebody. The so-called lockout was covered wall-to-wall with media and all the viewers saw was that it went peacefully and cooperatively. It looked like the most reasonable thing in the world to do—let's just throw the entire federal government out of the state, sure, no problem." The President took his high-backed seat at the head of the long oval table, already crowded with high-ranking military and policy advisors. Several high-definition plasma video monitors were mounted on the wall opposite the President, one split-screened to various maps and overhead real-time pictures of Montana, others occupied by the faces of generals and officials who had video-conferenced into the meeting. Fuentes found his seat and continued chattering. "The state Legislature is insane, I know, but whether we like it or not, they've been lawfully elected and have the full support of their constituents. And Governor Kane has his regular-guy act down pat. The man holds meetings in a bar, for Christ's sake! How could you *not* love that?" The last question brought a dirty look from the Commander in Chief, and several "shut up, you idiot," looks from others around the table. "The bottom line," he continued undeterred, "is we have nobody who can be easily or convincingly demonized, and no aggressive moves we can make without looking like the bad guys."

"Keep going," directed Henderson. "I want everybody to hear this."

"National polls," the Political Advisor pointed out, "show the guy's positives running well ahead of his negatives. They like him out there, west of the Mississippi in general, and in the Rocky Mountain States in particular, even if they disagree with some of his actions. He's standing firm for what he believes in against a vastly superior opponent. People like that. Now, common sense dictates those positives should plummet when the public hears he's got nuclear-armed, ballistic missiles targeted on New York and Washington." He looked around the room and shrugged his shoulders. "I hope. A lot of people in this country would enjoy seeing Washington and New York blown off the map. Throw Paris in there and they just might elect him king!"

Henderson turned to his military advisors. "What's the latest on the targeting?"

An Air Force three-star slipped on a pair of reading glasses and read from his prepared notes. "Mr. President, they've got three missiles targeted on us here in the Capital district—nine warheads—two missiles to New York, two to Los Angeles, two to Paris, and the last one is targeted smack square on the European Union headquarters in Brussels."

"Paris and Brussels," said the Chairman of the Joint Chiefs, shaking his head in disbelief. "Nice touch."

"Options?" asked Henderson.

"We've got a couple of dozen options but no good solutions," answered a Marine four-star. "We could send in airborne infantry, armored infantry, special ops teams, you name it. Their Guard troops are well equipped and motivated, and are well capable of kicking up quite a bit of dust, but if properly deployed, we could secure the area in a heartbeat. The challenge for us is the missile combat crew—they're in a hardened Launch Control Center sitting about 75 feet underground. They've severed their communications with us; they have their fingers on the button and are assumingly taking orders from Governor Kane. The missiles themselves are in a hardened, underground launch facility 80 feet deep and covered by a theoretically nuke-proof 100-ton blast door. We really don't have any clean force solutions here. Those facilities were designed to stand as our last defense in the worst-case scenario—nobody's supposed to be able to get into them or destroy them."

"And what happens if they launch?" asked Henderson. "If any or all of those missiles are launched, can I go out there and assure the public our Ballistic Missile Defense system will shoot them all down? What danger would those warheads pose if they're shot down over a population center and get blown apart without exploding?"

The military officers shot looks at each other. The pause in the conversation, though momentary, was obvious and ominous. The President spun his chair around and addressed the Secretary of Defense, loudly and directly. "We can shoot them down, right? Hit a bullet with a bullet? Isn't that the package we paid for?"

The SEC/DEF clasped his hands together and leaned heavily on the table. He looked up at the President and spoke deliberately. "Hitting a bullet with a bullet is actually an inaccurate analogy frequently used by opponents of the system. A bullet travels in a relatively straight line from gun barrel to target. A ballistic missile travels like a softball being thrown from center field to home plate—a very long, high arc. Intercepting an arcing missile can be both remarkably simple and terribly complicated at the same time. It's simple because it's just math. If we can determine a trajectory, we can plot an intercept. The complicated part is making it happen." The SEC/DEF turned to the CINC/STRAT peering in from one of the plasma screens. "General, could you briefly explain the complicated part for us?"

"Certainly, sir," responded the Air Force four-star from his conference room under Nebraska's Offutt Air Force Base. "Our Ballistic Missile Defense System uses what we refer to as a layered approach to disrupt the flight of incoming ballistic missiles. As the Secretary started to explain, these missiles follow an arcing trajectory that we break down into three distinct phases—the boost, midcourse, and terminal phases. The boost phase is the launch, the beginning of the missile's flight during which the rocket motor is firing and sets the missile on the path to its target. This part of the flight usually lasts about three to five minutes. Our submarine- and Aegis Cruiser-based missiles will try to take down the target at this launch phase, depending on where they're launched and the position of our Navy assets."

The CINC/STRAT cleared his throat and continued. "At the completion of the firing sequence, it's in the midcourse phase, the longest part of the flight. At this point the missile is just coasting toward the target. This can take as long as 20 minutes if it's coming to us from the other side of the globe—from Russia, for example— but, obviously, the closer the launch, the shorter the midcourse flight. We have about two-dozen ground-based interceptors positioned at Fort Greely and Vandenberg Air Force Base to take out missiles during this long, midcourse phase of their flight. But missiles launched from Montana won't be in the air long enough for us to fire those long-range interceptors."

He continued. "Most missiles, our Minuteman III included, shed their rocket motors along the flight to leave the warhead— warheads in the case of the specific weapons we're concerned with here—free to fall to the intended target. All we're left with then is the terminal phase where the warheads reenter the earth's atmosphere at very high speeds—over 2,000 miles per hour for these particular warheads—and drop onto their targets. We're left with a window of about 30 seconds to shoot down the incoming warhead before it strikes."

"Where does that leave us?" asked the President, quietly.

"Not with much, I'm afraid, Mr. President," confirmed the CINC/STRAT. "When the system was originally conceived and subsequently designed and rolled out over the years, our operational design assumed any ballistic missile threat would originate from outside our borders—from Russia, China, North Korea—the usual bad actors. Nobody figured we'd need to defend against a missile launched from one of our own silos."

President Henderson glared incredulously at the general's image on the screen. "Wonderful," he mumbled sarcastically. "That's just great. Are you telling me we have to stand by and watch our own cities go up in a nuclear fireball, but we can save *Paris*? Oh, that's going to go over *real* big with the taxpayers!"

"Well no, sir," offered the CINC/STRAT. "We have a shot. We have the advantage of knowing exactly how many missiles are targeted on a given city. We could ring the target cities with PATRIOT-3 batteries and we'd have about 30 seconds to take down any incoming warheads. You run the risk, of course, of the unexploded warhead falling into a populated area. If the warhead is struck directly by the interceptor—a long shot, but possible—then you could have a really bad dirty bomb situation. And even if the warhead isn't struck directly, there's still a real chance we're going to have a baseball-sized piece of plutonium rolling around on a highway somewhere."

"This can't be," muttered Henderson as he stood up and buttoned his jacket. "Gentleman, thank you for your input. Let me see your plan as soon as you reach a consensus. Thank you all." Everyone in the room stood as the President charged out the door. His Political Advisor and Chief of Staff chased him up the narrow stairway and followed him to the Oval Office. A uniformed Secret Service officer held open the door as the President and his two advisors streamed into the brightly sunlit office.

"Mr. President," started Fuentes. "Governor Kane hasn't yet gone public with this. When this gets released to the media—and that could happen any minute—and they start broadcasting pictures of uniformed soldiers setting up a secure perimeter in New York's Central Park and manning PATRIOT missile batteries, we're going to have a crisis on our hands without those Montana nuts having even fired a shot. The uproar will be relentless. Where are the warheads going to fall? Who's going to pay to clean them up? Senators will be demanding cleanup money and extra military protection before the day is over. House members will be asking why we don't preemptively attack Helena." The President's Political Advisor realized he was getting a bit loud and overly animated for the Oval Office, and dialed it down a bit. "Mr. President, we cannot go down this road. Our selection of options is poor, and none of them leaves us in a good place."

Henderson plopped down into one of the comfortable sofas sitting just off the center of the office. He exhaled forcefully, sat back, and held out his hands, palms up, clearly asking: *So, what do we do?*

"Economics," Fuentes continued, taking a seat in the sofa opposite the President. "Their cattle industry is collapsing, for this year at least. It's going to be very, very difficult for them to reconstitute it going forward. Keep in mind cattle provide over a billion dollars in cash receipts for a state without a whole lot of ways to employ people living in the middle of nowhere. It's their soft underbelly in this confrontation…economics. They're just not going to be able to hold out forever."

"Over a civil service bill…" sighed Henderson. "All this over a civil service bill."

"But I should point out," added Fuentes, "that despite all of the economic tension, new housing starts are up in Montana; people are moving into the state."

The President's Chief of Staff sat silently throughout the entire discussion. He sat back in the sofa opposite the President, alongside Fuentes, slouching a little, with a finger across his lips, as if to hold himself silent. His eyes were locked on the President. When President Henderson finally met his gaze, Cigala lowered his finger and clearly, but softly enunciated one word. "Deal."

CHAPTER 30
June 2014

It was an image becoming commonplace on television sets all over America—a lush open prairie, rolling, and heavily forested foothills a few miles back, framed with the towering, majestic, craggy Rockies in the distant background. Every news broadcast had its own version. Frequently there were cattle in the foreground, occasionally a few horses grazing. Some of the more intrepid crews managed to capture bison in the frame. Most reporters stood in the left of the picture, eyebrows dancing, rhythmically singsonging the story of the day, with a breathtaking expanse of Montana spreading out over their shoulders.

While the political tug-of-war crawled along, the need to fill airtime with human-interest side stories occupied much of the journalists' time. Talking heads debated the economics of cattle ranching, a morning show host tried her hand at fly-fishing, some spent a few days at dude ranches, others explored the state's abundant wildlife populations. Eventually almost everyone got around to the plight of the Indians and the tragedy of the reservations. Stories of grinding poverty, bleak futures, crushing alcoholism and drug abuse, and, of course, the occasional success story, appeared on all the major networks within days of each other, as often seems to be the case. A few even managed to observe the fact that the tribes, though sovereign nations, had effectively been welfare wards of the federal government for the past 150 years or so. But none could muster the insight to connect-the-dots from federal largesse with its accompanying smothering blanket of mandatory regulations to the tribes' stalled economic progress. The inevitable subtext of the stories was that somehow the central government just wasn't doing enough.

At the same time, over at the nation's capital, the White House press corps was getting hosed on a regular basis. The daily press briefing provided only the sketchiest of details relating to the Montana issue. Journalists asked, badgered, rumored, speculated, hypothesized, synthesized, and requested follow-up questions, but the press secretary tap-danced around the around the issue with a smile on his face and a nervous blink in his right eye. "We're in talks with Montana officials," he would intimate, and once cryptically added, "not everyone in Helena is enamored with Governor Kane's strategy," implying, but never saying, that some sort of a coup might be in the works. "Are there Special Forces on the ground in Montana?" several reporters screamed at once. "You'd have to ask the Department of Defense about any possible troop deployments," he responded, throwing gasoline on the rumor. "We're hopeful the situation will be resolved to everyone's satisfaction soon," he would say, then change the subject or leave the podium.

The President appeared twice in Rose Garden press events, once flanked by members of Congress jostling for position behind the Chief Executive as he signed a piece of environmental legislation, and again, a week later, accompanied by the diminutive president of a South American republic, who was clearly happy to be there for whatever the reason. Both times the press corps tramped past the story of the day and the accompanying human props to ask President Henderson about Montana and rumors circulating about the nuclear missile fields, rumors arising with regular frequency now. The President, armed with his patented smile and a sly comment, deftly sidestepped the questions, waved to the cameras and shuttled his guests along the colonnade back to the Oval Office.

For his part, Governor Kane had already sworn everyone on his end to secrecy, but the reporters were on the hunt, and he knew no secret could be secured very long in such a charged environment. His press briefings centered on statewide economic issues, and tended to be upbeat, stirring affairs. Each appearance served to remind Montanans how much they loved having him as their governor; even the press delegation was compelled to acknowledge enjoying this assignment, despite all the red meat and hay.

No one was more surprised than Lt. Gov. Pat Driscoll when the call came through. A staffer working on the President's National Security Council wanted to "run a few ideas" by him. The conversation was the first of several over the next few days, calls meant to test the waters for the shape of a deal that might bring the crisis in for a soft landing. Immediately after the first call, Driscoll briefed Governor Kane, who cautiously encouraged him to continue the dialog. There was at least some tepid satisfaction in the fact Washington was the first to look to play footsy, but Ben had no delusions about how this was going to play out. *We're gonna get humped, but at least everyone's gettin out alive. That's something...* He felt the way he had felt when he was a freshman assemblyman in the Legislature, those many years ago, when it had dawned on him that nothing was ever going to change. Back when he realized his role in the political process would be limited to pounding on his desk, raising his voice, getting his face all flushed and scary-looking and carrying the torch for the then-upstart libertarian movement. But nothing would really change. The reality had become a part of him, and he had accepted it. So he was surprised when the same feeling suddenly came over him again. There was something strangely comforting in revisiting the years-old realization again, and something incredibly distressing at the same time.

The deal making gradually wound its way up and around the political ladder. The initial trial balloons expanded into talking points, talking points firmed to mutually agreed upon concepts, concepts solidified into the framework of an agreement. Ben recruited Kim Lange to track and coordinate the various proposals. For days she could be seen racing down the long corridors of the Capitol, generally followed closely by one or two departmental analysts, bouncing from meeting to meeting with the agency heads attempting to nail down the potential impact on their operations.

Ben spent those days in his office, his right hand firmly anchored to a handsome tumbler of Scotch. He was way too busy to let himself get hammered, but maintaining a low-frequency buzz enabled him to get through the day without the burden of high-level thought. The tactical decisions and staff direction could be made on autopilot; he could see the events were already unfolding on their own, there would be no point in mucking things up by thinking about them too much.

He could hear Kim's staccato voice approaching. She paused in the spacious suite outside the door of his office, asking someone to please wait for her out there. One last sip of single malt slid down his throat before a smiling Kim appeared in the doorway and offered a polite knock on the rich mahogany doorframe.

"Yes, ma'am!" he smiled, sounding perhaps a tad too cheery for the occasion. "Bring it on in! Whatever you've got there, let's see it."

Kim stepped smartly into the office. "Hey, Governor!" She pulled up a chair and unloaded a 5-inch-thick pile of files, reports, and note pads on the Governor's desk. "I think we're there, Ben. I think it's as good a deal as we can expect. Better than we had a right to expect, between you and me." She pulled a sheet of paper from the pile and handed it to the Governor. "Here you go."

Ben, of course, was intimately familiar with the parameters of the ongoing negotiations, but many of the details changed hourly. The sheet now in front of him represented the latest locked-down points of agreement—issues both the feds and the Montanans had agreed were finalized.

"Let's see." He picked up a pen, settling down a bit. He sat back into the big chair and studied the sheet. "OK, they want control of the missiles back—there's a shock—and the One Nation legislation needs to go into effect within six weeks." He looked up at Kim. "Is that possible?"

Kim nodded affirmatively. "All of the department heads say it's enough time. A lot of the work was already completed last year."

"OK, what else?" Ben returned to the list and checked off the points as he read them. "General McDermott has got to go, but will be allowed to retire with a full pension, his court martial proceedings will be dropped and he'll will be granted full immunity from any further prosecution relating to the incident. Good. The elected officials—including yours truly—get to stay in office and are also granted immunity from prosecution. Good. The unidentified hacker who broke into the Pentagon computer will be granted immunity if he agrees to provide a written, detailed report of exactly how he did it. Excellent! How'd you get them to agree to that?"

"They want out, Ben. They want to make the whole thing go away."

"Excellent!" he repeated, and returned to the list. "We repay all back taxes, they reimburse all withheld funds; they reinstate Social Security payments and reimburse the state for whatever we shelled out when we picked up the expenditures. *And*, they agree to pay us an offset equal to the amount of state taxes we pay to them as required by the One Nation legislation. For three years! Excellent!

How'd you manage *that*?"

"They want out" she repeated, "and they're willing to pay. We have to keep it quiet, though. They're going to hide the payments in some existing program; you know, increase our highway money, or some such thing."

"Cool! Very cool. All right, I guess I need to call Barrett and Steere; I'm going to have to convene a special session of the Legislature to approve the tax issues. Barrett's gonna shit, he hates special sessions." He placed the paper down on his desk and leaned forward. "Thanks, Kim. You did a great job here. Really, it's better than I could have reasonably hoped for."

"I just did my part, Governor. It took about 30 people to knit this agreement together. And it's not over yet."

The receptionist sounded frazzled. "Governor, I'm so sorry. Chip Chadwell is on the line for you and he's being rather insistent. I tried to…"

"Don't worry about it," Ben interrupted. "Put him through." Chip Chadwell could be a real asshole without trying too hard. A former natural gas entrepreneur from Houston, the brash, eccentric billionaire had chosen Montana as the perfect spot from which to launch his second career. He'd settled into a cozy 130,000-acre ranch in the Gallatin River Valley, located just above Yellowstone in the southwest portion of the state. There he'd established the largest, privately held bison herd in Montana. He liked bison, he liked Montana, and he especially liked the fact he could get the governor on the phone virtually anytime he damn well pleased.

"Governor Kane? Governor, how are ya?! I've been meaning to give you a call, but I know you've had your hands full. Doin' a great job, by the way. Not takin' any crap from those Washington boys. Good for you! Those humps wouldn't know an honest dollar if they accidentally earned one. I like a man who knows how to make lemonade from a bucket of lemons; you know what I mean? You're doin' a great job! A great job."

"Why thanks, Chip, I..."

"Listen Governor," the irreverent billionaire continued, "I hope you don't mind my callin', but I have a situation down here with my herd, and you're just the man to run this by. Some people see problems everywhere, you know what I mean? People like you and me, we see opportunities. Opportunities everywhere! Am I right?"

"Well, sure..."

"Good! Governor, I've got 6,000 head of bison down here that've got an itch to wander. They're spread out about three, four miles west of the Gallatin—the Gallatin River; you know where I'm at down here, right? Anyway, they're spread out west of the river and are heading north. Now this wouldn't be a problem except I'm runnin' out of land! My boys can persuade them to go this way or that, but turnin' 'em around is gonna be a pain in the ass. There's a shallow in the river up there, and I want to run them across and into the grasslands on the fringe of the national forest, south of Bozeman. Do you know what I mean, Governor? Do have a map in front of you?"

"I could..."

"The problem, of course, is that it's federal land and I don't have a permit. Never could get one over there. But you've already solved the problem, right Governor? Screw them and their permits! If I can get them past Bozeman and across I-90, I think they'll run up to the northern parts of Park County. Beautiful grass up there. Beautiful grass. Almost nobody lives up there, the cattle are all gone and that grass is just blowin' in the wind. What do you say, Governor? What are we doin' with all the federal land, anyway? Might as well graze some bison. Did you ever try to turn around 6,000 bison? Do you know what they do? They either stampede or they keep going wherever the hell they please. Wherever they please. Right now they feel like goin' north. What do you say?"

Ben was wondering if he was going to see Trish this weekend. She had cooked him dinner in her small apartment the previous Saturday and he was hoping to return the favor soon. Things between them were progressing nicely, if slowly, which was certainly understandable under the circumstances. He realized Chadwell had stopped talking and it was likely his turn to say something.

"Yeah, Chip, how much time do we have? I'm in the middle of something with Washington right now."

"Three, four days. Five at the outside."

"OK, let me see how this thing shakes out and I'll have someone get back to you ASAP. Deal?"

"I'll be waitin' for your call. Thank you, Governor. You're doin' a great job. Great job. Thanks again." He hung up.

Ben flopped back deep into his chair. *Great! Now I'm going to have buffalo running wild all over the state.* He considered the idea for a moment. Somehow it really didn't sound so bad.

CHAPTER 31
July 2014

Like everything about his job, calling a special session of the Montana Legislature involved process, and Ben could be good at process. One foot in front of the other, work the checklist, make the calls, publish the notices, move from point A to point B to C to D and as far down the line as you have to go to get to the objective. Creativity and individual self-expression were the adversaries of smooth process, he knew, which is why it seemed to him most successful government officials tended to be dull, procedure-oriented, consensus-seeking team players.

Ben was a successful politician by accident, and he realized it. He'd gladly return to his restaurant business in a heartbeat, where he could be creative, intuitive, messy, and able (anytime it seemed appropriate) to tell obnoxious people to go fuck themselves and get the hell out of his bar. The whole rebirth of individual freedom and self-determination thing looked like it was shot to hell at this point, anyway. Might as well get lost in process.

Majority Leader Bill Barrett worked his way down the Grand Stair. Though the special session was called on short notice, he was in a chipper mood, waving and smiling to the hustling crowds of government workers crowding the Capitol rotunda. A couple of weeks of boating on Flathead Lake, some fly fishing, and a little hiking had left him rested, tanned, and even a few pounds lighter.

Almost all of the legislative staffers stayed around for what was called the "interim," the time when the Legislature was not in session, but when the various committees did their detailed research and investigations. So even with the short notice, every senator and representative had copies of the overall agreement reached between the federal government and the Governor. More importantly, they were all studying the final copy of the bill just voted out of the House Committee on Taxation, the bill needing to be passed by both houses and signed into law in order for the federal agreement to go into effect. The bill was virtually identical to the one turned back by the legislature the year before, at the start of the whole episode.

Barrett stepped lively down the corridor to the Governor's office. Ben would be a wreck, he knew, but he needed to see if it was going to be bomb-throwing Ben, or "I want to quit and go back to my restaurant" Ben. The endgame would be played out over the next few days, and Montana, Barrett suspected, would need its bomb-thrower.

Kim Lange came charging out of the Governor's suite just as the Majority Leader approached. "Hey there, Miss Lange!" exclaimed Barrett. "How are you this fine morning? And how is he?" Barrett nodded in the direction of the Governor's office.

"I'm great, Senator, thank you! You're looking rested—nice tan!" She wrinkled her nose. "He wants to quit and go back to the restaurant."

"Oh well," he sighed. "Hell, what fun would it be if we had the same old Governor every day? Variety is the spice of life, or so they say." He winked at Kim and walked past into the suite. "Have a good one!"

"You too, Senator. Good luck!"

Barrett stepped into the Governor's suite and greeted the

administrative staff. He was waved through to the Governor's office. Ben was seated behind his desk plowing through a small mountain of documents. He looked up. "Well, Mr. Leader, here we are again."

Barrett dropped himself leadenly into a chair and laughed. "Here we are again? Here we are *at all* should be good news at this point!"

Ben snickered and shook his head. "Hey, have you seen this stuff about a demonstration?" He handed Barrett a couple of printouts from a website. "A big one, right outside here. Apparently it's being organized on the internet. As soon as a vote is scheduled they'll appear outside our door. A just-in-time demonstration. How can you not love that?"

Barrett studied the sheets. "This is a protest *against* the passage of the bill. Just what we need. As if this wasn't going to be hard enough on its own. And look at these groups being represented," he flipped through the papers, "a lot of the usual suspects, but it seems there are a good many out-of-state people as well—Idaho, Wyoming, Utah. Look here! Saskatchewan, Alberta—the Canadians? The Canadians are going to come down and protest the expansion of the federal government?" He tossed the papers back on the Governor's desk and sat back.

"These here folks have had a lot of time to organize and they've been making hay," Barrett observed. "You remember how much pressure the Legislature was under last year?" Ben nodded. "Last time around it was a grassroots effort in every sense of the word—Ma and Pa Kettle writing letters and e-mails, making phone calls—a spontaneous outburst. The Legislature was overwhelmed, decided they were feeling their oats, and here we are again. Right back where we started."

Ben stood up and went to the window overlooking the campus. He imagined the massive crowd of protesters, the noise, the chants, the banners. The television coverage. The national television coverage. "Yep. It's going to be up to us, you know. It's going to be up to us to decide if this is a crisis, a problem in need of a solution, or an opportunity." He turned back to the Majority Leader and slid into his chair. "It'll be up to us."

"You're not expecting this bill to pass, are you Ben?" The Governor shrugged his shoulders unconvincingly. "Get yourself ready to make some difficult decisions, my old friend. The Government's given you a deal—it's a damn good deal, no doubt. But the issues haven't changed, Ben, not for our citizens, not for their senators, not for those thousands of people who are going to show up on our doorstep. And unless I'm misreading the look on your face, things haven't changed for you, either."

"What do *you* think?" Ben asked the Majority Leader. "What are the odds we get this thing passed and we can be trout fishing by the end of the week?"

Barrett shook his large bulldog head and looked out the window. "I don't know. The whip tells me the votes are there, but...I don't know why they would be. What's changed? Now, yes, they may well decide, 'hey, we've had our fun, we got caught, and are being given the chance to tiptoe out of here with our hides intact. We should take the money and run.' Live to fight another day and all that. But this is not a legislature with a strong track record in political prudence."

An aide rapped on the door and scampered in with a fresh pot of coffee. The warm, nutty aroma filled the room. "Thanks," Ben nodded and pointed to the small wet bar. "Why don't you just leave it there, we'll help ourselves."

"Man, that smells good!" declared Barrett, sniffing lustfully. They both got up and fixed themselves a couple of mugs and settled back in their seats. "I guess we're just going to have to wait and see what happens," mused Ben.

They didn't have to wait long.

Something big was happening, and the word was traveling quickly. Forty-nine states had long ago capitulated to the One Nation plan. Montana would be the last stand; opponents of the legislation had nowhere else to go. People from every corner of the state joined the out-of-state supporters pouring into Helena, and 150,000 squeezed into the capital city the Monday the Legislature opened the special session, with another 225,000 the next day. Helena, with its population of 30,000 citizens, hosted half a million people by Wednesday.

The protesters were far better organized than anyone had suspected. Local grocery stores, gas stations, camping outfitters and convenience stores were warned in advance of the oncoming hordes. Banks were advised so they could keep their cash machines full. Port-O-Potties lined the highways. Hotels, motels, B & B's, and camping grounds surrounding Helena had been booked well in advance; a rented convoy of buses shuttled thousands back and forth into the city from as far as 30 miles away. A Woodstock Festival energy quickly enveloped the event; the crowds were peaceful and cooperative, but determined in their solidarity. Television crews spread out along the crowded highways leading into the Helena area, interviewing pilgrims stuck in their cars. Traffic on I-90 was delayed for hours between Bozeman and Livingston waiting for Chip Chadwell's bison herd to cross the highway, bearing into the wind in search of fresh grass and water. Half a dozen mounted handlers fretfully controlled the roadway, focusing far more on working the crowds of onlookers than worrying about the bison. Those unfamiliar with the animals routinely tended to get a bit too close, not realizing an apparently lethargic bull could pivot on a dime and charge at 50 mph if provoked. And they were easily provoked.

Nearly a thousand motorists parked their cars on the highway and, armed with all manner of digital video, film and cell-phone cameras, walked up to watch the 6,000 buffalo meander from almost one end of the horizon to the other. Within minutes images of the migration were broadcast all over the world via the internet, and every evening news broadcast featured a reporter using the herd as a backdrop. Chief Running Wolf watched in amazement as the scene unfolded on his television set. He knew of Chadwell's herd and knew they didn't belong anywhere near there. He almost knocked over his beer reaching for the phone.

The echo of Speaker Steere's gavel had barely faded from the chamber when the Co-Chairman of the Joint-Select Committee on Montanan Self-Government stood to assert jurisdiction of the tax bill and send it to his committee. The bill, he claimed, threatened state security and was almost certainly unconstitutional. After a brief squabble on the floor, the bill was indeed referred to the Joint-Select Committee. There would be no vote today.

Outside, the demonstration's organizers were obviously keeping a close eye on the legislative schedule. The House had no sooner convened than the rally speeches stopped and the rhythmic chanting began. "KEEP MONTANA FREE! KEEP MONTANA FREE! KEEP MONTANA FREE!" Drums of all sorts, conga drums, bongo drums, snare drums, bass drums—there had to have been scores of them—enthusiastically pounded out the beat. The Capitol was surrounded, and it rocked.

Inside, with the tax bill off the floor, the people's representatives were now free to speak on any topic they chose. They chose to speak on state sovereignty. Speaker Steere sat stone-faced at the rostrum, the gavel clutched in his hand the only remaining manifestation of his authority. The House was a runaway train. He'd been sandbagged and he knew it.

A radical libertarian held the floor and was clearly feeding off the energy pulsing into the chamber from the massive throng chanting just beyond its walls. "...an effort to create a society where there simply are no adverse consequences to making bad choices in one's life. They do so by limiting the economic success some may have enjoyed if they've made the right choices in their life, and passing a percentage of those economic benefits to those who have made poor choices. It's nothing less than stabbing the golden goose that enabled us to develop this, the richest and freest society ever to inhabit the earth. Who do you blame? It's too easy to blame the politicians, the system, the government. No, you have to blame the electorate—they're the ones who vote themselves money every election. More service, more security, more entitlements. Let the neighbors pay for it. I say—*let* them spend each other's money, if that's their idea of heaven on earth, if that's their idea of freedom. We in Montana choose to define freedom differently; we choose to define responsibility differently. We have no voice in this national government, we have no faith in this national government, we have no future in this national government."

Speaker Steere smacked down the gavel. "You're out of order, Mr. Miller. Tone down the rhetoric."

"Ho-lee shit!" The Governor shook his head in disbelief.

Ben gazed through the office window, his vantage point placing him barely above the heads of the demonstrators. Those in his line of sight looked right at him, showing no aggression, smiling, waving, enthusiastically chanting "KEEP MONTANA FREE!" He waved back, pointing at amusing signs, applauding the frenzied percussionists, winking and smiling at the passionate multitude. *This is unreal. I wonder when the last time a crowd this big gathered to demonstrate for their freedom? East Germany at the fall of the wall? The Solidarity revolution in Poland? Ceausescu's*

Romania? And they all had everything the big government crowd said they should have—free health care...free state schools...state subsidized housing...guaranteed state employment...guaranteed monthly food rations...really small cars...what else could you want?

"KEEP MONTANA FREE! KEEP MONTANA FREE!" they answered.

He turned to the video monitors mounted on the wall opposite his desk. In the upper house the Senators were wandering in and out of the chamber, some milling around the dark, intricately carved mahogany rostrum, talking quietly in small groups. He could see Barrett bending over a freshman senator, one hand gripping his shoulder, the other pointedly jabbing the air as he made whatever point he was making. There was really nothing constructive they could do until the House passed the tax bill and sent it over to them.

The scene in the House was a whole other thing. The chamber was full, the atmosphere electric. Mitch Steere sat forlornly at the Speaker's platform, listening to another rambling speech, watching the agenda slip away from him. Ben studied the Speaker, a former Eagle Scout, with a sympathetic eye. *Poor Mitch,* he considered. *The guy's a nervous wreck. He really likes coloring inside the lines...this has got to be fucking up his head something fierce.* He would have liked to give him a quick call to lend a little support, but phones weren't allowed on the House floor. Ben returned to the window. He wasn't nearly as disturbed by the turn of events as was the Speaker.

The next legislator to hold the floor was no less passionate than the former. "...what was once a shining city on a hill, the greatest constitutional republic ever to exist on God's good earth, is inexorably being drawn into what can only be called a system of compassionate fascism..."

The crack of the Speaker's gavel pierced the chamber. "You're out of order, Mr. Harris," Mitch Steere interrupted. "Tone it down."

"My apologies to the chair, Mr. Speaker. The truth can sometimes be an ugly thing, I know. But there are times when the ugly truth must be recognized, and spoken out loud. The people assembled outside this building have no trouble recognizing the truth. The representatives of those people assembled in this chamber have no trouble recognizing the truth. The people in our neighboring states have no trouble recognizing the truth. In all candor, Mr. Speaker, my understanding is even our good neighbors in the Canadian provinces to the north have no trouble recognizing the truth! The federal government of these United States has gradually assumed and consolidated a dictatorial, centralized control of major public services and social support systems, many previously in private hands."

BAM! Speaker Steere smashed the gavel to the sound block. "You're out of order, Mr. Harris," he warned. "Your statements are bordering on treason. Tone it down, please."

"My apologies to the chair, and to my colleagues, Mr. Speaker. It is admittedly an emotional subject. The extreme statism engendered by the voting majority in this country, constantly seeking services, support and security paid for by the labor of other people, or other generations, has brought us to the impasse we face this day. Our politicians and judges, all sworn to protect and defend the Constitution, the founding document that so deliberately defines the limitations of the powers granted to the government we all serve, our politicians and judges act only as *enablers* for those who seek to shirk individual responsibility for the dark, suffocating shadow of collective responsibility. This is *not* the government of our founding! This is *not* the government of a *free* people! This cannot remain *our* government!"

BAM! BAM! "That's treason, Mr. Harris!" the Speaker

shouted.

Governor Kane was still in his office entertaining himself with the crowd outside his window. The sound of the crashing gavel in concert with the Speaker yelling *treason* caught his attention like a gunshot in a crowded room. He turned to the monitor behind him to watch the proceedings.

The representative holding the floor continued unabated. "It's been said, Mr. Speaker, the role of government is to do for people what they cannot do for themselves. A concept easily justified when considering the defense of a nation, the control of our country's borders, or the regulation of contract law and property rights. But precisely when, after 7,000 years of human artistic expression, did individuals become incapable of creating art without federal subsidies?" A murmur of approval gurgled up from the House floor. The Speaker tapped the gavel.

"Exactly where in the Constitution," he continued, "was the federal government granted the power to become the arbiter of compassion in society? As if confiscating the money of one person and awarding it to another could be fairly called compassion. If a *private citizen* tried that out on the street, it would be called *armed robbery*. But when his *elected representative* does the same thing in the halls of Congress, it's called *serving your constituency!*" A flutter of snickers shimmered across the body of legislators. Tap - tap.

The representative went on for a bit more, ranting about how the federal government used its tax- and subsidy-policies to pick the winners and losers in industry, in science and in energy production, and how newly discovered civil rights quickly morph into federally compelled patronage for alien or offensive lifestyle choices. "People have a right to live as they please," he insisted, "and no law should stand in their way. But neither should government force others to encourage or otherwise financially support them." Speaker Steere calmly but firmly proclaimed, "The gentleman's time has expired." Ben quietly turned his focus back to the crowd.

He'd noticed that there were small, scattered islands of federal supporters dotting the vast ocean of demonstrators. They were chanting and shouting and waving their placards in an effort to be seen by the news cameras patrolling the larger crowd. But they were few in number, and were being politely ignored. *They can't be having too good a day*, thought Ben.

His eyes returned to a couple who'd caught his attention earlier, if only for the fact they were so unexceptional. He was mid-to-late 40's, wearing a green John Deere cap and a neat, lemon yellow sport shirt. She appeared just a bit younger, in a red ConAgra cap and a souvenir tee shirt from a last year's Montana State Fair. *Farmers. Or maybe he's in agricultural supplies, maybe heavy equipment sales or service. She's raising the kids and probably holding down a part-time job somewhere.* He buzzed an officer from his security detail and requested he step into the office.

The Governor spent the next couple of hours picking the brains of a series of folks escorted into his office by his security people. As with the first couple, Ben would spot interesting looking people from his window and point them out to the security officer. They were brought in to see the Governor, most very enthusiastically, all totally surprised, two or three at a time. He spent about 10 minutes with each group.

Several of the visitors were from out-of-state, and were all generally pissed at their own state governments for going along with the One Nation legislation. The Montanans he spoke with were all proud of their government for holding out and were there to show their opposition to any deal. Few had any real awareness of the likely adverse economic consequences of forfeiting the deal. All expressed the view that Montana would be better off without the federal government. Ben pressed them on the financial consequences of their path—all felt, in essence, that the "payback" cost of the federal dollars, in terms of personal liberty and local autonomy, had gotten way too high. They'd rather be free to figure it out for themselves. Everybody was cheerful and optimistic and thrilled to be speaking with their famous governor right there in his office.

When asked how they heard about the demonstration, almost everybody referred to a website apparently serving as the organizing locus of control for the event. Eventually, Ben sat down at his computer with a couple of attendees, a pair of college students, and located the website.

It turned out to be far more than just a clearinghouse for coordinating the Helena demonstration. It was a "Free Montana" site, advocating the secession of the state from the union. Along with the expected articles, interviews, chat-room rants and progress reports, it provided links to the home page and e-mail addresses of every Montana state representative and senator—along with a brief description of the particular legislator's position on a free Montana. Ben thanked the two college students and excused himself; he wanted an opportunity to study the list alone.

"Son of a bitch," he whispered to himself. It took only a few minutes to realize that a majority of legislators, in both houses, at least claimed to support the idea of secession.

The Governor glanced up at the Senate monitor. Barrett was no longer on the floor. He bolted out of the office to find the Majority Leader.

CHAPTER 32
July 2014

Joe abruptly reversed course and ran back into his small office behind the bar to answer the phone. An acrid puff of smoke, easily recognized as the burning *cannabis sativa* plant, wafted out from the door. Ben hadn't been seen around the bar for four or five days and Joe thought it'd be safe to take a small breather.

Running Wolf was on the line. "Dude!" Joe answered enthusiastically. "How are ya? We're missin' you down here, chief. Hey, check it out—did you know if you look at the yellow and blue M & M's with blue-blocker sunglasses on they look black and white?"

The line remained silent for a moment. "No, I didn't, but I'll…a…I'll be sure to check it out. I take it things are…quiet down there today?"

"Oh yeah," Joe responded. "Ben's MIA—because of the crowd, I guess—and the guys are outside having a barbeque or something. But it's been nonstop ape-shit down here for the last couple of days." Since Helena had come under siege, Joe had been having a ball. He'd made a few calls, and, with the help of the Governor's security people, thrown some weight around and had Sanders Street closed to through traffic. A few more calls, and the street was lined with hundreds of motorcycles. The bar had been rocking for days.

"Yeah, I've been following it on TV," said Running Wolf. "Listen, maybe you can help me out with something. I've been making calls for two days—I tried BIA, Bureau of Land Management, the State Department of Agriculture, Fish and Wildlife, Department of Livestock, everybody. They can't tell me anything. They're saying the Governor made a decision on his own—what's going on with Chadwell's herd?"

"Oh shit! Have you *seen* that? Fuckin' AWESOME! We might ride down and check them out tomorrow. They're about two hours south of here, heading north a couple of miles west of Route 89. Biggest free-ranging herd of buffalo in the state for 100 years."

"Yeah, it's the free-ranging part I'd like to find out about."

"You know," Joe interrupted, "I met Chadwell once. He was in here, a little more than a year ago, I guess, meeting Ben for dinner. Pulled up in a burgundy Rolls Royce and parked right behind the Norton. Left me a $100 tip. How bad can he be? The guy's kind of an acquired taste, though; a little bit of a prissy ass-wipe. But he's swimming in cash, no doubt about it."

"Yeah, Joe," Running Wolf tried again, patiently, appreciative of Joe's state of mind. "Where can I find out what kind of deal Chadwell swung with the Governor?"

"Yeah, chief! Time to tear down the fences! Excellent! I...don't know when I'm going to see him. How about I leave him a message saying you called and were interested in what the deal is with the buffalo?"

"That would be fine, Joe. Could you write it down? I know you're busy," the chief allowed, generously.

"No problem." Joe scribbled the message on a note pad by the phone. "I'll call over there in a few hours, OK?"

"Thanks a lot, my friend." They spent a few more minutes bullshitting before Running Wolf was able to peel himself away and let Joe get back to doing whatever it was he was pretending to do.

"I don't get this. Where the hell have I been? How did this happen?" Ben, now sitting in the Majority Leader's office, was looking for something to throw.

"I don't know where you were," replied Barrett, "but two weeks ago I was belly deep in a cold brook, catching fish and wondering if I ought to climb back up on the bank to relieve myself or just go ahead and piss in the stream. The first I saw of the website is when you showed it to me. Sure I've been getting e-mail, *tons* of it. But who reads all that crap? I get a summary report from my staff, like everybody else. And I didn't read it, like everybody else. I'm as surprised as you are, Ben." Barrett pointed to the monitor on his wall. The sound was off, but Mitch Steere could be seen at the semicircular oak rostrum in the House Gallery, looking flustered, face red, pounding the gavel. "And as surprised as he was."

"Turn it up for a minute," the Governor requested. "The House Whip is speaking."

"Sure thing." Barrett tapped the video control panel. "What a joke. This guy's in the leadership; he's supposed to be working for Mitch. Did we all make a deal with the devil, or what?" The Governor just stared at the screen.

The young, handsomely dressed representative was addressing the chair. "Who is it, Mr. Speaker, who determines how your health care gets delivered, who may deliver it, and exactly what health care the doctor may deliver? The *central government* is the final authority. Who determines where your children get their education, who may teach them, and what they may be taught? The *central government* is the final authority. Who, Mr. Speaker, may possess firearms? Only the *central government* decides. What foods may you eat? How must they be packaged? How may they be prepared? How much fat or sugar may they contain? Who decides if your children are eating too much? The *central government* is the final authority. How much must you pay your employees? What benefits must you provide? The *central government* is the better judge than the business owner. And they'll send you to jail if you disagree. May you use tobacco? The *central government* is the final authority. What property rights may you retain? The *central government* is the final authority. And how do we describe our great nation? We say it's a *free country. A FREE COUNTRY!*" The speaker theatrically paused for a moment with an incredulous look on his face. "A free country? Will somebody please help me find the freedom here? Except for the fact, for the time being, I'm still allowed to stand here and address this body, Mr. Speaker, there's a lot more freedom here in theory than there is in fact."

"Sounds a lot like one of your old speeches, Ben," Barrett commented.

"Frightening, isn't it," the Governor admitted. "Except at the time, I was a lone voice shouting in the wilderness. Just another radical nut taking potshots at Washington. I wasn't in the majority crafting secession legislation—listen to this guy!"

At this point the speaker had really worked himself into a lather, raising his voice, and banging on his small podium to emphasize his points. The rhythmic incantations of the demonstrators could be heard clearly over the rising buzz in the House chamber. "In the name of HEALTH, they take our freedom! In the name of SAFETY, they take our freedom! In the name of SECURITY, they take our freedom! In the name of COMPASSION, they take our freedom! In the name of FAIRNESS, they take our freedom! In the name of JOBS, they take our freedom! In the name of the natural ENVIRONMENT, they take our freedom! In the name of PROGRESS they take our freedom! In the name of our CHILDREN, they take our freedom! My God, in the name of FREEDOM, they take our freedom! In the name of all that is good with the human spirit, this government encourages its citizens to vote themselves into an Orwellian box that neither fosters that goodness nor encourages it—it merely compels it."

Barrett pulled a bottle out from his lower desk drawer. "Drink?"

"Oh yeah."

"It's like a movie, or a National Geographic special or something!" Joel Spritzer exclaimed to his wife. "But should they be so close without a fence?" The only other time the Spritzers had seen bison was the small group of a dozen or so held at a three-acre compound at the Bronx Zoo. The Spritzers had traveled west to central Montana from their tony Westport, Conn., home to spend a week roughing it at the K Bar Ranch, a boutique dude ranch specializing in horseback riding and fly-fishing. The colorful brochure hadn't mentioned the thousands of buffalo milling about, just a stone's throw from their cabin. Joel Spritzer, a marketing executive, thought it strange.

The K Bar was situated about 20 miles north of Bozeman, just east of the small town of Sedan. It was long run as a traditional cattle ranch, until the owner died in 2007, leaving his wife, Michelle Clarke, in charge of the operation. She decided she'd had enough of the cattle business, leased out a good portion of the acreage, and built half a dozen rustic but very comfortable log cabins near the ranch house. She'd been running a successful dude ranch ever since.

The cabins were built facing a two-acre, man-made pond, previously used as an irrigation reservoir. She brought in a landscape architect to re-grade the ground elevations surrounding the pond for a more natural look. Clusters of ornamental native grasses, some strategically placed shrubs, and several clusters of cottonwood trees were allowed to grow out, encouraging wildlife to visit the pond. At dusk guests could sit on the small porches in front of their cabins, between 80 and 100 yards from the water, and watch the animals. Regular visitors included hawks and golden eagles, short-tailed grouse, red fox, mule deer, and pronghorn antelope. In the fall, the pond was a magnet for migratory birds, including bugling snow geese, elegant sandhill cranes and egrets, and the occasional boisterous family of trumpeter swans heading south from Canada to Yellowstone Park.

Bison, given favorable wind, can smell water from three to five miles away. They caught wind of Michelle's pond at some point in their northward meanderings and adjusted their bearing accordingly. They arrived gradually in the early dawn, heads bobbing in cadence with their muscular, rolling shoulders, the sparse leading edge of the herd nosing their way to the cool, clean water. The first to arrive waded partially into the water and drank greedily; calves rambunctiously plunged into the pond without reserve, soon followed by scores of dust-caked adults. The normally placid water was quickly boiling with the large, black shapes.

The frenetic din and commotion drew the guests from their vacation cabins earlier than usual. Families stood agape before the unfolding natural wonder. Many, like the Spritzers, wondered if the show was an unadvertised bonus feature included in their weekly rate. More than a few wondered about their safety.

Eighty yards is a perfectly comfortable distance to sit back in an Adirondack chair, enjoy a cold drink, and watch a fox, an antelope or a flock of exotic birds. But it's viscerally unsettling to see a large herd of active, bellowing bison at so close a distance. The bison cows really didn't seem much more threatening than traditional cattle in either size or demeanor. But every person standing there just *knew* that humans needed to keep their distance from the mature bulls. The large animals had a troubling sense of momentum when they broke into a gallop. There was just too much mass in motion for an animal leading with its horns.

Michelle took a deep drag on her cigarette and gazed at the

scene from her kitchen window. *Great*, she thought. *There goes my landscaping. You just can't keep anything nice around here...* She had followed the herd's progress on TV (there were no televisions in the guest cabins—part of the ranch's rustic charm) and anticipated their arrival. One of her wranglers was sent out on horseback to try to locate Chadwell's hands riding herd with the bison; another was sent around to the cabins to keep everyone calm and away from the dangerously unpredictable animals.

As one crowd built steadily around Michelle Clarke's pond, another was gradually dissipating around the state Capitol. A hard-core throng of about 100,000 was still surrounding the Capitol campus; more than enough to continue to stress the city's routine operations and vex the law enforcement officials, but the stragglers were generally cooperative and peaceful.

The Governor was still essentially being held hostage, more so by the Legislature's activities than by the crowd outside his window. He did the best he could, in the few, elusive quiet moments, to try to take care of some routine business. It was during one of those quiet moments that Ben finally got around to calling Chief Running Wolf.

They spoke for a few minutes about the crowds in the capital city, the restaurant, and laughed at how Joe Adams had managed to turn Sanders Street into an open block party for bikers. Eventually Running Wolf circled around to the business at hand.

"So, Governor, I understand Chip Chadwell has his herd running wild a couple of hours south of you."

"Yeah, at least I hope they're still a couple of hours away. All I need right now is a herd of buffalo running through Helena. Although I suppose it might help thin out this crowd some," he laughed. "Seriously, though, I did agree to let him move them around on federal land, since our permitting status with them is up in the air for the time being. It was sort of an off-the-cuff agreement; the departmental people are still trying to catch up and draw up some temporary guidelines. Chadwell's agreed to call ahead the best he can to private landowners to let them know they're coming through. Most of the ranchers have sold off their cattle—statewide we're down almost 2,750,000 head, I think—they're just hanging on to breeding stock. So we've got a lot of grass out there."

"What do I have to do to get in on some of that grass, Governor?"

"Go on," Ben encouraged.

"With this year's calves our bison herd is over 600 head. That's above the sustainable carrying capacity of the land they're on. The Crow, they have over 4,000 head with the same overcapacity problem. We could sell off the excess for meat, but we'd rather not."

Running Wolf cleared his throat and continued. "Governor, have you heard the term American Serengeti?"

"Umm, actually yes. It was an idea kicking around a couple of years ago…they wanted to take advantage of the depopulation of the central plains states by reintroducing wild buffalo herds. Restore the ecosystem, reintroduce indigenous plants and animal life, stabilize topsoil erosion, increase tourism, shine your shoes and cure cancer. It went nowhere because of ranching industry opposition. You're thinkin' now with most of the cattle gone, maybe something could be done along those lines?"

"Look's to me like you've already started, Governor."

"Yeah, but so far it's been more impulse than policy, chief. I'll tell you what, you may be right—there might be something here. Why don't you try to work something out with the Montana members of the InterTribal Bison Cooperative and Chadwell? You bring me a proposal; I'll bring it to the Legislature. Sound good?"

"Thank you, Governor, sounds fair. I'll get on it. I don't

suppose you have a phone number for Chadwell?"

"Sam, they *loved* it! They must have taken 10,000 pictures! I swear I'm thinking about getting a few of those animals myself." Michelle Clarke was talking to the president of the state chapter of the Chamber of Commerce. She had served as president of the county chapter for the past two years. "They've been lingering by the irrigation pond for three days now. Munched my shrubs all to hell. They just started moving north this morning. We've been taking the guests horseback riding around the fringe of the herd—I couldn't have cooked up a more perfect Old West experience with a Hollywood movie budget, I swear to you. People were in tears. *I* was in tears! I've already called my state senator and representative…would you contact the Governor's people, Sam? It'll sound better coming from you. They've got to let Chadwell keep these animals out here. Even if they just pass through here a couple of times a year."

CHAPTER 33
August 2014

The near-giddy visitors to the Oval Office were politely shuffled toward the door after posing for their souvenir photo with the Chief Executive. Smiling and still chatting spiritedly, the President escorted his guests across the room and said his goodbyes. Running his hand through his hair, he stepped back behind his desk and picked up a briefing document to prepare for his next meeting. His press secretary paused by the door for a moment.

"Mr. President, the daily press briefing is going to start in about 15 minutes. I've been ducking Montana questions all week."

The President didn't look up. "I don't know. Tell them we understand the legislative process is not usually a pretty one, sausage making and all that, but we remain confident cooler heads will prevail, and expect to strike a deal that will be satisfactory to all."

"Do we have any evidence there *are* any cooler heads? Someone's going to ask."

The President thought for a moment and softly chuckled to himself. "I suppose when Ben Kane and Bill Barrett become the cooler heads, we know we have a problem." He looked up at his press secretary. "I don't know, say something...elegant." Henderson, like everybody else in the national government, had seen the size of the crowds in Helena. There would be no military solution to this dilemma.

Barrett was to the point, his voice calm, resonant in his lowest octave. He clearly wasn't having any fun. "Ben, now's the time for a Hail Mary pass."

"I don't have a Hail Mary pass."

"Now or never. The House is voting a secession bill out of committee."

"Can't Mitch…"

"Steamrolled," Barrett interrupted. "Irrelevant. Kaput. Over. Just another floor vote—and I can assure you he's in the minority."

"So much for having friends in high places," muttered the Governor. "Assuming they pass it, what happens when it gets to the Senate?"

"They *will* pass it. Then, in the Senate, I can bottle it up for a few hours, a day maybe. But 60 votes shuts me up and puts the bill on the floor for a vote. And yes, the 60 votes are there." He paused for a moment. "Sorry, Ben, but it looks like democracy is going to run its course. You know what they say about watching out what you wish for."

"Yeah," replied Ben. "OK. Have someone keep me current. I'll talk to you later." The call ended and Ben punched the speed-dial code for Senator Nancy Taylor's Capitol Hill office. He was put right through.

"Nancy? Ben Kane. I just got off the phone with Barrett. The shit is officially going through the fan. I've been working the phones like a crazy person—I've spoken with every Governor in the Rocky Mountain and Great Plains states. We'll need all the friends we can find if this thing blows up." He paused and backtracked to assert the gravity of the situation. "Nancy, you understand what this means, don't you? If we secede, you and old Bud will be out of a job. They'll recall our entire Congressional delegation. So it's now or never if you're going to try to avert this."

Senator Taylor's voice betrayed her heartfelt concern. "Ben, I don't know how this works. If they pass a secession document, will you have to sign it?"

"I...honestly, Nancy, I'm not there yet. Maybe. Maybe not. Probably. I don't know...look, you need to get with the Senate delegations from Idaho, the Dakotas, Wyoming and possibly Nebraska and Kansas if they'll go along. Fourteen Senators—at least we'll pick up little weight there, right? Enough to make a little noise? You need to try an outright repeal of the One Nation legislation, or try to amend it, postpone it, seek an exception for us, anything you can think of. Nancy, when you speak on the floor, you need to use the strongest possible terms. The bleakest, most apocalyptic language you can muster. Unload both barrels. It's now or never."

The Senator sighed. "Fire and brimstone has never been my forte, Ben, but I'll give it my best. We'll kick up a fuss, enough to get some attention from the press, but, well, the President fought hard for that legislation. It's the centerpiece of his administration, and I don't see him backing off. I hope this isn't your last option, Ben." Her sincerity was sobering.

Ben glanced outside at the thinning crowd beyond his office. The sky was clear, the sun brutal. The pounding August heat, now climbing into the 90's, was taking its toll on the crowd, many of whom were drifting away in search of shade and air conditioning. The Capitol groundskeepers were, little by little, taking advantage of the situation by picking up discarded signs, posters and other trash, and emptying overflowing garbage receptacles. One was crumpling up a 10-foot long "Keep Montana Free" banner and tossing it into a large dumpster they had trucked to the grounds.

The Governor shifted his focus back to his conversation. "Last option or not, nobody will be laying this on your doorstep, Senator.

All I can ask is for you to give this your last, best shot.

"Look," he continued, "there's no question we're facing a terrible, life-altering decision here. There are many, many very real, rational reasons to just walk away from this, to fold our cards and quit. We know the easy way out, Nancy, hell, any bonehead looking at the facts would. The question is—what is the *right* decision? And to make matters worse, if and when this lands on my desk, I'll be asked to make a decision with woefully incomplete data. What does secession really mean? Will we be treated as a hostile nation? Will Washington impose an economic embargo on the state? Will they blockade truckers? Are we going to keep using the dollar as currency? Does the Federal Reserve continue to set our monetary policy? Are we going to need passports to travel over the border to Idaho?" The Governor paused to take a sip of water.

He took a breath and lowered his voice a notch. "And what happens if they do come in after us and start arresting people? Resist? Shoot back? Once we cross that bridge, we lose. If Henderson decides to screw the reelection politics and chance a shooting war on live TV, we lose, period. If he's willing to sacrifice an election and take casualties to 'save the union,' then all we will have done is gone ahead and really fucked up life for a lot of people. God knows, I'm not doing this for any supposed legacy, or for history or any such crap. But I sure as hell don't want to be remembered as the guy who got thousands of dreamy-eyed kids killed because I couldn't back off from a little overheated political rhetoric. I need to decide if this is real or not." He let the last statement sink in for a moment. "Any suggestions?" he asked playfully, trying to defuse a way too serious moment.

"Sorry, Ben," she answered solemnly. "I do appreciate your careful formulation of the problem, though. At least you won't go down in history as the guy who made an impulsive decision."

"I hope not," Ben responded, knowing full well he was entirely capable of doing just that.

"Easy big fella," Kim Lange cooed, scratching her horse affectionately and trying to get him settled down after the indignity of a three-and-a-half-hour trailer ride. The big animal snorted and shook his long head. "Oh poor baby! I know, I know, Mommy's been so *mean* to you! Keeping you locked up all day. Come on horsy, let's walk around a little."

Kim's evening would be spent on the edge of Hardin, a small town east of Billings, just a few yards from northern border of the Crow Reservation. She had reservations at a highly recommended, family-owned equine motel—a motor lodge with a clean, spacious barn available to the guest's horses. The guest stalls each had attached, fenced, outside paddocks, allowing Kim to let Cato stretch his legs while she went to the office to check in for the evening. By the time she got back out to the barn, one of the owners had Cato set up with fresh water and a little feed, freeing Kim to get herself settled in for the night. "Rest up, sweetie," she whispered to Cato, stroking his mane. "Big day tomorrow."

Kim stepped out of her room into the still dawn. The temperature was already climbing into the 80's, the air heavy with grass and dust and distant pine. She took a deep breath of the thick, sweet air and checked her watch. Pulling her hair back into a ponytail, she strolled briskly over to the barn to check on Cato. *Time for a quick breakfast, and then we need to hit the road...*

"He's a beautiful paint horse, Miss Lange. A magnificent animal." Gordon Bird-in-Flight thumped Cato's haunch warmly. "I hope he doesn't spook easily." He helped Kim straighten the saddle pad draped across Cato's back.

"He's been around bison, if that's what you mean. I have two back home, so at least he's used to their scent, and he knows to keep his distance." She hoisted her saddle over the pad. Bird-in-Flight helped with the cinch and strap. When the saddle was snug he turned and walked over to his truck.

Kim continued to ready her horse for a long day. A handsome, hand-tooled leather scabbard was secured on the left side of the saddle. Her just-in-case Winchester Model 70 was slipped inside. Dark leather horn bags were draped across Cato's shoulders, and a matching pair of saddlebags was buckled behind the saddle. The Crow riders had well-worn ballistic nylon bags, more utilitarian than Kim's pricey leather gear, if somewhat less fashionable in fading hunter's orange.

A flat, tepid wind, offering no relief from the growing heat, gusted across the rolling brown prairie. Rain was generally scarce in August, and this year was no different. The only moisture in sight could scarcely qualify as cloud cover; thin, ephemeral whisks of vapor scattered high throughout the vast blue dome. Any visual poetry in the postcard vista was lost on Kim, who undid a third button on her sleeveless denim shirt. *It's going to be hot today...* She lifted the flap on one of her saddlebags and reached in to check her water bottles. The trucks accompanying them would carry plenty of water, but she liked to have a couple of quarts on board to avoid dehydration and to rinse the dust out of her mouth.

"Nice bags," commented Bird-in-Flight, returning from his vehicle. He handed her a two-way radio. "Here you go; keep this handy. It's a five-watt unit; plenty powerful for open land. We'll be on channel 77." They spent a few minutes reviewing the operation of the various knobs and buttons. "It's a nifty little gadget," he continued. "It has a GPS indicator. When you're talking to somebody, the person's name pops up here," he pointed to upper left corner of the small digital screen, "and this little compass indicator arrow shows you where and how far they are in relation to your position; one and a half miles northeast, half mile south. You get the drift."

"Cool!" She slipped the radio into one of her horn bags.

After breakfast at the motel Kim had driven about 20 miles south into the Crow reservation. She met Gordon Bird-in-Flight at a prearranged spot on I-90, just a bit north of the Little Bighorn Battlefield, and followed him west for another five miles along a rough, unpaved road to the Crow bison herd. A dozen Crow cowboys, along with a good number of small Jeeps and grubby 4x4 pickup trucks laden with supplies, were already waiting for them.

By the grace endowed by virtue of her connections with the Governor, she had been offered an opportunity to spend a couple of days and ride on a historical roundup, or at least an attempt at a historical roundup. They were going to try to push the Crow bison herd almost 200 miles in hopes of merging with Chip Chadwell's herd.

TV crews from all over swarmed the area. Local news, national news, the National Geographic Society, Discovery Channel, even the History Channel—everybody felt obligated to document the event. It was the first time this kind of massed, national media presence had appeared on Crow land. Of course, most were there for the buffalo, not the people, a fact not lost on the Crow. A representative from the IBC patiently explained to the producers how there wouldn't be much to see—there would only be stampeding bison, galloping cowboys and gunshots fired if things went terribly wrong—but the crews had schlepped all the way down there and clearly weren't leaving, so the Crow officials decided to make the best of it.

Bird-in-Flight gathered the news and documentary producers, feature reporters and a couple of university wildlife scientists around the back of one of the pickup trucks. He spread out a map on the open tailgate, drawing the crowd in tightly around him. Kim quietly snuck up to the edge of the group. The out-of-towners wouldn't place her but some of the local reporters would know who she was. She was counting on her packer-brimmed cowboy hat, dark glasses and lack of makeup to keep her incognito for the time being.

Bird-in-Flight turned to face the crowd. He clapped his hands sharply to command their attention. "OK kids—let's get started. Thanks for coming today." The group settled down.

"I don't know what it is you think you're going to see here. I'm here to tell you what we think we're going to try to do." He smiled. The group grunted appreciatively. It was still early and coffee was proving difficult to find.

"We're right here," Bird-in-Flight turned and pointed to a red circle on the map. "The bison are scattered in this prairie here in front of us." He used his finger to trace a rough oval on the map, then turned and pointed to a cluster of animals about three-quarters of a mile away. "That's the last group we're looking at over there. Normally bison graze in groups of 20 to 50 animals. Large herds only assemble during migrations. Right now they're stretched out about, oh, I don't know, maybe five miles up there through the valley."

He turned away from the map and faced the group. "The first thing we need to do is to coax the groups into a herd. They're too spread out to work with now. We just toss some food from a truck and get them walking. We'll start with the groups in the rear and start them walking to the group just in front of them. Then we'll move up and start the next group walking. We just keep going until we get the whole herd tightened up and moving together. It could take a day; it could take three days...I don't know. It might be tricky—the rutting season is mostly over, but there are still a few bulls tending cows out there. They can be very dangerous."

Bird-in-Flight turned back to his map. His silver ponytail,

playfully poking out from under his black cowboy hat, flicked gently in the wind. "The plan is to walk the animals 40 miles west across our tribal lands," he traced a line across the Crow Reservation on the map, "and emerge somewhere south of Billings to cross I-90. Then we'll turn northwest and walk 120 miles or so to meet and join Chip Chadwell's herd somewhere southeast of Helena." He tapped a second red circle on the map.

The reporters had been twitching for minutes and could no longer hold their questions. A petite, perky female journalist out of Billings popped first. "You're going to be passing residences, towns, highways, farms. How are you going to keep the animals safely away from private property? And how are you going to handle crossing federal land?"

The Crow elder nodded. "There's plenty of open land between here and our destination. We've secured easements from a number of large, private ranching operations. There'll be cowboys on their flanks the whole way, keeping them back a safe distance from places they shouldn't be, and discouraging them from spreading out too much. They're not like cattle, you know…you can't *make* them go where you want them to go, but you can encourage them. As long as we keep the herd leaders moving in the right direction, the rest will follow. The herd instinct is very strong in these animals."

He continued. "Politically, the Crow Nation is not going to involve itself in the difficulties between the federal government and the state, except to take advantage of any opportunities presenting themselves. We've been assured all treaties between our nation and Washington will be respected, and been advised to treat all land not in private hands as state land. And we've been granted permission to allow our herds on state land."

"How long will it take to reach the second herd?" another reporter asked.

"We have no way of knowing—nothing like this has ever been

attempted before, so far as we know. Normally, free-ranging, grazing bison will wander a quarter mile to, maybe, three miles while eating during the day. If it's time to move on, for better grazing or for water, they can travel 10 to 12 miles overnight. In the old days, a bison herd would migrate several hundred miles in a year." He shook his head, as if to say it was all a mystery to him. "But we don't know. We're hoping for a favorable wind. We think once they catch the scent of Chadwell's herd they'll move toward them on their own. So—three to six weeks, maybe?" Bird-in-Flight shrugged. "They'll get there."

The reporter followed up. "10,000 buffalo total, am I right? Does it mean the Crow are partners with Chadwell?"

Bird-in-Flight nodded. "That's right. Chadwell has a bit over 6,000 head, and we'll be moving about 4,000 to join him. So we're roughly 60-40 partners at this point. The animals contributed to the herd by investors will be identified by ear tags; new offspring will be owned by the partnership, with shares apportioned according to the initial contribution. The lawyers have it all worked out; they say it's going to be sort of a mutual fund with livestock."

"Our animals all have yellow ear tags," he continued. "The Blackfoot are in the process of tagging their herd. At this point the plan is for them to bring their animals down to join the big herd late in the spring, when their new calves are strong enough. They should have over 1,000 head by then. With our spring calves, we should have a single herd somewhere between 17 and 18,000 animals. There's been nothing like it on this continent for over 130 years."

The producer from the History Channel asked an unexpected, but not unwelcome, question. "Sir, can I ask what this project means to your people? Is this just a shrewd financial deal? You know, maybe a chance for the tribe to take advantage of Montana's political problems with Washington and partner up with a tycoon like Chip Chadwell? Or is there something more involved here?

Why are you doing this? "

"A very good question," Bird-in-Flight responded sincerely, "and I thank you for the opportunity to answer it." He methodically folded up the map and stuck it in his back pocket. He closed the tailgate and gave it a little shake to be sure it was latched securely.

Bird-in-Flight leaned back against the tailgate and folded his arms across his chest. "This agreement, this partnership, is a win-win, as they say, all around. There is certainly something in it financially for our partners and us. There is something in it spiritually for our people, for all of the native people in the state, and something in it economically for the state. And it's good for the land."

He kicked at a little pile of dirt with a dusty, scuffed boot. "Our culture is centered around the idea of living in harmony with the earth. We have been ripped from that life since we were moved to the reservations. Having the buffalo back will restore balance to the land and to our relationship with it. Our nation will never be what it was; this we know. But if the spirit of our people can be made whole again, we can go forward in harmony, in balance. We can make our way." The media folks fell uncharacteristically quiet.

"Our people, our children, suffer the sickness of a lost soul. Many are lost in drink, drugs, hopelessness. For generations we have been holding on to a memory, to the rituals and customs of a proud people. It's good to be proud of where you came from, of your ancestors; and we teach our children to respect their history. But it's better to be proud of who *you* are *now*..." he jabbed his finger in the air for emphasis "...an attitude made more difficult when the essence of your civilization is more a memory than a reality. The buffalo will restore the connection to the land for the Crow nation, and for the Blackfoot, and for the other nations affected in this way."

He paused for a moment and looked out at the dispassionate

black animals dotting the rolling landscape. "For years we have kept buffalo on our reservations. They were kept behind fences, like our people. Maybe now, with our brother buffalo once again roaming free, the spirit of the native people will be freed along with them, though we still remain behind fences."

Kim, thankful for her dark glasses and lack of makeup, was sobbing quietly.

Bird-in-Flight pointed to a small cluster of Crow cowboys standing around a crew pickup parked a short distance away. They were also studying a map. "Let me introduce you all to the drive foreman," he smiled, "and let's see if we can't get you folks a front row seat."

Kim inconspicuously stepped aside and allowed the media contingent to pass. Still using her hat to shelter her identity, she stomped through the dry, dusty grass over to Cato to complete her preparations for the historic ride. The early morning sun still sat low in the east, but already the heat of the day was upon them.

CHAPTER 34
August 2014

The kitchen door kicked open hard. Before it closed, the crashes and shouts of the barely controlled chaos beyond flashed into the dining room. The harried expeditor could be heard rushing completed orders out to the front of the house. He stood hunched in front of the dual-tiered, stainless steel shelving separating the sweltering cooking stations from the frenzied food servers, coordinating the cooking staff's efforts and sliding completed plates onto oversized trays waiting to be carried out to the dining room.

"Station 3—burger's up! That plate needs a baked potato! Station 5—shrimp cocktail's up! Where's the prime rib? I'm waiting for a prime rib here!" Servers crashed through the swinging doors shuttling hot food to waiting patrons. Busboys rapidly cleared tables and lugged precariously overflowing bins of soiled plates and silverware back into the kitchen. Handwrought, western motif iron fixtures hung from the high ceiling Each fixture held a dozen low-wattage bulbs; each lamp was covered with a tiny shade and bathed the diners below in a distant soft, warm evening light. The packed dining room of the American Outback Brewing Company was crackling with positive energy, and Governor Kane and his inner circle were enjoying the evening right smack in the middle of it.

Though the last remnants of the demonstrators around the Capitol building had finally dissipated some time ago, Sanders

Street remained closed to traffic between Sixth and Eighth Avenues, essentially protecting the Governor's watering hole from the horde of remote broadcasting vehicles still holding the Capitol campus under siege. It also allowed the Governor's expanded security detail to keep the increasingly annoying national media mob at arms length. The Governor and his colleagues took advantage of the added security by indulging in a well-deserved night out.

It was a night out with a purpose. After a week of strident debate and a torrent of supportive public input, the state Legislature had just passed a bill declaring Montana to be a free and independent state, severing all ties with the United States federal government. The Declaration of Independence for the State of Montana sat on the Governor's desk, awaiting his signature.

This was Ben's first appearance in the public dining room at the restaurant in weeks. Joining him for dinner was his usual cadre of conspirators—Kim Lange, Lt. Governor Driscoll, Senator Taylor (who flew out of Washington as soon as the legislation was passed), Majority Leader Bill Barrett, Speaker Mitch Steere, and General McDermott. The cross-table banter was a blend of animated shoptalk and well-lubricated gallows humor.

Kim, her arms still bright red from two days on horseback, leaned over her gazpacho to Mitch Steere, who was sitting across from her readying a forkful of fragrant sautéed mushrooms. "So, Mr. Speaker, what was it that finally brought you over to the dark side?" she inquired playfully.

He chuckled and savored a mouthful of his appetizer before responding. "Unity," he said. "In the end, we all felt it should be a unanimous vote. You know, hang together, or we will surely hang separately, or however it goes. I got the chance to say my peace. Everyone did." He seemed at ease with the outcome.

Senator Taylor tried to engage General McDermott, who was distractedly picking at his free-range roasted chicken and sinking deeper into a second tumbler of scotch. "General, you were the talk of the town a while back. The Chairman of the Armed Services Committee was livid. He wanted the Secretary of Defense fired for not sending the Marines in after you! I'm glad things have worked out for you so far...I know the Governor would go to any lengths for you."

General McDermott hadn't been out much lately and wasn't sure if the turn of events warranted celebration or not. "They went too far this time," he muttered. "They just went too damn far." He looked up at Senator Taylor. "I just can't believe we're the only ones who said *no*." He shrugged his shoulders. "We're the only ones."

The Senator patted his shoulder. "It's not over yet, General," she said softly. "I don't believe we're the only people who feel this way. I just think we're the only ones crazy enough to take the first step."

Senator Barrett attacked a succulent grilled elk chop almost the size of his head. "MmmMmm—good stuff, Ben. I don't know *why* you felt you needed to go into politics! You should have stayed in the kitchen."

"And stayed out of trouble," the Governor added. "Don't rub it in."

"Hey," the Lieutenant Governor chimed in, "all of the financial advisors on the networks are speculating that Montana could turn into a domestic tax haven for the continent—U.S., Canada *and* Mexico! We should start thinking about charging admission," he joked.

Barrett shook his head. "They'll never let it happen. You know what they used to say, only a true welfare state needs to keep poor people out and rich people in." He sat back and drained his mug of dark beer. "It has *forever* seemed perplexing to me how, to this day, the economic collapse of the Soviet Union is celebrated as a victory for the American way, yet we apparently aspire to the very collectivist economic model leading to their failure. Do people not understand the collapse of the Soviet Union was economic? It wasn't a victory of democracy over totalitarianism. It was a victory of free market capitalism over government-managed collectivism. It's like Washington is in a mad rush to smother the greatest economic engine in human history in a dusty old entitlement blanket. Collective economic systems are simply unsustainable."

"I thought places like Sweden and Denmark were the new model societies for the economic utopians?" Driscoll asked.

"Oh, I think you're right," Barrett answered, "but Sweden and Denmark are not serious examples of effectively working socialist systems. Come on, they barely qualify as countries. They're really just very exclusive, ethnically and racially uniform, limited membership communes. Sort of like Vermont. Hell, you can do anything with a couple of thousand people—live in teepees, sit around the campfire, share the women, share the wine—the whole bit. But if you're an outsider, *try* to become a citizen of one of those countries, and see how easy it is to get full membership benefits. Or, if you're a Swedish company, just *try* to relocate to another country to avoid the perpetual cradle-to-grave responsibilities you assume when you hire somebody. Oh, you can leave…they won't stop you at the border. But you're going to have to leave your company and your money behind. They are no more countries than is the Mafia— it takes a lifetime commitment to get in, and no one gets out."

"Besides," Ben added, "they're lousy examples because they're *not* working. They're failing states. Over 30 percent of all employment in Sweden is public sector. The remainder is a farm industry staggering on the balls of its ass since the European Union reduced farm subsidies across the board, and an industrial sector moving to China along with everybody else's. All they're left with is a government taxing its own civil servants to pay their own salaries. Not exactly a visionary plan for stoking the economic engine."

Kim wasn't about to sit out a discussion on creeping socialism. "I don't see the U.S. ever rolling back entitlements. Free stuff is a one-way street; you only get more of it, never less. Why take less when somebody else is paying? It's just not in our political DNA. So all we're left with is what history tells us will eventually happen—total systematic economic collapse, per East Germany, the Soviet Union, every South American neo-socialist government and the soon-to-be collapse of Western Europe. The writing is on the wall; look, even the economy of New York City has been unsustainable without state and federal subsidies for the past 20 years. Too much fixed overhead in the local government, too many civil servants, a school system accepting practically every parental responsibility associated with raising children and failing at almost all of them, too many people on the public payroll—either directly, through salaries, or indirectly, through entitlement programs—and by the shrinking percentage of productive members of their society. Think about it. The economy of the largest, greatest city in this country is unsustainable on its own, and nobody seems the least bit bothered by it."

"Well," Speaker Steere interrupted, "the truth is, the taxpayers of New York City pay more than enough in taxes, if you count what they pay out to their state and federal government. If they could hang on to their own money, they'd be in fine shape. But then the state and federal officials wouldn't be able to pass out the free cookies to people in other jurisdictions."

"Yeah," nodded Kim, acknowledging the correction. "But isn't that just symptomatic of the overall entitlement Ponzi scheme? It may take 40 years, it may take 60 years, but only one result awaits this nation if we continue down this path—total, catastrophic, economic failure. Once we get there, it'll be easy to end entitlements—they'll be insufficient jobs, a dwindling tax base, not enough money going to the government, so no checks coming back from the government. Then maybe we can start over."

She turned to the Governor. "Ben, whatever the difficulties we're going to face going it alone, I believe you save the state from eventual economic failure with the rest of the states. You'd be saving the state, Ben." She paused for a sip of red wine.

"All we're really going to do," she continued, "is get a head start on the other 49 states in trying to re-establish and rebuild our economy. Personally, I think we can do a killer ecotourism thing with the buffalo. Worldwide ecotourism. Let the buffalo roam, let the pronghorn and elk wander, and let the wolves and coyote chase them. And let people watch and take pictures, and leave their money behind. It's a real opportunity, and it's doable."

"Who's talking about a utopia now?" Barrett grunted.

"Come on!" Kim retorted. "Granted the Indian nations have an emotional investment in the project. But that aside, it's just a nonsubsidized livestock industry using native animals instead of Southeast Asian imports. With the built-in potential for an ecotourism component." She glanced at the Governor for support.

"We'll see," Ben offered. "Chadwell tells me he's received a number of inquiries from traditional ranching operators about getting a piece of the bison herd. There's a lot of uncommitted money floating around out there since they sold off their cattle earlier in the season…it's got to end up somewhere. We have the land, they have the investment capital—why not put it in bison?" He looked up at Barrett and over to Mitch Steere. "But tradition dies hard. This is heresy for most ranchers, not to mention the unfortunate racial component associated with the involvement of the native tribes. We'll see what shakes out."

A busboy cleared a few plates and refilled the empty water glasses. Ben gave him a wink and a silently mouthed thank you.

Senator Taylor politely waited until the young man hustled away; then she presented the Governor with a question. "Ben, you were fighting this fight before most of us even realized federal encroachment *was* a serious issue. How do you think it got this far? How did 275 million people let themselves be led around by the nose, like lambs to the slaughter?"

Ben took a deep swig of beer and cleared his throat. "I hate simplifying these things, you know? But to me it's like a young child's unconditional love for an irresponsible parent. The child is innocent, naive. The parent is undeserving of the child's devotion, but the child has known no other parent. If the relationship runs its course, the parent usually ends up doing irreparable damage to the child.

"People *want* to trust their government," he continued. "Oh, they may not trust it when the opposing party is in power, and they tend to trust it all too much while their guy is at the helm. The plain truth of the matter is our representatives have squandered any trust they've been allowed; they don't deserve it, at least in my view. They've constructed, and work within, a system doing irreparable harm to the country and its citizens." He shook his head and rapped his knuckles firmly on the table. "This state isn't going to take it anymore. We're not going down with the ship."

"So?" inquired Trish, tapping her fork playfully against her plate. "Tell me the truth. And if you don't like it, you can leave now! No pressure."

"Oh good," said Ben. "No pressure would be nice for a change." He dug into a steaming plate of rigatoni, prepared the traditional Italian way with a spicy tomato sauce and a generous sprinkling of coarsely grated Romano cheese.

Getting the Governor alone had proven close to impossible for Trish. She had held open an invitation for a home-cooked dinner at her modest apartment for more than a month now. Ben thought tonight, the night before he'd scheduled another live broadcast to address the state, would be the ideal time for a quiet evening.

"This is world-class sauce," he declared, sitting back from the table and taking a breather. "Really, this is great; it's the real thing. Where'd you get the recipe?"

"Thank you!" Trish tapped her forehead. "It's in here. I used to watch my dad cook when I was a little girl. Cook by taste. You know, a little of this, a little of that. The real secret is to cook it forever—I let it cook about three hours. How's the wine?" She served a six-year-old Chianti Classico Reserva per Kim Lange's suggestion.

"Fabulous! Here, watch this." He expertly swirled the deep, blood-red liquid around the sides of the glass, and then took a good sniff. "Mmmm—generous, open bouquet: nice, round fruit; black cherries…"

"Stop! You drink beer!"

"I know," he snickered, and swallowed an ample mouthful. "Kim keeps trying to teach me wine talk. It's good, though. Really."

After dinner, with the promise of ice cream for dessert, she hustled him off to the living room to watch a movie. She left him to tinker with the electronics and returned to the table to clear the dishes. The conversation meandered around to his upcoming TV broadcast. She knew better than to press him for details, rather she was more concerned with his personal well-being under the stressful circumstances.

"You're not going to be left holding the bag for this little adventure, are you?" she asked as she sat down next to Ben. He was still goofing around with the remote control.

He shook his head vigorously. "Oh God, no. I've asked for any trouble I might have coming. The bill was passed unanimously. I really don't even need to sign it. If I do nothing, it becomes law on its own 10 days. If I veto it, they have the votes to override my veto."

"But," he continued, "If I *were* to veto it, it would send a message, for sure. They respect me," he nodded philosophically. "A veto would get everyone's attention. I'm sure I could slow this thing down, if I thought it was the best path to take."

"Wow. No pressure there," she deadpanned. "Sounds like a fair day's work. How do you make a decision like that?"

"I don't, really," he answered. "I just sort of let the pieces fall into place, and pray I have the common sense to see the answer spelling itself out in front of me. What's been clear from the beginning in this episode was not so much the trail we should be taking, as much as the trail the feds insist on taking us down. For me, the real question is the meaning of national loyalty. You know, a soldier goes off to war knowing he may be asked to give his life for his country. That's loyalty. What I've been stuck on is the question of whether loyalty extends to my having to lead civilians on a march over a cultural and economic cliff if my government tells me to. If you can't take a stand here—where do you take it?" Trish sat down next to Ben and faced him attentively. Her hair was set in a long ponytail, pulled back tightly away from her soft oval face—sort of like a high-end European countess. She looked good. She looked *really* good. He softened his voice; his shoulders visibly relaxed.

He went on to finish his thought. "In the final analysis, a country is a compact, a promise, an agreement among people to live together under a common set of laws, under a mutual understanding of the common values, and under some guise of a common culture. There's a constant give-and-take with the values and culture, but there's generally more holding things together than pulling them apart. If it stays together long enough, then you have a common history, the heroes, the triumphs, the tragedies overcome. All told, more reasons to stay together than to drift apart.

"In the last 50 years or so here in the U.S., values have become highly polarized, and our common culture reduced to fast food outlets and blockbuster movies. History has been rewritten, the heroes are now dirtbags, the triumphs are now someone else's tragedies, and the tragedies, well, now they tell us they were our own fault...we had those coming. So all we're left with are the laws. And when those laws are written and enforced by someone you have next-to-nothing in common with, didn't vote for, and don't like much, well, here we are." He sank back into the sofa and threw his arm around her. "You said something about ice cream?"

CHAPTER 35
August 2014

Ben stood quietly amidst the mounting chaos once again engulfing his dining room. He appeared, even felt, rather bookish, wearing an off-white linen jacket, his reading glasses parked halfway down his nose, and clutching several overstuffed folders against his chest like a slightly bemused college professor. Kim Lange stepped to his side and touched him lightly on the elbow. "Governor. Why don't you sit down and relax for a while. They're going to be another half hour."

"I can't," he joked, pointing to his regular seat, presently crawling with lighting technicians. "Someone's in my booth." They both laughed.

"Don't worry about it," he said. "I need to shake off some nervous energy. Besides, this is as close as I get to meditation." He looked around the room. "Where's Barrett? I thought he was going to be here tonight."

"He's holding court up at the bar," Kim responded. "Very entertaining."

"Son of a bitch!" the Governor laughed. "Do me a favor and make sure he doesn't start cheering or applauding in the middle of the broadcast. This will probably get picked up worldwide and I'd like to at least *pretend* we're serious about this."

"Oh, he's serious about this! No doubt about it. He'll be a good boy, I'm sure. By the way, why the dining room? I remember it polled very well with Montanans the last time you did it, but the out-of-state talking heads thought it was a bit suspect. Don't you think broadcasting from the Capitol would add a little—panache?"

"Panache? Good word use," he cracked, then whipped off his reading glasses and used them to jab the air for emphasis. "No, look, this is not one government against another government. It's not a governor against a president. This is the people against their government. I sit with the people." He swept his open arm across the knot of onlookers crowding the room. "My people. My friends. Screw the talking heads."

The mobile video production crew worked quickly but deliberately. Having broadcast from the dining room once before, and on shorter notice to boot, the entire crew had adapted the nonchalant "been there, done that" demeanor of professional journeymen who've seen it all. They had the Governor sit down for a few minutes of lighting tests, then released him to mingle up at the bar until five minutes to air, 6 o'clock, Mountain Time. It was as good a time as any for what would certainly be picked up as a national broadcast, putting him on live at 5:00 P.M. on the West Coast, 8:00 P.M. on the East. The frenetic media machine was already nearly spent in anticipation. Cable channels had been wall-to-wall with Constitutional scholars in dark suits and historians in turtlenecks practically spitting up on themselves in anticipation of what they thought they might hear. Nineteenth Century secessionist arguments were being dusted off and replayed for the 21st Century audience. Lincoln's motivations were questioned, as were Benjamin Kane's. Cattle futures inched higher.

When the time came, Ben settled into the booth and walked through another brief sound test. His makeup was touched up. This was the big dance, and everybody had a camera. In a few minutes the final adjustments were made, and the live image of the Governor of Montana filled the airwaves.

"Good evening. I'm speaking with you once again from my establishment in the Helena Capitol district. I'm here, rather than in my office, because at a time like this I'd rather be surrounded by my friends than by the trappings of power. I am sorry to have once again found it necessary to invite myself into your living room. I promise not to stay long. We just have some paperwork to wrap up…"

The Governor took a few minutes to review the string of events transpiring over the past year taking them to this spot. He revealed there had been ongoing talks with the administration concerning control of the Great Falls missile fields. He left unmentioned that as a show of good faith, the missile targeting systems had already been reset to their original coordinates, and Montana was finalizing plans to hand back control of the weapons to the federal government. It was then time to get down to the business at hand.

"We've been talking for years," the Governor said, "about reducing the size, scope and influence of government. Well, I'm happy to report tonight that with your help, indeed, at your insistence, we're about to cut the cost of government by over two-and-a-half trillion dollars."

The Governor reached to his left, out of camera, and slid a handsome, dark leather folder to position before him. It was close to an inch thick. He solemnly opened the cover and turned the first few pages. Brushing his hand across the open page, he gently caressed the paper, as if reading Braille, or assessing the quality of a fine garment. Without looking up he said, "This document already has the signatures of every elected Senator and Representative of this state." He slowly lifted his gaze back to the camera. "The action we are about to take is not unprecedented, and perhaps not even unexpected. But it *is* serious, and we owe the world, and certainly, our countrymen, an explanation for our actions.

"Our political history in the past half century has shown a clear and unambiguous trend away from the country's founding principles of a limited government of constitutionally enumerated powers. We've evolved from a society based on the concept of individual liberty, liberty needing to be protected and fostered by government, to a society based on legally delineated rights, those rights being regularly uncovered, discovered and recognized by the courts, defined by the legislature and selectively enforced by the executive branch. Until, of course, they change their minds and discover somebody else's right trumps your right. We, in Montana, choose liberty. We choose the freedom to act for ourselves, over the right to demand from others." Governor Kane deftly slipped on his reading glasses and read from the document in front of him. "To this end, we offer the following rationale for our separation from the United States federal government:

"The ever-increasing encroachment of federal power is antagonistic to the concept of self-government.

"The federal government has usurped the state legislature's power to regulate education, law enforcement and general social policy, effectively eviscerating the state's ability to be responsive to its citizens.

"Federal officials have treated the state's concerns in an arrogant and dismissive manner, enforcing, rather than providing protection from, the tyranny of the majority." He paused and looked back up at the camera. "This nation's founders declared to the world that governments derive their powers from the consent of the governed. Nobody let *us* know when their seminal idea had been tossed aside." He went back to the document.

"The federal government has used its constitutional power of taxation to threaten and goad the citizenry, by taking the citizen's hard-earned money and returning portions of it only under specific conditions, and only for use in those particular purposes defined by the federal government.

"Federal economic policies have used tax credits, tax loopholes, subsidized loans, direct subsidies, bailouts and other methods of 'corporate welfare' in a continuous attempt to plan and control the economy—acts that misdirect private investment, stifle innovation, weaken unsubsidized industries and put people out of work."

Ben again glanced up at the camera to emphasize the point. "Look, it didn't work for the former Soviet Union, and it won't work here. Winners and losers in agribusiness, in energy production, in transportation, in high-technology, and in pharmaceuticals should be picked by the marketplace, not by the U.S. Congress. They're all big boys now, and have topnotch executives who get paid millions of dollars for making the tough decisions and managing those businesses. They don't need the taxpayer's hard-earned dollars to help them compete in the open market." He returned to the text.

"They have subjected our mountains, waterways, forests and grasslands to a series of politically driven management policies to benefit national constituencies and political contributors, rather than native-state concerns and interests.

"They have accepted, encouraged, and enforced economic principles of collective entitlement—principles which have historically led to the economic downfall of otherwise stable nations, both friend and foe alike." Ben removed his glasses and looked up at the camera. His voice rang clear. "We separate from this union to seek the constitutionally promised concept of self-government. It was the federal government's responsibility to safeguard the sanctity of the uniquely American notion that government is beholden to the people. In our view, they have failed.

"At the demand of the citizens of this state, and through the actions of their lawfully elected representatives, I hereby declare

Montana to be a free and independent state, to be from this time forward unbound from all ties and obligations to the federal government of the United States of America." Without hesitation, Governor Kane uncapped a fountain pen and affixed his signature to the document.

"It's done."

He recapped the pen and placed it back on the table. The mesmerized audience, crowded into the dining room, erupted into thunderous applause and boisterous cheers. Barrett had squeezed into the dining room and stood shoulder-to-shoulder with Mitch Steere and other legislative officials, all whooping and hollering their approval. Kim and Trish, both in tears, stood nearby clapping wildly. *The bomb thrower is back*, Barrett smiled. The Governor waited for the commotion to settle down and continued.

"Before the fireworks start, we need to acknowledge our recognition that this new birth of liberty can be taken away from us as swiftly as the federal government chooses to act against us. If they choose to force the issue," he nodded soberly, "they can win a fight, be it physical or economic, there's no question about it. But they cannot win fairly. They've got the brute force to bring to bear, but not the winning argument. I challenge the President, and the other 49 states to tell us we're wrong. Tell us the preservation of the union of states means more than living the values upon which the union was founded." Ben was feeling his oats now, and had one more thing to get off his chest.

"I'd like to say a word to the younger generation out there— anybody who intends to be in the workforce 30 or 40 years from now. When I was a kid, the great generational outrage was the draft, the Vietnam War. You may well think your generation has no draft." He cracked a wry smile and shook his head knowingly. "Oh, you have a draft all right—if you intend to be working and paying taxes for the next 30 years, believe me, you've been drafted. You've been drafted into a *lifetime* of paying for *my* Social Security, *my* medical care, *my* prescription drugs, *my* long-term home care, and *my* nursing home care. And for a kicker, longevity increases every year. Entitlements—I love that word, don't you? Just being born, or crossing over our border, *entitles* you to reach into your neighbor's wallet and have him cover your educational, medical, and retirement expenses. What a deal! Well, anyway, entitlements already make up 60 percent of the federal budget, and my generation outnumbers yours two to one. At the present rate of growth, entitlement spending will grow to 80 percent of the budget by the time you retire in 2040. Oh, you've been drafted, all right. They just haven't told you yet." He took a sip of water.

"The baby boomers are retiring as we speak. And they'll be retiring as the best educated and wealthiest generation to ever walk the earth—and *you* will be paying our freight for the next 20, 30 or 40 years. The boomers are the largest demographic block in history—76 million strong, 30 percent of the country's population—*and they vote*! So you think your generation had no draft? Welcome to your economic Vietnam, kids!

"Why? Why are you all being drafted into making this draconian, lifelong economic sacrifice? So today's politicians can get elected. Period. So they can get elected promising their constituents free stuff, paid for with someone else's money; or even better—another generation's money. Well, my young citizens—it's *your* money!" The Governor flashed a broad, theatrical smile and winked. "And we all appreciate your support!" Laughter tittered through the audience.

"Forty years from now, the federal government is going to have to drain so much money from the economy to carry this entitlement load that the benefits will simply not be sustainable. Just like the promised benefits weren't sustainable in the former Soviet Union, in Cuba, in Eastern Europe, and now in Western Europe. Their economies collapsed under the weight. We've had our own revolution here today—yours may have to wait 30 or 40 years, but you *will* have yours. You'll have to.

"Collective entitlement and centralized control of local government functions are Marxist remnants, nothing more. These failed philosophies were designed to oppose liberty, self-determination and free-market capitalism, not to complement it. Here in Montana, we've made our position on the subject clear. We've shaken off the siren song of the collective utopia and struck out on our own. We hope not to remain alone for long." He reached for the secession document still in front of him and gently closed the cover. "I'm sorry for taking so much of your time tonight. Thank you for listening." He held his eye contact with the camera until the red light switched off. He wormed his way out of the booth to the deafening applause and tears of everyone watching.

He pointed to the front of the house. "To the bar! Drinks are on me!"

A blistering rain blew hard across the West Wing colonnade and rattled the French doors leading into the Oval Office. It had been an exceptionally wet summer in the nation's capital, and was showing no sign of letting up, certainly not on this evening.

Robert Henderson swung open the heavy twin doors and stood gazing into the dark rose garden. The night air was warm, warmer than the air-conditioned Oval Office, but not uncomfortable. A gusting wind drove the heavy rain into the President's face. He made no effort to move. He welcomed the warm, wet contact, the rich, moist, soaking late summer air.

The Oval Office was dark, softly illuminated in spots by several well-placed nightlights. At night, the room felt more akin to a national chapel, lit only with the dim, warm fire of votive candles, than it did an after-hours executive office. It was late, a bit after 11:00 P.M., just about three hours after Governor Kane's historic broadcast. Along with most of the country, the President had watched. Unlike most of the country, it would be up to him to decide what to do about it.

"Mr. President?" The President's Chief of Staff, Marty Cigala, quietly entered the Oval Office. He was a little uneasy finding the Chief Executive standing in the open doorway, getting soaked. Henderson grunted in acknowledgement, but didn't turn around.

"Mr. President. Are you OK, sir?"

"You know," Henderson responded quietly, still talking to the rain, "the Chief Justice tells me under the circumstances, martial law wouldn't be too extreme an option."

"How would it work, sir?"

"Who knows?" Henderson shook his head. "There'd be a military occupation and policing, we'd have to arrest or otherwise remove all offending elected officials and replace them with some sort of temporary ruling council or board, and reopen the federal courthouses; we'd have to find a way to somehow reinstate federal tax collection…" Henderson hung his head and mopped his wet forehead with his bare hand. "We'd have to force them to do everything they're supposed to be doing—at gunpoint. Precisely as the Governor told the world we'd have to do. He practically dared us to roll tanks into the state."

The President went on. "The Secretary of Defense tells me they're cooperating fully on the missile fields. We're essentially back in control—our men are in the silos, communication networks have been re-established and…" he laughed sarcastically, "…secured, or so they tell me. There are some training issues, some musical chairs with the chain-of-command, endless Congressional hearings," he rolled his eyes, "as if nobody was expecting *those*. But it's all being worked out."

"What about the hacker?"

"Same deal we put on the table before, I believe. Full pardon in return for a full, detailed disclosure of his methodology." Henderson finally stepped back from the open doorway and wiped the water from his face with both hands. The Chief of Staff ran to the private restroom a few paces away through the pantry corridor and grabbed a dry towel. "Here you go, Mr. President."

"Thanks." The President accepted the royal blue towel, embellished with elegant gold highlights and the Presidential seal, and vigorously dried his head. He walked to the rest room and looked at himself in the mirror. "Did we poll after the speech?" he asked as he roughly worked his hair back into place with his hands.

"Yes, sir. Generally, people disagree with the act of secession; they think the Governor is extreme; they think his actions have been extreme. But at the same time they for the most part agree with his reasoning...they think the federal government overregulates, limits liberty, steps on state's rights, is too intrusive, blah, blah, blah. They disagree with the secession but agree with the reasons for doing it. We don't have a lot of room left to maneuver."

The President nodded in agreement and continued running through the situation they were facing. "They've recalled their Congressional delegation, and shut down all of the federal courthouses in the state. Apparently, an amendment to the Montana Constitution is working its way through their Legislature. It would dissolve any controlling legal authority presently commanded by U.S. Court of Appeals and Supreme Court decisions—in essence eliminating two centuries of Supreme Court precedents and with it, any and all settled federal rights. Montana's judicial system would stand on its own." He shook his head. "Ben Kane really knows how to throw a party. Did we issue our statement?"

"Yes, Mr. President. We were out there within minutes of his broadcast—kept it short and simple. We refused to recognize the fact of secession; we assured the public that the missile fields remain under our control, and that we think the Montana state government has behaved irresponsibly, and has let its people down. And, per your suggestion, sir, we made no mention of the word *treason*."

"Good," said Henderson. "I don't want to poison the well for a smooth reconciliation at a future date." The President tossed the towel into the rest room and picked up a few documents to bring back with him to the residence. "Anything else?"

"We were going to leak some information to a *Post* reporter concerning the financial hardships we think will be imposed upon the ordinary people in Montana as a result of this action. We want to get the facts out there—soften the ground a bit—before the press turns on us."

"Good," the President agreed, "Let's do it." President Henderson stepped out of the Oval Office onto the colonnade leading back to the residence. The rain let up a bit. "I'm done for the night. See you in the morning."

"Good night, Mr. President."

The sun was just setting on a beautiful, cool, mid-September evening. Governor Kane, anxious to be on time for a dinner date that had been hopping around his schedule for a week now, turned the corner of Sixth Avenue and started up Sanders Street to the American Outback Brewing Company. His security detail was back down to one officer, and Ben was enjoying his newly recovered freedom to move about as he pleased. The media hoards were long gone. They were off chasing an early hurricane slamming into the South Carolina coast—human tragedy, physical devastation and general mayhem made far better stuff to stick in between commercials than did politics. The evening news was filled with images of rain-soaked reporters, hanging on to light poles against the 100-mile-per-hour winds, reporting to the world that the weather down there was indeed really, really bad.

The weather in Helena, Mont., in contrast, was quite nice. September brought with it warm, sunny days and crisp nights. The green was still clinging to the deciduous trees in town, but the colors would be changing in weeks. *No rush*, thought Ben. *Winter will be here soon enough.*

The Crow bison drive took just over three weeks to rendezvous with Chip Chadwell's herd. The event resulted in a renewed flurry of news coverage—Native Americans had received more press in the last month than they had since the 19th Century. They hadn't seen such positive press since, well, ever.

Politically, the state remained at a stalemate with Washington. There was no representation for Montana in the federal legislature; they sent no money to Washington, and Washington sent none to Montana. Except for the Great Falls missile fields and a few administrators from the Bureau of Indian Affairs, there were no federal employees working in Montana. Federal courts were not operating; federal laws and regulations held no sway in the state. The state continued using U.S. currency because nobody said it couldn't.

Tourism picked up a little over the previous year's numbers, agriculture was weak, natural gas, oil and coal production remained strong, but overall, the state's economy, long propped up with federal dollars, was touch-and-go. The federal government had for years been the second largest white-collar employer in the state, so unemployment was on the high side (though many of the impacted workers—especially law enforcement and security personnel—were offered the opportunity to rotate out to a more receptive locale). Ben was speaking with the state's lawmakers about trying to more aggressively attract outside, even international, business to the state with their strong free market and low-regulatory policies.

Ben pulled open the door to the brewpub and stepped into the cool, sweet, malty atmosphere. A modest midweek crowd filled the dimly lit barroom. Trish, identifiable from his vantage point only by her bouncing, lush brunette mane, was sitting midway down the bar, surrounded by a thick cadre of attentive, well-dressed men. He greeted the pretenders gracefully and gave her an affectionate peck on the cheek. "Hey, kiddo!" he whispered. "Look who finally showed up for dinner." After a friendly hug he casually draped his arm across her shoulders.

Joe gave them a moment then discreetly slipped a coaster in front of his boss. "Hey, Joe," said Ben. "Why don't you get me a glass of whatever Mark is going to be giving away this Friday?" He was referring to the "special brews" occasionally cooked up by the brew master that were, now and again, a little less than successful.

Joe shot a quick glance around the bar to see if anyone else heard the request. He locked eyes with the Governor, pursed his lips and shook his head, clearly indicating he didn't think it was a good idea.

After having his first pitch waved off, the Governor tried again. "Uh, OK, just get me a draft Outback. Thanks." As he turned back to Trish, he noticed Kim Lange sitting at the far end of the bar, also surrounded by well-scrubbed male admirers. "Hey, lady!"

Kim excused herself from her troop of feverish devotees and shuffled over to the affectionate couple still clutching her wine glass. "Howdy do all?" she bubbled.

Ben swung his unoccupied arm around Kim, and now had both ladies under his arms. "My girls!" He gave them both a little squeeze. "One for work, one for home!" Both their faces grew wide with exaggerated shock and in unison they threw off his arms in protest.

"You can have him," said Trish, straightening her jacket, feigning insult.

"Nope, he's all yours," parried Kim.

"And they wonder why I'm still single," observed Ben, half seriously. "How's your pet buffalo?" he asked Kim, hoping to change the subject. "Are you ready to set them free yet?"

"You know," she started after a sip of wine, "I've really been giving the idea some thought. I love them to death, but after seeing the giant herd, I feel so bad seeing them all alone. It's just the two of them…" She took another sip of wine.

"They're looking for partners, aren't they?" asked Ben. "Talk to Bird-in-Flight, I'm sure he'll let you in on the deal."

"Uh-huh," she looked up at the ceiling, as if running the numbers in her head. "My contribution would make me a two ten-thousandths of a percent partner. Hey, it's not as if I can't use the investment. Without Social Security I have to start worrying about my retirement portfolio," she grinned mischievously.

"Don't remind me," said the Governor, rolling his eyes. He looked over to Trish with his best naughty puppy dog look. "Ready for dinner?"

"I'm not talking to you. Go to your meeting."

"Very funny. Come on, aren't you hungry?" Ben drained his glass of beer and prepared to head into the dining room.

"Go to your meeting!" she gave him a little baby push.

"What meeting?" The Governor looked around at his friends, having no idea what she was talking about. "We have a dinner date, don't we?"

Trish looked over to Kim. Ben shot Kim a questioning glance. Kim arched her eyebrows and looked back at Trish, then over to Joe, who motioned with his head to the back of the dining room.

"What?" asked the Governor, now getting a little agitated. "Who's back there?"

Kim looked at Joe. Joe looked over to Trish. Trish looked back to Kim.

"Who's back there?" Ben asked again, his voice now rising a bit. "Will somebody please tell me what the hell is going on?"

"Oh, you're gonna *love* this!" said Joe, finally.

"Top this off for me, will you?" He slid Joe his empty glass and waited for him to fill it up. Beer in hand and shaking his head, Ben turned and walked into the dining room. He smiled and greeted a few familiar faces and made his way back to the storeroom they used to plot the revolution. Pausing at the closed door, he could hear muffled voices in the back room.

"What is this?" he muttered under his breath. He pushed open the door.

The room fell silent as soon as the door opened. Governor Kane stood motionless in the doorway, his hand still on the knob. He recognized all of the deadly serious faces now turned to him, but was simply dumbfounded as to what they were doing there.

Still nobody said a word. As awareness overcame shock, Ben decided it would be up to him to break the ice. He took a couple of gulps of his beer and noisily cleared his throat. He looked around the room at the collected governors of Idaho, North and South Dakota, and Wyoming. Sitting beside them were the premiers of the provinces of Saskatchewan and Alberta, Montana's Canadian neighbors to the north.

"OK then—what are you guys drinking?"

* * * * *

~ Author's Note ~

Foremost, I should be clear about the fact that so far as I know, the good citizens of Montana have no particular attraction to either buffalo or revolution. I had to set the story somewhere; Montana just seemed so much more likely a place than say, New Jersey (no offense to New Jersey). The operating minutiae pertaining to the Minuteman III intercontinental ballistic missile system has been appropriately researched and presented as accurately as possible. Thankfully, I was unable to uncover any details as to how one would *a*ctually hack into the Pentagon's fire-control system. Someone might know, but I don't.

I tried to do justice to, and handle with all due sensitivity, issues involving the tribal nations. I was always aware of being an outsider looking in, and tried to be fair to an indigenous culture growing increasingly dilute in the homogenizing blender of popular American society.

The Libertarian Party (www.lp.org) is the oldest, largest and most successful third party in American politics. Currently, over 600 Libertarians hold elective office across all 50 states, more than all other third parties combined. Unlike the characters in *The Third Revolution*, actual flesh-and-blood Libertarians do not advocate revolution; rather they promote a platform of less government, lower taxes, and more personal freedom. They feel people should be free to make their own choices, provided they don't infringe on the equal right of others to do the same. In the Libertarian's world, the government's only role should be to protect people's right to make their own choices in life, so they can reap the rewards of their successes and bear personal responsibility for their own mistakes. Wake me up as soon as that happens...

Printed in the United States
26686LVS00001B/424-444